The Rel

Copyright © 2025 Valicity Elaine

All rights reserved. No part of this publication may be reproduced, distributed, or transmitted in any form or by any means, including photocopying, recording, or other electronic or mechanical methods, without the prior written permission of the publisher, except in the case of brief quotations embodied in critical reviews and certain other noncommercial uses permitted by copyright law. For permission requests, write to the publisher, addressed "Attention: Permissions Coordinator," at the address below.

ISBN: 978-1-957290-64-5 (eBook)
Print: 978-1-957290-65-2

This is a work of fiction. Any references to historical events, real people, or real places are used fictitiously. Names, characters, and places are products of the author's imagination. Inclusion of or reference to any Christian elements or themes are used in a fictitious manner and are not meant to be perceived or interpreted as an act of disrespect against such a wonderful and beautiful belief system.

Cover designed by Valicity Elaine

The Rebel Christian Publishing
350 Northern Blvd STE 324 - 1390
Albany, NY 12204-1000

Visit us: http://www.therebelchristian.com/
Email us: rebel@therebelchristian.com

Contents

AUTHOR'S NOTE i
Prologue 1
1. 2
2. 13
3. 25
4. 36
5. 49
6. 65
7. 80
8. 91
9. 102
10. 114
11. 122
12. 141
13. 153
14. 163
15. 176
16. 184
17. 195
18. 206
19. 213
20. 226
21. 236
22. 249
23. 258
24. 266
25. 279
26. 283
27. 297
28. 309

29	319
30	329
31	339
32	348
33	355
34	370
35	378
36	390
37	403
38	413
39	426
40	433
Epilogue	439
Enjoy these mafia love stories!	451
More books by Valicity Elaine & TRC Publishing!	451
ACKNOWLEDGEMENTS	453
The Rebel Christian Publishing	454

Run, Darling

A Low-Spice Mafia Romance for Christian Women
By Valicity Elaine

A Rebel Christian Publishing Book

AUTHOR'S NOTE

please read this entire note

CONTENT WARNING:

Hello! If you are new here, then you may not know what to expect from this book. Dark Christian Romance, sometimes referred to as *Clean* Dark Romance, is a dark love story without erotic scenes, vulgar language, or excessive violence. Because it is Christian, it also includes openly Christian characters and a message of faith, but **please do not take this story lightly. This is still a dark romance**, meaning, it will cover dark topics including, but not limited to, **mafia activity, kidnapping, alcohol consumption, violence**, and more.

This is NOT an erotic novel, but **there is** lovemaking in this book. It is not explicitly detailed but if you are uncomfortable with any more passion than kissing/handholding, this may not be the book for you.

Target audience is 18 or older, Christian or non-Christian. Reader discretion is advised.

LEGALITY:

There is a very unorthodox marital arrangement featured in this book. **Please understand it is only fictional and is not meant to be glorified or romanticized in any manner.** The marriage was included to show you the depths of darkness the protagonist faced and why she turned to God for help, because only He could help her.

The marriage between the two characters happens at a young age but **there is no physical contact between them until they are both legal adults.** After much research, I learned that such a marriage is, in fact, legal. There are a few states in the US which do allow lovers to marry under the age of eighteen. You would be shocked at how low the age limit is—I was shocked to learn that, shamefully, some states **have no limit.**

I get more into the legality of the marriage in later chapters, so please keep in mind that this is a much larger picture and problem that I want to bring awareness to, **not** glorify or romanticize.

CULTURAL ELEMENTS:

This story takes place in modern-day California, but it contains references to the Irish culture, language, and history, including references to the history of the Irish Mafia. I want to remind readers that this is a work of fiction and is not intended to portray any culture in a bad light.

I did a lot of research while writing this story. My goal is to present that research as accurately as possible, but for the sake of the story, some changes were made.

The Irish crime organization, the *White Hand Gang*, did exist. It was formed and operated in the United States between 1900-1925 as rivals to the Sicilian mafia called, the *Black Hand*. As police began to crack down on crime, the White Hand eventually dissipated and was considered eradicated by 1930.

White Hand leader, *Dinny Meehan*, was murdered in his own home on March 31, 1920. This day happens to be my birthday and was a fun fact to learn while researching this crime organization. According to police reports, White Handers blamed Meehan's death on Italian mobsters and began a war that would last for nearly a decade; however, it is unclear if the Black Hand was actually involved in the assassination. No matter who is responsible, Meehan's death did not *directly* cause the downfall of the White Hand. The aftermath of Meehan's death is a fictional element I added to the history of the White Hand for the sake of the story.

I do not know if the White Hand (or the Black Hand) still exists today in any capacity or if it ever ventured beyond the borders of New York City. I also do not know how exactly the White Hand operated. In this story, the organized structure of the White Hand and its presence in California is entirely fictional. The mafia organization called *Panthers of LA* is entirely fictional, but it was inspired by the controversial history of the *Black Panther Party*, a political organization which sought to challenge police brutality against Black Americans between

1966-1982.

The Black Panther Party has a somewhat complicated story that involves both activism and allegations of criminal activity. It is difficult to say whether the allegations against them are true since many who opposed the Black Panthers also opposed the Civil Rights Movement as a whole and would have greatly benefited from their dissolution. Whatever the case, many American scholars consider the Black Panthers to be one of the most influential organizations to inspire Black Power and excellence in America while some also label the party as nothing more than a historical nuisance.

I used the history of the Black Panthers to create the modern-day Panthers of LA purely for entertainment purposes. There is no solid evidence to suggest the party was anything close to a mafia organization and I do not wish to portray them as such. The Panthers of LA is an entirely fictional mafia group. Other than being founded in California, it has no true relation or connection to the Black Panther Party.

Lastly, the Irish language is known by a couple different terms; **Gaeilge**, **Gaelic**, or sometimes **Irish Gaelic**. To the best of my knowledge, the Irish people simply call their language **Irish**. I chose to use all four terms throughout the novel and did my best to find the most accurate spelling and translation of Irish words and names. This was a bit difficult because the pronunciation of some words and names depends on the dialect and even the region of Ireland.

I do apologize if there are any linguistic mistakes. Please

understand it is my goal to be as accurate as possible when including culture in my work, especially a culture that I am relatively unfamiliar with.

According to a DNA test, I am about 5% Irish—which is really cool to me! But that isn't the reason I included this culture in this book. I was drawn to the Irish people out of a simple love for diversity and rich history. This book was written in love and joy, and I pray that I presented the Irish culture in a positive manner.

NAME GLOSSARY:

Irish names are rich with history and beauty, but many of them may not sound the way they are spelled. I chose to keep the traditional Irish spelling for these names, rather than the anglicized versions to stay true to the heart and beauty of the Irish culture. This guide may help with pronunciation as you read.

Caolán: *Kee-Lin*—sometimes pronounced *Kay-lin*. I chose the softer pronunciation of *Kee-lin* because I felt it fit his persona better.

Aoife: Ee-fa

Aifric: Af-rik

Tadhg: TIE-G, like the word "Tiger" but without the "R" at the end.

Balor: Bah-lur

Prologue

Caolán

All I ask is that you don't judge me when it's over.

1

Ria
Before

What did you do for your 9th birthday?

I bet you had a Barbie themed party with vanilla cupcakes and bright pink frosting; even served pink lemonade to match the theme. Or maybe you were a tomboy. You had a chocolate marble cake like a rebel and removed your Power Ranger mask to blow out the candles. It was the Pink Ranger mask, but still. A Ranger, nonetheless.

Happy birthday.

For my 9th birthday, I got married.

I hadn't known I was getting married at the time. The celebration was about a week after my actual birthday, so I thought it was just an elaborate party to make up for being late. My father had a lot of elaborate parties and was always late for family events and holidays. He was a wealthy businessman, so his time was divided between work and more work. When he was around, the celebrations were grand. Sometimes even celebrities had lunch with him in our estate gardens. But my 9th birthday was different. Special.

I wore an all-white dress that'd been custom made just for me. I had a bundle of flowers from the family garden in my hands, fingernails painted pale pink. My mother let me wear a bit of lipstick, even showed me how to pucker in the mirror. Then she pinched my cheeks to work color into them and smiled when she was finished.

"Let me braid your hair back," she'd said, turning me around in my chair.

I wore a crown of flowers in my hair and then she placed a veil over my head and pulled the front wing down to cover my face. I had giggled and made a joke that we should play peek-a-boo. It was childish, I know. I was turning nine, for God's sake. Peek-a-boo was for children. Like my little brother Darren who'd waited outside in a three-piece suit. He looked sharp, and I'd told him this when Mother finished my hair, and we left the dressing room. But he hadn't cared. All of his six-year-old attention was taken up by the iPad in his hand, which our mother snatched away with a *tsk!* and a threat to have Father spank him later.

Darren got a lot of spankings from Father.

"Are you ready?" my mother had asked, taking my bouquet as she gazed into my veil.

I nodded. "Ready Freddy."

She'd smiled, remaining silent for a long moment, a moment that seemed to stretch and stretch, like a rubber band pulled taut. Then, inexplicably, she clamped a hand over her mouth and let out a sob. A nasty wet sound that scared me, like something was stuck in her throat.

"*Catherine.*"

We both turned sharply to find Father at the end of the hall. The sight of him immediately dried my mother's tears. She wiped both her cheeks and reached for my hand which I took without a word. Her grip was shaky.

Father walked toward us, making the long hallway seem shorter than it was. He was a tall man, not just to my nine-year-old eyes, but tall in general, towering over Mother, towering over the servant women who poked their heads out of the dressing rooms and then quickly shut the doors. He was even taller than his own bodyguards who walked closely behind him. But for all his might and fortitude, Father greeted me with a charming smile as he squatted and gingerly lifted my veil.

"Let me look at you." His voice was warm and deep. I could feel his breath brushing against my nose as he spoke. It smelled of coffee with a bit of cinnamon. "You're going to make this family proud."

That made me happier than any gift I knew was waiting in the foyer. They'd set up a table and had filled it with beautifully wrapped boxes before I'd even arrived at the venue. I remember walking past and gasping, being filled with excitement so strongly I was trembling.

"Are we almost ready?" I asked my father.

"We're ready," Father said, rising. He seemed to stretch on forever, like a great mountain growing before me, his trimmed beard a white cloud at the top, his smile the radiant sun.

I loved my father with every fiber of my being. Loved him as rain loved the earth and plants loved rain and bugs loved plants and birds loved bugs and humans loved birds—the kinds to eat and the kinds to watch. I loved him as if he were the center of my world. I didn't care that he punished Darren so harshly. I didn't care that my mother always flinched away from him. I cared that when he was near me, I only felt protected, cherished, and strong. Like one day, I could be as mighty as him.

Father took my hand, but Mother called his name, and he stopped. "Darren, there's still time—"

"No, Catherine."

"We can make other arrangements—"

"I said *no*."

Even the guards behind my father jumped at the sound of his voice. I squeezed his hand, feeling tears prick the backs of my eyes. One of the lady servants cracked the door to the side of us and Father snapped his fingers at her. She knew exactly what to do; in a pale pink dress, she swept into the hall and scooped Junior up so she could carry him away.

"Let's go," my father said, and he only said it once.

Mother remained silent from that moment forward.

"Is it time to blow out the candles?" I asked.

"In a bit. First, we want to have a ceremony."

"What ceremony?"

I'd already been baptized the year before, and I hadn't bled yet. We had a ceremony for my older sister, Bethany, when she began to bleed for the first time. I don't remember much of it because I was only two years old back then. But I know it was really nice; she got to wear a white dress just like mine, and there was cake afterward. I think she liked the party, but I never got to ask. Beth moved away after that. I never saw her again.

"We're going to have a dedication," Father told me, patting the top of my head. "Just repeat the words Reverend Moore says, and you'll do fine, Glory."

"Okay," I said, squeezing his hand.

I would do as I was told. I would attend the dedication. I would repeat after Reverend Moore. And I wouldn't question it.

The dedication was quick. I walked down the aisle with Father right beside me. At the end, a gentleman waited for me. He reached for my hands when I made it to him, but I shied away, grabbing for my father. That made the crowd chuckle, voices seeming to rise from a white void I could not see beyond. The veil suddenly felt like a cage, and I stumbled backwards, clawing at it.

"Easy," my father said in my ear. "It's all right, Glory."

The nickname calmed me as much as his confidence did. I didn't know who this man was, and he wanted to take my hands. Men weren't allowed to touch me. Not even the bodyguards who kept my father safe. For some reason, this man wanted to hold my hands in a room full of people. But Father said it was okay, so I took a calming breath and reached for this stranger. I couldn't see him well because of the veil, but I could tell he was older. Maybe early twenties. Bethany would be around the same age if she were still alive.

When I looked down, I could see the man's hands clasping mine. Since I couldn't see his face, I focused on those instead. They were so large, my hands disappeared inside of his. His palms were warm but calloused, the knuckles scarred on top. I wondered what sort of man had scarred hands. Someone who worked hard. Someone who was strong.

My father had scars on his hands.

Numbly, I repeated the words Reverend Moore spoke. I didn't understand any of them, but the crowd clapped once it was over, and then the man lifted my veil.

He *was* older. But that didn't scare me, how could I be afraid of his smiling face? He looked so kind, with fiery red hair and blue eyes, full lips that curved upwards even as he spoke.

"Happy birthday," he said.

I'd almost forgotten about my birthday. The sudden mention made me gasp and say, "It's time for cake!"

The crowd laughed and Father patted my shoulder. "It's time for cake, Glory."

He led me out with the strange man who walked beside me. He remained by my side throughout the rest of the night. I blew out my candles with him standing next to me. Then he helped me slice my cake. Even fed me a piece. Someone in the crowd said I should serve him a piece, too, and they all waited for my reaction.

"Here." The man cut a tiny piece off my slice and then placed the fork into my hand. He took my hand and raised it so he could eat the cake off the end. I stared at him. I could feel my cheeks heating with shame, and I didn't understand why. I fed my father food all the time. He loved to join me for tea parties when he was free.

But this man wasn't my father. And the crowd seemed to like that he was eating cake from my fork. They clapped and took more pictures when he finished, but I just stood there staring at the piece of strawberry he'd bitten. It was deep red, sweet juice spilling out onto the vanilla frosting. It looked like blood.

After the cake, it was finally time for gifts. Again, the man sat beside me the whole time, collecting the wrapping paper and the loose ribbons I tossed aside. I got clothes, toys, jewelry, sculptures, a set of pearls, a tiara encrusted with diamonds, a massive emerald, a painting from the Victorian era—worth millions.

Such strange gifts for a birthday, but I accepted each one with a smile, peering out at the crowd of adults I barely recognized. I could see family members. Cousins, aunts, uncles. But there were others there, too. People with the same fiery red hair as the strange man beside me. A sea of green eyes that crinkled to match the smiles on their faces. I didn't know those people, but they'd come out to my birthday party and had showered me in expensive gifts. It would be rude not to say thank you. So, I nodded at each person who stepped forward and presented me with a box. I shook hands. I smiled for more pictures. One woman even did the sign of the Cross over me and said a prayer. I accepted that, too.

The last gift was from the mysterious man beside me, but he didn't want to give it to me there in front of the crowd.

Instead, he leaned toward me and whispered, "Let's go for a walk."

I shot a look toward my father, but he didn't protest. In fact, his face darkened when I didn't move.

"Don't be rude, Gloria. Go with him."

Without a word, I hopped down from my chair and walked outside with this man I didn't know. It was dark out, but the moonlight was bright enough for me to see dozens of cars lining the pavement. In the middle of the driveway loop was a fountain. It spurted to life right in front of me, spraying cool mist into the air.

"Let's walk," the man said, tugging my hand to guide me away.

We walked across the green expanse surrounding the property, guards following at a lazy distance. Trees dotted the property, as strong and sturdy as the men my father assigned to protect me. I could see birds drifting down to rest on their branches, squawking at the chill that settled with the evening, almost in protest of the cold.

When the grass began to stain my white ballet slippers, the man stopped and squatted in front of me. His breath came out in a cloud. "Are you cold?" he asked, taking off his jacket. He placed it over my shoulders before I even answered. I snuggled into it, enjoying the smell of his cologne. It was different from Father's but just as heavy.

"Thank you," I murmured.

"I wanted to give you my gift in private."

I nodded as he pulled out a golden chain from his pocket

and held it up so I could see the heart-shaped pendant dangling at the end. It was pretty, the prettiest necklace I'd ever seen. But I was already wearing a silver crucifix, so I didn't know if I should take it off or not.

The man sensed my hesitation. "How about we switch?"

"Y-You want my necklace?"

"Don't you think I deserve a gift on this special day?"

I didn't know how this day had been special to *him*, but I nodded anyway. How could I tell him no?

He took off my cross necklace and then clasped his gold one around my neck. I reached up and clutched the pendant, turning it over to read the inscription.

"What does it say?" the man asked.

"See you soon, love."

He poked my nose. "That necklace is a promise. Remember it."

I nodded.

"Caolán."

We both glanced up to see my mother. She stood twenty feet away, just past the guards, unsure if they would let her through. I didn't speak because I was shocked at the word she'd spoken.

I think that's the man's name. It was sharp and pronounced differently from the name I'd seen on his guest card at our table. Mom had pronounced it as, *Kee-lan*, a stark reminder of his Irish heritage. I could hear it in his accent. Every word rolled at the end, like it tickled his mouth to speak.

Caolán nodded and the guards let my mother approach.

"I've come to get Gloria," she said, hugging herself. Her voice broke with a sniffle when she spoke again. "Please let me have her."

Caolán stared at her. In the evening light, I could see that he wasn't smiling. His face was like a stone, expression blank and unbothered by the crying woman before him. I didn't know what to make of him. He'd been smiling and happy and kind all night, and now he looked at my mother like he couldn't stand her.

With a sigh, he said, "I've decided not to take Gloria with me. She will remain with her family until she comes of age."

My mother broke, falling to her knees with a cry. "Thank you," she sobbed. "*Thank you*, Caolán."

Caolán took me by both arms and turned me to face him. "It's time for me to go, little one."

"Okay."

"What does your necklace say?"

"See you soon, love."

He smiled that kind smile once more. "That's a promise." I nodded as he turned me again, this time to face my mother. "Time to say goodbye."

"Okay..."

"Once I leave, you're going to hear a lot of things about me," Caolán said into my ear. "They're all lies. Remember that."

"All lies," I whispered back.

"Now, go to your mother."

He let me go and I ran forward, crashing into my mother's

arms. She wept into my hair, hugging me tightly. Instead of comforting her, I craned my neck to peer around my mother. I wanted to see Caolán. Wanted to glance back and wave at him before he left. But I couldn't and I knew I *shouldn't*. He promised to see me soon, so why did I need to wave goodbye? But also ... I didn't wave because of his last words.

Just as he released me, Caolán whispered one last thing in my ear.

"Run, darling. And don't look back."

2

Ria

Present

Your eyes are winter ice. Your hair is spring fire rose.

That was the first line of my final exam for the Fall semester. It was for a creative writing class where I decided it would be a great time to share poetry from my journal. The scribbles of my soul. I'm sure I got an A, but the fact that I wrote it at all disturbs me.

Eyes like winter ice. Hair like spring fire rose. A man who is both fact and fiction.

I know that man. I know every part of his face and body. I know the curve of his lips, the straight edges of his square jaw. I know the flattened plane of his forehead as easily as I know the backside of my hands. I know *his* hands. Hard, calloused hands with scars across the knuckles.

I haven't forgotten a single detail about him in all these years, and yet, I've only seen him a handful of times. He is a stranger and a companion at the same time. Both a child's obsession and a woman's nightmare.

I did not choose my husband.

I understand that now. What happened to me at such a tender age was neither normal nor moral, but it was legal. Did you know four states in the US have no minimum age requirement for marriage? No matter your age, if you have parental consent and the approval of a judge, you could get married as an infant if you wanted. Or if your family wanted.

California is one of those states.

I was legally married at the age of nine. To a man fifteen years older than me. I had no say in the matter. I had no idea what was even happening. But it was legal and it was done and it will be finalized in less than three weeks. After I turn eighteen. By finalized, I mean it will be consummated.

For the last nine years, I've wondered what it would be like to be held. Touched. Kissed. Loved. I have wondered because it's never happened to me. I might have gotten married at age nine, but I was never touched. Not by my husband or any other man. I was surrounded by women my entire life. I was pampered. I was spoiled. I was coddled. I was treated as a precious gem, yet I was firmly disciplined, constantly watched, highly educated, and kept on a strict diet.

My father is a very rich, very important man. Everyone in my family is. Until a few years ago, I thought we were just a wealthy family of business owners. I thought my father was a multi-billionaire because he owned two airlines and had just launched his own cruise line. All of that is true. But the planes and boats are just devices. Tools used to ship the real function of his business.

My father is a drug dealer. A mafia crime boss. And I am his princess. Mafia royalty.

This revelation took longer than it should have to sink in. Maybe because I was so pampered and so childishly spoiled. Maybe because my mother kept me in expensive, private Christian schools where I learned about God and Jesus and she always told me I didn't just have a guardian angel, I had the Holy Spirit. She told me our family needed His protection and when I got older, I would need the redemption I'd been given through Christ.

As a child, I had no idea what any of this meant. I just accepted it because it's what I was taught. But when I learned the truth, everything changed. Everything clicked. My family needed God's protection because we were awful people. And we needed redemption because our sins were so black, we deserved all the dangers we faced.

None of this was clear to me until I had my first period. That was when I learned the truth.

After getting married at age nine, Caolán allowed me to remain with my family. It was not out of the kindness of his heart. He let me stay to keep the peace between our organizations. Previously, our families had been at war. My sister, Bethany, was married to Caolán's older brother. When he killed her, chaos ensued, but my marriage to Caolán ended the fighting and united our families once again.

I cannot let this marriage fail or else the fighting will start again. For nine years we have lived on the edge of a knife, tiptoeing around a sense of peace so fragile, the wrong look could shatter it. Caolán let me grow up in my mother's house to strengthen that peace. But he came for me when I began to bleed at age fifteen.

I remember my parents fighting over it. The fierce whispers that crawled from my father's office, riding the waves of tears spilling down my mother's cheeks. In a nightgown and my first pair of period panties, I padded down the hall and pressed my ear to the large door.

My father's voice was the one I heard first. "She has to go, Catherine," he told my mother. "Caolán's requested her."

"You told him?" My mother sniffled. "You *told* him?"

"She bled all over her sheets! If I didn't tell, the housekeeping would. He would have found out no matter what. You know that."

I felt a sharp prick of embarrassment puncture my dignity. I hadn't spoken to my father at all that day, hadn't even seen him, yet he knew one of the most intimate details of my life. And he'd shared it with another man. Like gossip.

Why did it matter if I bled all over the sheets? What business was that of Caolán's? I hadn't heard his name since my thirteenth birthday, when he showed up at my party unannounced. He presented me with a gift and then kissed my cheek and asked if I was a woman yet. My mother had tripped over herself to answer before me, stuttering, "N-Not yet. She … She's still my little girl."

I had frowned. "I'm thirteen, Mom. I'm not a little girl anymore."

"In some ways, you are, darling."

I hadn't understood what she meant or what Caolán was really asking until I woke up two years later with blinding pain in my lower abdomen and bloody sheets. That day, I had expected a party. When Bethany bled, we celebrated with food, drinks, and gifts. It was luxurious and grand and filled with so much joy. Most of it my own.

When I think of Bethany's party today, I don't remember her smiling. I don't remember her laughing or dancing or enjoying her cake. I just remember her being there. And doing what she was told.

She left when the party was over, and I never saw her again.

I started bleeding, but there was no celebration. Instead, there were whispers and tears and my mother begging my father to please speak to Caolán. To please do something.

"Don't let him take her," she had wept.

Something crashed in the room, the sound of shattered glass.

"He wants her!" my father had shouted. "That is his right."

"She's our daughter. Our *only* daughter left—"

"He could have taken her when she married him. You know that, right? On her ninth birthday, he could have taken her home with him. But he showed us mercy."

I'd backed away from the door, staring at the red wood, trying to comprehend what I'd just heard.

When she married him...

Ninth birthday...

Showed us mercy...

None of it made sense. So, I stormed inside for answers. Both of my parents stopped talking and blinked at me in shock.

My mother spoke first. "Gloria—"

"Is it true?" I asked. "Am I married?"

They exchanged panicked glances, but the fear rolled into calm as my father exhaled and told me everything. Each word stirred the calm, pushing it further to the edge until I couldn't hold on any longer. I remember my knees buckling. I remember my mother hugging me. I remember us both shedding tears.

I had become a woman. That meant I could bear children. That meant Caolán had every right to claim what had been promised to him.

Mercifully… He was kind to us again.

Caolán did not take me away from my family when I was nine years old, and when word reached him that I had begun to bleed at age fifteen, he chose not to take me again. I would be allowed to live with my family until I turned eighteen. Then, without question, I would be his.

My eighteenth birthday is just around the corner. I will be given to Caolán shortly after, on the day of our wedding anniversary.

I wish I was a child again, believing all the lies I'd been told. My life was better when I thought my family was strict because of our money and our business. Not because we were in the mafia. The lies were evil, but I wanted to believe them. I *wanted* to believe my father was good, and my mother was independent, and that my faith was true. Not some desperate scapegoat. But even that was a lie. I don't know if I have faith anymore. I don't know what I believe. Because if I choose to believe in God, then I must accept my family's fate. God punishes evil. So my days are numbered. I deserve what's coming for us as much as anyone else. I *want* to be held accountable because that's the only way I know I was ever truly free. If I accept that this was all a choice, then I can believe I had one to begin with.

I know I didn't, but slaves don't like being called slaves. Many of us are satisfied with the mere illusion of freedom. That's why I've been at boarding school overseas. Building my own illusion.

Caolán came to see me when he heard about my bleeding, but he did not take me with him. Strategically, he allowed me to remain at home and gave my parents yet another kindness they did not deserve. Now, they owed him. He had bestowed more than one mercy upon our household. It had started to make us look weak. Like we needed handouts.

My family needed something to justify all the free kindness they'd been given. Boarding school was the answer. My mother and father let me enroll in school overseas and told everyone Caolán valued my education and that was why he didn't take me. No one believed the lie, but that didn't matter.

I've been at a prep school in England for over two years now. My sophomore, junior, and now senior year. I've loved every second. Over here, I have freedom from my mafia family. For about three more weeks.

Once I turn eighteen, I will drop out of school and live with

Caolán. I will give him three sons, as our contract states, or I'll keep having children until we get there. I will accept my fate as a mafia princess. I will take my place beside my husband. I will live in a world of sin and await my judgment.

My only solace is that I did manage to make friends. I have no regrets in my dull, controlled life, because I got to spend two and a half years living vicariously through my best friend, Aoife.

Aoife is my roommate. She was born into the Irish mafia; because of our families, we have a lot in common. A lot of secrets that only we can speak of. A lot of restrictions we live by that no one else understands. Despite what we have in common, she is my opposite in every way. Outgoing while I am shy, tall while I am short, completely aware of who she is while I was kept in the dark until I bled and demanded answers. This is because our biggest difference is that I am mafia royalty, and she is a mere grunt.

Aoife's family is tiny, most of them are employed by larger families as security guards or hitmen. In fact, Aoife wouldn't have been able to afford this boarding school if she weren't engaged to a higher-ranking man. It happened over the summer, and her family agreed to let her finish school like mine. After graduation, she will honeymoon in the Caribbean and return with a child growing in her belly. If she's fortunate. Her contract is only one son, so there's no rush but Aoife wants to get the hard part over with so she can move on with the rest of her life.

I wish I could be that bold and headstrong. I wish I could

have hope for my future the way she does. But right now, all I've got is a suitcase to pack; I've been stuffing clothes into it for the last hour.

Aoife clicks her tongue when she enters our room, she glides across the floor in a sweeping skirt and click-clacky heels. She is perfect with long legs and skin the color of pearls. Her eyes are emerald green, and her hair is the pale dust of a natural blonde, like ashen rivers flowing over her silky skin. The gentle waves cascade down her back as she walks; I wonder how heavy her hair is, if I could cut it off and weigh it like a basket of spun white gold.

In the Bible, King David had a son that was very beautiful. The Word says his hair was so long because he only cut it once a year, and it weighed 200 shekels. Today, that's about 5 pounds of hair. Could you imagine that? I bet Aoife has 5 pounds of hair. She pulls it into a ponytail now as she tiptoes over my piles of clothes, complaining the entire time.

"Honestly, Ria, I thought I told you to start packing days ago?"

Ria is my nickname, short for Gloria. Aoife started calling me that because it *almost* rhymes with her lovely Irish name, pronounced EE-FA.

She says my name again. "Ria, are you listening?"

"Yes. Sorry. I'll be packed soon."

"Want me to help?"

"No," I say quickly. Firmly. Packing up feels like digging my own grave. Allowing Aoife to help would be like asking her to grab a shovel. I can't do that to her.

Aoife kneels beside me, staring at my unfolded clothes. "It won't be so bad. Maybe he's a great guy." She plants her green eyes on me, and I reflexively look away. I feel her soft hand on my cheek, brushing my hair behind my ear. Revealing my face. "Great guys won't care about this." She runs her delicate finger over the puckered scar on my face. It starts above my left eyebrow and curves around my eye, digging into the side of my nose and carving a crooked line across my cheek to end at my jawline.

It happened when I was fifteen, right after I started bleeding. I haven't seen Caolán since then, so I don't know how he'll react to seeing my ruined face now. But if he's still the charming man from my memories, then Aoife is right. I have nothing to worry about, and that's what scares me.

I'm not afraid of how Caolán will treat me. I'm afraid of how I will treat him. I'm afraid I will like him. Maybe even love him. The nine-year-old girl in me still does. Her heart flips at the thought of seeing that smiling, charming man again. The one who gave me a necklace and a promise.

See you soon, love.

What does God do with hearts that long for darkness? I don't want to know. I'd like to think that maybe Caolán is an answer to a prayer I hadn't whispered before. A dark knight come to rescue me from the shadows of sin.

"You can't help me," I tell Aoife. "This is my battle."

"Battle?" She lets go of a very feminine laugh, and when she stands, I catch a whiff of her rich, botanical perfume. "You're turning eighteen and marrying a rich man. This isn't a battle at all!"

If only I could see this the way she does. To Aoife, marriage is a one-way ticket to money. From the moment she says, 'I do,' her only responsibility will be to look pretty and produce the next heir to the family fortune. Aoife sees no problem in this. She's even excited about it, so my hesitation confuses her. It might even annoy her. But I outrank her ten times, so she doesn't voice this. Instead, she offers comfort.

Aoife pulls out her phone and types out a long message, then she grins at me. "I just let my family know I'll be spending Christmas with you."

My eyes bulge. "You what?"

"I'm going to Los Angeles with you. Don't argue." She holds up a manicured hand. "The deal is done."

"But isn't your fiancé expecting to see you for the holiday?"

"Actually, he'll be out of the country on business, so this works out."

Oh… I have no idea what Aoife's fiancé does within the organization, but I know his family is ranked much higher than hers. High enough to afford her education and to pay for the private jet that will take us both to my home in LA.

When I first met Aoife, she was borrowing money for lunch. Now she's got a private jet. If there is one thing the mafia has given us, it's money. But that money comes with strings. *Shackles*. Aoife doesn't seem to mind them, but that's because she grew up poor. I'm not impressed with money. Despite living in luxury, my marriage is nothing but a trap for me. Soon, I will be locked in place. *Caolán's* place. But I won't have to do this alone. Aoife will join me for the holiday break. She will be my comfort—my strength—and just maybe, I'll manage to smile through it all.

3

Caolán

Abhartach. That's the Irish word for vampire. When I was a child, my wrinkled grandmother told me an Irish folktale about a vampire who only drank the blood of virgins. He had red hair because of the fresh blood that flowed through his ice-cold veins. In the sun, his hair turned into fire, and if you made eye contact with him, your very soul would burn.

Eyes like winter ice. Hair like spring fire rose.

What an interesting tale. I am positive my grandmother told me this story to scare me, but it had the opposite effect. I became obsessed with vampires. Obsessed with blood. Maybe because I have red hair, but also because, as a young, foolish boy, I thought drinking blood might be cool.

To be clear, I have never drank blood, but I did try. When I was 10 years old, my father caught me trying to slit the throat of a street cat I'd found. I didn't want to kill the cat, I just wanted to taste its blood which I couldn't do without killing it. Needless to say, he beat me senseless and made me raise the cat as my own. To teach me compassion.

I named the cat Dracula, and he lived to the ripe age of 16.

That beating taught me two things: the first is that I shouldn't drink blood. The second is that if I wanted to shed blood, I couldn't get caught. Because getting caught got me beat. So, I decided that day that I would become a hitman. Because then I could shed blood all I wanted, and I'd get paid to do it. Good thing my family is mafia.

Over the years, my obsession with blood eventually died out. My job was no longer a weird fetish, it had somehow become a skill. It takes expert effort to kill someone and not care. It takes immeasurable self-control to take a life and feel nothing afterward. But I've done it. Over and over and over.

I am numb to death. It does not scare nor intimidate me. In many ways, it is the only thing that makes me feel alive. When you spend so much time around dead people, you begin to question the difference. What *makes* me alive? I still haven't quite figured that out, but I feel a flicker of life each time I pull the trigger. I feel alive because, in that moment, I know I'm not the same as the guy bleeding on the floor.

There's a man before me now, on his knees with his hands tied behind his back. He is naked and bloody, and his face is disfigured. Two black eyes, a busted lip, a broken jaw. This is not my handiwork. The guy arrived at the warehouse like this, delivered by my own cousin, Billy O'Rourke. Billy's a hitman, like me, but he's much more dedicated to his job than I am. I'm not sure if I envy him or not.

"How am I supposed to verify his identity?" I ask, pulling

on a pair of black leather gloves. The man hardly looks human anymore.

"It's him," Billy insists. "You think I'd beat up an innocent guy?"

One time Billy got angry and broke a guy's neck because he overcharged him on his tab at the bar. The guy lived, but still.

"Yeah, Bills, I do think you'd beat up an innocent guy." I turn around. "Are you sure it's him?"

"One hundred percent." Billy gives me a thumbs-up and flashes an ugly grin. He's sitting on top of a deep freezer, swinging his skinny legs over the edge like a child. When I roll my eyes, he lets out a howl that's supposed to be a laugh. It echoes around the warehouse like a nightmare that won't end.

"Well, let's get this over with."

My gun feels heavy as I tug it from my waistband. Cold metal in my cold palm. I press it to the man's forehead and exhale a shaky breath. When I look into his eyes, I see a stranger. I don't know this man. Can't even remember the sin he committed, but I know his name. That's all I need. A name and a price. In this world, knowing your name is like knowing your darkest secret. Because once I have your name, I hold your life in my hand.

Outside, they call us assassins. Hitmen. Enforcers. But behind the shadows of the mafia, inside the wrought iron gates of the graveyard, we call ourselves *reapers*. I am the weapon they use when silence isn't fast enough.

This man is my target, and I've come to collect.

"Are you afraid?" I ask.

His reply is a whimper.

"I see…"

His head drops like he's given up. He has nice hair. I stare at the curls stained red with his own blood while I give him a few moments to get things right with God, at least that's what I tell myself. The truth is that my hand is shaking. It's shaking too badly to pull the trigger.

I can't stop it.

It's been a long time since I performed an execution, almost 12 years. I retired after replacing my older brother as the heir to the O'Rourke head family, trading my pistol and knives for a suit and jacket. My days of hunting and killing are supposed to be over, but I made an exception today. My wedding anniversary is coming up, which means I will officially inherit my portion of the family business. Once that happens, my little brother, Nolan, will have to step up. But he isn't ready. Apparently, neither am I.

I am not against killing. This is what I was raised to do. But this is my first kill in over a decade, and my last one didn't end so well. I messed up.

I *messed* up. And I'm still paying for it today.

When I look at this man and his unrecognizable face, my mind lies to me. It fills in his bloody features and I no longer see a stranger. I see my older brother on his knees, a gun to his forehead. *My* gun. *My* job. *My* voice bouncing off the walls of the room, asking the same question: *Are you afraid?*

I don't remember his answer.

"Running out of time," Billy drawls behind me. "I got plans, mate. Best hurry up with this."

I can't hurry up. I can't stop my hand from shaking.

With a huff, I yank the gun away and turn around. Nolan is leaning against the deep freezer beside Billy, his hands crammed into his jean pockets, his shoulders bunched. As soon as he sees me facing him, his demeanor changes. He relaxes his shoulders, lifts his chin. Tries to look tough, but I see through his act. Nolan is a 17-year-old kid who was cursed with natural kindness. He doesn't belong in the mafia at all, not with his bowl cut blonde hair and freckles smattering his cheeks which always seem to blush. Some days he looks more like my pretty little sister, but then he blinks, and I see our oldest brother's face and then I feel like I can't breathe.

Nolan shouldn't be here.

Our parents think he's out running errands with me, which, technically, he is. But they don't know that errand involved finishing one of Billy's kills. He needs this as much as I do. We're in the mafia whether he likes it or not. I love my baby brother enough to hate the world he lives in, but this is our life. This is the cup we've been given. We must drink from it, even if it poisons us.

I reach for Nolan. "Come here."

When he realizes what I want, he starts shaking his head. "Please no."

I nod at Billy who obeys the unspoken command without hesitation. He laughs as he hops off the deep freezer and grabs Nolan by the back of the neck.

"Off ya go!" he says, dragging the boy over to me.

Nolan fights him, twisting in his shirt, slapping at Billy's hands until he shoves him to the ground in front of me.

I squat and hold out the gun. "Finish him, Nolan."

Nolan doesn't move. He keeps his head down so his blonde hair falls into his face. From this angle, he looks like a girl. So small and delicate, too thin for his age, too fragile for this dark world. I reach forward and lift his chin, not at all surprised by the wetness that streaks his face. He blushes when I run my thumb over his cheek, catching a tear.

"Please don't make me, Caolán." Nolan sniffles and sits forward so he's on his hands and knees. "Please don't make me kill him."

"Goodness." Billy snorts. "What'll we do with this one?"

I honestly don't know.

In Ireland, my great grandparents farmed sheep. Whenever one of them got sick, they'd try their best to nurse it back to health but once it reached the point of no return, they'd take it out back and put a bullet through its skull. They didn't sell or eat the meat, fearing that it would make them sick.

It was worse when it happened to a baby. At least a sheep would have given them a few coats of wool. It'd earned its keep while it was alive. But a sick lamb hadn't done anything except eat and die. It'd been a waste of time and effort.

My little sobbing brother is a lamb. But I can't take him out back and shoot him. All I can do is take care of him until he gets better.

"Nolan," I say, and he cuts me off with a hiccup, crawling forward to latch his arms around my middle.

"Please don't make me!" he shouts.

What an awful position to be in. My first kill was not as dramatic as this, and it happened when I was four years younger than Nolan is now. But Nolan is nothing like me. He did not grow up harboring an obsession with vampires, using the mafia to feed his bloodlust. He lusted after books and video games, shutting himself in his room and pretending his family wasn't a group of ruthless killers. He had that privilege as the youngest in our family, but he is not a child anymore. He can't hide from this.

With a sigh, I pat the back of Nolan's head. "At least watch me do it."

Nolan stiffens but after a moment, he pulls back and wipes his nose, then he slowly nods. "Okay."

"Turn around."

He listens, as obedient as a frightened pup. Nolan stands beside me, straightening his wrinkled clothes as I once again press the gun to the man's forehead. He groans in agony, though I can't tell what pains him most; his extensive injuries or the fact that he's dying. If I'm being honest, I don't really care.

"Are you afraid?" I whisper.

The man groans again. Nolan holds his breath. Billy laughs somewhere behind me.

I pull the trigger. It's over in a flash.

The man falls forward, which scares Nolan so badly that he jumps back and shrieks, but Billy is behind him and gives him a hard shove to keep him upright. Nolan trips sideways and whirls around, face red with angry embarrassment.

"Stop it!" he shouts.

Billy laughs while I clean my gun off. "*Stop it!*" he mocks in a high-pitched voice, then he grabs Nolan by the collar and tugs him into a headlock. The two fumble around while I remove my gloves and take a picture of the dead body. I have to deliver proof of the kill to my boss by the end of the day. This is the boring part of being in the mafia—the paperwork, if you will.

"Caolán!" Nolan cries as Billy pummels him. He's on the floor now with our cousin kicking him in the ribs. Normally, I would make Billy stop, but Nolan needs to toughen up, so I pretend I don't hear his cries as I snap a few more pictures and then walk to the deep freezer across the warehouse.

"That's enough," I say.

By then, Nolan has a bloody lip but he's alive, so I don't see an issue. The look in his eye is full of betrayal, like he can't decide if he wants to cry or scream. He's angry that I didn't stop Billy from beating him, glaring at me like a petulant child.

I roll my eyes. "Put the body away, Billy."

Billy groans. "Me? I hate cleaning up!"

"I'd stay and help but Nolan and I have plans. You know that."

"Dinner with the new wife." Billy grins. "I heard she's in town."

Gloria *is* in town, but I don't have plans to see her yet.

"Dinner with my family," I reply.

Billy's grin is serpentine. "Tell dear *Aintín* Aifric I said hello."

I will never mention Billy's name to my mother. She hates him, almost as much as she hates me.

"I'll try to remember," I tell my cousin, then I motion for Nolan, and he follows me outside without a question or complaint. In fact, he doesn't speak until we get home.

"I'm sorry," he whispers, the words are barely audible over the loud whine of the garage door closing behind us. "I'll do better next time."

"It's fine."

"Are you going to tell Mom?"

"*Mháthair*," I correct in Irish, only because she hates the word, *Mom*. Nolan made the grave mistake of adapting too many American English words into his vocabulary for our mother's taste. When I was a kid, she'd made me suck on a lemon wedge each time I said *Mom* instead of *Mháthair*. She's too entranced with Nolan to touch a hair on his head, but still. Doesn't hurt to keep her in a good mood.

"Mháthair," he mumbles, then he looks up, eyes still large and watery. "Are you going to tell Mháthair?"

It's funny that he's more afraid of our mother knowing of his failures than our father, but I shake my head anyway. Mother has no idea he was at the warehouse today, if she finds out, she'll have me whipped.

"I'll keep this to myself," I say, like I'm doing him a favor.

Nolan smiles. It breaks my heart. God, he looks just like Aidan.

"Let's go inside." I take off my seatbelt, but Nolan stops me before I can open my door.

"Why do you question them?"

"What?"

"You asked him twice."

Are you afraid?

The question drifts into my head, and with it comes the same answer I always get. A groan, a whimper, or a sharp string of swear words. No one ever answers.

"I don't know why I ask," I mutter, staring down at my hands. "I guess it's a reminder that we're all the same. No matter how much power we hold in this organization, we're still weakened by the same thing."

"What thing?"

I glance over at him, taking in his large round eyes and his babydoll lashes. They're so blonde they're almost white, like winter snow has fallen on his face.

"What do you think weakens us, Nolan?"

He pauses. "Fear?"

"Yes."

"But he never answered," Nolan says.

"That doesn't mean he wasn't afraid."

"So ... Was he?"

I nod slowly.

"How do you know?"

My answer comes out at the end of a sigh as I shoulder open my door and get out of the car. "I could see it in his eyes."

They weren't wide like Nolan's or filled with tears. That man's eyes were dull, void of emotion. They looked just like mine. That's how I know.

4

Caolán

I drop Nolan off at his bedroom and stalk down the hall to my own. I can smell dinner even from my quarters, but I need a shower and a drink before I can muster the mental fortitude required to face my parents. First, I need to get the blood off my hands as much as the guilt. What am I doing to Nolan? Why does it matter so much that I toughen him up?

I grunt as shower water bleeds down my back, burning with every fierce drop. Steam clouds the bathroom until I cannot see my reflection in the mirror on my shower wall. My lion's mane of red fire is gone, my blue eyes have faded, I can't even see the straight line of my jaw.

Good. I don't want to see myself.

I whip my hand out of the shower and slap the light switch, plunging the bathroom into darkness. Exactly how I like it. Darkness is my purpose. It's where I'm comfortable, even when I'm not working.

As a reaper, I have mastered the shadows. I have learned to

be unseen. I have harnessed the power of silence, and I wear it on my shoulders like a cloak of invisibility. My first kill was at age 13, my initiation into the White Hand Gang. Any normal 13-year-old would have been playing video games and stealing glances at pretty girls, but I was far from normal.

The White Hand Gang is my world, a graveyard caged by five cold, dead fingers. Each finger is a Clan. Clan Cullen is the largest family, representing the Thumb of our Hand, strong soldiers who keep the organization afloat. Clan Fitzpatrick is our leader, the Pointer Finger. Clan O'Connor is the smallest, representing the Pinky Finger. Despite their size, they are extremely old, demanding respect for their deep Irish roots. Our richest Clan is the Ring Finger, Clan Hughes, making them the bankers of our organization. Finally, Clan O'Rourke, my family. We are the Middle Finger of the White Hand. The arsenal. When the Pointer Finger picks a target, it's my family's job to take them out. That's what I was doing earlier with Billy.

As you can see, the White Hand Gang is very structured. It's an old organization originating in the streets of New York. We rose to power in opposition of the Black Hand, a Sicilian gang that thought much too highly of themselves. Unfortunately, the White Hand was defeated when our leader was shot in the head while he slept. At that time, the Hand wasn't as strong as it is today. Our Fingers weren't united, we could not form the fist we needed to fight back. So, when our leader was shot, everything fell apart. It would be nearly a century before the White Hand resurfaced here in California. My great grandparents relocated with other mafia refugees and made a home for themselves here. Far away from Italians. There are other crime organizations in California, but the only one that threatens us is the Panthers of LA, a mafia run by the Jackson family. My wife's family.

I am not afraid of the Panthers. I wear the white hand of death; five fingers tattooed onto my flesh to mark me as a Clansman. Middle finger raised. I have cut, killed, maimed, and tortured my way to the top of my organization. I'm good at what I do. I'm good at killing people. That's what I was raised to do.

You might be wrinkling your self-righteous nose now but let me remind you that peace isn't free. Someone has to do the dirty work. When you're second in line to the family inheritance, the dirty work usually falls on your head.

For a long time, I didn't mind doing the dirty work. I still don't mind doing it. But circumstances have changed. I am no longer second in line to the O'Rourke head family. I am now the sole inheritor.

Twelve years ago, my older brother died. Some would say his death was justified, considering he murdered his own wife. That event sparked outrage from his dead wife's family. The Jacksons. That rage called for vengeance. Vengeance led to war between the Irish mafia and the Panthers of LA.

My brother died in that war. A war he started.

I ended that war by marrying the Panther Princess, a nine-year-old girl. Gloria Jackson is next in line to the Panther throne; when she turns eighteen, our union will turn two great mafia organizations into one powerhouse. The White Hand will hold the leash of the Panther. At least, that's what we hope. For the last nine years, there has been no fighting. No unnecessary deaths. No more cries for vengeance. The Panther businesses have skyrocketed, and O'Rourke banks have benefited because of it. Marrying Gloria Jackson was a good idea. Now, it's time to consummate.

My wife will be flying into town this evening. I've already double checked her flight schedule. Plus, I have eyes on her. I've always had eyes on her. Gloria belongs to me. She does not have the luxury of privacy. Not unless I say so.

I think of her as I get dressed, wondering what our reunion will be like. I never visited Gloria much as a child. I was very careful about maintaining a certain image with her. She does not know I'm a hitman. She doesn't know I murder people for a living. To her, I'm a happy, smiling man who has only ever been kind and charming. That's the image I've upheld since we were first married, but a lot has changed over these nine years.

Like Nolan, Gloria is not a child anymore. It's time for her to grow up as much as him. But I'm just as stumped about dealing with my wife as I am my little brother. Nolan must mature to survive and carry on the family legacy. But Gloria needs to grow up for a different reason. She must stand by my side, give me an heir, and help me lead this family. I don't know if she is the sort of woman who can handle it. I suppose I'm going to find out this week.

My phone buzzes now as I swing open my bedroom door, fully dressed and ready for dinner. I walk down the wide hallway of my family estate, tapping the screen of my phone. I know it's an update from my informant.

I'll be flying with her.

Interesting.

I pocket my phone without replying and open the double doors to the grand dining room. My family is already sitting in their respective chairs, my father at one end of the table, my mother at the other, and Nolan in the middle. He's also freshly showered, the ends of his hair slightly curled at the tips. He's done a good job covering his busted lip with a bit of makeup. I wonder what lie he told our parents to explain how he got it.

I sit across from him and offer a smile. He doesn't smile back, nor does he smile when our mother flashes him a grin. He just sits there, staring at his plate of pot roast.

Part of me thinks Nolan hates this family, but so do I, so join the club.

"You are late, Caolán," my father, Charles O'Rourke, says in his thick Irish accent.

My mother adds something in honest-to-God *Gaelic*. Do you know how old the Irish language is? More than a thousand years older than English. Think about that for a second. My mother, intelligent Irishwoman that she is, is completely fluent in Irish Gaelic. I grew up hearing ancient cuss words screamed down the halls. I heard folktales in their original Celtic tongue. I even learned to recite the Ten Commandments in Irish, much to the joy of my very Catholic grandparents.

Aifric O'Rourke is a queen wearing a pristine white dress that makes her look angelic with her pale skin and crystal blue eyes. Her hair is a creamy shade of blonde, like the dust of angel feathers, gathered into threads and spun upon her head. Every part of my mother's appearance is perfect, painstakingly pruned with plucked eyebrows, smooth, glassine skin, and makeup applied with a delicate hand. She comes from the Pinky Finger, meaning, her side of the family is *old*, old enough to recall the days when Christianity was first introduced to Ireland. That was like, 400 AD, just to put this into perspective. My maternal ancestors were pagans who converted to the Christian faith but did not forget their cultural roots. So, my mother was born into a family of proud Irishmen and women whose deep roots outranked my father's deep pockets. Call it old money versus new.

In this world, you can achieve status in three ways: Numbers, Money, or History. That's it. The large organizations rule through brute force, they have the manpower to overtake anyone. The rich organizations rule through coercion, no one can resist a deal that'll get them rich. While the old organizations rule through loyalty, it's hard to betray someone when you're bound by an alliance that was established before you were even born.

So even though my mother's side of the family isn't very rich, they hold a lot of authority simply because they've been around for that long. There's a saying within the Hand, *The O'Connors never lie.* It basically means their word is truth because no one is old enough to remember otherwise. The Pinky Finger remembers alliances, they remember secrets, they remember lies, they remember deceit. So, while my mother's family is short on cash, they are very rich in information. They have intel on every major family and organization within the Irish mafia, which makes them a weapon all on their own.

I suppose she was a perfect match for my father, leader of the Middle Finger. Her secrets helped me land kills. Her information kept me one step ahead. I was good at my job because of her. But I set all of that aside to take my brother's place after he died in the war. My family is the head of Clan O'Rourke, that means we don't have to do the killing ourselves. We are the ones who *assign* assassins, so I've been retired for the last 12 years. I am my father's right hand now. That's why he's got an attitude about my tardiness.

"I expect the Jacksons will reach out soon," my father says, sipping his whiskey.

"I'm waiting for their call," I say.

"Why not reach out to them?" Nolan clears his throat across the table.

"I don't think that would be wise."

"You're already married. What does it matter if you reach out first?"

Our dear mother interrupts. "This is not just a marriage, Nolan, it is an alliance. If we appear eager, some might think we need this alliance more than the Jacksons do and could very well attempt to use that against us."

"I see," Nolan mutters softly, then he stares into his pot roast until our father speaks.

"Whatever the case, her birthday will be here soon. I expect you to spend this time wisely, Caolán."

"Of course."

"I will make arrangements for the ceremony," Mother says. She smiles, and I wonder if it hurts. I have vague memories of my mother smiling during my childhood, but it was never at me. Not the way she smiled at Aidan or Nolan. Now she winks at me over the rim of her glass, like a faerie casting a spell. "I'm going to make sure Gloria is the most beautiful wife you've ever seen."

It dawns on me then that she's talking about the active ceremony. The part where we seal our marital vows in virginal blood.

"What exactly do you have planned?" I prod.

My father suddenly takes a deep interest in his dinner, sawing at a hunk of potato like his life depends on it. Nolan also busies himself with food. I don't blame either of them. We're talking about my wedding night and which one of them will have the honor of watching. Yes, that happens in our world. Someone has to witness the consummation to testify that it happened, and that blood was shed. Our contract promised me a virgin and three sons. Before we get to the sons, we've got to confirm I had a virgin to begin with.

"You will learn the details when it's time," Mother says. "Just know that it will be marvelous."

I have no idea what could possibly be *marvelous* about watching your own children have sex, but I've seen weirder things in this world. Unfortunately.

"How many witnesses?" I ask.

"Three from each family," my mother says, and when Nolan blanches, she quickly adds, "Uncail Rory will stand in as our third."

"*Uncle* Rory," I whisper in English. I'm not against Gaelic vocabulary, really, I'm only correcting my mother to annoy her. It's my own petty way of deflating her little bubble of joy. She has far too much power for a woman in this industry and it's clearly gotten to her head. Most of that is thanks to my placid father who hands all the tough decisions to his wife because he cannot be bothered to *think* without having a glass of whiskey first. No matter. I am his right hand now, that means I outrank my mother and can very well override any decision she makes.

The tricky part is making sure my mother doesn't retaliate. She is allergic to the word *no* and doesn't take kindly to disagreement. Challenging her authority could start a different sort of war I'm not sure I'm prepared to fight.

If I can be honest with you … I'm not good at fighting. In my business, you don't call my name when you want to fight. You call me when you want to end the fight. I'm not a soldier; I'm an *assassin*, remember? Besides, I don't want to fight my mother, but I will not sit by and let her take over my marriage. I won't let her take Gloria from me. She is the only thing in this world that is mine. I won't give her up.

"I won't have to witness the ceremony." Nolan exhales as color returns to his face.

It's probably for the best. Knowing my brother, he'll end up fainting and ruining the mood. Then our family would be shamed for having such weak men.

It isn't his fault he's so pathetic. The war changed him. He was just a child when everything went down. The most crucial and confusing years of his life were riddled with violence, death, and pain. To top it all off, we lost Aidan in the war. We could have released hell's fury after that, but my father was tired of fighting. Because Aidan started this war, the other Fingers of the Hand did not back us in the fight. We were alone and out of options. Mercifully, so were the Panthers. They lost their heiress; we lost our heir. It was time for a ceasefire.

I was shocked the Jacksons agreed to the marriage at all. The deal was better than we deserved. Aidan murdered the Panther heiress. His actions brought shame to the O'Rourke name and nearly ruined us. My family's reputation was in shambles. The White Hand was *this* close to amputating its Middle Finger. If the Jacksons hadn't agreed to this marriage, we might have lost everything. But they don't know that. The Panthers were blinded by their grief and the ever-looming threat of the other Fingers joining the fray. They didn't know the rest of the Hand had abandoned us, and that worked in our favor.

The truth is that we need this marriage to work far more than the Jacksons do. That's the reason I was so lenient with Gloria's family. By showing them mercy, I appeared to have the upper hand. I planted the seed of mystery in their heads, making them wonder what I was up to and when my mercy would run out. The Panthers were so caught up in their grief over losing Bethany, they never noticed just how badly we were struggling. That's why love is such a dangerous thing in this world. It blinds you. Weakens you. Allows others to take advantage of you.

My family flourished because of this alliance. Marrying Gloria gave me control of her entire inheritance, and since the will Aidan left behind rewarded me with the inheritance he'd gained from Bethany, I effectively control 30 percent of business within the Panther mafia. Critically high numbers for a man who isn't related by blood. Those numbers reestablished the O'Rourke family as the head of the Middle Finger once again. For nine years, my family has lived in luxury because of this marriage. But we've only been testing the waters. Until the marriage is consummated, I am still an outsider to the Panthers. This alliance could fall apart at any moment, and my family would once again fall into disarray.

This must work out. There is no other choice.

"When will she arrive?" my father asks, swirling his whiskey.

I check my watch, then my phone. The message from my informant is still there, a pleasant reminder. **I'll be flying with her.** That wasn't the plan, but it works all the same. Gloria should never be left alone.

"She will arrive soon," I say confidently.

"Are you prepared?"

That almost makes me laugh. I have waited for this day for nearly a decade. Without thinking, I reach up and clutch the cross pendant around my neck. Gloria gave me this all those years ago. I still have it. Never took it off, just like I promised I wouldn't.

I run my fingers over the cool metal of the pendant. "I am more than prepared."

"Do not mess this up," my mother warns. It sounds like a

simple reminder of how important this whole thing is, but I know her words are deeper than that. She knows how badly I messed up before. And she remembers how I promised I wouldn't let it happen again.

"I'll be fine," I mutter.

"Excellent." Mother swirls her wine. "I will make arrangements to have her visit us here."

"No," I say. "I want to meet her myself first." No offense to my family but they all kind of suck. Bringing Gloria here would be a terrible idea.

"Caolán," my mother coos, "this is something I should handle—"

"Last I checked, she was *my* wife, Mháthair. Not yours."

"I didn't ask what you checked." Aifric bristles, but then she quickly softens, glancing at my father to gauge his reaction. Charles looks so disinterested, I'm not even sure he's heard any part of this conversation. He sniffs and takes a sip of his amber alcohol. His indifference only feeds my mother's ego. Her face twists into a victorious smile. "This is a delicate matter, Caolán. Allow me to handle it."

No. I don't want my mother to handle anything that involves Gloria. She wants to take over. She wants to control this. It'll start with dinner parties, then the consummation ceremony, and then she'll start sticking her hand into Gloria's life, then she'll try to control the children. It will never end. But I can't tell my mother no or else she may retaliate and make things even worse. She will have her way, no matter what.

I grit my teeth. This is my *marriage*. The mafia has every

other part of my life, can't this one thing be mine alone?

"I'll take your silence as a, '*yes*?" Mother says. "I've already got the day planned anyway, just clear your schedule and put on a smile. This will be fun."

Fun. Yeah.

5

Ria

"Happy birthday!"

My family is gathered in the dining room wearing starched suits and expensive dresses. I arrived home just last night, but my mother doesn't care about jetlag, she insists on celebrating. She had our in-house chef prepare all my favorite foods and even baked a cake. It sits on display with a sparkler sputtering fire into the air, lighting up the faces of my parents and cousins and everyone else called out to pay respect to the Panther princess.

I have had many birthday parties over the years. Naturally, my family has attended each one. But so has Caolán. He has been a constant figure at birthdays and events, like a yearly reminder of our contract deal. When I was a child, I didn't understand who he was or that we were married. I didn't even know my family was mafia. So I would look forward to Caolán's appearances. To me, he was not my husband, he was a mysterious, kind man who gave me more attention than I deserved.

For my 10th birthday, Caolán arrived just as the party was wrapping up. He took pictures with me and then gave me a present; a bundle of morning glories that he called *the most beautiful flower in the world*. I had beamed, standing on my tiptoes so he could kiss my cheek. I'd seen my parents kiss, had seen my Aunt Nina kiss her husband, and had even watched when my tutor would kiss my father after our sessions were over. She would meet him in his office and then quickly leave before dinner, chin tucked, head swiveling for witnesses. She never saw me by the staircase. Never knew that I saw her with my father, heard the noises they made inside.

Caolán never kissed me. When I stood on my tiptoes, he smiled and patted my head, making me feel very much like the child I was. And then he said, *Happy birthday*, in his deep, husky voice, and left me there with my overbearing mother and my lying father. But he always came back. Every birthday. Every year another chance for a fateful kiss. I cannot help but wonder if this year, my eighteenth birthday, will be it.

I casually skim the crowd as my mother guides me toward the table to greet everyone. *Don't look for him*, I tell myself, but I can't keep my eyes from wandering. I shouldn't want to see him. I should be running for the hills, plotting my escape from this marriage and, ultimately, the mafia. But I know as good as any other woman in this world that there is no escape. The best I can do is pray for a husband who will be kind and live my life one day at a time. Searching for the little joys. The things that make me smile. There had been a time when Caolán made me smile, before learning the truth about our arrangement. Before realizing I had no choice but to marry him. Then that affection turned into fear, but my fears melt as my mind is flooded with pleasant memories of our birthday reunions. Nostalgia so sweet, it wipes away the bitter fear.

At the table, I am greeted by my brother, his sweet boyish face grinning widely. I see my father, his face void of emotion. I see my Aunt Nina wearing a smirk and holding a drink. As always. But I don't see *him*.

Mother walks beside me as she presents me to distant cousins and uncles I haven't seen in years. They knew me before the scar, so seeing me now is awkward. At first, I keep my eyes averted and greet each guest with a shy nod, but then I get annoyed. I am the Panther Princess, I am not going to let anyone make me feel bad in my own home.

With a huff, I pull my shoulders back and brush my hair behind my ear as I greet my Aunt Nina. She stares and then pulls me in. "Get 'em girl," she whispers, hugging me tightly, but when I pull away, my mother looks horrified and quickly grabs my face. She yanks on my hair as she guides me away.

"You foolish girl."

"You're working her too hard!" Aunt Nina jokes behind us.

I glance back to give her a smile; she's got her glass of champagne raised in salute. I can't stop myself from grinning at her, but it's wiped away when I finally see *him*.

In the back corner of the room, almost hidden by the sea of familial faces, is Caolán O'Rourke. For a second, I'm not even sure if what I'm seeing is real. Caolán leans against the wall with his arms folded; so casual, so perfectly calm.

When I stare for too long, blinking in shock, he comes to life and smirks. It's barely perceptible, the corner of his mouth twitches and his eyes fill with confidence as if to say, *Yes, it's me, darling.*

My heart thuds.

"He's here," I whisper.

My mother tugs my elbow just to keep me moving. I hadn't realized I'd stopped walking.

"He's here to wish you a happy birthday," she says. "Be sure to thank him."

"Right now?"

My mother's eyes are big and there's a small sheen of sweat on her forehead. She's as nervous as I am. Great.

The crowd begins to mingle, enjoying drinks and hors d'oeuvres from the staff walking through the room. I squint through the mass of bodies to find Caolán moving toward me. My breath freezes as he pushes from the wall and glides through the crowd. Every step makes it harder for me to breathe. He's wearing black jeans and a black long-sleeved shirt. So casual for such a high-ranked man.

"He's coming over," I tell my mother.

She turns and quickly wraps me in a hug. "Just smile and thank him for coming."

I can feel her heart beating against mine, it's fast but steady. Mom pulls away and cups my cheek. Her smile is motherly, but it smoothly shifts into something businesslike, and she suddenly can't look me in the eye as she fixes my hair, making sure my scar is covered. I stare at her as she does it, reminding myself that Catherine Jackson will always be a mafia queen before she is my mother.

My scar doesn't just ruin my face, it ruins our family. If the marriage hadn't already been performed, it would never happen. Not with my face like this. And the fact that Caolán hasn't seen it yet only makes everything worse. If he thinks I'm too ugly, he might try to have the marriage dissolved. And even if he doesn't, this is still a stain on our family's reputation. We lost a war, surrendered the last living princess to the O'Rourke family, and then allowed her face to be ruined. Mafia princesses are supposed to be beautiful. Right now, I am anything but, and my mother cannot stand it.

"There we go," she says softly, adjusting my hair one last time. It's dark, and thick enough to create a curtain over the left side of my face. If you don't look too closely, you'd never know the secrets hidden beneath the heavy curls.

"Gloria." The voice is hoarse, like he isn't used to speaking, but the accent is rich and vibrant. It makes me come alive, alerting every part of me to his presence. His nearness. His eyes on me. When I look up, peering through my heavy bangs, Caolán is watching sharply. His gaze focuses on the left side of my face, and I hold my breath, waiting for him to tell me to push my hair back. I'd have no choice but to listen and reveal my full face, but he does no such thing.

Caolán inclines his head. "Happy birthday."

I swallow. "Um ... Thank you for coming."

"I'm afraid I can't stay. I only came to see you." He nods.

"And now I have."

"Right. Thanks anyway."

He reaches up and brushes his thumb along my jaw. "We'll talk soon." His eyes shift to the side, and I realize that statement was for my mother. From my peripheral, I see her nod.

"Of course," she says quickly.

His eyes return to me, and he shocks everyone in the room by leaning forward. I inhale so sharply, I catch a whiff of his breath. It smells like smoke and mint. "Goodnight, then," he mutters against my lips. It's the closest I've ever come to a kiss, and it nearly makes me faint.

In that moment, I am blinded by memories of each birthday. Each time he could have kissed me and chose not to. Each time he said I was too young. That I wasn't ready.

This year is no different.

Caolán is so close, if I tilt my chin just a bit, I could press my lips against his. But I don't move, and neither does he except to pull away. Like he always does.

When he releases me, I stumble back, and my mother catches my elbow again. Caolán chuckles. "My apologies," he says, and then he turns and leaves. Not a soul moves until the double doors shut behind him.

My mother loudly clears her throat, reminding everyone to return to their mingling. The crowd obeys and chatter rises like water, slowly filling the room. She takes my hand and squeezes. "You did well."

"Thanks."

"Now, let's finish the night."

My mother keeps me by her side until dinner is served, then I sit beside my father who takes his place at the head of the table. Father does not speak to me. We stopped talking years ago when he finally told me the truth about everything. I've had nothing to say since. My mother held out hope that we would return to the father/daughter pair we used to be, but then I got this scar and that solidified the wall between us.

My mother tries to steal me away again after the cake is served, but Aoife, God bless her, distracts her with questions about her attire. "You look so beautiful in green!" my friend says loudly. "Is it to celebrate the upcoming anniversary?"

I laugh as my mother stumbles through her answer. I can't hear much of what she's saying because Darren, my little brother, appears beside me just then. He greets me with a fist bump and a wink. He's fifteen now, though he tries to look much older with a finger of whiskey in his hand. I wonder when our parents started letting him drink, and then I notice the black polish on the pinky finger of his right hand, the one holding his glass of alcohol. That's the first step of initiation into the mafia; the painted nail represents a claw of the panther. Once you earn five claws, you're in. I don't know the steps for attaining a claw, I'm a woman, so my status within the family was sealed at birth. But the men must earn their place within the organization. Initiation happens for all of them and begins at the same age.

I watch my brother closely as he tells me all about how school is going and how he hopes I love the gift he got me; a gaming PC. He's still such a kid, yet he's drinking our father's whiskey and training to join his gang, hoping to eventually replace him. He's got the claw to prove it. He might be a cub for now, but it's only a matter of time before Darren grows into a panther. Mighty, powerful, feared by all. Even me.

Darren waves his hand in front of my face. "Ria, you're spacing out."

"Sorry." I force out a laugh. "I'm just tired."

His shoulders bunch and a beat of silence yawns between us where he tries not to stare at the left side of my face. "Hey," Darren finally says, "I've got a surprise for you."

He leads me to the back of the dining room, only stopping to glance at Aoife who is still speaking to our mother. The fifteen-year-old part of him kicks into full gear as his eyes glide down her body, Adam's apple bobbing in a dry swallow. I don't blame him. Aoife looks beautiful in her short evening dress with sky-high heels. She's wearing all black like me, but her dress has a split all the way up one side. It isn't the sort of dress you'd expect from a good mafia daughter, but Aoife doesn't seem to notice the stares she's been getting since we arrived. I doubt she even cares. Darren certainly doesn't.

"Hey," I pinch his arm, "stop staring. You look desperate."

Darren gives me a lopsided grin. "Sorry. I just—your friend is really pretty."

I love the way he blushes; it makes him look more like a kid and less like my father's apprentice.

"You remember Aoife, she's visited before."

"Of course, I remember her."

I roll my eyes and move toward the door before he starts begging me to give her his number. Darren is the type who wouldn't care that she's years older and engaged.

We walk into the lounge connected to our dining room, the chatter behind us hushes to the crackle of our large fireplace. There's a servant stoking the fire when we enter, he stands and nods before leaving—except that he doesn't leave. He walks right up to me wearing a grin I only notice once he's close enough for me to see past his fully grown beard.

"Tony?"

"The one and only," he says, and I throw my arms open and shamelessly hug him.

Anthony Jones has been my friend since I was a child. He was originally my personal bodyguard, raised side by side so he would develop a protective sense of responsibility for me. We're three years apart, so when I left for school, he reluctantly stayed behind. My family was not happy with the idea of me walking around England without a bodyguard, but I reminded them that I was going to a normal school with normal people. Not some mafia owned university where crime bosses usually send their children. Those places do exist, by the way. They're the breeding grounds of criminals which is exactly why I picked a very quiet, very Christian boarding school across the pond. I wanted nothing to do with the mafia. I wanted to go to a school where a bodyguard wouldn't be necessary. But, *gosh*, did I miss Tony!

Tony gives me a bear hug, lifting me from the floor and spinning me around so my skirt billows out. I feel his laughter in his chest, right before it bubbles up his throat and erupts from his mouth like a sudden burst of joy. As I listen to it, I cannot help but laugh with him. Our cackling fills the lounge, but we have to calm down before we draw attention.

"Happy birthday." Tony pokes my forehead. "And welcome home, Ria."

I reach out and squeeze his arm. "I've missed you."

"Same here." Tony smiles warmly but I notice how his eyes drift to the left side of my face. This is the chasm between us. This scar disrupts more than the smoothness of my skin; it has marred every relationship I have. My father is worried about his reputation. My mother is worried about my marriage. Everyone else thinks I've been attacked. I wasn't, but the truth isn't any brighter.

Tony clears his throat as I stare at my shoes, then he produces a flower from the pocket of his suit jacket. When I look up, I am greeted by his sheepish smile. It's accompanied by a shrug of his broad shoulders. "I'm sorry I couldn't bring you a better gift. This is all I could think of."

It's a daisy. Slightly crumpled and missing a few petals from being kept in his pocket, but it's still beautiful.

"Where did you find this in the middle of winter?"

Tony grins. "I have my ways."

"Still doesn't beat my gaming PC," Darren says from across the room.

I snort. "When do you think I'll have time for video games, D?"

He looks away and I regret the question. I guess I'm not the only one who isn't looking forward to the ceremony. At least Darren and Tony won't be forced to witness it. I'd die of shame if they had to stand in the room while it happened. It's already enough that my mother will be there.

"Let's return to the party." I cross the room and use the silver plate hanging on the wall as a mirror so I can place my daisy into my hair. I purposely secure it on the left side of my head so at least now it'll look like people are staring at the flower and not trying to see the wicked scar carved into my flesh.

When I turn around, Tony's eyes are filled with wonder. "Nice," he says softly.

"Thanks."

Darren clears his throat. "Let's go. You've got plenty other gifts to open."

He isn't wrong about that. The next hour is spent opening gift after gift, each one seemingly getting more and more expensive. There is jewelry, clothes, invitations to exclusive balls, my uncle gives me keys to a car I will never drive. I don't have a license; no woman in this organization does. My father says we don't need them because we have drivers to take us everywhere, but Aoife says it's so that we can't travel without our husbands knowing where we're going. *If you want to go somewhere he doesn't approve, your driver won't take you. And since you can't drive yourself, you're trapped. Totally at his mercy.*

It's funny, Aoife hadn't seemed bothered by this when she told me. She'd said it with a smile.

I thank my uncle for the new car and pass the keys to my

mother who is beaming. The luxurious gifts are proof of our family's approval of me. In their eyes, I have grown into a woman worthy of gold, diamonds, and brand new cars. I have made them proud to call me their princess. Granted, they purchased all these gifts before seeing my face, but it's not like they can take them back, so this is a win/win situation for my parents. Even my father seems in a better mood, nodding as he inspects the car keys.

At the very end, my Aunt Nina produces a card that says I have complimentary lifetime membership at a country club I have never been to. I think she owns it, so I'm looking forward to going.

"If you ever need a break from all the greenies," she whispers with a wink, "you can take a load off here."

Greenies is the word she uses for the Irish mafia.

My smile is genuine. "Thanks, Aunt Nina."

My mother takes the card and reads it, then she passes it back to me. It's the only gift she's allowed me to keep for myself. She's taken everything else and sorted it neatly on the gift table.

As my father escorts our guests to the lounge for drinks and cigars, I turn to her. "You don't need this one?" I hold up the card.

"It's best if the O'Rourkes don't know about that one. Thank God Caolán left before she gave it to you, though that won't make much difference."

"What do you mean?"

"Your mother-in-law has requested I ship all of your gifts

to her for approval."

"What?" I stand and cross the room. "They were given to me. Why does she get a say in what I can and cannot keep for *my* birthday?"

"She gets to decide what comes into her house, Ria."

Her house. It hadn't dawned on me until just now that I'll be living with her.

"Caolán doesn't have his own home?"

My mother looks at me like I'm stupid. "I am certain he has an apartment or two, but you'll never see the inside of them."

"Why not?"

"Because they aren't for you. They are for his mistresses."

I watch her walk around the gift table, sorting my things. The revelation is too blunt for me to digest. I can't wrap my head around the idea of Caolán having a mistress and keeping an apartment for her. Not the Caolán I know. Not the man who stroked my cheek and told me goodnight and nearly kissed me in front of my entire family. *That* man has a mistress? I won't believe it.

"That's why I let you keep the country club card," my mother says. "You're allowed some secrets and that should be one of them."

"I don't want to keep secrets from my husband."

"You're so young." She walks over and plucks the daisy from my hair. "And stupid."

"Give me that back."

With a roll of her eyes, Mother tosses it into the trashcan beside the gift table. I watch it roll down to the bottom below piles of expensive wrapping paper.

"Every woman in this organization eventually needs a break, Ria. You are fortunate to have the status to actually take one."

"Did you need a break from Father?"

She stares at me for a long moment. Before she can reply, the lounge doors open and I hear Darren's voice across the room. "The ladies were just dismissed," he says. That means it's time for the men to enjoy their drinks in private. As the lady of the house, my mother could entertain the women in the ladies' lounge down the hall but if she declines, the wives and other female guests will be escorted home by their drivers. Their husbands will return home when they're ready.

Aoife and two other women have entered the room, all three of them stare at me pleadingly.

"You can't leave a birthday celebration early." I laugh. "Right, Mother?"

She blinks. "Darren, please take the women to my lounge and arrange for treats. I'll be there momentarily."

He groans out a complaint about doing *women's work* and then leaves with a troop of ladies.

When the doors are shut, my mother says, "You won't be entertaining the guests. I'll tell them you got tired."

"Why?"

"I don't think we should give them the chance to ask any questions about your face."

"Mom—"

"You managed to survive the night, Ria, but don't push it."

"No one cares about the scar."

"I do. We're fortunate Caolán didn't see it earlier. You have no idea what that mark could do to this family."

"Honestly, the mafia is far too old fashioned."

"I agree. But we don't make the rules—"

"No, Mother, as women we don't do anything except what our husbands tell us to do."

She shakes her head and marches away. "Hopefully, your husband tells you to keep your mouth shut."

"If he doesn't, my mother certainly will."

"And if you don't like it, you'll cut yourself up again!" Her demeanor breaks and she shouts the last part of her sentence, silencing me with a gasp.

"Maybe I should retire early," I mutter.

"Yes," Mom agrees. "You have an early morning anyway."

"I do?" The question jumps out of me even though I don't want to speak to her anymore.

"I didn't get the chance to tell you. As your birthday gift, the O'Rourke family has invited you to their estate. You will have brunch with the family and make plans for the upcoming Christmas Ball together."

That is their birthday gift? Why didn't Caolán tell me this himself? I think of the last words he said to my mother. *We'll talk soon.* Did he tell her then? Why didn't he tell *me*? The question burns me and leaves a sour taste in my mouth. I don't want to spend the day with Caolán's family. I'm not even sure I want to spend the day with *Caolán*. Clearly, he chooses when to speak to me and what to share with me. I suddenly feel like a child again. Like that nine-year-old girl who thought the world of that mysterious, smiling man.

I fear I have been fooled. Terribly.

"I don't want to go," I say softly.

"You will go," my mother replies. "You will behave yourself. You will impress Caolán's family. And for the love of God, Gloria, you will keep that awful scar covered."

6

Ria

Mother makes me wear green to the O'Rourke family gathering. I tried to tell her that was unnecessary, that Irish people would be as annoyed with me wearing green as I'd be with them serving fried chicken for dinner. But Mother wouldn't have it. So here I am, walking up the front lawn of their massive mansion in a bright green dress with matching shoes. I've even got a shamrock hairpin in my head. I feel like a fool.

A maid answers the door when we knock; she's an older woman with a strict face and small eyes that widen when she sees us. Her silver eyebrows shoot to the top of her head. "You must be the Jacksons."

I wonder what gave it away.

We are led through a massive foyer decorated with statues, paintings, and a chandelier that is bolted to the ceiling by thick metal poles. I try not to tilt my head back as I walk under it, watching the diamonds shimmer.

Music spills down the hall, a mellow tune with low vocals. I recognize the song, something I've heard on the radio a hundred times already. Apparently, my mother has heard it too. That's what makes her nervous as she realizes how foolish we look dressed like this.

When we get to the lounge door, she glances at me and laughs. "Nice song."

"Were you honestly expecting tavern music?"

She chews her bottom lip, and I wonder if that's her way of admitting that, yes, she truly had been expecting some medieval song with a red headed bar wench crooning on a stool and someone stomping through an Irish stepdance in the corner.

The maid smiles and opens the double doors for us. I hear chatter over the music, but it immediately hushes when my mother and I walk inside. We are greeted by no less than 25 Irishmen and women who stare at us with pressed lips and wide eyes, as if withholding laughter. I would laugh at myself if I could muster the courage.

"Welcome!" says a voice lovely as silk.

The crowd parts to reveal a beautiful woman. She is tall, elegant as a swan, and moves with the grace of a lazy angel drifting through the room. Her dress is white which makes her pale blonde hair seem almost silver, pulled back into a ponytail that swings back and forth as she walks toward us. She is so pristine, I half expect her heels to be glass slippers.

She must be Caolán's mother, I conclude, *queen of the White I land.*

"Aifric O'Rourke." Each one of her pearly white teeth is

visible when she smiles and holds out her hand. It's positioned with the fingers down, like she wants me to take it and kiss it.

"Um, Gloria Jackson." I reach for her hand, but my mother nudges me aside and takes it instead. She squeezes her fingers like an old friend and doesn't dare incline her head. We may be in their house, but my mother is still a mafia queen. That makes her Aifric's equal.

The woman's smile seems etched onto her smooth, porcelain skin. For a long moment, she neither speaks nor moves. She just stands there blinking, like she cannot believe we didn't kiss her hand.

"Well," she finally says, "welcome to your new home, Gloria."

"Thank you."

"Allow me to introduce you to your new family." Aifric sweeps her arm out to the watching crowd. Their faces have relaxed so they don't look ready to laugh at us, but I'm not sure their expressions are much better now. They look unimpressed, each pair of eyes staring at the side of my face, covered by my thick curly hair. I feel my palms begin to sweat.

"My husband," Aifric motions to a man the size of Santa Claus with a red beard and thick red hair.

He thrusts his mitten hand at me. "Charles O'Rourke."

"Call him Father," Aifric says and everyone pauses, staring at me.

"H-Hi, Dad," I mutter.

My mother shifts her weight from one foot to the other, as uncomfortable as I am.

"And this is your brother, Nolan." Aifric reaches for a small blonde boy who takes my breath away. He's so pretty I can't even speak for a moment. Baby blue eyes, round as marbles, and straight blonde hair cut into an old-fashioned bowl. It would look embarrassing if he weren't so cute. When his eyes meet mine, I feel all of my mother's shameful stereotypes drift through my head. I suddenly hear the tin whistle and the bodhrán and the Irish harp playing somewhere in the distance, and I see the carpet fade away, replaced by lush greenery and rolling fog.

Looking at Nolan is like looking at Ireland itself.

This *is an Irish prince*, I think, reaching for his hand. He shocks me by kissing it, his lips soft and warm as they peck the skin. "*Dia duit.*"

His accent is so beautiful I hardly notice he's spoken another language. I'm mesmerized by his mere presence, as is his mother who hovers nearby, close enough to catch his hand and interlock her fingers with his when he steps away. She's smitten with him. I wonder what she thinks of Caolán, but she doesn't bring him forward. When Nolan steps back, Aifric announces it's time to serve breakfast and sweeps an arm in the direction of the door for us to leave.

She must notice the confusion on my face because she says, "Don't worry, Caolán will join us soon," then she floats away, humming to herself and dragging Nolan along. Charles follows at a leisurely pace, the crowd flowing around him like a rock in water.

"That wasn't so bad," my mother says beside me.

I don't reply.

Breakfast is an array of foods. There's a buffet where the children run like starving victims and stick their hands into the candied plums while the adults reach over them with tongs and spatulas. They pile their plates with bacon, grilled tomatoes, black and white pudding, baked beans, brown bread, poached eggs, apple oatmeal, and finish with strong black coffee.

I hardly know where to begin, so I take a saucer and settle for a poached egg with toasted soda bread. My mother does the same, adding coffee with rich Irish cream. She sits on my right side with Aifric beside her. I'd expected my mother-in-law to sit beside me, but the seat on my left is occupied by a slender man who glances at me once he sets down his plate.

"Tadhg," he says.

For a moment, I think he's greeting me in Irish, then I realize he just said his *name*. It's pronounced like TIGE, as if saying *Tiger*, but without the 'R.'

"Gloria," I say back.

He takes his knife and starts cutting into a thick sausage. "I know who you are. You stand out like a sore thumb here."

I feel my cheeks burn. "I know."

"Well, you *almost* fit in." He laughs. "With all the green."

"Please don't remind me."

"Whose idea was it?"

"My mother's."

"Figured. Parents are awful, aren't they? Especially in this business." He laughs and chops the tip off his sausage with his sharp teeth. "My father told me I had to find a wife by the end of summer or else he'll cut me out of his will."

"Sorry to hear that."

"He gave me a tough timeframe because he knows I'll cave and let him arrange the marriage for me." Tadhg shrugs. "I'm not opposed to an arranged marriage. Looks like things worked out for my cousin, at least."

By *cousin*, I'm sure he means Caolán, so I smile and nod, but I keep my head down because as soon as I look up at him, I see his dark eyes laser to the left side of my face. He's staring shamelessly, even sets down his fork and knife and leans toward me.

"Well … Things *almost* worked out."

I look up.

"You're almost pretty," he says, nodding at my face. "And you almost fit in." He nods at my awful green outfit. "But that's where it ends."

I swallow my bite of toast, but it's thick and dry and I nearly choke on it. I hadn't grabbed a drink, so I reach for my mother's coffee, but Tadhg grabs my other wrist and holds me in place. His breath is hot on my ear, the heavy smell of sausage burns my nose as he hisses, "Why are you here *without* Caolán? Where is he?"

"Let me go." I try to tug my arm free, but he holds tight, twisting my wrist a little further. We're sitting so close, it looks like he's simply holding my hand. Tadhg has mastered the art of intimidation; his face is impassive, his eyes cold but charming. By the look of his face, you'd never know he was hurting me.

He leans even closer, so I feel his breath on my cheek, rolling over my bumpy scar. "Did you scare him away already?"

"I said let *go*." I twist my arm away, but he shoves me at the same time, and I collide with my mother. Her dishes clatter as she jumbles against the table, catching everyone's attention. The room is all staring at *me* instead of looking at Tadhg, the real culprit. He's gone back to slicing his sausage, pretending nothing happened between us.

My face is hot, and I feel the backs of my eyes burning. Before any tears can form, I bolt to my feet and mumble something about the bathroom before rushing out the door. My footsteps echo down the hallway like claps of thunder as I practically run away from that room. I'm not crying because I'm hurt or even embarrassed, the tears are there because I'm angry.

Who does Tadhg think he is? He called me ugly and unfashionable, then he put his hands on me in a room full of people. Did no one notice? Or did they simply refuse to acknowledge what was happening?

He grabbed a mafia princess without worrying what the repercussions would be…

Who is Tadhg? The question haunts me as my feet slow and I stop in the middle of the hall. Caolán's family is head of the O'Rourke bloodline, but there are four other Clans in the White Hand. Which one is in charge of them all? I have no idea, and I don't have time to figure it out. I don't even know where I'm at right now, forget the stupid Hand.

I glance down the hall, turning in a slow circle. I've got no idea where I am.

"Great," I mutter.

There's a stretch of doors in either direction, I pick one and begin stomping toward the largest set of doors at the end of the hallway. "That should be the dining room," I say aloud.

A voice behind me replies, "That's my father's office."

I jump and turn to find Nolan at the other end of the hall. He stuffs his hands into his pockets as he approaches, looking less like an angelic prince and more like a lazy kid with each step. Suddenly, his face isn't as mesmerizing as I remember. His eyes are faded blue, his hair falls into his face in choppy bangs, and he quickly brushes them back with an annoyed huff. Up close, he doesn't look mesmerizing. He just looks tired.

"Bathroom is back this way," he jerks his head.

"I don't really have to go," I admit.

"I figured you didn't." He barely has an accent now, unlike before when he kissed my hand and spoke Irish. It makes me wonder if some part of Nolan's appearance is just a performance. Something he does to please his overbearing mother. "Was it Tadhg who got to you?" he asks.

"Just nerves."

"You don't have to protect him."

"Seems like everyone else in there was protecting him."

Nolan looks uncomfortable.

"You knew he was messing with me, but you didn't intervene. You only stepped in after I left." I take a step closer. "Who is Tadhg?"

Nolan runs his hand through his hair. "He's the prince of

Clan Fitzpatrick. Underboss of the Pointer Finger of the White Hand."

Even I know the Pointer Finger must be the ones in charge. If Tadhg is their prince, then he's a powerful man. Powerful enough to do whatever he wants in a room full of people.

I just don't know why he targeted *me*.

"Technically, Tadhg is a distant cousin," Nolan continues. "I mean, everyone in the White Hand is related somehow."

"I guess manners don't run in the family."

He chuckles. "Don't mind Tadhg. He's always been a jerk, and he's only messing with you to irritate Caolán."

"Why?"

"Because my brother is popular with the Pointer Finger. During the war, he did what Tadhg couldn't."

"Which was?"

Nolan shrugs one shoulder. "Ended it."

I get it now. Caolán made Tadhg look incompetent; that was years ago, but Tadhg is the prince of the Pointer Finger. As mafia royalty, he doesn't get to mess up. It was his job to end that war, but he let Caolán step in and do it for him. He's been living with years of failure on his shoulders ever since. Now Tadhg finally has the chance to exert his dominance. To make Caolán feel as small as he's felt all these years after the war.

I'm the perfect target. The prize of the war itself.

I resist the urge to hug myself as worry floods through me. Nolan's voice brings me back into focus. He sounds sincere. "Caolán won't let him touch you again."

"That's a great promise for the future, but what am I supposed to do until then?" I reply. "Where is Caolán?"

"I wish I knew." Nolan glances away but then his eyes return to mine, and they're suddenly filled with mischief. "Wanna check his room? He might have left clues."

My heart flutters and I can't stop myself from grinning as I answer, "Absolutely."

To be honest, I'm not really interested in rifling through Caolán's sock drawer. I want to see his room because I don't want to go back into that dining hall to face Aifric or my mother. Not to mention Tadhg.

I'm happy here with Nolan. With his mischievous smile and his tired eyes, he looks nothing like the boy I met earlier, but I think that's what draws me to him even more. Both of us have roles to fill here in the mafia. Neither of us likes it.

I wonder if being his mother's puppet is any better than being my family's mascot.

Nolan leads me to Caolán's room, smirking and glancing back over his shoulder the whole time we walk. I lift my skirt and take quick little steps on the balls of my feet, trying to quiet my footsteps. We're both grinning like old friends, like we've done this together a hundred times. I love it. I love the rush of adrenaline, knowing that I'm breaking the rules, that in some small way, I'm taking something the mafia has denied me. Freedom.

I started sneaking away when I was eleven, ducking into crowds when my mother wasn't looking, and her handmaid was distracted. When I was twelve, I slipped away at a banquet where my father had gathered with men in suits and my mother stood with pretty women I did not recognize.

I snuck off because I wanted to see if the pool was open. Eventually, I found it, but someone was already there.

It was Caolán, but he wasn't alone. There was a woman with him, wrapped in his arms and pressed against the stone wall. She wore the same uniform as the other banquet staff members, her name tag, *Ashley*, glinted in the sunlight as Caolán ruffled her shirt, sliding his large hands beneath it. She'd gasped and thrown her head back, and he'd covered her mouth with his own to muffle the sound. I was entranced. At twelve years old, I had seen people kiss before. But not like that.

Hidden behind the palm trees dotting the grand pool, I pressed myself against the bark and watched with silent, adolescent intrigue. I was at the edge of puberty, excited by feelings and sensations I couldn't explain or comprehend. And there was the man I'd dreamt about for years, kissing a woman. I couldn't look away. Couldn't unsee the way his lips covered hers, the way his jaw moved, flashes of his tongue sliding into her mouth. And then he finally pulled his hands from beneath her shirt, and gripped her bottom, lifting her from the ground. She had laughed and latched her legs around his waist, but her laugh was cut short when she glanced up and looked right at me.

"Wait!" she gasped, pulling away from Caolán.

He looked confused when she jerked back, but I never got to see his reaction beyond that. Before he could turn around and spot me, I hopped to my feet and dashed away.

"I thought I saw someone," the woman had said as I ran.

I returned to the party in time for lunch to be served, but I wasn't hungry. I was breathless and nervous and shaking. Caolán was late for the banquet. He arrived after lunch, just as the dishes were cleared. I never told anyone that I saw him. Never told anyone that he was late because he'd been by the pool with *Ashely*, gasping and moaning against the wall. I kept all of that to myself, like my own little secret. And later that day, when he finally came to see me, I smiled like nothing had happened.

When his visit was over, I did the same thing I always did. I stood on my tiptoes for a kiss—but not on my cheek. I wanted to be kissed the way I'd seen him kiss *Ashely*.

But he denied me yet again.

Caolán took my hand and kissed it. "It was nice to see you again, Gloria."

"Is that all?" I'd asked, frowning.

He had laughed and patted my head. "That's all for now."

That's all for now... words that'd haunted my twelve-year-old dreams. *For now*, I was not a woman. *For now*, I wasn't enough for Caolán. *For now*, he could not kiss me.

I spent six more years waiting for a kiss, hugging my pillow at night and thinking of the red headed man and his full lips and the way he'd held *Ashley*. But those fantasies became nightmares when I turned fifteen and learned the truth. That the charming man I'd yearned for was a mafia boss. The brother of the man who'd killed my older sister. Suddenly, I didn't want kisses anymore. I wanted nothing to do with the mafia at all.

But here I am, sneaking down the hall to get into Caolán's bedroom. Grinning like I'm a child again. When we finally reach the room, I can't help but wonder what I will see inside. What secrets has my Prince Charming been keeping?

Caolán's bedroom is locked but Nolan learned to pick locks before he learned to tie his shoes. Shamelessly, so did I. No, I don't condone breaking into anyone's bedroom, but I can't deny the fact that I was raised in the mafia. There are some skills you learn in this business that aren't so bad.

Nolan grins when he gets the door open, and we tiptoe inside with our lungs full of held breath.

Caolán's room is dark. Not the décor, I mean, *there is no light in here*. The light switch doesn't work and there are no lamps on the bedside table or the desk across the room. I don't even see a candle. Nolan has to open the curtains for us to walk around without tripping over anything. Once the sunlight pours in, I almost wish he hadn't yanked the curtains back. I almost wish I hadn't entered the room at all.

The walls are dirty, stained with splotches of red. It's on the floor too, like someone flung a paintbrush around the room. The carpets have slashes in them, there's even a knife stabbed into the floor right beside the entrance to the balcony. On the desk is a display of guns, they're all dismantled and set out like dismembered bodies. Even from the doorway, I can tell they've been polished. They're the only clean things in the entire room.

Standing here now, I feel a sudden sense of guilt wash over me. Like I've crossed a boundary, stepped into a place I was never supposed to see. But now I can't *un*see it.

Fear chases the guilt away and devours my heart. I need to leave. What if Caolán found out I was here? What if he found out I've seen all of this madness?

"We should go," I whisper to Nolan who looks just as frightened. I'm guessing this isn't the sort of décor he'd been expecting either. It makes me wonder if this is the first time he's ever been here.

I turn around to retreat and pause, my eyes landing on Caolán's bed. I can't breathe as I stare at it.

"No-Nolan," I mutter, "why does Caolán sleep in a coffin?"

Nolan takes a cautious step forward but his shoulders sag in relief and he lets out a sigh as he nears the bed. "That's not a coffin. It's too big."

He's right. The bed is king sized; they don't make coffins that large. That's the only thing that gives me peace. The whole bed is glossy black; there isn't a headboard and the slats of wood on the sides come up enough to make the bed look like a coffin, but I take Nolan's word for it. The mattress is bare and torn to shreds, like someone took that spare knife to it. Tried to cut out all the springs. The sheets are missing entirely, but there's a blanket thrown across it that's threadbare and stained with that mysterious red liquid. The whole thing looks wrong. It might not be a coffin, but it's still a monstrosity.

The *room* is a monstrosity. A scene of chaos.

"Let's go." Nolan pulls me out the door and slowly shuts it

behind him.

Now that we're in the hall, neither of us knows what to say or think. We just stand there breathing and blinking and wondering what the heck we just saw, but we don't speak on it. After a few moments, Nolan nods like he's just come to some sort of conclusion, and then he walks away.

"We should get back," he says over his shoulder.

"Nolan, wait—"

"Just forget it." He shakes his head. "Everything you saw in there, just forget it, Gloria."

I want to. I really do. But how?

7

Caolán

I hold the blade against the man's throat and repeat the same words, like a ritual. "Are you afraid?"

The man says nothing, but that isn't surprising. He can't speak because he has no tongue. Still, I give him a moment with God because I don't think the Lord requires a tongue to hear your prayers. Then I slide the blade across his throat.

Eoin Greene dies slowly. I watch his life drain from his eyes and I wonder where he goes. Surprisingly, the Irish mafia is very Catholic. We need a way to balance the darkness so we raise our children in the Church, praying that one day God will be merciful and save their cursed souls.

I grew up memorizing the Ten Commandments and reciting the Lord's Prayer. I fasted for Lent and took Communion every First Sunday. I was Christened and circumcised at birth and baptized at age 12. Then I was initiated into the White Hand Gang at 13. I don't know how much of the Bible I believe, but I do believe in God Himself—if only because I believe in the devil. I have seen the evil of this world. I have partaken in it. I know that if there is something called Satan roaming this earth then there must also be a God whose light outshines the darkness.

That is what I choose to believe. That, in the end, there is somewhere for Eoin Greene to go. That God was merciful enough to let him through those pearly gates.

As he dies, he fills the room with an awful noise, finally succumbing to his injuries. Normally, the target doesn't sustain injuries. I end things with a single bullet, no time for them to react let alone *feel* anything. But Eoin is different. Eoin was a snitch, and snitches don't get to die a painless death.

"Strong as an ox!" Billy O'Rourke cackles loudly. He's here once again, waiting in the back of the warehouse, by the deep freezer that already holds one body.

Reapers rarely work together but I've gotten rusty over the years, so when I picked up the name, I thought I'd need Billy's help because this wasn't just a kill; I had to torture him. It's not something I have a problem with, but Billy is an expert at this. He loves blood more than I do, and since I have plans today, I had to push things along. So here we are.

"Tough guy, right?" Billy says to me.

"That took longer than it should have," I say back.

My cousin shrieks as he slaps Eoin's dead shoulder. His body flops forward in the chair he's tied to, blood gushes from his empty mouth. I cut out his tongue. He'd been using it against us, so we took it back. I'll have Billy deliver it to the Pointer Finger tonight. I have no idea what they plan to do with it and neither do I care. My part in this gruesome mess is over.

"Nolan missed a good one," Billy says.

"He didn't need to see this," I murmur.

"Yes, he did. You can't shield him from this forever. This is who we are, Caolán. Nolan needs to accept that."

Honestly, it's my mother I'm more worried about. She's one of the reasons Nolan is so soft. She's coddled him since he was a baby, never fully explained who he was or what his life would be like in this family. It's like she wanted him to live as a civilian while holding the title of a mafia prince.

People like us don't get to live in both worlds. We have to pick one. I chose the mafia, it's time for Nolan to choose too. And for my wife. Seeing her yesterday put a lot of things into perspective. She's not a child anymore, but she's just as wide-eyed and innocent as my little brother. I could tell just from looking. She knows nothing of the world she was born into, and running off to a Christian boarding school certainly didn't help expose her to it. Now she's going to get a firsthand look at her in-laws on this awful date my mother has set up. I have half a mind to skip it altogether but I'm not so cruel as to leave Gloria there alone.

But ... What am I going to do with her?

I shake my head, vowing to figure it out later. "Will you handle the clean up?" I ask Billy. "I've something I need to do."

Billy makes a face. "I cleaned up the last guy alone."

"I have plans. You know this."

I was supposed to see Gloria for brunch earlier, but I was here instead. Technically, that isn't Billy's fault. I took the kill when I knew I didn't have the time, but I also didn't have a choice. I needed this kill. This outlet.

Believe it or not, my last outlet was worse than killing people. My relief came in the form of a silvery powder called *fog*. It's a drug the White Hand produces right here in California. It got its name from the powerful illusions it gives the user, clouding your mind with fantasies that are so vivid, I nearly killed to stay in them.

That was my outlet. A little bag of powder that left me staggering on my feet, stumbling into the house at night, slurring my words, obsessing over things that weren't there. I tore myself apart with fog and death, killing and snorting and vomiting up my miseries. Then doing it all over again. I messed up. But I got myself clean sometime after Aidan's death. I left the drugs and the killing alone. I'm better now.

I think.

"You're already late," Billy says, pulling me from my thoughts. "Another hour won't matter."

"I need to shower and change." There is blood on my shirt and a little staining the toe of my polished shoes. "I can't let her see me like this."

He scans me from head to toe and then shrugs. "Let her see the real you. She'll find out one day."

Not this day. I've worked too hard to make myself appealing to Gloria. She needs to grow up, just like Nolan, but she will do it on my terms. Not Billy's and certainly not my mother's.

I can't say this to Billy, he'll think I've gone soft, and maybe I have. I spent nine years watching my wife grow into a woman. Hidden in the crowd, I watched her walk to her piano lessons as a teenager. From a safe distance, my spies saw her celebrate every birthday. And through a pair of binoculars, I saw her leave for the airport when she first flew to her boarding school in England. That was when I noticed the scar. I don't know how she got it; it must have happened when my spies weren't tailing her. That's the only thing in her life that I have ever missed. It took everything in me not to brush her hair aside last night and see it up close, but I didn't want to do that to her. She would never forgive me if I embarrassed her like that.

"Just take care of this, will you?" I motion to Eoin's body, but Billy's already a step ahead of me. He's got a hacksaw out and is sawing at the man's leg, dismembering him. A snitch's death is a gruesome thing.

"This'll take all day!" he calls as I leave. "You owe me!"

I sure do.

When I finally make it home, I try to sneak in through the back entrance, but my mother outsmarts me by placing her assistant, Quinn, by the door. When I enter, she's waiting with a smile that says, *You're cute.*

My shoulders slouch. "Does she know I'm here?"

She holds up her phone. "I let her know the moment security cameras picked up your car entering the garage."

"Let her know I'll be down in twenty minutes—"

"Your mother said you are to report to her as soon as you arrive." Quinn smiles. "She already knows you're here; you shouldn't keep her waiting."

Quinn is a shrewd woman who loves exerting what little power she has whenever she can. When I was a child, she would grin when I got into trouble, twisting my ear or pinching my arm until I screamed. If I had been a mafia prin*cess* instead of a prince, she would've had her fingers removed for such cruelty. But my parents thought the extra discipline would toughen me up. In a way, it worked. If Quinn ever slips up, I will gladly choke her to death without batting an eye. I think that's tough enough, right?

No matter how I feel, I can't kill Quinn in the middle of the hallway unprovoked.

I stifle a sigh and gesture down the hall. "Lead the way, Quinn."

She takes me to one of the small lounges just down the hall from an equally small dining room. Just before she pushes the door open, I adjust my suit jacket and hope there's no blood on my sleeves. I wasn't supposed to be on a job in the first place. It's bad enough that I'm late, to show up with my kill on my clothes would be unforgivable. And sloppy. But I push all those thoughts aside as Quinn guides me into the room.

It's empty except for the feminine figure resting on the fat chair by the fireplace. I know it is my mother because of how stiff she is. Like a creature carved from ice, she is cold and hard and breathlessly beautiful. Her hair is blonde and long as her body, swaying in a ponytail that brushes her hips. Her neck is slender as a swan's, her mouth is pink as a Barbie's, her eyes are dead like mine.

She inhales and I wonder if she can smell the blood on my clothes because she says, "You took a job."

"Yes."

Her scowl is devilish. "I told you no more."

"I know."

"I told you that is beneath us."

"I *know*," I say again. She has made this more than clear for the last fifteen years of my life, constantly reminding us that she came from a respectable family of the Pinky Finger.

My mother expected to marry into luxury or power, but her father signed a contract with Charlie O'Rourke, and she found herself the queen of a lowly clan of murderers instead.

Despite being a hitman, my father was still rich. Aifric used his money to invest in businesses and made our family even richer. Then she raised Aidan to be the perfect heir and secured a marriage to the Panthers—a powerful deal that managed to impress the leaders of the Pointer Finger. And finally, her greatest handiwork was me.

My mother did not like the fact that I continued the family business by becoming an assassin, but she found a way to use even that to her advantage. She made me good at my job. She taught me how to extract information, how to sniff out fear, how to track my target. She fed me intel, secured information on my behalf, and gave me targets that others thought impossible for me to get to.

I completed every assignment, and each time I pulled the

trigger, she hated me a little more. That hatred became palpable when I got addicted to fog. I was everything she couldn't stand about the Middle Finger. A lowly grunt doing the Pointer Finger's bidding. I was an embarrassment to her, a daily reminder of who her family was at its core. Despite all the fancy things she'd bought to cover that up.

The hatred was easy to handle because I was making her all the money she'd ever wanted. It was easy to handle because I was living in the shadows, keeping my shameful ways hidden in the darker corners of our world. It was easy to handle because I was high all the time on fog. But then Aidan died, and his crown was laid on my head. I was suddenly in the spotlight, a place never meant for a crackhead murderer like me.

My mother cannot stand it. Not just my job as a hitman, she cannot stand that I took the assignment that changed our lives forever. Her murderous son has replaced her perfect heir. The boy she'd groomed and cultivated since he'd spoken his first word. He's gone and I'm here. Not her perfect boy, but her perfect failure.

Neither of us likes it. Neither of us has ever gotten used to it. But what else can we do?

"I told you *no more*," Aifric says again, her voice high and cracking. "I told you not to miss the family brunch. I told you that you needed to be here for your new wife."

"Mháthair, it was only brunch. Gloria will still be my new wife tonight at dinner."

"That's not the point!" she yells, throwing her hands up. "Is it impossible for you to behave as you should, or must you kill every chance you get?"

I surrender an easy smile, brushing my bangs from my face. "How should a mafia underboss behave?"

"With class. With authority."

"The authority to remind you of your place?"

Oh ... She doesn't like that one bit. Her face curdles and floods red with rage. "You think you have authority?"

"That's what it means to be the underboss, right?"

"You have no idea what it means. You have no idea what it's like to rule."

I cannot stop myself from chuckling. "Sadly, Mháthair, neither do you. And you never will."

"Do not mock me," she hisses as I turn toward the door. "I have run this family for over thirty years, I will not let your bloodlust tear it apart!"

"I needed an outlet. One kill doesn't count as bloodlust."

She scoffs. "Murder is your outlet."

"Murder is how we get paid."

"And what do you use your money on?" she challenges. "Are you using again?"

I pivot and storm to her in three strides, forcing her back a step. "Don't you *dare*."

She laughs in my face. Like I'm nothing but a joke to her. "No. You aren't using. You would've struck me down by now if you were."

She ... She's right. I wasn't myself when I was using. I wasn't normal. My obsession with blood was insatiable. I'd take kill after kill and go to sleep covered in crimson. I loved jobs that required stalking, and I lived for torture. I'd volunteer for cleanups, dismembering bodies with a smile on my face, mysteriously waking up from a high with amputated fingers in my bed. Blood stains on the floor. Gouged-out eyes left in my sink. I've no idea who they belonged to, most days I didn't even remember taking them. I *couldn't* remember taking them because of the fog. That's what it did to me. Fogged my memory, blurred the lines between illusion and reality. I wasn't even sure if I was killing names on my list or just murdering random people. *Innocent* people. But at the same time, the fog hushed the voices. Quieted the screams. Fog gave me peace in the very chaos it'd created.

It made me a good reaper. Maybe even turned me into a serial killer. That's why I keep my room veiled in darkness. I can't stand to see the mess I once made. The monster I'd been, caged in that prison cell. Where I belonged. Regardless, I will not allow my mother to insult me for an addiction she fed. She hated the fog, yet she supplied me with it, knowing it helped me get through each job. Then she turned on me when I became too much for her to handle.

"I'm a murderer," I tell her, stepping ever closer, so I can get into her face. "But murder is how you can afford your big house and your pretty dress and your blonde extensions. Don't you dare look down on me for what I've done for this family. For what I've done for *you*."

She shoves me away. "Look at what your job has turned you into. The sort of man who brushes off family events to kill people. The sort of man who disrespects his mother." She spits—literally spits—on the floor. "Aidan would have never—"

"Aidan is dead," I say flatly. "You should know that better than anyone."

For a very long, very quiet moment, my mother does nothing but stare at me. Before she can think of something to say, a knock sounds at the door. It is gentle, hesitant, like the person knocking doesn't really want to enter.

"*What is it?*" I call over my shoulder.

Quinn's voice responds, "Dinner has been served. Your guests are waiting."

Mother composes herself, fixing her ponytail and smoothing the wrinkles in her dress. "We'll be right there," she says, and her voice is strong as stone. Solid. Firm. Like nothing happened in the last five minutes. She's back to the icy woman of my childhood nightmares. But I'm not a child anymore. That's something she's having a hard time coping with. She can't bully me like she did with Aidan, and she can't control me like she does with Nolan. But she wants to. And she's trying to.

As my mother brushes past me, she gives me a look that says *this isn't over*. We will finish this conversation later, and when we do, she will have the final say.

8

Caolán

The smell of garlic and roasted meat hits me hard as I enter the dining room. Everyone is already eating, but they look up from their plates and stare in silence as my mother and I find our seats. My entire family is here. This is something I wasn't expecting. When Mother put the schedule together, she mentioned brunch and family activities, followed by a fancy dinner in the evening. I thought all of this would happen with just the four of us and Gloria. Not half my cousins and their spouses and guests from other Clans. No wonder Aifric was so upset I'd missed the morning and afternoon. She'd wanted me to be here for all of her esteemed guests.

My eyes scan the room. I see members from every Finger, but my gaze lingers on Tadhg Fitzpatrick the longest. He is the failed prince of the Pointer Finger, and he looks eerily happy to see me. When he notices my gaze, he lifts his glass and then adjusts in his chair. It's at that moment that I realize the chair beside him is empty, but it isn't saved for me.

My mother crosses the room and sits next to Tadhg. She even smiles at him like she's happy about it. Deep down, she probably is. This is her chance to kiss up to the Pointer Finger, praying it makes a difference for our family, but I know it won't. Tadhg hates me. He hates that I, a drug addicted lunatic, ended the war while he abandoned us. He isn't here to pay his respects to my new marriage, he's here to try to ruin it. In front of my entire family.

I take a seat across from Gloria and exhale slowly. My mother is announcing the menu, but I'm not listening. To distract myself, I take this moment to study Gloria. She's wearing a green dress that matches her mother's, they look like a pair of overripe limes. She must feel awful in that cheesy getup, but when she sees me, she smiles and inclines her head like nothing is wrong. The sight of her almost hurts. Gloria still looks at me like I hold the world in my hand. The *White Hand*, but she doesn't need the details. I make an effort to smile back.

As young as she is, I can see the woman Gloria has become. Her lips are full, and her smile is practiced; it almost reaches her eyes. They're large and hazel, bright against her dark brown skin, and her hair is a shock of natural coils that spring out in every direction. She's parted and tamed them, so they appear as dark clouds puffing around her shoulders. They're thick enough to cover the left side of her face. The side with the scar. She doesn't know I've already seen it, so I'm not surprised when her confidence slips as I shift my gaze to focus on her left side.

"Good evening," I say to her alone. "I'm sorry I'm late."

"It's alright." Her voice is soft. Sweet.

"Did I miss much?"

"Only half the day," my mother says. "What an impression you've made."

Gloria's mother laughs loudly. "Oh, Aifric, we've enjoyed ourselves so much we hardly noticed his absence!"

It takes great effort for my mother not to roll her eyes. She busies herself with a sip of wine and then dabs at the corner of her mouth. "I am glad he hasn't dampened the mood, however, we had a schedule for the day."

"I had work," I say flatly.

"I told you to be here. You know how much I hate excuses."

"You hate a great many things, Mother—"

"Now that you're here," my father wisely interrupts, "let us enjoy our meal."

The room falls silent, and I try my best not to fill it with screaming. My mother is pushing my buttons, trying to assert dominance where there is no need. She's doing this for Gloria's sake, letting her know who really runs this family. And for Tadhg's sake, putting on a show for the Pointer Finger.

"Your home is beautiful," Mrs. Jackson says nervously. "Thank you for having us today. It was amazing to meet your family."

"And amazing for us to meet you," Tadhg inserts with a smile I do not trust. His eyes glow as they fall onto my wife, consuming every part of her. It's like watching a wolf lick its chops. "Welcome to the family, dear."

"Thank you," Gloria says.

"Let's raise a toast." Tadhg stands and Aifric stands beside him, motioning for the staff to pour everyone a drink.

When a woman steps beside me to pour wine into my glass, Tadhg clears his throat. "Caolán, there's water for you. No need to indulge."

I raise an eyebrow. "I'm fine with wine."

"Are you certain you should drink? I thought addicts were supposed to abstain—"

"I'm not an *addict*." My voice is sharp, cracking through the room.

Tadhg smiles, letting the silence devour me. Every eye blinks in my direction, even Gloria's. She is staring at me like she has no idea what's going on. I'm not surprised. She doesn't know who I truly am, that I'm not the Prince Charming of her childhood dreams. That man was a fantasy, one I created *without* fog.

"I'm sure Caolán can handle a toast," my mother says, not to my defense but in defense of the O'Rourke family. Everyone in the Hand knows about my past addiction, but announcing it like this is so disrespectful, it'll leave tongues wagging. Something my mother certainly does not want, especially with the Jacksons here. They could make a strong case to pull out of the consummation and the marriage if they think I'm not a fit husband for Gloria.

"We've all had a little wine," my mother goes on. "You know it isn't as strong as other drinks."

"Wine may not be so strong to you because you drink so

much, Aifric," Tadhg replies, "but Caolán is different, as a recovering addict."

My mother, Aifric O'Rourke, Queen of the Middle Finger, blinks.

Had she really convinced herself that allowing Tadhg in this home wouldn't be a problem for everyone? I'm happy he's embarrassed her too. Now she knows how it feels to have your faults thrown into your face.

Tadhg motions to my glass of water. "Won't you toast with that?"

"Don't try to—"

"I'm toasting with water," Gloria says suddenly.

I fall silent, staring at her raised glass, slender fingers squeezing the stem.

"I don't drink alcohol either," she whispers.

Slowly, I reach for my glass of water. My chest aches as I lift it. I'm standing in a room full of people I hate. Family who enjoys watching me suffer. But here is Gloria, defending me in this small way. The only way she can.

What an unexpected spark of light in this awful dark world.

Tadhg makes a toast I don't listen to and then sets down his glass. "This wine is exquisite. We should do another toast, but I don't want to get anyone drunk."

My stupid mother laughs.

"How does the water taste, Caolán?" Tadhg asks.

I look up to find him smiling. I would spit at him, but I doubt it'd make it across the table, so I settle for staring at the wall over his shoulder like I didn't hear him.

My mother quickly tries to change the subject while she can. She looks at Gloria and says, "I'm sure we'll see more of you after this, right? Considering you'll be living here soon."

Gloria presses her lips together. It's a tiny reaction but more than enough to let me know she doesn't like this arrangement.

"We haven't made any decisions yet," I say.

My mother looks confused. "What do you mean?"

"I mean I was thinking I'd like to live outside the estate."

"I'm sure you think a lot of things, Caolán," Aifric answers, "but this family has resided at this estate for generations. That tradition will not be broken."

"Tradition is important," Tadhg echoes.

My mother jerks her chin down in an awkward nod. "It most certainly is. Right, honey?" She looks at my father who replies with a grunt. He truly does not care, but Aifric is glaring at him, and Tadhg is waiting, so he's got to say something, if only to placate my mother's demand for his support.

He rubs his temple and rests his eyes on my face. He looks like a man who is tired of his family. A man who just wants to eat his roast beef. "Tradition is important," he says plainly.

"So important." Tadhg shakes his head like he's deeply moved.

"You're right," I agree. "*Traditionally*, the Pointer Finger leads the White Hand. Unless it involves winning a war."

The color drains from Tadhg's face, he even chokes on his food and reaches for his wine to wash it down.

Because I'm petty, I add, "How does failure taste?"

Aifric does not respond, leaving my father to jump in and

save my life. Everyone in this room knows my comment could cost me my tongue, but Tadhg won't do anything so drastic so long as the Jacksons are here. He might not like me, but he knows the Hand needs this alliance. If he is credited with ruining it, his father will punish him. Severely.

My father points his fork at me like I'm a child, his voice comes out in a dark, dangerous tone. A rumble of thunder, threatening a storm. "Do not disrespect your elder."

Tadhg lifts his hand as if to wave all of this off. "I'm hardly Caolán's elder. My birthday is only two days before his."

"You are still an honored member of Clan Fitzpatrick," Father says, almost robotically. "Please forgive my son's harsh tone."

"Apologize," my mother says, finally finding her voice.

"Sorry."

Mother jerks to her feet and motions to Tadhg. "Apologize *properly*."

She wants me to kiss his ring.

Before I can refuse and get myself killed, Tadhg surprises me by shaking his head.

"All is forgiven," he says, then he motions to Gloria. "I hope this display hasn't put you off. I promise we're nicer than we seem."

"Every family has squabbles." Gloria stares at her plate. "If it's alright with my husband, I'd like to live here anyway. I like this house."

That's a lie, but I don't challenge her on this. I know Gloria is only speaking up to keep the peace.

"How agreeable." Tadhg nods at Gloria and then opens his hands, gesturing at the table. "I think it's time for dessert. Let's enjoy something sweet while we discuss the Christmas Ball."

We have no choice but to follow his lead. Even though this is our house, Tadhg is still in charge here. As the Prince of the Pointer Finger, he's in charge wherever he goes.

Mother forces a smile and claps her hands. The doors behind her open and servants pour in to set down plates of cake.

There's a single candle in Gloria's slice, the flame lights up her face as she smiles. "How sweet."

"Happy belated birthday," Tadhg says. "I hope you don't mind me giving you this small gift."

Gloria shakes her head. "I don't mind at all."

"Make a wish," Tadhg insists.

Gloria glances between him and my mother, but she obeys the order without question. We all watch as she closes her eyes and then leans forward to blow out the candle, but Tadhg holds up a hand. "Wait!" His voice cracks with panic. "Your hair, it'll catch fire if you aren't careful."

"Oh..." Gloria laughs. "I won't lean forward so far."

"No." Tadhg places a hand over his heart. With his dark hair and picturesque features, the gesture makes him look like a noble prince. "You are a mafia princess. I will not risk an accident here. Just pull your hair back to be safe."

The suggestion robs her of words. Gloria's eyes wildly search the room for a way out. They skitter to my mother who watches with a reserved smile, like she's so concerned. They fly to my father who is eating his own cake, paying us no mind. And then they land on me, and I stare at my plate.

I cannot help her now. If I do, things will only get worse for her later.

"Mrs. Jackson, you would be so upset if something happened, and Gloria's face was marred. Wouldn't you?" Mother says, but Mrs. Jackson doesn't respond, so my mother digs her claws into Gloria. "You understand, right, sweetheart?"

Gloria slowly nods. "Yes. I understand."

My mother smiles. "Then pull your hair back."

Gloria's shaky hands reach up to pull her curly hair away from her face, but Tadhg stops her yet again. "Caolán, why don't you help her?"

How cruel...

I grip my tiny fork. It's supposed to be for cake, but I want to ram it into my mother's eyes. And then Tadhg's. They're doing this on purpose. Humiliating Gloria to punish me.

Tadhg has hated me for years. He would rather hurt my innocent wife than put a bullet in my skull, because a bullet would be quick and painless, but this is long and torturous. This will haunt me for the rest of my life. That Gloria was punished when I should have been. That she was forced to reveal her darkest secret to my entire family, and I had to help her do it.

I stand and button my suit jacket. The walk around the long dinner table feels like a mile, my heart is pounding when I stop behind Gloria's chair. She's sitting perfectly still, staring down at her cake, watching the candle flame shimmy back and forth. She doesn't even react when I reach down and place my hands on both her small shoulders. She remains still. Like she's not even there anymore.

I lean down and speak into her ear so no one else can hear me. "*Tá aiféala orm.*" It's an Irish form of saying 'I'm sorry.' I know Gloria doesn't understand a single syllable, but I say it in my language because I know it better than English. This is the best apology I can give her, even though she doesn't know it.

My hands shook when I shot that man in the warehouse. They shook as I slid the blade across Eoin Greene's throat. They don't shake now as I reach for Gloria's puffy hair.

Are you afraid?

The words dance into my mind, and I almost pause. I have no business thinking of that question; this isn't an execution. But it certainly feels like one, like the death of the chance we had to find love in this marriage. For nine years I stayed away from Gloria, only visiting when necessary. I wanted her to see me as a charming man, but I didn't want to groom her. I stayed away from Gloria to protect her from myself. And now I'm the one who is hurting her. Revealing her darkest secret to a room full of people.

The table holds in a collective gasp once Gloria's face is revealed. Everyone is stunned—except me. I've already seen her scar. I've known about it for years. I even know it's the reason her parents shipped her off to boarding school. They weren't being progressive mafia parents; they were hiding her from the public so no one could see the shame she'd brought them.

With my hands in her hair, Gloria leans forward and safely blows out her candle. It dies with a hiss and smoke rolls over the table, acrid and bitter against the smell of chocolate and sugar. In that moment, I feel like her light goes out with the candle. The flicker in the darkness is gone, and now it's pitch black all around me.

I let her hair go.

"Happy belated birthday," Tadhg says again.

Mother echoes him. "Happy birthday, darling."

"Aifric." My father's voice is deep enough to shake the table. The sound of it draws my mother's full attention.

I glance at him and see the irritation in his eyes. He isn't stopping her because he thinks what she did was wrong, he's intervening because he's annoyed. Whatever. I'll take it.

"Let's move on to the Christmas Ball," he says, waving his hand. Servants practically sprint out to gather our plates, though no one has eaten. "Make this quick, I've grown tired."

At my father's words, the dinner is over, and my mother has been tamed. I steal a look at Gloria as she stands and mutters something about the bathroom. I try to catch her gaze, but she won't look at me. I don't blame her. She's just realized I am not the man of her childhood dreams. That man would have intervened and stopped the taunting. But I didn't. I sat there and let it happen. She will never forget that.

9

Ria

I want to go home, but I can't say that because Caolán's witchy mother or his awful Clan leader will find a way to humiliate me for it. Aifric and Tadhg forced me to expose my face to their entire family. Then they made it worse by making Caolán help.

That's the part I don't understand. He had all of that fire ready for his mother and his distant cousin at the start of dinner, but when it came to me, he remained silent.

Why didn't he stand up for me? The man who showed so much mercy during my childhood has taken a step back, built a wall between us. I thought he would protect me from the dangers of this world. My dark knight. My own guardian angel. But he isn't an angel at all.

Who is Caolán O'Rourke?

I'm slowly learning he is not the man of my dreams. His room was a frightening nightmare. His silence was my own personal hell. His smile is like a wicked reminder that I've been played for a fool. I have married a man I do not know, and I cannot escape it.

At least this is almost over, I tell myself. After the cake incident, Charles moved everyone to a small lounge. The children and most of the women have gone home, leaving only a handful of family members to rest on the sofas and chairs. The fireplace has been lit, cigars are being smoked. This is supposed to be an hour for us to unwind, but relaxation is the farthest thing from my mind.

I'm sitting beside my mother as she goes over the plans for the Christmas Ball with Aifric. Everything has already been arranged, but they're discussing the finishing details just to be sure.

"Gloria is wearing a red dress," my mother says chirpily. "Though I did consider getting her a white one at first, to remind everyone of the wedding."

"The *consummation*, you mean?" Aifric raises her eyebrows.

My mother silently nods.

"Which of your family members will be attending the ceremony?"

Mother speaks slowly, like she doesn't want to discuss this. That makes two of us. "I will attend, my sister will also be a witness, as well as her husband.

I know it's customary for a number of witnesses to watch the ceremony, but the thought of it still makes my skin crawl. Our mafia tradition requires two women and one man from the wife's side of the family and one woman and two men from the husband's. Two witnesses from each party must be directly related to the couple, others can be there for business reasons or as a show of support.

My father cannot witness the ceremony because it is improper for him to see his daughter in such a position. So my uncle will stand in as the male witness for the Panthers. I already know Aifric will be a witness, but I wonder who else from Caolán's family will be watching us have sex.

"Charles and I will be witnesses," Aifric explains, laying a delicate hand on her husband's knee. "We will have my brother—"

"I'd like to be your third witness, if you don't mind." Tadhg smiles at the room, but his eyes are on me. I don't have a choice in this, so I know he isn't staring for approval. He wants to see my reaction.

I try very hard not to squirm at the thought of him seeing me naked.

Tadhg doesn't take his eyes off me. They're darker than his hair, like drops of ink spilled onto his face, disrupting his even complexion. He is the color of a ghost, so pale I can see a long, blue vein in his jaw, wiggling over his hairless chin. If I believed in them, I'd call Tadhg a vampire, though I doubt he lusts for blood. Tadhg feeds on *shame*. He finds it irresistible, like he cannot help but insert himself into every part of my marriage. Even the most intimate.

"I think it would be an honor to have you witness the consummation." Aifric inclines her head to Tadhg. "Honored Fitzpatrick."

I half expect her to take his hand and kiss it but she only grins, flashing perfect white teeth.

"So, it's settled then," Tadhg says.

My eyes flick to Caolán across the room, praying he'll speak up. That he'll say *something*. But he doesn't. To his credit, he looks like he wants to. He's the only one of us who isn't sitting, instead, he's planted himself by the drink display, three fingers of whiskey in his hand which is clenched so tightly around his glass, I'm sure he wants to smash it against a wall. But he doesn't. Caolán doesn't do anything. He accepts this fate—*my* fate, because I'm the one who'll be shamed the most here. For Caolán, the ceremony is a show of masculinity, proof that he can father a child. For me, it is evidence of my innocence. Apparently, the only value I add to this awful dark world.

My mother tries to change the subject. "About the music—"

"I want the couple to share a dance," Aifric says quickly.

Now, Caolán speaks up, grunting from the other side of the room. "I'm not dancing."

"It's important for the couple to spend some time together." Aifric looks at Tadhg for support, instead of her husband.

He obliges. "Dancing is a great part of our culture. What better way to demonstrate your union before both families?"

"We're united now," Caolán says.

"I don't know any official dances," I add. "So, maybe dancing isn't a good idea."

"You truly cannot dance?" Aifric asks me.

I can do the Cupid Shuffle, but I don't think that's the sort of dancing she has in mind.

"No," I say.

Aifric smiles and then motions for one of the young ladies sitting in a nearby chair. The girl nervously stands beside her, unsure if she's about to become a victim or not.

"We'll show you how to dance," Aifric says. "Caolán, why don't you demonstrate with your cousin, Mona?"

A muscle in Caolán's jaw spasms as he clenches it, but he doesn't say *no*. After a moment, he tosses back the rest of his alcohol and stomps across the room. "We'll do the waltz," he says, grabbing Mona's hand.

She gasps, but it's overshadowed by Aifric's grunt of disapproval. "You would perform a German dance before your Irish family?"

"Why not perform a Céilí?" Tadhg asks. "It's far more traditional."

Caolán's voice is flat. "This is not a Riverdance shindig. We're doing the waltz, or we don't dance at all."

He yanks Mona away from the group and barks for everyone to clear the area, so they have room to dance. Quinn, Aifric's maid, is in the far corner, twisting knobs on the sound system. She frantically punches buttons to find a suitable song for the dance and then dims the lights.

Watching Caolán dance is mesmerizing. He is far more graceful than I expect; despite his temper and the fact that he didn't want to do this, he moves with the easy ebb and flow of cool water. He pulls Mona close and holds her not like an expert, but like a lover. His hand is pressed to her back, his arm is stretched out to lead her. Mona follows Caolán around the room with a nervous look on her face, but it soon melts into warm pleasure as she learns to trust him. Their dance is beautiful, and somewhere deep inside, I feel jealous.

Where was this kind man when I needed him?

I turn away from their performance to find a corner to sulk in, but Tadhg bumps into me before I can make it two steps. "Leaving?" He tilts his head to the side.

"Just getting some air."

"You'll be dancing next. Stay close."

"The room isn't large enough for me to get lost in." I almost roll my eyes but catch myself at the last second.

"Okay," Tadhg says, stepping aside, but as I move to pass him, he shoots his hand out in front of me to block my path again. This time, however, something is in his hand.

It's a ribbon.

"Why don't you tie your hair back again?" he asks. "You know it's proper to perform a waltz this way."

Hair doesn't matter to the dance as much as he thinks but this isn't really about that, and we both know it. Tadhg is still on his power trip, trying to hurt me to get to Caolán.

I snatch the ribbon from him and yank back my hair, glaring at him the entire time. My eyes burn and I bite the inside of my cheek so hard, I taste blood. I'm not holding back tears, I'm trying to keep it together, so I don't spit in Tadhg's face.

How much of this am I supposed to endure?

"Lovely," Tadhg murmurs, then he leans close and strokes my scarred cheek with the back of his hand. "I can't wait to see more of you."

I don't reply. I don't even look at him as I walk away, but I do catch my mother's desperate eyes flicking between me and the *Honored Fitzpatrick*. Her expression breaks my heart. She wants this. She *needs* my marriage to work because the Jackson family must repair its reputation. We lost Bethany, and then we lost the war to defend her honor, then we were given handouts for years. We look like a mafia charity case.

I release a long sigh. Just yesterday, I wanted to show off my scar just to annoy my mother. Now I'm being forced to reveal it against my will. Frustration weighs me down as I settle against the far back wall. Caolán is still dancing with his cousin. I can't help but watch, trying to imagine myself in a pretty dress gliding around a ballroom floor, but I can't. Not when I look like this. I wouldn't be a beautiful dancer; I'd be an embarrassment. And Aifric would watch with a smile on her face as I was humiliated before everyone. She's smiling now as we all watch the demonstration. Caolán isn't. His face is impassive, as if he has removed himself from this whole situation.

When the dance is over, he scans the room, only stopping when he sees me. *Was he looking for me?* I glance away as chatter fills the room; Aifric's voice rises above the rest, discussing song choices with my mother. Naturally, Tadhg is there to weigh in, but I tune all of that out when Caolán crosses the room to stand beside me.

He keeps his eyes forward when he speaks. "This isn't how I wanted the night to go."

I don't reply.

"You're upset," he says.

I still don't speak.

He shifts his weight from one foot to the other and I catch a whiff of his cologne and ... something else. There is a bitter smell mingled with the woody fragrance. Something dark, something that makes my nose itch. I can't place the smell, but I know it isn't normal.

"My mother is doing this on purpose," he says.

"You think?"

"She's punishing *me*, not you."

"You're the underboss of your family's faction within the White Hand."

Caolán understands what I'm saying. That he shouldn't be afraid of his mother or of his distant cousin.

His voice is edged with annoyance. "Things are complicated."

Does he mean his drug addiction? I can't outright ask him, but I also can't pretend that I didn't hear what Tadhg said in there. That's what upsets me so much. I spoke up and defended him as best I could, but when his family turned on me, he didn't mutter a word.

That's not complicated, that's betrayal.

I lower my chin, staring at the floor like the carpet can give me confidence.

I just want to go home...

Caolán grunts. "Hold your head up."

"How can you tell me that?" *When my face looks like this...*

He huffs, crossing his arms and leaning back against the

wall. "It's just a face," he mutters. "Not even a bad one."

After everything that's happened, I shouldn't feel anything for his compliment, but my heart betrays me and double thumps in my chest. I am starved of compliments. I am desperate for affection. My face is a problem for everyone around me. A tool for Aifric to use against me or an image of shame for my mother to hide. But Caolán looks at me as if he doesn't even see my scar. Even now, he glances down and catches my gaze, but just as quickly, he looks away. *Bored,* not disgusted.

It's just a face. My heart thumps. *Not even a bad one.*

I try not to stare at him as he stands beside me, silence swelling between us like a fat balloon, ready to pop. Caolán has his arms crossed, but I can see his hand gripping his sleeve, long fingers digging into the material of his suit jacket. His knuckles are still scarred, just as I remember them, but the backs of his hands are covered in tattoos. Those are new.

Bold black lines form the outline of a skeleton's hand over his own, each middle finger is tattooed completely black. I wonder if that represents the position of his clan. The Middle Finger of the White Hand.

Caolán notices me staring and glances down at his hands before unfolding his arms and slipping them into his pockets. "I know they're ugly."

I don't think they're ugly, honestly, but they are shocking—more than mere decorations, they're *markings*. Like he's written his name and position on his own flesh in a code I don't understand.

A skeleton. What does that symbolize?

Death.

"A man of my position shouldn't have such gauche tattoos. But I wasn't supposed to be the underboss."

That's right. Caolán is replacing his older brother. My sister's killer. That means when his brother was alive, he didn't have to present himself as a respectable businessman or wear an uncomfortable suit all day. He didn't attend business meetings or represent his Clan the way his brother had. Caolán had been free to do whatever he wanted, including stain his skin with ink. He probably hadn't even planned on getting married. But his brother's sudden death sealed his fate. And mine too.

"What were you before you became the underboss of the White Hand?"

He stares straight ahead, his jaw clenching and unclenching.

"You don't have to tell me," I whisper.

"In time, I will."

"Do you think I can't handle it?"

Caolán removes his hands from his pockets and stares at them—at the blackened middle fingers. "No," he says, "I don't think you're ready to know everything."

"Will I ever be?"

"I don't know."

"Well, hurry up and figure it out. I haven't got all day."

The corners of his eyes crinkle, his lips flatten with pressure. His version of a smile. A real one. It's hidden behind a wall he has carefully built around himself, but I see the weak spots.

The parts that threaten to crack.

Caolán almost smiled at me.

But just as quickly as that little grin appears, it's abruptly gone and he's staring forward again like it never happened. I suddenly feel like I've just caught a glimpse of him I wasn't supposed to see. My heart softens. Caolán is complicated. He appears calm but his body is stiff to the touch. His eyes are oceanic blue, but his expression is always dead cold. His hair is shockingly red, nothing like the warm auburn of his father's locks. Caolán's hair is carmine, like the color of a bloodstain. His mouth smiles easily, but I'm slowly learning those grins are mechanical. Rehearsed. He smiles because he must, not because he wants to. *Those* smiles are reserved. But I almost got one.

"I'm sorry I let them insult you," he says to me, voice low, barely audible.

When I look up at him, he's staring right at me, and I almost can't catch my breath.

"I won't let them do it again."

I nod. "Thank you."

"Gloria! Caolán!" Aifric calls. "Come now, it's time for your dance."

Caolán pushes from the wall and leaves me there. As he moves, I catch a whiff of that strange scent again and it isn't until he reaches up to brush his hair back that I realize what it is. I see it on the end of his shirt sleeve, poking out from his suit jacket. A smudge of red.

Blood. Caolán smells like blood.

I can't look away from him as he leaves. *God, what have I gotten myself into?* I feel bad for praying, like I don't have the right to ask for God's help. Most days, I barely even think of God except to say that I expect His judgment and punishment to flood into my life soon. Maybe Caolán *is* His punishment. Or maybe I'm wrong about all this.

Caolán apologized and said he wouldn't allow me to be embarrassed again. I've chosen to trust that apology and give him a second chance. So, if my mafia husband can be a gentleman then who is to say that God cannot be a good Father?

Maybe my faith needs a second chance, too.

10

Ria

Christmas is coming. I've barely had time to breathe. My birthday and all that it brings has almost overshadowed the precious holiday. Even my parents seem to have forgotten the reason for the season. I should not be surprised, despite their claims to be Christian people, they don't live like it. We are a mafia family. God is part of our culture, but not so much part of our actual lives. That would be inconvenient. How on earth would we deal with traitors if we truly honored the whole, *Thou shall not kill* thing?

Whatever their beliefs are, my parents have not totally forgotten about Christmas. They're throwing a ball to honor the birth of Baby Jesus and to bring our families together. The Jacksons and the O'Rourkes.

"Caolán O'Rourke." Aoife whistles behind me. She's lying on my bed, fingering through my jewelry box. We're supposed to be picking out accessories to match our ballroom gowns for the dance, but mostly we've just gossiped about all the misery

Caolán's family put me through at their outing. "My cousin met him once," Aoife says.

That catches my attention. "Tell me more."

"She said he was nice to her. Quiet and very serious. But nice."

That adds up. Despite how awful that dinner was, I'm not afraid of Caolán. I've never feared him. Even when I first realized we were married, I thought, *at least it's him. Caolán won't hurt me. I won't end up like Bethany.* That has been my goal in life. To live. To survive. Because my sister did not.

"Why did your cousin meet Caolán?" I ask.

Aoife glances up from my jewelry and smiles. "She used to work for a Chief in our Clan. Eventually, she was connected to Caolán. She said he's very quiet. Doesn't waste time. And doesn't show much emotion." Aoife sighs dreamily, and my gaze slides over her once again. She's hugging one of my pink pillows and playing with a string of pearls. Her words come out as a whisper. Lips puckered. Eyelashes fluttering. "She only saw him once. But she said it was worth every second."

My heart stops. It had not occurred to me what sort of meeting Aoife's cousin had with my husband. But the dreamy look on her face lets me know exactly what happened.

"Your cousin is a prostitute," I say.

Should I feel offended? I hardly know Caolán, despite being married to him for nine years now. Do I have any right to lay claim to him? To be *possessive* of him?

Whether I have the right or not, Aoife's gossip annoys me. She's smiling now, still hugging my pillow and prattling on about how handsome Caolán is. She sounds like a silly high school girl who just caught wind of a dirty little secret. Normally, I wouldn't mind the juicy gossip. At an all-girls boarding school, stuff like this was all we ever talked about. But this is different. This secret is about me—and I didn't even know it. How long has *she* known?

I stare at Aoife as she holds up a string of pearls. She's in the mafia, too. The *Irish* mafia. Just like Caolán. But she isn't from California; she grew up in upstate NY, living off the poor remnants of what's left of the Hand up there. I hear they're barely a gang and regularly ask the California division for help. How is it that a lowly grunt could know such precious information before me? I almost ask her, but when she stands and crosses the room, I lose my courage.

Aoife passes me the pearl necklace. "Wear this tonight."

I shake my head, reaching up to grasp the golden chain I've worn nearly all my life. It was Caolán's. I still remember the inscription: *See you soon, love*. A promise. It shouldn't mean anything to me, but it does.

You'll hear a lot of things about me, Gloria, he'd said that day, *they're all lies.*

I believed him. I believed that Caolán was good. I still believe that, but my faith in him is slipping. His room is a chamber of nightmares. He didn't defend me against his mother. And he smelled like blood.

Who is Caolán O'Rourke?

I give Aoife a very practiced smile, the one I use on my parents. "You wear the pearls. They go much better with your dress, anyway."

She beams. "Really?"

"Of course."

"Help me try them on?" Aoife turns and sits at my vanity, lifting all her heavy blonde hair so I can clasp the necklace for her. I see her reflection in my mirror, smiling, but not at me. She's gazing at herself, already imagining how the pearls will look around her slender neck.

"They're perfect," I whisper. As I secure the necklace, I see Aoife's secret written on the back of her neck. A tiny shamrock tattoo.

Almost every man in the mafia has tattoos but none of the women do, not before marriage at least. Mafia men are soldiers. They get their hands dirty and mark their souls for death carrying out the sins of this world. But the women are meant to be precious gems. Priceless and innocent and pure. The men in our world pay million-dollar contracts to marry virgin women with smooth skin, to kiss lips that have tasted no wine, to make love to an untouched body. Aoife's tattoo could get her killed, but she's always been a bit of a rebel.

Maybe I'm giving her too much credit. Aoife is a mafia girl, yes, but she isn't royalty. At most, her parents expect her to remain a virgin until marriage. I doubt they know about the tattoo but the worst it will do is earn her a good beating.

I brush my thumb over Aoife's tattoo, and she giggles, leaning forward. "Your hands are cold!"

"Sorry."

She turns around, still smiling. "I'm thinking of adding a

leaf after I get married."

Shamrocks are three-leaf clovers, *four*-leaf clovers are rare and even considered magical. I don't know if Aoife sticks to her Druid roots or follows the beliefs of her Catholic Clan, but she seems very superstitious about the shamrock. She told me about adding another leaf before, says it will bring her good luck which she needs if she wants to give her husband a son.

I don't believe in luck. As a Christian, I believe in God's favor and in His blessings. Either way, I don't think the shamrock will help Aoife. She's from a very low-ranking family. Technically, she *can't* add a fourth leaf to her tattoo because that honor belongs to high members only. So, even if luck is real, the clover won't help her.

I don't have the heart to remind Aoife of any of this. I'm not even Irish, so I don't think it's my place to comment on it anyway. Instead, I smile and say, "Let's put on our dresses."

I have a strapless red gown with a sweetheart neckline. The waist is ruched, so the skirt spills out around me. It looks beautiful when I twirl. Aoife's dress is very form-fitting, cut low to show off her cleavage and pure white to give an air of innocence.

I open my mouth to give her a compliment, but someone knocks on my door and cuts me off. Thank God I haven't put on my shoes yet, so I get to the door in my bare feet and yank it open.

Anthony Jones stands in the hall wearing a grin that becomes a gape in his face when he sees me. "You look amazing," he breathes.

I blush. "Thanks, Tony." I can't hold his gaze as he stares at me; inside, I'm waiting for his eyes to drift to the left side of my face, as they always do. My mother insisted I do as Tadhg says and wear my hair pinned back for the ball, so my face is on full display now. Aoife helped me out by applying my makeup; the scar is still visible, but it does look better. Good enough to earn a compliment from Tony, at least.

I hate to admit it, but a small part of me wonders what Caolán will think when he sees me. Despite him not defending me, it was his last words that gave me the confidence to tie my hair back today.

It's just a face. Not even a bad one.

My face isn't bad.

"Wow," Tony says, still staring at me.

"You look great too." Aoife appears in the doorway and Tony loses all interest in me. I don't really blame him.

"Nice to see you, Aoife." Tony nods.

She nods back. "Same."

"I'm guessing you two were getting ready for the ball."

"I thought that's why you came," I say. "To escort me."

"I wasn't sure you still needed an escort. I mean ..." he glances away. "I heard your husband will be there."

"Right," I say.

Tony and Aoife watch me closely. Aoife is nervous because I'm her ticket to the ball. She might wear the shamrock crest, but she has no business attending this event, not unless she's there to serve the drinks. Tony, however, can go anywhere he wants. He isn't royalty, but being my bodyguard gives him a place at my dinner table for life. He was raised by my side, grew up in my house like my own brother. One of the perks of sacrificing your child to the head family is the elevation of your own. Tony's life of servitude bought his father the title General and earned his family a higher rank within the Panthers organization. All because he decided to be my friend and protect me when necessary.

Tony steps closer, tugging my elbow. He's the only man who has ever touched me so intimately. Every gesture makes my heart ache for more of his nearness, but I quickly close off that part of my heart. I don't want such intimacy from *Tony*. I want this closeness from Caolán. But Caolán's already let me down once. I'm not sure what to expect from him tonight, especially since Aifric and Tadhg will be there yet again. Will he protect me if they try to put me on the spot again? Or will he stand by and watch like last time?

"You don't have to see him tonight if you aren't ready," Tony tells me.

"Might as well pull the bandage off," Aoife says.

"Really?" Tony turns to her, but I shake my head and stand between them.

"Aoife is right. Caolán is my husband; I want to see him tonight."

There's a nine-year-old girl inside of me who just won't let Caolán go. A little girl who believes in all her heart that I've got it all wrong. Caolán is the charming gentleman I remember. He messed up, but he's going to prove himself tonight. I know he will.

"I guess I'd better get my shoes," I say, turning away from Tony.

"I can have the car pull around front," he offers.

"No. I want to visit my sister first. I'll meet you guys there when I'm finished."

Tony hesitates. He doesn't like it when I travel alone, but I'm in my own home. He knows my father will likely escort me to the dance himself, so he turns and offers his hand to Aoife. "Shall we?" he asks, like the perfect gentleman.

She blushes. "Give me five minutes and I'll be ready."

11

Caolán

"Be on your best behavior," my mother says, checking her makeup. We're in her dressing room, inhaling the scent of her Parisian perfume. She sits at her vanity while I sit on the edge of her bed, waiting like an obedient pup for her to finish up and go. This is a scene I have lived through many times, watching my mother fluff her hair, apply lipstick, or pick out a bracelet for whatever event we were attending. When I was a child, I would sit on the floor in my kid-sized suit and the only view I had was of her legs. Most of my memories are filled with my mother's knees and the lower half of her dress. Stockings, pleats, designer heels. My very first example of what a woman should be was dropped into my head by my mother.

What has she taught me over the years?

"Did you hear me?" she asks.

"I'm always on my best behavior, Mháthair."

She glances up and I stare at her reflection, watching the ice in her eyes grow even colder. I cannot remember a time in my life that I ever felt warmth from her. There are moments from the past that summon warmth, but only the feeling. The memories themselves are blurry, so obscure that I cannot say if they are real or just illusions created by fog, snippets of desperate joy snatched from my hallucinations and held hostage by my heart. My mind lies and calls them memories, I pretend not to notice. Pretend that her smiles in those dreams are real. Pretend that the sound of her laughter is real, that it'd once happened, that she had once loved me. But I know that isn't true.

Mother's gaze narrows. "That dinner was not your best behavior." She gathers her white dress to cross the room. "You've taken on more jobs since then."

"Who told you that?"

"Are you really so stupid as to think you could get anything over my head?"

I hate the look on her face now, a smirk with bundled cheeks and easy eyes. I don't see a single wrinkle on her face or forehead. I never have. She is dangerously close to her 60s but looks like an old-fashioned model from the 1950s. Marilyn Monroe would be jealous. The way she moves is glacial, slow and smooth, every problem and obstacle parting or crumbling before her. She could sink a ship if she wanted; stab it in the side—or the back—and then watch it drown with the smirk she's wearing now.

I hate her face, but even worse, I hate how right she is. I should have known my mother would find out about my activities of late, but I couldn't help myself. I needed those kills.

Needed to see the blood like a vampire needs to drink it. That sounds dark, doesn't it? But the blood is better than the fog.

Like a child, my eyes fall to the floor, and I stare at the tip of my polished shoes. "I needed a distraction."

Mother sighs and walks over to me. Her hand is cold as she strokes my cheek, but I close my eyes anyway, yearning for warmth, for *something*, from her. She loved Aidan so much. So easily. She dotes on Nolan and even has her moments with my father. But she has never loved *me*.

I peel my lids back to see my palms open in my lap. This is why. She hates what I do, even though she made me into this shadow. Now I've been dragged into the light, and she *still* hates me, but I know it's deeper than that. It wasn't just my job that she hated, it was my last kill. The one that ended the war.

"I'm sorry," I mutter. Not for Eoin Greene or any of the other names I've kept a secret. I'm sorry for the last name. The name that she gave me.

I'm sorry I messed up.

When I look up, her expression is pinched. She knows what I'm apologizing for, but she wipes it away with a roll of her eyes. "No more distractions. Focus on Gloria."

"I have been, but you're getting in the way."

"Did you honestly think I would stand by and let you mess this up?"

I wince at her words. "I can handle my own marriage, Mháthair."

"No, you cannot." She laughs, the sound full and resounding, soaking up all the joy in the room. There wasn't much to begin with, but she finds it, drags it out of hiding to savor this moment where she shames me for existing. "Look at you, Caolán. You're an up-jumped crackhead who cannot even make it to dinner on time."

"I'm not using anymore," I mumble.

"But you did use. And you made a name for yourself because of it. This is your bed, lie in it. I'll handle things while you rest."

"I don't want to rest."

"Then what do you want?" Her eyes slide up and down my face, searching for the answer I cannot give her. She figures it out anyway, and I'm rewarded with another of her haunting chuckles. "Oh, Lord. You want Gloria to fall for you."

"She is my wife, after all."

"She's a frightened doll who's spent the last two years at a Christian boarding school. The only reason she is in this marriage is because she has no choice." She lets go of a noise that might have been a laugh. "If it weren't for that awful scar, she would be out of your league. Thank God she looks gruesome."

She doesn't look gruesome. Not to me. And she doesn't seem to mind my face either. Before the fog, I might have been a handsome man, but the drugs left my cheeks hollow, my eyes stained with dark circles, and my face scarred with ribbons left by my own hands. Nails scraping my cheeks as I wailed in the throes of withdrawal. I am not a handsome man anymore, but Gloria has never frowned at me. Has never looked away except in her own shyness. She doesn't think my face is awful, not any more than hers.

"You must not confuse duty with emotion," my mother says. "That will be your downfall."

I don't speak, staring down at my hands, wondering how right she is. Maybe Gloria doesn't care about my face, but if she knew the real me—the one who killed and tortured—would she still look at me the way she does? With her eyes filled with wonder and life. Maybe she never looked at me that way at all. Maybe her smiles are foggy dreams too. That seems to be the only happiness I've ever found in this life, as if the very concept of joy itself is a lie.

"Regardless," I tell my mother, "You've allowed Tadhg to stick his hand into our lives."

Aifric teeters across the room, her heels stabbing into the thick carpet. "I'm being assertive. The Hand is meant to *grip* power, Caolán, not let it pass through its fingers."

I watch my mother turn and leave. She doesn't care if I follow, doesn't even look back. I stand there so long, the motion sensor lights flicker off, startling me. Annoyed, I pull out my phone and send a text to both of my informants. They should be with Gloria. I need them now more than ever. If I cannot stop my mother or Tadhg, then I must approach this differently. Maybe I can't protect her from my insane family, but I can prepare her so she's ready for whatever they have planned.

O.O.O

Gloria is visiting her sister's memorial. She's sitting on a stone chair beside an empty pond. In the summer, there are fish in the water, but her mother has them removed once the weather turns. I know because it's my job to know everything about the Jacksons.

I like watching Gloria. I like even more that she doesn't know when I'm watching. I get to see her as she is. Unfiltered. I watch her in silence across the expanse of her lawn. I came out here just to see what she looked like before we go to the ball and my mother sinks her fangs in. I have binoculars, but even without them, I can make out Gloria's red dress. She looks pretty, but I'm not so much interested in her appearance. I like Gloria in anything. I like Gloria because she's mine, though I'm not sure she feels the same. After that dinner, I am positive she hates me. That won't change anything, but still. I would prefer to get along with my wife, if possible.

I had years to get along with her, but I chose not to. It would have been so easy to groom her. To mold her into the woman I wanted her to be. But I am not a monster. Although, I will admit I'm not an angel either. I wanted Gloria to become her own person because I enjoy the challenge of breaking her. Then I can rebuild her and see if I like her that way.

The truth is that I don't know how to live with Gloria in a perfect, peaceful marriage. Perfection is something I have never known—and how could I? I was raised to kill people and I've gotten very good at it.

Don't you see? Chaos *is* my peace because without it, I have no purpose.

So, I don't *want* Gloria to be broken. I need her to be. I'm a hitman. The only time anyone has ever acknowledged me is when they needed me. And even now, wearing my brother's secondhand crown, I am only here because I must be. Because my father needs a better heir than Nolan.

Without a need, I don't exist.

I *need* Gloria to be a problem so that I can fix her. I *need* Gloria to be weak so that I can be strong for her. I *need* her to fight this marriage—to hate me—so that I can get her to love me. That's the only way I can function.

That might sound cruel, but this is the fate I've been given. The Hand I've been dealt. Maybe Gloria didn't ask for this, but it's not like there are women lining up to replace her. Unless you volunteer.

Would you like to be my broken girl?

I lower the binoculars and sink into the shadows of the nearby trees. This is quite unnecessary. The Jacksons have no idea I'm on their property. It's my job to be stealthy, but security is pathetic around here. It is shockingly easy to get on and off the grounds.

I move through the trees until I reach the west side of the mansion. Gloria's family estate is rather large, so this takes me a few moments but once I'm close enough, I emerge from the brush and move across the lawn to the backyard patio. Her bedroom is on the third floor, like a princess in a tower. I'm in good enough shape to climb onto the first-floor window and hoist myself up to a second-floor balcony. I gingerly hold onto the drainpipes and scale the house until I'm on her floor, then

I shimmy to her balcony and swing my long legs over the stone railing. It only takes a pocketknife and good hearing to unhook the pin in her balcony door lock. Then I'm inside.

The room smells of coconut. I know she uses the oil in her curly afro hair. The scent reminds me of warmer weather, tropical beaches, and women in bikinis. I have never seen Gloria in a bikini before.

For a long moment, I stand in the threshold between the balcony and her bedroom, simply looking. Admiring. The carpet is the color of champagne, fluffy enough that it feels criminal to walk around in shoes, but I take my first step inside and listen as the noise around me hushes, like walking into a library. All that is left is the memory of her. The laughs I didn't get to hear. The tears she shed in my absence. The secrets she whispered to her diary at night.

I know she has a diary. I've watched her enough to remember it. In England, she kept the journal in her bottom drawer, underneath her sweatpants and oversized shirts. I wonder if that has changed.

I walk to her dresser and squat, but a voice stops me. "Her top drawer."

I glance at Gloria's bed, where I know the voice came from. Sure enough, on the dark side of her room, in the shadows cast by the dressing wall in the corner, is a woman sitting on Gloria's blankets. She clutches a pink pillow to her chest, wrinkling her white gown.

"Aoife." I stand and smile. "You look lovely."

Her eyes sharpen into daggers, but it's her words that cut

me. "You look dangerous. As always. Like you've come to kill."

"That is my job, isn't it?"

"You told me to meet you here. What do you want?" She gets to the point. "Ria is expecting me soon."

"She's still visiting her sister. We have time."

Aoife adjusts on the bed, still hugging that stupid pillow like a child. That's one of the reasons I chose her as my informant, because she looks young enough to pass as an airheaded teenager.

Aoife is 23 years old; she's been working for me since she was 19. I took her from a club in NYC where I found her working a pole for the German mafia. Initially, I was interested in her beauty but when she spoke to me, I realized she had an Irish accent. Not a German one. So, I kept her for myself.

It wasn't sexual. I mean, *yes*, I did sleep with Aoife that night. But that's what I'd paid for. I don't believe in wasting money. Since then, I've had other uses for her, and she's excelled. If you're not driven by lust, you might learn that hookers are good at more than one thing. They are excellent at gathering information.

Aoife was perfect. She was young, beautiful, and was familiar enough with the mafia to slide under the radar. She wasn't originally from the mafia; she was simply an Irish immigrant who came to America at the wrong time. Right now, the mafia rules NYC. Political upheaval led to New York officials defunding the police which handed immeasurable power to underground forces. Basically, the mafia took over. Aoife arrived in the Big Apple as a young teenager just as this chaos unraveled. She had dreams of getting her citizenship, going to college, and making something of herself. But that never happened.

In a lawless city, the best you can hope to do is simply survive. Aoife had no skills. No money. No connections. But she had a beautiful face, and she was a virgin. She used what she had to stay alive. And that's where I found her. Putting herself to use.

Desperation made it easy to take advantage of her. I gave her a place to stay and a check to cash. All she had to do was gather information on the men I sent her home with. It was simple work, until the Jacksons told me about Gloria's boarding school. That's when I sent Aoife to England. For the last few years, it has been her mission to keep an eye on Gloria. She didn't have to become her best friend and roommate, but I suppose that made it easier to stay close to her.

Aoife has been doing an excellent job, but now her job has made her hostile toward me, as if she is protective of Gloria. She glares at me from Gloria's bed, like I've done something wrong. Even her voice comes out as a hateful whisper.

"Is there something you need, Caolán?"

I should wrap my fingers around her slender throat for speaking to me that way, but I let it slide. She's emotional. I get it. Consummating the marriage will be the end of her friendship with Gloria. Or maybe she's angry for another reason. Maybe she thinks it's wrong for me to solidify a relationship with such a young woman. Or maybe she's angry because I haven't solidified anything with her.

I know that's what she's always wanted, ever since she had a taste that night we met. It was a wonderful night. Aoife has always been good at her job. Every single part. But that isn't what I've hired her for. Aoife is a prostitute. Women like her cannot marry high-ranked men like me.

In case you haven't figured it out yet, she isn't engaged. *I've been footing the bill for all her expenses.* Once she 'turns 18' she will drop out of school because she isn't supposed to be there in the first place. That's the story Gloria needed to believe. Apparently, she also believes Aoife's little shamrock tattoo is an act of rebellion, but it isn't.

I gave her that tattoo.

It isn't to portray her affiliation with the White Hand, it's to label her as a whore. All of them have the shamrock tattoo, three leaves to represent their three uses. Beauty, pleasure, and pain. The shamrock is inverted to symbolize their position within the mafia. Beneath us.

Aoife wasn't raised in the mafia; she doesn't know what the shamrock truly represents. She doesn't know the order of our business and that she cannot ever be more than what I've marked her as. She doesn't even know she's been marked. She thinks she can add a leaf to her tattoo once I consummate my marriage. Her way of saying, *Job well done!*

There will never be a fourth leaf, and her job will never be over. Not unless I say so. After I've finished this business with Gloria, Aoife will move on to the next assignment or she will wait for me to call on her. For personal use. That's it. I know it's a cruel life, but this is better than doing tricks on a pole for dollar bills. She should consider herself fortunate I took her in and not some lunatic with a depraved appetite. I've seen what happens to women like Aoife in my world. It isn't pretty. But *she's* pretty. Pretty enough to bat her lashes and fool my lovely wife for over two years. She's done a wonderful job; I just need her to cooperate a little longer. I've paid her enough to cooperate for life.

When I bought Aoife, I had to pay the owner of the club she danced at. Nearly a quarter of a million dollars for a skinny Irish girl with natural blonde hair. I had the money, but still, that was pricey for a girl who'd been used so much already. This is why I hate the German mafia. They think they own everything because they took over NYC and ran the cops out of town. It's a lawless city over there, either your worst nightmare or a dream come true. Depends on the poison you enjoy. How badly it burns.

Aoife stands and walks over to me, drawing my attention. "Get out of your head."

She's right. I think too much.

"Is she having any second thoughts?" I ask.

She shrugs, but the bedroom door opens before she can reply.

I turn and smile. "Anthony, took you long enough."

Anthony Jones sighs. He looks annoyed but I don't care, I'm paying him way too much money to be concerned about his sensitive nerves. It isn't my fault he wants out of the mafia. Who on earth gives up such luxury to go to college and get a real job and live like a normal nobody?

I guess that's what you do when you aren't raised as an assassin with a taste for blood.

Anthony wants to leave the Panthers, but his rank is too high for him to simply walk away. He knows too much. Has seen too much. A bullet is the only way out for men like us, but he's convinced he can disappear and change his identity with the right connections.

I have those connections. And I've got the money he'll need to start over. Once I consummate the marriage, I'll have no use for him, so I'll set him loose. He's been my spy since he was a child, I'd say he's earned a fresh start.

"Ria will be there soon, we have to go," Anthony says.

I roll my eyes. Gloria is always the excuse they give me when they don't want to chat for long. "She'll be fine. Unless you lied about her father escorting her."

Anthony swallows, shooting a glance at Aoife but she has no reaction. She's not going to help him.

"That's what Ria said before she left. Her father will escort her to the ball."

"Then you won't be needed for a while."

His shoulders sag. "Sure. I guess not."

"Regardless, meeting here is dangerous." Aoife sits on the edge of the bed and crosses her legs. They're smooth and bare, perfectly exposed between the high split in her dress that travels up to her thigh.

Anthony stares at her bare legs. I wonder if they're sleeping together again. It's so cute that they think I don't know.

"There's a reason I wanted us to meet here," I say.

Anthony finally looks away from Aoife's legs to nod at me. "What reason is that?"

"To remind you of your jobs. You are here for Gloria. You exist for Gloria. But this part of her life will end. You're supposed to make that easier for her."

"She's not having second thoughts," Aoife says. "She seems nervous, but we've been encouraging her to do what's best." She looks at Anthony. "I have, at least."

"The heck does that mean?"

Anthony fumbles for words. "I-I told her that—well—I told her she didn't have to meet with you tonight. If … If she wasn't ready."

"And why would you ever tell her something so stupid?"

He shrinks. Even takes a step back. "She needs to know we're on her side. If we push her too hard, she may end up—"

"End up what?"

"End up doing something drastic."

I raise an eyebrow. "The only drastic thing she can do is run away and you know that isn't possible without help. So, unless you plan to betray me, we have nothing to worry about. Correct?"

Anthony licks his lips. "Correct."

"Good. Now, go to the ball and have fun. At the right time, guide Gloria to the balcony. I'll be there to meet her." I reach into the pocket of my suit jacket and retrieve two thick envelopes. The first one goes to Anthony who greedily counts the money inside right in front of me. The second goes to

Aoife. She has the grace to wait a moment, but then she can't take it any longer and starts flipping through the wad of bills, her lips moving quickly as she silently counts. When she's finished, she glances up and frowns.

"This is too much."

"There's extra. For me."

She flicks her eyes to Anthony who is staring with flared nostrils. Her chest rises as she inhales, looking back at me, wondering what I'm going to do next. She has no words. For this, I am always given blind obedience, if not desperation.

"That's all, Anthony." I wave at him, but he doesn't take the hint. He's still staring between me and Aoife, probably heartbroken.

"We will see you at the ball." I turn to him, and the annoyance on my face must be clear because he startles and finally moves toward the door.

"Right. Sorry. See you there."

Once the door is shut, I'm left in silence with Aoife who is watching me closely. She doesn't speak until I remove my suit jacket. I place it on the back of Gloria's vanity chair and loosen my tie as she warns, "We shouldn't do this here. In her room. On her bed."

"I can take you on the floor."

Her eyes dart to the fluffy carpet and I watch her throat bob as she swallows. "No."

"The bed then." I stand before her. "This will be quick."

Aoife nods. She's still sitting on the edge of the mattress, but the bed is high, and she is tall. I don't have to lean down very far to kiss her forehead. The contact is gentle. Brief. But it's enough for her to fall back against the blankets, a tired gasp peeling from her lungs like a creature that'd been trapped. Finally set free by a simple kiss.

"Lift your dress," I say, then I chuckle as she obeys without question.

I lean down, hovering over her body and she lets out a gasp of pure desire. There is a gentle smile crawling over her face, claiming her plump lips. My next words wipe it away.

"Did you honestly believe I would take you here—in my wife's bed?"

Aoife's eyes shoot open. She doesn't blink as the silence stretches on. "I-I thought—"

"Get up." I step away, adjusting my tie. "I just wanted to speak to you alone, Aoife. Without Anthony."

She looks beyond disappointed, grasping the edges of heartbreak. "What is it you want?"

"Your loyalty."

I shouldn't have to sleep with her to get it, but that's how Aoife functions. I can't blame her, not when I have a history of blood and drugs and every foul thing you can imagine. Aoife was there for a lot of it—the *worst* of it, if I'm being honest. She cleaned me up more nights than I can remember—there are nights I *can't* remember, and she won't talk about them. I'm glad.

It was those late nights with her dragging me into the bathroom, peeling away my bloodstained clothes, wiping vomit from my mouth, sponging me down when I was too high to do it myself, those nights built the connection we have. But that connection became strained each time she crawled into bed with me, like a reward for her commitment. I let her do it because I felt bad for turning her away. Some nights I wasn't conscious enough to turn her away, but I'm not sure I would have, regardless. There is a part of me only Aoife has seen, I will never take that from her. But I can't ignore that she's allowed the sexual part to cloud her judgment.

She didn't clean me up because she cared, she cleaned me up because she knew it was an easy ticket to my bed. It worked until I got clean. For the last few years, we've been stumbling through a relationship that is strictly business, and it isn't working as smoothly as I would like, but this is my fault. I let Aoife have her way, now I've got to put my foot down and remind her that I'm not her cracked out boyfriend. I'm her boss, and she will do as she's told whether she likes it or not.

"I need you by Gloria's side," I say.

The look on her face is one of annoyance. "That's where I've been for over two years, Caolán. You don't have to remind me."

I look her up and down. She's still lying on the bed, leaning back on her elbows with her legs open so I can see straight up her dress. "Yes, I do."

She smirks. "You don't have to fight this so hard. I know you miss me. And I've missed you."

"As much as you missed Anthony?"

That silences her for a few seconds. Confusion and then shock takes over her features, but she covers her surprise with another grin. "Are you jealous?"

"You're a whore, Aoife. Why would I be jealous that you're doing what you do best?"

"Wow. Married life has made you cruel." She stands and smooths the wrinkles from her dress. "I remember when you liked my job. That was why you hired me."

"That's not what I pay you for anymore."

"But you miss what you paid me for."

"No, I don't."

She drops her gaze to my crotch and laughs. "Yes, you do."

Crap. I turn toward the door and adjust my belt to cover the tent in my pants. I'm not ashamed to admit it happened. Aoife is a beautiful woman whom I used to sleep with. This is the sort of reaction anyone would get in this situation, but that doesn't mean I have to act on it. I *won't* act on it because I'm married. Technically, I've *been* married, but my wife is of age now. We don't have long before we consummate and make things official. I want to be loyal to her. She's been loyal to me, sticking up for me the best way she could at that awful family dinner. I owe it to her not to sleep with her best friend behind her back. Not anymore, at least.

"I need people I can trust," I tell Aoife, turning back around to face her. "Tadhg Fitzpatrick will be at the ball. Get his attention. Find out what he has planned."

She doesn't look interested. "You're sending me to sleep with some guy who hates you."

"I'm sending you to gather intel," I correct her. "How you do that is up to you."

"There's only one way I can do that."

"Just get the job done," I grunt. "Can I trust you or not?"

She watches me for a long moment. "You already know the answer to that question."

"I want to hear you say it."

Aoife closes the gap between us and steps into my personal space. She wraps her arms around my neck and kisses me on the lips. I let her do it, and when she pulls away, I stare down at her. "You can trust me," she whispers.

I choose to believe her.

12

Ria

Spending time at Bethany's memorial usually leaves me in a somber mood, but today I feel light and hopeful and jittery. There is something in the air, something that buzzes with excitement. Perhaps this is the beauty of Christmas, of a precious gift given to us which we do not deserve. I think about all of this as I ride to the Christmas ball; it isn't far from my home, about a ten-minute drive to a fancy hotel. My parents ride with me and when we arrive, we're swept into the splendor and luxury of the night.

Ladies tiptoe in high heels, the skirts of their dresses flowing around them like angels drifting through the dance. Men walk with their shoulders back, chins up, their suits crisp and their bowties perfectly straight. There are servants carrying Christmas themed food on trays, tart cranberry wine and sweet cream puffs dusted with wintergreen mint. There is a lamb leg on a spit, a fire blazing beneath it, and an assortment of cheese, olives marinated in oil, and flatbread served with hummus—

so many foods native to Bethlehem, where baby Jesus was born. I wonder if He would've eaten the lentil soup bubbling in a pot beside the lamb, or if He would have preferred the roasted fish and baked loaves I see the chefs wheeling out on a cart.

The crowd parts when we enter, staring at my parents and then gaping at me. At my scarred face. I ignore their wide eyes, staring straight ahead as I walk. My mother reaches for my hand, but I know it's more for herself than me. When I glance sideways, my heart breaks. Her eyes are huge, her jaw is clenched shut, her chest filled with held breath. She's embarrassed. Because of me.

I peel my hand from hers and step aside when my father stops to greet a general from the organization. My mother stands next to him, pretending not to notice me slip away. I'm sure she's happy to see me sink into the crowd.

I find my way to a corner of the room, by a table of hard meat and crackers. The salty smell makes my stomach growl, so I turn to make a plate, but Darren's voice stops me.

"Eating already?"

"I'm hungry," I say.

"Hungry or hiding?" He reaches past me with his long arms and snatches up a little pickle.

"I'm hiding," I admit. "How'd you get the vultures to leave you alone?"

He shrugs. "I'm not important until Dad officially names me as his heir. Until then, I'm invisible."

"So, what kept you from arriving on time?"

A grin slides across his boyish face. "I was busy."

"With a girl?"

"Sometimes my business needs to be mine."

I snort out a laugh, but it's cut short when I notice the way Darren's face darkens. For the first time in my entire life, I don't see the goofy little brother I grew up with. I see my father's shadow. His jaw clenches and his eyes narrow.

"I thought so," Darren mutters. "The White Hand is here."

My blood runs cold, and I turn to get a look, but Darren grabs my arm and holds me in place. "Don't," he says firmly.

"I need to see." I have to see Caolán before he sees me. I have to know what to expect, but Darren won't let me move. "*Please*," I say, but his grip only tightens.

"Not now."

"Why not?"

"Because you look desperate."

I stare up at him and the stony look on his face makes me realize how much I'm trembling. I can feel my body shivering like I'm cold.

Darren pulls me closer. "Father says panthers can smell fear. That might be true, but the White Hand ... it can *grasp* fear. Hold it. Choke it." He leans down and whispers, "Don't let them see your fear, Ria. They'll use it against you."

Suddenly, he lets me go and turns around with a grand smile on his face. "Tony!" he says, extending his hand for a shake.

I take a deep breath before I face my security guard. I hadn't noticed his arrival. "You made it," I say.

Tony's smile is tight, like it hurts his mouth to do it.

"Where's Aoife?" I frown. "I thought she was with you."

"I walked here, hoping she would catch up, but I guess not."

That doesn't answer my question, but as I open my mouth to press him, I am silenced by the sea of green eyed, blonde-haired people pouring into the grand hall. They look like ghostly saints, something beautiful yet frightening, like a herd of vampires.

Tadhg enters first, pausing in the doorway so the Jackson generals can greet him. I hate the way they line up to grovel, inclining their heads and shaking his hand. Tadhg eats this up, grinning with a spark of fire in his eyes.

"What a jerk," Darren mutters. "Who is that guy anyway?"

"Leader of the entire White Hand," Tony answers, but I correct him.

"His daddy is the leader."

My brother and my guard both stare at me for my boldness, but I ignore them, watching the Irish procession flow into the room. Behind Tadhg is a stream of Clan leaders I don't recognize, but I count them off on my hand. One finger at a time. And then, finally, I see him.

Caolán O'Rourke walks in wearing a very bored expression, like he wants nothing more than to turn around and walk back out. He is unimpressed with the people who greet him, uninterested in the idle small talk offered by pretty women who vie for his attention. Like a proper mafia boss, he inclines his head, shakes hands, and smiles when needed, but I can see the deadness in his gaze. Sadly, it's still there when he looks at me.

Caolán's blue eyes fall on me like a stone hitting water. I freeze, even suck in a little gasp, and stare back—but before I can make anything of our connection, it's gone. Caolán looks away from me, just as bored as he was when he first entered.

Aifric appears by his side. As she walks, she holds her hand out for him to take, and he does so without even looking, like he knows what's expected of him. Then he kisses the back of her hand and passes her to his father. Charles is a lumbering giant, three inches taller than Caolán with crimson hair trimmed into a beard. He looks like he doesn't want to be here, then again, I've never seen him look any other way.

"Well, they look rich." Darren sighs.

"Those are the O'Rourkes," I say.

"Caolán has a little brother." Darren points, but I quickly slap his hand down.

"Pointing is rude!"

"Sorry." He shrugs.

I don't have the bravery to search for my brother-in-law, I'm too afraid of seeing everyone's disgusted frowns because of Darren's pointing. Instead, I try to change the subject. "Caolán looks handsome tonight."

"Great," Tony grunts.

He seems annoyed, and I have no idea why. Even Darren gives him the side eye, but he doesn't comment.

"I want to speak to him," I say.

Tony's entire face wrinkles. "Right now?"

"No. Tomorrow."

He doesn't like my sarcasm, but you know what I don't like?

I don't like the way his eyes land on the left side of my face before he says, "Are you sure you want him to see you like this?"

I walk away without replying. *It's just a face*; Caolán's words echo in my head—in my *heart*—but they're cut short when Tony grabs my elbow.

"Hold on," he says, "Aoife just walked in. Wait for her, at least."

I glance back to see my best friend walk through the doors at the very end of the Irish procession. For a moment, I'd been worried about her, but now it all makes sense. She's in the Irish mafia too, of course she would arrive with them. I just wish she would've told me.

She sees us right away but doesn't bother coming over. I watch her enter the crowd, greeting Irish Clansmen and even stopping to kiss the ring of Tadhg Fitzpatrick. His eyes glow as they swim down her body, lapping up her curves, wetting his palate with fantasies of the blonde beauty who meekly inclines her head and then offers him a curtsy.

"She's really playing it up," Tony mutters.

"Well, he is her mafia leader," I remind him, though no one has ever curtsied to *me*.

Tony mumbles something back, but I don't hear it because Darren is talking over him. "Aoife looks amazing," he exhales. "As always."

I choose to ignore that comment; so does Tony, who busies himself with a handful of cheese cubes from the display table. He crams them all into his mouth and then motions for a server to bring him wine to wash it down.

"Slow down," I mutter.

At this point, Aoife has finally arrived, Tony doesn't bother with cordial greetings, he gets right to the point, blurting, "She wants to see him now."

She makes a face, her expression annoyed. It's the first inkling of irritation I have ever seen on her, but it's gone the next second, replaced by a smile so warm I wonder if I imagined the look.

"Don't you want to eat first? I think they're serving dinner soon," she says.

"They're roasting a leg of lamb." Darren sounds hungry.

"Why don't you see what table Ria has been assigned?" Tony suggests, just to get Darren out of here. Even I recognize he's being sent away, but there's nothing Darren can do. He isn't needed here and it's only a matter of time before our father expects him to stand by his side. One of the pros *and* the cons of being his heir.

The three of us watch as Darren slinks away, banished from the grownup party. Once he's disappeared into the crowd, Tony says, "Let's get some fresh air on the balcony."

Aoife mutters something about getting a drink and then pushes into the crowd before either of us can stop her. I don't miss the fact that she goes to the drink display closest to where Tadhg is standing.

Outside, the air is cool, and I shiver as I walk to the edge of the balcony, near a little round table with a cushioned chair beside it. There's a bundle of flowers left on the table, tied together with a string of white yarn and a card with a hole punched through, so it's looped onto the string. These were left here for someone. It isn't until I'm holding the bundle that I realize the flowers must have been left for *me*. They're morning glories, my favorites—and not just because we share a name, I like them because they're the flowers Bethany planted by the pond when I was just a child. I wonder if these flowers were taken from the pond. More importantly, I wonder who left them here for me now.

"You found them," Tony says, and I feel my heart flip. Are these from him? Like the daisy he gave me for my birthday. My mother threw it out, but now I have these.

I clutch the flowers to my chest. "Is this why you brought me out here?"

"Yes."

"They're beautiful."

"Great."

The word seems so flat.

"Is there a reason you left them?"

Tony and I have always been close. Close enough for me to wonder what my life would be like with him, but I've been married for half my life. Since childhood, I have known that I would never have room for any other man besides Caolán O'Rourke. Tony has known this too. So then ... Why would he get me flowers? Is this his way of confessing? His last chance to tell me how he's felt all along?

Tony curses softly.

"Tony, it's okay," I tell him, stepping forward.

"Things have been crappy tonight."

"I know. You've been drinking a lot."

"I drank one glass of wine."

But Tony never drinks. His job requires him to stay alert at all times, so he rarely indulges.

I let out a nervous laugh. "Sure, it was just one glass. But that's one more glass than I've ever seen—"

"Well, my life doesn't revolve around you."

My laughter dies in my throat, choking me of words. I'm left standing on the balcony as Tony glares at me like I've just spat at him. I have no idea what's going on. I don't understand his anger.

"Tony—"

The balcony doors open and Aoife pokes her head in, holding a glass of wine. She passes it to Tony and his shoulders visibly relax, but he looks at me before he takes a sip, like he isn't sure he should drink it in front of me.

"I'll be right back," he says quietly, shuffling back into the party. He stands at the door with Aoife as he sips his drink, his head tilts toward her while she speaks. I can't hear what they're saying, and I'm not sure I want to, but my legs move on their own and I walk the perimeter of the balcony until I'm standing right beside the door. I'm hidden by the large white curtains hanging inside, so Aoife and Tony will have to turn all the way around to see me, but I know they won't. They're completely consumed by their conversation, fierce whispers I can barely hear over the party chatter.

"... Meant something to you," Tony says.

"You think I wanted to stay back with him?"

"Yes, I do."

Aoife's voice is muffled for a second, but I catch the end of her sentence. "... Do what Caolán says."

My eyes widen. *What is she talking about?* I clutch the flowers tighter and the corner of the card pokes into my finger. I'd almost forgotten about the card. I hold it up now and stare at the creamy white paper with loopy handwriting. My breath cuts short when I read the words.

See you soon, love.

Those were Caolán's words... One of the last things he said to me, inscribed on the pendant of my necklace. I reach up and touch it without thinking. These flowers aren't from Tony. I've had it all wrong. So then ... What's up with my friends?

They're still whispering to each other. Tony's wineglass is empty now; he holds it up and points it in Aoife's face—that's when I see it. The anger in his square jaw, the way he grips his glass so tightly I fear he'll crack it. The defensive way Aoife leans back from him, like they're fighting. Having a lovers' quarrel.

Is he angry because of Aoife? Because he *meant something to her?*

I feel like an idiot. My two best friends have been sneaking around right beneath my nose, and I had no idea. But even worse than that, Caolán is somehow involved.

Without thinking, I stomp forward and yank open the balcony doors. The frigid air slaps Aoife and Tony, breaking their conversation. They stare as I march past them, shouldering through the crowd. I make it to the hallway before I feel someone grab my arm.

I tug away hard, but my anger softens when I pivot and see Aoife instead of Tony. "What's wrong?"

"I'm going home." I turn away again, but she doesn't let go.

"I thought you wanted to speak to Caolán."

"Not anymore."

"We shouldn't keep him waiting," Tony says.

"Why not?" I snap. "Because you've got to do what he says?"

Aoife pales while Tony's mouth flaps open and shut like he wants to speak but doesn't know what to say. I don't care what he has to say. I throw the flowers onto the floor and twist my arm free.

"I'm leaving. Don't follow me."

"Tony," Aoife looks at him and he pulls out his phone. "What are you doing?"

"Making a call."

"That won't help," she says sharply.

"Let me handle this!" Tony snaps back.

Handle this? I am not a problem to be handled. I am not an issue you can fix with a phone call. With a huff, I turn to leave again, but I don't make it more than two steps. As soon as I begin walking, the door ahead of me opens and I'm face to face with my husband.

Caolán's presence silences everything. I can't speak. Aoife looks too afraid to say anything. Tony just tucks his phone away and then straightens his tie. We look like three idiots who've just been caught doing something wrong. None of us can tell what this *wrong* thing is, but we all feel the weight of our guilt, nonetheless. That's how intense Caolán feels. His expression is flat yet full of emotion, his mouth hasn't opened but I feel as if he's spoken a thousand words. And his eyes are dead, like blue stones set in a marble statue.

"You found the flowers," he murmurs, staring at them.

"Yes, I found them," I whisper.

"But you didn't like them."

"I did."

"Then why are they on the floor?"

I don't speak as he walks forward and stoops to retrieve the abandoned bundle. His touch is gentle, delicate, he even brushes the petals with his thumb, like it might have gotten dirty. I watch in muted shock, wondering how a man could be so gentle yet fill my heart with fear. The fear is familiar, it's the exact same feeling I get around his mother.

First, he ignored me. But now he's come to find me, and I have no idea what he plans to do now that he's here. *Who is Caolán O'Rourke?* I'm not sure I want to find out.

13

Caolán

I stare at the bruised flower petals, running my thumb over the deep indigo color. No one has spoken in almost a full minute. Aoife and Anthony are complete idiots who are too afraid to speak, and now their fear has bled into Gloria.

I glance up to see her wide-eyed stare and it pisses me off. She looks like she wants to run away, after throwing my gift on the floor. What did my flowers ever do to her? Why didn't she like them? I thought this would be the apology she wanted for how my mother and Tadhg treated her and how I sat quietly and let it happen. But it's not enough. She's still angry.

"Why did you throw them away?" I ask. My voice is darker than I mean it to be, but I don't care. I'm allowed to be angry, too.

Gloria takes a step back and flicks her large eyes toward her friends, but neither of them offers help. When she swallows, her slender throat bobs up and down. Her neck is so small, I bet I wouldn't need both hands to choke her.

"I was upset," Gloria whispers.

I grip the bundle of flowers in my hand. There are tiny little thorns along the sepals and stems, they stab into my calloused palm, pricking the insides of my fingers. I ignore the sharp pain. For a moment, I want to squeeze even harder, break the skin and draw blood. I'm not particularly angry, if anything, I'm just annoyed. But I'm used to shedding blood when I'm annoyed, and now, beneath my frustration, there is a pinprick of confusion.

I wanted Gloria to be a problem because that gives me a purpose. If she has a temper, I can dampen it. If she has an attitude, I can adjust it. If she has a need, I can fulfill it. Every single one. But she isn't the problem here. *I* am—and I can't fix myself.

"Why are you upset?"

The question stuns Gloria and she stumbles over her words like she can't really explain it. "I—W-Well … Uh … I was c-confused."

I raise one red brow.

"It's my fault," Anthony interjects but I snap my fingers at him.

"Let her speak."

Anthony needs to learn his place. I don't miss the way he looks at her, like he meant what he said. That this is all his fault. That he blames himself for her pain.

My blood freezes. He hurt her… and she responded by throwing the flowers down. Because she thought they were from him.

The thorns of the morning glories stab into my flesh a little harder. Why would my pretty wife expect flowers from another man?

"I see what's happened here," I say smoothly. All that attitude Gloria gave me over my mother and her silly scar, but here she is throwing a tantrum over another man. Throwing my flowers down over another man.

"You have forgotten who you belong to," I say softly.

When I look up from the flowers, Gloria is staring at me like she has no idea what to expect next. I don't either, but I step toward her anyway. She steps back. Her hazel eyes are wide with fear, the fear I had initially expected, and that sends my blood racing. This is an emotion I can handle. This is something I can fix. This is the side of Gloria I want to see.

Every step toward her is one step back, shifting our connection from husband and wife to stalker and prey. She looks like she's about to bolt. Dear God… I hope she runs. Just so I can chase her.

The excitement ends as her back hits the wall and I take one last step to close the gap. My hand presses against the cool cement just above her head, caging her in. She looks at me like she isn't sure if I'm a protector or predator. I'm not sure either.

I hold up the flowers. "Take them. I bought them for you."

Her small hands grasp the bundle, slim fingers brushing against my own. In that brief moment, I know that her hands are soft and warm, nothing like mine. I want to reach out and hold her hand, to feel curve of her palm and kiss the supple skin. But just as the thought enters my head, she winces and snaps her head down to stare at her hand. She cut her finger on a thorn.

"Ouch," she murmurs. A red dot swells on her finger and then runs down the side, bright red against her smooth brown skin. She is the color of chocolate with a mane of afro curly hair she's tamed into an elaborately braided bun. Away from her face. I like that. I like that she isn't afraid of her imperfections.

Gloria lifts her finger, but I grab her hand and shock her by pressing her finger to my mouth. The blood is warm and has a sharp metallic taste. It's funny, I've always wanted to be a vampire and now I've finally tasted blood. Fitting that it would be hers.

She gasps but doesn't pull away. The sound that leaves her mouth is soft, barely more than a whisper, like she's afraid to speak. When I glance up, her eyes are on me, and her lips are parted. Without thinking, I let go of her hand and lean forward, pressing her against the wall. My mouth hovers over hers, so close, I wonder if she can smell her blood on my lips. I am *this* close to kissing her, I *want* to kiss her, but she isn't ready.

"Better?" I whisper.

I feel her breath brush against my lips as she says, "Yes."

"Good girl."

I finally pull away and have to stop myself from smiling when Gloria releases a heavy sigh. Subconsciously, she reaches up to clutch her necklace and my eyes laser to it.

"You're wearing it," I say softly.

She nods and I wonder why that makes my chest tighten. I

already knew she wore it every day. Seeing it in person, though, seeing it up close instead of through reports or binoculars is entirely different. She really is mine. She sees herself as mine, or else she would've taken the necklace off.

I turn to look back at Anthony. He's staring between us with an expression that makes me want to laugh. Maybe he didn't have feelings for Gloria, but he certainly cared for her, and he knew that she cared for him, probably more than she should. But that is about to change. No matter how much fear runs through Gloria's mind and body, that necklace is proof of where her heart resides. In my palm. In the grip of my bloody hand.

"I'm sorry for the confusion," I say, making Gloria tilt her head to the side. I nod at the flowers. "You must have thought they were from Anthony."

She doesn't speak.

"Did it disappoint you to learn they were from me instead?"

"I'm happy to receive flowers from you."

"Please don't throw them down again."

"I won't."

"To be fair, Anthony *is* the one who clipped them and left them for you. So, technically, he did bring you flowers."

Gloria's eyes stretch and she looks at Anthony before returning her vision to me. Disbelief is written all over her face and it clouds with anger when I say, "I told him to place the flowers there for you."

"You told him…?"

Anthony shifts like he wants to say something, but I speak

over him. "He works for me. I tell him to do a lot of things."

She looks at Anthony again, and then at Aoife, unsure of her own best friend now.

"I don't understand."

"We'll work it out after the ceremony."

Gloria makes a noise, I'm not sure if it's a word or a groan but the look on her face lets me know she understands what I'm saying. This isn't her business, and I don't intend to give her any more details until the ink of our contract has dried—and it won't dry until it's signed in blood.

"I should go," I say. "The party expects me."

"Me as well," Gloria replies.

I hope she doesn't see the surprise on my face as she walks to the door. I had expected anger or maybe even an outburst, but Gloria is more mature than I give her credit for. She knows her place, even when she doesn't like it.

With a straightened back, my wife walks past me, completely ignoring Anthony and Aoife. She doesn't even pay *me* any attention as I walk beside her. I'm not sure if that annoys or excites me, but I feel something stir in my chest.

"I'm surprised," I say when she stops at a table and snatches an olive from the display.

She raises one eyebrow at me.

I don't really know how to explain that she's stronger than I thought she would be. That she's shocked me by not breaking down at the news of her friends being spies.

I say, "You wore your hair pinned back."

Gloria pauses mid-chew, like she's just now realized this

herself. "Yes. I did."

"I like it."

That catches her off guard. She turns and blinks at me, but before she can form a response, the band begins the music for our dance, and I smile. "That's our cue."

"This doesn't change anything," Gloria says as I extend my hand. She takes it and lets me guide her onto the dance floor, leaving the food and her flowers behind. The music hushes as the crowd gathers to watch us. I pay them no mind, neither does my wife. In this moment, we are obsessed with each other, unable to acknowledge anything else or anyone else around us. I hardly hear the music begin when the band starts to play, it's Gloria who starts moving and I shuffle the first few steps to keep up.

"You're still angry," I say softly.

She doesn't speak as I twirl her, catching a whiff of her perfume. It's lemony and sweet. When she turns back around, I pull her close. "I keep telling you things are complicated, why can't you see that?"

"When I was a child, you were the man of my dreams," she whispers.

That hurts more than it should. It stings and burns and turns my anger into desperation.

"I'm still that man," I say, dipping her. She's flexible and leans her head back toward the floor as the audience claps softly. I pull her back up. "You've changed just as much as I have."

"I haven't changed. I've grown up."

"So have I."

"Grown into a man who plants spies into my life."

"A man who is in the mafia." I grunt. "Don't judge me for becoming what I was raised to be. Not all of us got to scamper off to a fancy Christian school. Not everyone can escape, Gloria."

She's silent, and I take the moment to twirl her again. It isn't in the choreography, but I don't want to look at her right now. I just want a moment to gather my thoughts. Gloria isn't just judging my actions; she's judging who I am.

"If you give me a chance, you might see that I'm not much different from the man you knew as a child," I tell her.

She doesn't look convinced. "The man I knew as a child would have defended me against his mother."

"The girl I knew wouldn't hold my sins against me."

That seems to surprise her, she screws up her face but doesn't speak.

"We're getting to know each other," I say, "So, I'm not surprised there are things you don't like about me. But you aren't perfect either, princess."

Her eyes become circles as she gapes at me. The color drains from her face and she turns stiff in my arms. I know from her expression that I've messed up. I said the wrong thing.

She thinks I'm talking about her scar.

"No." I shake my head. "That's not what I meant." But it's too late. The music stops and the crowd begins to clap again. Gloria steps away from me, pulling out of my arms. She faces the mass of family and friends and gives them a smile that holds neither joy nor confidence. Then, before the clapping is even finished, she turns and leaves.

I follow her.

"Gloria," I call, but she doesn't stop. "Gloria!" I grab her elbow and yank her through the double doors to the balcony before she can fight me and make a scene. It's cold outside, my words come out in silvery puffs. "I didn't mean what you think."

She tries to twist away. "Let me go!"

"No."

Her head snaps up and her eyes meet mine like a strike of fire, a match lighting a storm. "I'll scream," she says.

"See if that helps you." Anger flashes through me and I yank her into my chest. She presses her hands against me, trying to stable herself, but I grab both her wrists and hold her there, my hands like shackles over her own. "You don't get to walk away from me like that."

"I just did," she whimpers.

"You belong to me, Gloria. You might not like that. You might not like *me*. But that's the way it is. Do you understand?"

She doesn't speak.

I shake her.

"I don't belong to anyone!" she says quickly, fiercely.

"You can lie to me if that makes you feel better. But don't lie to yourself." My grip on her wrists slackens. I pull her a little closer. "You feel it. Same as I do."

She shakes her head. "I feel *trapped*."

"Say you hate me," I murmur. "Say it, and I'll walk away."

She doesn't speak.

"We're in this together. Do you understand?"

Slowly, Gloria nods. "I understand."

But I know she doesn't. I can see it in her face, in the tears swelling in her eyes. She doesn't believe I'm any different from Tadhg or my mother. She doesn't trust me when I say her scar doesn't matter to me—so I try to prove it to her.

I lean down and kiss her.

Gloria's entire body goes stiff, like she has no idea what's happening, but she catches on pretty quickly. My wife melts. Her mouth opens slightly, and I deepen the kiss, smiling when she gasps against my lips. Her arms latch around my neck, and I go from holding her hostage to holding her up. She is breathless and trembling when I pull away, her eyes fluttering as she looks up at me. Her mouth opens and then closes. She doesn't speak, just stares.

"I didn't mean what you think," I say.

She nods, eyes wide and unblinking. "W-We have to go back to the party."

I step back and untangle myself from her arms, then I watch as she tiptoes to the balcony doors. She glances back before slipping inside, looking equally frightened and amazed. She's probably confused, unsure if I am the man of her childhood dreams or the monster she thinks I am. Honestly, I have no idea.

14

Caolán

Tomorrow is my wedding day. Technically, it's my *anniversary*, but we're treating this like a fresh wedding and celebrating with a bachelor party. I'm sitting in a pub with a mug of Irish Red Ale, surrounded by the men I've spent my life working beside. Assassins and spies and gravediggers, all the things the Hand wishes to toss away despite how much they need us. These are the guys I call my brothers, the ones who know what it's like to live in the shadows. The only difference between us is that I've been dragged into the spotlight. I'm an underboss now, and tomorrow night with Gloria will solidify that.

I scan the crowd that has gathered for me. The pub isn't very large, built nearly a hundred years ago by the first members of the White Hand who crossed from the east coast of the US. The floor is cracked cement, patches of rundown carpet still clinging to life in the far corners of the room. The walls have been repainted so many times, I'm sure it's a few inches thick now. The lights are dim, and the chairs are flat and covered in cracked leather. It is a place of grime and darkness, and it's exactly where I want to be.

Ahead, there are women dancing on poles with clusters of wolffish men gathered to watch. Instead of throwing money, they throw horseshoes, a slightly updated version of an old Irish wedding tradition. The horseshoe represents good luck; it's customary to have one present at each wedding to bring luck to the couple as they begin their new life together. Some brides will include a horseshoe in their bouquet, carrying it around all day like a magical charm. Today, we're throwing them at hookers. If you snag a pole, you get a free lap dance. Snag her twice, you get a free private show. Snag her three times and she's yours for the night.

If it makes you feel better, I didn't make up these rules. I'm just here to watch the dancing, though it is entertaining when the guys miss and occasionally whack a hooker in the hip. One dancer gets so angry, she stomps down from her platform after being hit three times—once in the face. I feel for her, I really do, but trying to leave is a bad idea. The rule of the pub is not to touch the dancers, but if you're not on the pole, then you're not a dancer. You're just fair game.

As soon as the woman steps down from her platform, one of the guys wraps his arms around her waist and hoists her over his shoulder.

"Are you going to help?" Nolan asks beside me. He's sitting with his hands in his lap like he's afraid to touch anything, even the drink I got him. He's too young to appreciate the ale, so I'm not angry about wasting money on it, but still. I've never seen a teenager pass up a drink or a stripper before. Nolan truly doesn't belong here.

I take a deep breath. "How exactly should I help that woman, little brother?"

He turns to watch the scene. The dancer screams and slaps her palms against the man's back, but he pays her no mind, marching straight through the club toward one of the back rooms.

"It doesn't matter anymore," he mutters, and he's right.

I sip my drink. "You're too sensitive, Nolan. Kill that side of you before it's too late."

"This side of me may come in handy one day."

When I look at him, he's wearing a serious expression, like he's determined to be kind for the rest of his life. No matter what. If he weren't my brother, I would admire his passion. But that sort of attitude will get him killed in the world we live in. I can't let that happen.

"Nolan, listen—"

"Party's getting started already!" Billy O'Rourke flops into the chair beside me and howls out a laugh. Without asking, he reaches forward and grabs Nolan's cup, downs the drink in four big gulps and slams the mug down hard. "That's good ale, mate!"

"Indeed." I take a sip of my own.

"You've got to be the saddest looking bachelor I've ever seen." Billy leans toward me, staring at my face. His eyes are sharp, or at least the one he has. Billy's left eye has faded to grey, compliments of a target who almost got the better of him.

The fight was brutal and left him with a scar through his eyebrow and a dead eye. Shockingly, it hasn't harmed his appearance much. Billy's always been ugly. His face is narrow, each feature sharp and small. His hair is never combed, he's skinny as a rail, and when he smiles, you can see that all his little teeth are sharpened into points. He did that right after losing his eye. Apparently, the fight was so bad, he killed the guy by biting his throat and ripping out his windpipe with his teeth. Had them sharpened afterward because he said the job would've gone much easier if he'd done it before. Never mind the fact that he looks like a walking shark now. I doubt he's bitten anyone to death since then, but at least he's prepared.

"You don't look like you're having fun," Billy says.

"I'm enjoying my drink."

He grins and the horseshoe tattooed onto his chin stretches. "I got something a little stronger, if you wanna get crazy tonight."

I watch as Billy pulls out a little clear bag of silver powder. Fog. He sticks his finger inside and then places the powder beneath his tongue. Billy likes to take fog before and after kills. The first dose helps him enjoy the blood, the second brings him back to reality. Helps him accept that it's over.

I used to do the same thing, doubling or even tripling the dosage when the kill had to be brutal. I didn't need a strong high to get through it, I needed a strong high to get through the nightmares that came after. To smother the screams I could hear in my sleep. To silence the weeping that never seemed to stop.

The powder clouds my vision now. Dangerous relief. But I can't go back to that, not when I'm so close to having something real in my life. I don't need illusions or hallucinations to enjoy Gloria. She's mine without the brainwashing drug. For once, reality is better than the lies I used to snort up my nose.

"I don't want any fog," I say when Billy holds up the bag.

He tilts his head to the side. "You sure? You've really racked up the kills lately."

I've taken more names in the last week than I have in the last few years. But I don't need fog to survive the aftermath. Not yet at least.

I glance at Nolan, wondering what he's thinking, wondering if he'll be like me or Aidan when he's finally able to pull the trigger. I became an addict. Aidan is dead. Maybe it's better if he's nothing like us at all.

"I don't want any," I repeat to Billy.

"Married man," he says. "Getting all responsible and stuff! I like it." Billy slaps my shoulder and licks his lips. His tongue is long and split at the end, like a snake's. "Do you want a dancer?"

I sip my ale in response, and for some reason, this makes him laugh again.

"Oh, I know what you need."

Billy shoves to his feet and disappears around the corner for a few moments. When he comes back, he's escorting a beautiful woman. She's dressed like a dancer, but as she steps closer, I recognize the planes of her face.

"Aoife," I say softly.

A sultry smile dances across her perfect lips as she sits on my lap and wraps her arms around my neck. "Surprised to see me?"

I glance at Billy. "Did he convince you to come out here?"

"This was her idea," he says innocently.

Of course it was. I haven't seen Aoife since the Christmas ball. I told her to gather intel on Tadhg and she ended up going home with him. We typically cease communication when she's with a target, so we don't raise any suspicions. I figured she would give me a report once we met in person, but Tadhg surprised me by keeping her with him until now.

Even so, I'm not happy to see her. Aoife is one of the reasons my wife is angry at me. I underestimated how deeply Gloria cares for her. Her betrayal to my wife as my own spy has cut her far more than I thought it would. If she knew I've also slept with her over the years, she would never let me touch her again. I've hardly touched her now.

That kiss we shared had been sudden, if not forced, but it was enough for me to know that she wants me. Deep down, beneath the anger and resentment she feels toward our marriage, I know there is a darker feeling inside my wife. Desire. Lust. Need. I felt it all when she folded into my arms, melting from the heat of our kiss. I felt it as she wrapped her arms around my neck, as she let me pull her close. Gloria wants me, and she hates it. How could she not? She was forced to be with a man she barely knows, groomed to perfection so that I would be pleased with her. She has never had a choice in any part of her life. But I care enough about her to give her a choice.

I want Gloria to love me. I want her heart because it's the one thing not included in our contract.

Aoife reaches up and strokes my cheek, leaning forward to whisper along my jaw, "This is perfect, isn't it?"

"Do you have anything to tell me?" I ask in a gruff voice.

She looks annoyed. "You could be happier to see me."

"If you don't have anything, then you should be with my wife. Have you even apologized to her?"

She's blinking at me like I'm crazy. Like she can't possibly figure out a reason why she should ever say sorry to Gloria.

"You pretended to be her friend. You spied on her—"

"For *you*," she says sharply.

"And I will pay my penance, but you seem to have no interest in paying yours." Calmly, I reach up and grip both of Aoife's shoulders, pushing her away from me. "You should go."

"What?" She clutches my shirt. "I just got here."

"Funny. You weren't supposed to come at all."

I stand, forcing her to her feet, but before I can get Billy to take her back to wherever she came from, there's a commotion in the pub and all three of us stare into the crowd, trying to figure out what's going on. Even Nolan watches, sitting silently beside me like he wants to hide in my shadow.

In the crowd at the entrance, I can see a familiar figure moving through the bodies. His dark hair is hard to miss, but it's his grin that gives him away.

"What's Tadhg Fitzpatrick doing here?" Billy curses and then stands, even straightens his wrinkled shirt like he cares what Tadhg thinks.

"Why do you think he's here?" I ask.

Tadhg walks right up to me, and I have no choice but to stand and acknowledge him. The prince of the Pointer Finger took time out of his busy day to celebrate my wedding; tongues will wag if I don't show him proper respect. They're *still* wagging after the spat we had at dinner, but I suppose this is his way of extending an olive branch. As annoying as his presence is, I have to admit I'd rather have Tadhg as a friend than a foe, so when he's near, I button my suit jacket and hold out my hand for him to shake.

He looks at it and then extends his hand, but it's positioned with his ring up. He wants me to kiss it.

My gaze narrows. "What are you doing?"

"Greeting you."

Like this? In front of everyone. At my bachelor party.

I should have known an olive branch was the last thing Tadhg wanted to offer.

"I don't know who you—"

Nolan cuts me off with a jolt. He shoves to his feet and nearly knocks me over as he brushes by me to get to Tadhg. Before either of us can even figure out what's happening, Nolan grabs his hand and kisses the ring. In my place.

"Greetings, Honored Fitzpatrick," my brother murmurs. "Clan O'Rourke welcomes you to the party."

He isn't the underboss, but Nolan *is* a prince of Clan

O'Rourke. His official greeting and welcome is just as good as mine, so Tadhg is forced to retract his hand after a beat of tense silence. His fingers twitch like he wants to wipe them on his pants.

"Thank you," he says, then his eyes drift to my side and land on Aoife who shifts her weight from one foot to the other. I don't know what's going on between them, but I don't plan to find out either.

Instead of offering Tadhg a seat or a drink, I slide my hands into my pockets and say, "Thanks for coming." It's a subtle way of telling him his presence is unwanted, but he doesn't take the hint.

Tadhg's lips curl backwards in an ugly smile and his eyes light up with wicked joy. "I have a gift for you, Caolán." He retrieves a slip of paper from his pocket and passes it to me.

There's a name and address scribbled on it. A target. The night before my wedding.

When I glance up, he's beaming. "I'm sure you'll take care of this."

Billy tries to rescue me. "I can take care of that, boss. No need for Caolán to get his hands dirty right before the wedding."

Tadhg doesn't even acknowledge he's spoken. "I expect proof of kill before sunrise."

He leaves in silence. Neither Billy nor Nolan speaks for a long while after he's gone. We return to our seats and I stare at the paper in my hand, trying to figure out what the heck I'm supposed to do. Handing me a target is an insult to my position as an underboss, but everyone knows I've been taking kills again anyway so it's not as low of a blow as Tadhg wants it to be. That's why he gave me a name he knows will tear me apart. Or tear my wife apart.

"Just give it to me." Billy reaches across the table and takes the paper from my hand. "Tadhg will never know I did it."

"He will," I mutter.

Billy frowns. "Who is Anthony Jones?"

Aoife's head snaps up; she's no longer sitting on my lap but has settled beside me in the booth. Her eyes are huge, blinking between Billy and the paper he tossed onto the table. She's itching to grab it, to verify that she heard what she heard, but she knows her place and keeps her hands clasped on the table instead.

"Anthony is someone who works for me," I confess. "A spy from the Jackson organization."

Nolan leans forward and takes the paper. "That can't be right. Why would Tadhg want you to kill him?"

"To make my wife hate me," I mutter.

"You can't do it, then." Nolan folds up the paper. "We can notify Darren Jackson. We don't have to—"

"We *cannot* defy the Pointer," I hiss.

Our family started the war that nearly tore the Middle Finger apart. After almost a decade, we finally have the chance to stitch things back together. We cannot let anything ruin the fragile peace we've built. Not even this.

"But…" Nolan stares through watery eyes. "This will hurt Gloria."

More than that, it could start the war over again. Unless Tadhg plans to cover up what he's asked me to do. He could hide the body and then release it later; make it look like Anthony was killed by someone else. Or he could reveal the truth; that Anthony was working against his own mafia. That alone would get his name on a list in the Jackson organization. So, technically, Anthony's death would be justified, but that won't remove the pain it will cause Gloria. And if she ever found out I did it, she would never forgive me.

I shove to my feet and storm out of the booth. Nolan, Aoife, and Billy all run behind me, following me out into the cracked parking lot in the back.

I'm fumbling with my keys when Billy approaches. "Let me do it, mate." He slaps my shoulder to get my attention, and I look down to see the little bag he's offering yet again. "Take the night off. Have some fun with Aoife. It'll all be over in the morning. I promise."

Aoife… The sound of her name clicks everything into place. The moment my eyes land on her, I feel hatred swell inside me.

How did Tadhg find out about Anthony?

She sees the question in my eyes as I turn to her, and she doesn't have an answer. The guilt on her face *is* an answer. I told her to get his attention at the Christmas ball, but I didn't tell her to start spilling secrets.

"What did he promise you?" I ask her.

Nolan and Billy stare in disbelief.

Aoife shakes her head, gasping as tears run down her face.

"I didn't have a choice."

"You said I could trust you."

She drops to her knees right there in the parking lot; jagged rocks dig into the soft flesh of her legs. She winces but ignores the pain, reaching up to take my hand, kissing my fingers the way Nolan kissed Tadhg's.

"I had no choice," she whispers against my hand. "He took me to his home that night. I was trapped there—he wouldn't let me go unless I told him something."

I know she's right. Aoife's just a whore while Tadhg is the prince of Clan Fitzpatrick. She truly had no choice but to do what he said, just like I have no choice now. But that doesn't mean I'm not angry. And it doesn't mean she won't pay for this.

I pull my hand away. "Billy, please take Aoife to your place for the night."

Both of their mouths drop open. Aoife looks horrified but Billy looks excited. He's a twisted man with twisted tastes, I'm sure a night with him is fair punishment for getting Anthony killed. Plus …

"I owe you for helping clean up Eoin Greene."

Billy's laugh is wicked. He pulls Aoife to her feet and slaps her bottom. "When do you need her back?"

I blink at her. "I don't."

Aoife's lips move, but for a few seconds nothing comes out, then a word tumbles from her mouth. "Caolán—"

"Have fun," I say, looking only at Billy.

"Oh, I will."

I swear he growls as he pulls her away.

I could feel bad for what I've just done to Aoife, but the truth is that I don't care. The only thing that makes me pull out my phone is the image of Gloria's face that pops into my head. She cares about Aoife, despite her betrayal as my spy. So, for the sake of my wife and her gentle heart, I send Billy a text.

Send Aoife home by midnight.

One night with him is punishment enough.

Once I'm done, I put my phone away and glance at my little brother who looks like he's about to cry. I don't have time for his tears tonight.

"Get in the car," I grumble, marching past him. "You're coming with me."

15

Caolán

The drive to the warehouse is silent and sullen. I know Nolan wants to say something; his unease is as obvious as the blaring red light I blow through before turning into the lot. But he doesn't say anything. For once, it seems like he finally understands how things work. That nobody *wants* to do these things, but most times we have no choice.

I punch the ignition button and the car goes dark, engine purring as it settles.

We sit in silence.

"Nolan," I say after what seems like forever, "you can sit this one out. If you want."

I hear his seatbelt click and I turn to stare at him. "I want to go," he says, and then he opens his door before I can ask if he's sure.

The warehouse looks abandoned, like most kill sites do. I almost trip over a crack in the pavement as I walk to the door where Nolan is already waiting. He doesn't look afraid like he normally is, but he doesn't look as brave as he's trying to be. He won't look at me. And once I unlock the door, I hear him suck in a long breath, hold it, and then slowly exhale.

The lights are out inside, and they flicker on with a bright scream when I slap the switch. My eyes burn for a moment, and when my vision clears, I see a man on his knees in the middle of the room. There's a bag over his head, but I can see the blood staining his white button-down. They beat him and then left him here for me to finish the job.

"Wait by the door," I tell Nolan, but he shakes his head and follows me over to the man.

He's letting out a wheezing noise I can hear well before I get to him. *They must have broken his nose when they kidnapped him—* that's what I think until I get close enough to see his tie wound around his neck. It's been tightened so much that it's choking him, but very slowly. He can't take any more than shallow breaths, and even those are labored. His hands are tied behind his back so he can't loosen the tie himself. If I hadn't come to finish the job, he would've eventually choked to death anyway.

Nolan runs forward and grabs the tie, gingerly pulling on the knot with shaky fingers.

"Stop," I tell him, but my voice is quiet, a breath above a whisper. "Stop, Nolan."

He doesn't listen.

"Nolan!" I find my voice and it comes out as a bark that bounces around the empty chamber.

My brother jumps and whirls around. "Why shouldn't I help him?"

"What difference will it make? I still have to kill him."

The man starts weeping, and with his tie loosened, I can make out his voice now. It's definitely Anthony.

Nolan doesn't reply; he just turns around and begins to carefully pull the black bag over Anthony's head. I take this moment to prepare the gun they've left for me. A pistol with a silencer I have to attach myself. It's sitting on top of the deep freezer by the door. I'm supposed to kill him, take a picture, and then stuff his body inside for the cleanup crew to deal with. Maybe Tadhg will have him dismembered, maybe he'll burn him up later, or maybe he'll just hold on to the body for months, pretending the boy went missing. He might even make me help with the search, torturing suspects for information I know they don't have. Because I'm the one who's about to pull the trigger.

I don't have any gloves to put on, so the gun feels cool in my hand, smooth metal clenched in a scarred, calloused palm. My body feels like it's moving in slow motion as I approach Anthony, still on his knees, muttering to my brother. I hear Gloria's name fall from his mouth and it stops me in my tracks. They're talking about my wife.

"Tell her I'm sorry," he says to Nolan, who nods emphatically, clutching that black bag for dear life.

My brother looks up at me when I'm close enough, hovering over them both. "Please don't," he whispers. "You don't have to do this. We can find another way."

"Move," I say.

He doesn't.

Fine, he can watch him die up close.

I press the gun to Anthony's head, and he obediently closes his eyes, muttering what I know is a prayer, though I can't make out the words. They always pray when they know they're about to die. Just like Aidan did.

The thought of him nearly stops my heart. Suddenly, I see my brother on his knees. Not Anthony. They have the same posture, the same bowed head, the same engulfing silence in their last moments.

"Are you afraid?" I whisper.

No one knows I'm asking myself.

Anthony doesn't reply, or maybe he does but I can't hear it over Nolan's loud pleading. "Don't, Caolán—please!" he blurts, but it's too late.

I pull the trigger.

And nothing happens.

The gun clicks, but there is no bullet, no blood sprayed into the air, no head whipping back. Anthony is still there on his knees, his eyes squeezed shut, his lips still moving in a silent prayer.

Nolan blinks at me. "What happened?"

I step back, staring at the pistol, then I eject the magazine and laugh. It's empty. And scratched into the metal casing are the words, **You passed.** I flip the clip over to read the other side, ***Take a picture.***

This was a test. Another chance for me to prove my loyalty to the Hand. If I had refused the kill and escaped with Anthony, they would have hunted me down. I had to pull the trigger, because only then would I have realized the gun was empty and checked the magazine to see the message they left for me.

I drop the gun. "We're done here."

Anthony exhales a groan of relief. There's a dark stain on the front of his pants, so I don't blame him when he slumps over and closes his eyes. He's exhausted. Drained.

Nolan reaches for the gun, turning it over in his hands. "I don't get it."

"Did you want him to die?" I snap. "We're done. Let's go." I march toward the door, not caring if he follows or not. As expected, I hear his footsteps a few moments later.

He's right behind me when he says, "Are we just going to leave him?"

"Yep."

"Won't you get in trouble for not finishing the job?"

I don't reply until we're both in the car, snapping our seatbelts into place. "I was never supposed to kill him, Nolan." I hold up the empty magazine and he curses in Irish as he takes it from me, reading the jaggedly carved words.

"I can send photos to Tadhg for you."

"No, it's got to come from my phone."

"Okay," Nolan says, and then he stares at me.

I stare at my hands clenching the steering wheel.

"Caolán—"

"What?"

"This is good, right? You didn't have to kill Anthony after all. And you passed the test."

"Yeah, it's good."

He shifts in his seat, unsure how to say his next words.

"Just spit it out, Nol."

"If it's good, then why are you so angry?"

He doesn't get it. This wasn't just a test; it was a message. That Tadhg is in control. At any moment, he can stick his hand into my life and force me to do things I don't want to. Force me to hurt my wife or the ones she loves.

She isn't safe here, but there's nowhere I can take her. Nothing I can truly do to keep her away from Tadhg. I thought my mother had been the greater threat but she's just a bitter, power-hungry woman. The most she wanted was to rule the household, make me and Gloria listen and obey. She was annoying but she wasn't dangerous.

This ... I lift my eyes to stare at the warehouse. *This is entirely different.*

Anthony stumbles outside in a daze, he takes one look at me in the driver's seat of my car and then starts a slow jog in the opposite direction, like he isn't sure if I'm going to catch up and finish the job.

"This isn't good," I finally reply to Nolan.

"How can I help?"

"You can't."

"Yes, I can—"

"Could you have pulled the trigger in there?" I motion to the warehouse. "Would you have found the strength to do what I just did?"

"I don't have to," he whispers, dropping his head. "I'm not

like you, Key, I know that. But that doesn't mean I'm useless." He looks up, scowling like he's actually angry at me. It's almost cute. "I don't have to be a murderer to serve our family."

He'd be right if he were a woman, but he isn't my pretty wife, he's the prince of Clan O'Rourke. A clan of reapers; so, *yes*, he does have to be a murderer to be useful to us.

I don't say any of this to him, however. This is the first time he's ever stood up for himself. He isn't turning out the way I want, but he is learning.

I throw the car into drive. "Let's go home."

Nolan doesn't speak to me during the ride home, but I'm fine with that. My mind is too busy with everything that's happened. Aoife has sold my secrets. Anthony was almost killed. Tadhg knows I've got people working for me. And Gloria…

What do I do with my wife?

I have to keep her safe. Gloria is the only thing in my life that is mine. The only thing that is real. I like her. I like being around her. Every other clip of happiness I've had has been a lie. Joy stolen from foggy dreams. But Gloria isn't a hallucination. She's real and she's mine and I won't let the Hand take her from me.

We can't live under Tadhg's thumb like this, but there's nothing I can do that won't make things worse. He's even taken over our wedding night, inserting himself as a witness. He'll get to see my wife naked, watch me make love to her, and then examine the bloody sheets afterward.

I've known how consummation ceremonies work my entire

life. I've witnessed three already as the underboss. I've heard the complaints from bitter women who have a hard time accepting their place in our world. But I've never paid them much attention. To me, the ceremony didn't matter. It was tradition. Nothing to be ashamed of.

But how could I have seen it any other way? I'm a man. It means nothing to perform my duties before a crowd. If anything, it's a chance for me to show off the gifts of Clan O'Rourke. But now I get it. Now I can feel the burning sense of shame my mother and female cousins have suffered. Now I understand what Gloria must feel. And I hate it.

He can't take this away from us. He's got my job in his hand. He's a leader of the entire White Hand. But he can't have this. Anything but this.

Nolan tells me goodbye and then slinks into the house. I sit in the car until the garage lights flicker off, then I punch the steering wheel in anger and hit the ignition button again.

There's only one way to solve this. It will make or break my marriage.

16

Ria

This is my last day of freedom. With a sigh, I rise from my cushioned seat and close the book in my hand. I've been hiding in the library of my family estate all day and half the night. This place used to be my escape. As a child, I would run here—not to read the books—but to hide from my father's booming voice when he yelled, or to shut out my mother's sobbing when the yelling stopped. There was something about the muted atmosphere that made me feel at peace. The plush carpets squishing between each toe, the way you have to whisper once you come inside. The outside world ceased to exist in the library. The only noise allowed in was that of books and stories, the sound of pages turning and adventures playing out. That was my peace as a child, but I've learned that my life is not a storybook. I've got to find *big girl peace* now, somehow.

As I walk toward the exit, I pass the front display. It's been the same all my life, an old King James Bible sitting on a white stone pillar. It belonged to my greatest elders, passed down through the generations. If you look in the front, you can see our family tree listed until there's no more room to add names. Some of the oldest names on the list were former slaves who taught themselves to read and used every penny they could find to purchase the precious Book. Others were preachers, and then civil rights activists. What a shame that my family has become this monstrous force now. Owners of a mafia organization.

The Panthers of LA began as *Black Panthers*, the activist organization founded in California in the 1960s. Originally, the Panthers fought against police brutality and corruption. But over time, political corruption stood in their way, internal conflict tore them down, and eventually, the Panthers were consumed by their frustrations. What started as an inspirational movement became an organization of radicalized ideology. Racism was no longer their only enemy; the Panthers hated the *world*. To them, injustice couldn't be defeated through marches and political change. They believed you had to beat corruption at its own game.

That's how a group of activists became mafia bosses.

My family is part of the corruption that poisoned the original Black Panthers. I'm glad there isn't room for more names to be added to the family Bible. No one deserves to have their name placed beside the people who actually did great and wonderful things for our family. The ones who stood for something and loved their families and honored God. What we have now is a shell of what we used to be, and I'm not sure we could ever return.

I run my fingers over the page of the Bible, it's always left open in the same spot, **Matthew Chapter 5**. I know this chapter. It's famous for the *Sermon on the Mount* where Jesus Christ described what we call *The Beatitudes*. As a child, I had no idea what any of this meant, but attending private Christian school all my life helped bring things into perspective. *Beatitude* means *supreme blessedness*. So, the Beatitudes are the people Jesus calls supremely blessed. As wonderful as this sounds, my eyes skip over that segment. I'm drawn to verse 14, when Jesus says, *Ye are the light of the world*. That's what He thinks of us.

My eyes blur as I continue reading, going over the words that describe absolutely nothing about me. Verse 16 nearly makes me sob, *Let your light so shine before men, that they may see your good works, and glorify your Father which is in heaven.*

I am not a light. I am not a city on a hill. I do not give light to anyone or anything around me. In my entire life, I've done nothing that would encourage anyone to seek God's face. I know I'm not the best Christian. In many ways, I don't even know what I believe in anymore. But even if I *did* believe, I know there's simply no way I could live a life of faith here. I can't be a light in the mafia; the darkness is too strong. They would snuff me out in a heartbeat. They already have.

I turn and leave the Bible on its stand, dragging myself to my bedroom. I should be out celebrating instead of moping, but I don't have it in me to even pretend I would enjoy a bachelorette party. The only people who'd come would be lower ranked women only there by obligation, and then Mother and Aoife. Those are the last two people I want to see.

My mother, the woman who sold me. And Aoife, the woman who betrayed me.

My bedroom door opens with a silent yawn, it's warm inside so I drift to the balcony doors and grasp the handles. *Something's wrong...* my body stiffens. The doors ... they're already unlocked. I take one step back from the balcony doors and gasp.

There's someone in my room. A shadow that comes alive and peels from the far wall. It takes up more room than it should, long legs stretching before it to form the figure of a man. A man I recognize.

"Caolán," I whisper.

"Darling," he says. His voice is low and husky; it always sounds like he has a sore throat and paired with his Irish accent it's almost difficult to understand him. But I hear his next statement loud and clear. I hold it in my head and swallow each word—each *letter*—transporting them to my heart.

"I've missed you."

I look away, embarrassed by how much I want to smile right now. We haven't seen each other since he kissed me, but this is about more than just the butterflies in my stomach. This is the man who had my best friend and bodyguard spy on me for years. Caolán turned Tony against his own mafia, a betrayal punishable by death. Even worse, by telling me about Tony's lies, he's put me in an impossible situation. If I rat out Tony, I have to watch my personal guard die. But if I remain silent, I'll have to live knowing there is a rat in my family, in my home, and I did nothing to stop him.

"You shouldn't be here," I say.

"Tell me to leave."

I can't. I don't want to. And I hate myself for it.

Caolán extends his hand to touch me, but I take a step back and shake my head. "You're still upset with me," he murmurs.

"You've been lying to me. Everyone around me is a spy for *you*. You act crazy when you're angry. Then you apologize like you're nice again. And you suddenly kissed me like that was supposed to make it all better."

I look away as I finish that statement, hoping he can't see me blushing. That had been my very first kiss, not a moment of passion, but an explosion of heat and rage. I'd loved every second, but some part of me won't admit that aloud. I can hardly admit it to myself. I like Caolán, exactly as he is. But I shouldn't.

"I don't want to see you right now," I whisper.

"I see," Caolán says softly. His eyes go from cat slits to almonds, as close as he'll ever get to being wide-eyed. It's a strange, unnatural expression on him.

"Who are you?" I ask softly.

"I'm your husband."

"But who is Caolán O'Rourke?"

"What do you mean?"

"My husband is a man with a charming smile and a gentle voice. But that isn't who *you* are. Caolán O'Rourke is someone entirely different. I've realized that lately."

"Did Aoife tell you that?" He steps a little closer.

I scoff. "Aoife doesn't speak to me anymore. I had my

maids pack her bags. She lives in the staff quarters now. Apparently, that's what she is anyway. At least for one of us."

"Yes, she works for me, but that isn't so bad."

"Being spied on isn't bad?"

He looks exasperated, as if dealing with an annoying child. "You went overseas, Gloria. Did you think I wouldn't want to know what you were up to?"

"You didn't have to plant people in my life to do that. You didn't have to force my own bodyguard to betray his organization."

"How else should I have done it?" His voice is sharp, cracking with anger. "How should I have kept an eye on my wife who knows nothing about this world? Tell me, Gloria, since you are so full of ideas."

I frown. "You could've visited me and asked how I was doing! You could've written me letters and kept in contact! You could have done so many other things!"

"I did it the only way I knew how. You can't blame me for that."

"You're right," I sneer. "I don't blame you for being exactly what you've always been. I blame myself for not seeing it before. For being fooled by your charming demeanor."

His face darkens and his voice becomes a whisper, each word a menacing threat. "Let me remind you that this is the mafia, Gloria. I don't have to be so charming, if that's what you prefer."

"I prefer the truth—"

He's across the room before I can even blink, moving like

a phantom, like he was made for the shadows. *No*, like he was made *by* the shadows—and when he steps into the pale moonlight spilling in through the balcony doors, he seems out of place. Like a ghost caught wandering in daylight. But this ghost is real. His anger is real, and he releases it through his hand which wraps around my throat.

I squeeze my eyes shut but they pop right back open once I realize I can still breathe. He isn't choking me. But I can feel each one of his fingers on my neck, holding me in place. The message is clear. He could choke me if he wanted to. He could squeeze the life right out of me, cut off my cries and my airways too, and leave my body for my dear mother to find.

But he isn't. He's just holding me, looking at my face, watching my reaction.

"This is the truth," he whispers, running his thumb over my windpipe. "This is who I am."

"My husband."

"A hitman for the White Hand. I'm a murderer."

"You don't have to be."

"You know I don't have a choice. And neither do you." His eyes flick down to my lips. "But that doesn't matter, does it? Because even if you had a choice, you'd still be here. Wouldn't you?" I blink and Caolán leans forward but stops short of kissing me. The proximity brings back every childhood memory of him. Every clap of thunder between us, every moment I stole. Happiness snatched from his iron grasp; cold hands wrapped over his steel heart.

Is that all? I'd asked as a child.

He'd smiled each time. *That's all for now.*

And what about here? What about *now?* With his lips so close, his words dance across my mouth like a cold kiss. "You're not upset because you don't know who I am," Caolán says. "You're angry because you *do*, and you like me anyway."

I suck in a gasp, but it's swallowed by a kiss. Caolán's lips press against mine roughly, desperately, like he can't control himself. He groans as I tilt my head back, slipping his tongue into my mouth, running his hands down my body until he grabs my waist and pulls me closer.

I don't fight him. I can't even imagine pushing him away because he's right. Despite his betrayals and his possessive nature, I still want Caolán. I don't dislike *him*; I dislike the *mafia*. I dislike the darkness that surrounds him. But you can't have one without the other. He's a custom wrapped package.

That is what I hate. That I'm walking into the shadows with my eyes wide open, and as I wrap my arms around Caolán's neck, I don't have a concern or a worry about it. In that case, I'm just as bad as him, aren't I? Maybe even worse.

Caolán's kiss burns, his mouth is hot, and his breath comes out in pants. My hands tangle into red fire and Caolán grunts as I yank his hand back. His blue eyes are cubes of ice that cool us down for a moment. We stare at each other, breathing, watching, wondering what happens next.

Caolán dips his head, and I stand on my tiptoes to meet him halfway. This time, the noise he makes comes from deep inside, a growl that starts in his gut and swells through his chest until it rumbles out his mouth. It sets me ablaze and I pull him even closer. We're inseparable, like two bodies turned into one. How is it possible for us to have such passion for one another?

Perhaps it isn't passion at all. Maybe all of this is lust.

That's what pulls me away, tripping backwards and wiping my mouth. Caolán stares, a veil of uncertainty blanketing his features. His brows are drawn down and his jaw is set in a hard line.

"We have to stop," I whisper.

"We're already married, Gloria. It's okay—"

"They have to witness it." My skin crawls as I say that, but we both know it's true. We have to consummate the marriage before witnesses to honor the contract. Those witnesses must see blood. If I don't bleed tomorrow night, then the contract will be null. My virginity cannot be broken before then, not even by my lawful husband.

"I thought you'd be willing to risk it."

"We've already risked enough."

We could be whipped for what we've just done.

"We can't do this," I whisper.

He steps closer, stroking my cheek. "It's just us," he says. "We have this moment."

"But we can't—"

"Do you really want Tadhg to take this from us?"

I blink. Tadhg who told me I was almost pretty. Tadhg who forced me to tie my hair back, even had Caolán participate. And Tadhg who added himself as a witness. He volunteered to watch me have sex. He's a sick pervert if I've ever seen one.

The thought of his smirking face makes me shiver, but I'm

still afraid. What will happen if we do this?

"We—We can't," I whisper again.

Caolán cups my chin and lifts it. "Then tell me to leave."

My heart seizes in my chest. "No."

He leans down again, but I meet him halfway, kissing him like my life depends on it. In this moment, I don't care about Tadhg or Aifric or the mafia at all. The only thing I want is this moment between us, a moment no one can take away.

Our kiss is a spark of fire that erupts into a storm of searing wind and flames. It sends electricity shooting through me, my chest, my gut, my legs which tremble as I rise on the balls of my feet. Caolán lifts me from the floor and carries me to the bed. His hands are rough, calloused palms gripping my waist, sliding down to my thighs, slipping beneath my skirt. I gasp and he covers my mouth with his own, only pulling away to whisper, "Let me show you who I am."

I'd be a fool to argue.

How gentle can a murderer be? When he undresses me, he treats me like a princess. Precious. Cherished. When he lays me against the pillows, he watches like a hawk, his eyes predatory, but his hands delicate, masterful. When I cling to him, his body reacts from head to toe, every muscle tightening, coiling with passion. And when I dig my nails into his back, his voice is the softest I've ever heard. My name is on his lips like a whimper for release. We find it together, and then we crash in a bundle of warm, sweaty limbs.

After a moment, Caolán rolls off me and onto his back. His eyes are closed; his chest rising and falling. Slower, *slower*, until he catches his breath. I watch the apple in his throat bob as he swallows, hypnotized by it. I want to roll over and kiss him there, but I stay in place, afraid to move and shatter the moment.

"Thank you," he whispers finally.

"For what?"

"For thinking I was worth it."

17

Ria

Thanks for thinking I was worth it...

I replay Caolán's words in my head; over the memories of the passion we just shared. He *was* worth it, but...

I roll onto my side so I can look at him fully. "I did it for me just as much as you."

"What do you mean?"

This wasn't just about making love, it was about taking back some sense of control. Dignity. Something the mafia has denied me for so long.

I don't know how to say that, so I just rest my head on Caolán's bare chest and sigh. "I did it because I wanted to. That's the first time I ever did that. Made my own decision."

"Me too," he murmurs, and I sit up to stare at him.

How can that be true? How can a mafia underboss not be allowed to make his own decisions? My eyes fill with all my questions, but Caolán doesn't answer them. When he looks down at me, his eyes focus on my scar, like he's seeing it for the first time.

He leans over and brushes his thumb along the bumpy skin. "I never meant this was one of your imperfections."

"You told me already."

"But you didn't believe me."

"I do now."

He stares at me—at me face. "What happened?"

"I did it to myself. I didn't want to be a mafia princess. I didn't want to be married. I thought the only way I could get out of it was to make myself unattractive. So I cut my face up, hoping that you would call off the marriage when you saw me again." I sigh. "But that never happened. I left for boarding school before we could meet again."

"I saw you," he says, and I stare at him in shock.

"When?"

"You know I've been watching you for a while, Gloria. I saw you when you first flew to England. I've known about the scar all along, I just didn't know how you got it."

He's known. All this time, Caolán has known about my deepest secret. The one thing I've tried to hide from the world. That means when Aifric and Tadhg made me pull my hair back, he wasn't surprised by what he saw. And when he said I had imperfections, he really didn't mean the scar.

It's just a face, he'd said, *not even a bad one.*

Without thinking, I lean over and kiss him. My eyes flutter shut when he groans and slides his hand down my leg. He grips my thigh and drapes it over his waist, pulling me into him so we can make love again. This time is faster than the first, we're finished hardly before we get started. Caolán grunts out three solid minutes of this passionate dance and then his body tenses and he hisses through his teeth, almost like he's angry.

When I pull away, he can't look at me, ears burning redder than his hair. "I'm sorry," he mumbles, "I didn't mean to—"

I cut him off with a laugh and a kiss to his cheek. "Honestly, I'm flattered."

Is this how things could be between us? If we learned to love each other. If the mafia didn't stand in the way? I can't imagine my life without the Panthers and I'm sure Caolán can't imagine his without the White Hand. But I think of the scriptures I read earlier as I run my fingers through my husband's hair. *You are a city on a hill...* maybe if we leave the mafia, we could build our own lives. Our own cities. Is that possible for us? For these creatures of darkness.

Where can we build our city? my heart whispers to God, and it feels like a fruitless prayer because there is nowhere we can go that Aifric or Tadhg wouldn't find us. We will never have peace—our fate is as black as the tattoos that cover Caolán's skin.

Now that he's fully naked, I can see there are so many more tattoos than just the ones on his hands. His chest is covered in the ribs of a skeleton, there are even black lungs behind the tattooed bones, but the heart is missing. When he'd taken off his shirt, I had nearly gasped, but then he turned to toss it away and I caught a glimpse of his back. It's covered in a life-size reaper; a black phantom holding a scythe, ready to collect souls of despair.

I would ask the inspiration behind his markings, but I already know. He told me as much earlier, that he's a hitman for the White Hand. Death is his inspiration; murder is his purpose. That's the man I call my husband.

Is this okay? I ask God. It's funny how many questions and prayers I have now, *after* sleeping with him. But I didn't see all of this before. I didn't know what he was hiding beneath his clothes; taking them off was like opening a coffin.

When I was in school, my Bible study classes went over all the *fun* things high schoolers love to do. The class was an attempt to dissuade us from drinking and smoking or having sex, complete with scriptures sprinkled through the slideshows of blackened lungs and DUI car wrecks. The only part that stuck with me was the tiny little slide we had to read about tattoos.

I hadn't cared about getting inked because I'm a mafia princess, regardless of my faith, I'm not allowed to have them before marriage and even after, I can only get one Caolán approves of. But that lesson didn't talk about tattoos being a sin, it talked about them being an *altar*.

"Idolatry is a sin because it places something higher than God. Sometimes we do this without thinking. We idolize our jobs, our partners, our favorite celebrities, but there is something that takes this a step further." She leaned over her desk, speaking in a serious tone. "Some people build an altar to worship their idol. When you build an altar, you shed blood on it as a form of worship." She let that sink in. "Tattoos are no different. You put the needle to your skin and shed blood to the idol you've created. It could be a cute butterfly or your favorite anime character, when you cut your flesh for it, you are offering a form of worship to it."

I had almost raised my hand to ask about Christian tattoos—images of scriptures or crosses—but my teacher beat me to it, answering before the question could pass my lips.

"There is no such thing as a Christian tattoo," she'd said, shaking her head. "When you shed blood for a tattoo, you are making a sacrifice to the idol you have created. Shedding blood to draw a cross onto your arm does not please God, it *mocks* Him—because the ultimate sacrifice has already been made. Christ shed His blood on the altar two-thousand years ago. He does not need you to shed it again, and certainly not as a form of worship. If you dare to build an altar on your imperfect flesh and shed your imperfect blood to get it, you mock the sacrifice that has already been given." She'd looked around at all of us, ignoring the ones who were rolling their eyes. One boy even rolled up his shirt sleeve to show off the tattoo he already had. I understood the knee-jerk desire he had to be defiant, but he was missing the point.

My teacher wasn't trying to shame him; she was trying to inform him. Sometimes you don't know you've made a mistake until it's been revealed, because no one around you sees it as a mistake to begin with. And sometimes you can't accept that your behavior *is* a mistake because you aren't ready to.

My teacher had smiled at that boy. "The wonderful thing about God is that He isn't angry with you when you build these tattoo altars. He will forgive you. He will overlook them. That's why Christ shed His blood. So that when God looks down from Heaven and sees us, He doesn't see ink or man-made altars, He sees the Blood of His Son, Christ Jesus, and that's all that matters."

That's all that matters, I tell myself, tracing my finger along the curve of ink on Caolán's chest. I can feel his voice vibrating when he speaks, like a low hum against my ear.

"What are you thinking about?"

"Your tattoos."

"Oh…"

"How old were you when you got them?"

"I started around thirteen."

"*Thirteen?*"

Caolán swallows. "That's how old I was when I was initiated into the White Hand. My father was proud, but my mother didn't like the ink."

"Why does she hate you so much?"

Caolán pauses. He's lying on his back, his fingers slowly moving up and down my waist, to my ribs and back. Every so often his hand moves up high enough to brush his thumb over my breast. It makes me shiver each time. "Because I killed my older brother."

That is not the confession I was expecting, and I don't know how to react. So, I just lay there on my side, staring at the tattoos on his chest and arms. The skeletal fingers of his hands.

Caolán fills the silence with his story. "Aidan was my mother's favorite. He was the heir to the O'Rourke head family, and he listened to everything she told him. She'd groomed him to take over the family business so that he would rule as she wanted him to. But Aidan messed up. He fell in love with Bethany."

I stiffen. That can't be true. Bethany was murdered by her husband.

"How could he love her if he killed her?" I whisper.

"He didn't kill her," Caolán says slowly. "Bethany … She— She didn't like the mafia."

"What are you saying?"

"She wasn't happy here."

"What are you *saying*?" I demand, sitting up and staring at him.

"She killed herself, Gloria. Bethany took her own life to get out of the mafia."

"I don't understand." I turn away and hug myself. I can't even look at Caolán right now. None of this makes sense. "The official word was that she was murdered. Why would you keep the truth a secret?" I whirl around. "Why would you keep that from *me*?"

His face is impassive. "You wouldn't have believed me."

I wouldn't have. I hardly believe him now.

My chest rises as I take a breath. "Does my family know? Am I the only fool here?"

He shakes his head, and I feel like I can breathe again. "No. I chose to keep that a secret. It's a lie I bear alone."

"Why? Why cover up something like this and make your brother out to be a heartless murderer?"

"It was what he wanted." Caolán blinks slowly, undoubtedly thinking of Aidan. "My brother truly did love your sister. But he couldn't make her happy. In the end, he blamed himself for her death. He said her suicide was the same as murder since he was still responsible in some way."

"So, he let our families fall into war because of that?"

Caolán shakes his head. "The war was better for the Panthers, Gloria. You know how the mafia feels about suicide."

I do. Even an airheaded princess like me knows it's considered a terrible sin. A betrayal to the organization. If anyone had found out Bethany took her own life, my family would have been ostracized for raising weak children. In some twisted way, Aidan's lie helped us. Even though he knew that lie would label him as a violent woman beater, he told it anyway.

"So then…" I whisper, trying to piece it all together. "Why did you kill him?"

"To end the war."

I swallow.

"The Panthers were stronger opponents than we thought. Your family was winning the war, Gloria. It had to end, or we would have been ruined. My mother knew this. So, she did something about it."

My eyes bulge. "No…"

Caolán nods, confirming the worst. "She ordered a hit on her own son. And I fulfilled it."

"She hates you for carrying out the order."

"No. She hates me for keeping her secret."

"Secret?"

"Targets are placed anonymously within the Hand. The contract is requested and approved by our leaders, then a hitman is assigned to the task. The Pointer Finger agreed to place the mark on my brother because they knew the war had to end. They blamed Aidan for starting it in the first place, so the hit was valid." He sighs. "They chose me on purpose. They gave me my own brother's name and forced me to choose between saving the organization or saving my family."

It was a test of his loyalty. And he'd passed.

"When I brought Aidan's body to the Pointer, to prove I'd finished the job, my mother was there. She had no idea I would show up in person and see her guilty face. And she's hated me ever since." His voice darkens. "Because I know what she is. I know the sin she's committed."

"Caolán—"

"One day, we will both pay for what we've done. We must."

I can't stop myself from asking, "Will she try to kill you?"

He chuckles. "I'm the new heir to our family name. If I die just like Aidan, we will look weak. So, I doubt my mother plans to order another hit anytime soon. But that doesn't mean she will ever like me. Every time she looks at me, she sees the ugly truth, and she can't stand it."

"What about you?" I ask, and it earns me a blank stare. "What do you see when you look at yourself?"

Caolán takes a long time to answer. "I don't know."

He murdered his own brother. He chose to honor the

White Hand over his kin. But he did it *for* his kin. Killing Aidan saved his family's reputation, and it buried his brother's secret. Allowed him to take Bethany's shame to his grave, so she could be remembered as a victim, not as a weakling.

Aidan loved her. He loved my sister.

But it wasn't enough. Despite the love he had for her, Bethany still took her life. She saw death as a reprieve from the mafia.

Do I hate the mafia that much too?

I feel the bed shift, and I glance up to see Caolán swinging his legs over the edge of the mattress. He starts grabbing his clothes and says, "I've got to go now."

"Just like that?" I didn't expect us to have dinner in bed, but how can he casually leave after everything we just discussed?

Caolán pulls up his underwear. "I have to get ahead of this."

Oh. Right.

Caolán and I had sex. Twice. *Before* the ceremony. Now, he's got to fix the problem we just created. This could ruin everything. The O'Rourkes might even get angry enough to annul the marriage and cancel our contract. They'd have every right to do that since we broke the terms. To make things even worse, Caolán wouldn't suffer much from this. He's a man, and he's still the underboss of Clan O'Rourke. He could remarry and sign another contract next week if he wanted. But I'm broken. My virginity is gone, and I lost it before the consummation ceremony. That makes me untrustworthy.

In the mafia, trust is worth more than gold and it is paid in blood. Virginal blood. Which I don't have anymore. Its currently staining my champagne sheets, smeared across both my thighs. That would've been perfect tomorrow night, but right now it marks me as a traitor and a whore.

"What have I done?" The words are just a whisper, but Caolán hears them and kneels on the corner of the bed to answer.

"You made love to your husband. You did nothing wrong."

"You know that isn't true. They'll cancel our contracts."

They'll kill me for this. My family will kill me just to remove the stain of failure.

"Gloria," Caolán's voice brings me back into focus. He's staring at me, his cool eyes sharp and focused. "Let me take care of this."

I nod, but I have no intention of letting Caolán handle anything. What could he possibly do? He might be able to get himself out of this, but he can't truly help me. Not unless he convinces his entire Clan to accept our marital contract despite us breaking it. If it were any other family, I'd believe in him, but I've met Caolán's mother. And I've met Tadhg. They will not overlook what we've done.

So, there is only one thing I can do now. But I don't tell this to Caolán. As he buttons his dress shirt and leans down to kiss me once more, I simply lean into him and whisper, "See you soon, love."

I won't, but he doesn't need to know that.

18

Ria

The night air feels cool against my dewy skin. This is what it feels like to be a woman, slick with sweat, muscles sore, body aching with a numbness so pleasant I can hardly call it pain. Every part of me feels different now. Every part alive with a sense of joy and confidence I didn't have before. I made love to my husband. Desperate, passionate love that awakened parts of me I didn't know existed. It wasn't a pretty dance. There was pain as much as pleasure, but that was overshadowed by the intensity of the moment. Overshadowed by the knowledge that we were doing this forbidden act together. That it had been my choice.

I think that's what I loved about it most. That Caolán placed everything in my hands. The underboss of the Middle Finger laid all power at my feet. In that moment, for *just* a moment, I was in full control of myself. I made that choice, and I don't regret it, but now I must face the consequences of that choice.

A sigh falls from my mouth as I stare over the balcony. If I squint, I can see the foliage along the perimeter of the backyard. It shimmies as a dark figure moves through it; Caolán retreating to his home. It feels so scandalous. Having a boy sneak into my window at night, without my parents knowing, without any permission—mine or theirs. But I welcomed him without an argument, and he stayed until he was satisfied.

"But Caolán is not a boy." The words make me shiver as I whisper them to the wind.

A boy did not sneak into my bedroom, a man did. My husband did. And now he's leaving to fix the broken pieces of our marriage. I want to stay in this moment a little longer, want to bask in the warmth that still lingers from our connection. His flesh pressed against mine. His hands on every part of my body. I belong to him now, in every possible way, which only makes what I'm about to do even worse.

I leave the balcony and shut the doors behind me, quickly moving into my ensuite bathroom. I'd love to relax in a bubble bath but there's no time for that. I have hours before sunrise, hours to make this work, hours to get away.

The shower water stings, burning away the pleasure from before. It runs down the drain in a red-tinted stain, taking virginal blood with it. Blood that I must hide.

My shower lasts ten minutes, then I rush back to my bedroom so I can dress and rip my stained sheets from the bed. But when I open my bathroom door, I freeze in place. Someone is in my room. Sitting on the edge of the bed.

"Aoife," I whisper.

She looks up, her face illuminated by the dim lights in the room. She helped me hang the trail of Christmas lights above my bed, wearing fuzzy socks we'd stolen from stocking stuffers, our bellies full of hot cocoa and marshmallows, breath sweet with peppermint. We'd joked and bumped shoulders, bouncing on the mattress and giggling like the schoolgirls we were. That was mere weeks ago, but it feels like years now.

We are not those girls anymore.

"Aoife," I say again, and as I step toward her, I get the feeling that something is wrong. Her face is streaked with tears, snot running from one nostril, pooling along the curve of her upper lip. She's hugging herself, shoulders bare and bruised with angry red marks. Her dress is tattered, her stockings ripped—one leg is completely bare—and she isn't wearing shoes.

I clutch my bath towel. "What happened to you?"

"Caolán did."

"That can't be true." The reaction is automatic, not because I feel the need to defend him, it's because of the red stain in the middle of my bed. A stain Aoife hasn't noticed yet.

Her eyes reach mine for the first time. I see the anger in them. The hatred. "He did this," she hisses.

"He couldn't have."

"How could you know?"

I pause. "Because he was here with me."

Aoife blinks. Her expression is something I have never seen before, an odd mixture of confusion and understanding. Like the answers and the questions both pop into her head at the exact same moment. She adjusts on the bed, looking me up and then down. In my bath towel. My hair pulled up into a bun, the strands curling at the ends. I wonder if she can see the glow about me. If she can smell the change that's happened. I can. I smell it in the room, still warm and heady, like our breaths were caught in the blankets, moans trapped in the pillows.

The proof is all around us, but the most damning evidence is the red stain in the middle of the bed. Aoife sees it now as she turns around, eyes wide and darting left and right, like she knows what she's looking for. And fully expects to find it.

"What have you done?" she whispers, staring at my sheets.

"I don't understand."

"Caolán will fix it—"

"He doesn't even love you."

I tilt my head to the side. I don't think I love Caolán either. I spent my life infatuated with the idea of him, but when we met, he was nothing like the man of my childhood dreams. That nearly ruined things for us, but we've managed to build a shaky bridge between us. It isn't perfect, but it's better than what we had before. Regardless, Aoife's response is not what I was expecting. She isn't angry that we've doomed ourselves, she's angry that it happened at all.

New questions bloom in my head. "Why do you think Caolán is responsible for what happened to you?"

"Because he sent me with the man who did this."

"What did he do?"

Aoife shakes her head. She's still staring at my bed, eyes filling with bitter tears. "Whatever you think he did."

I want to ask who did this to her, but I doubt I'll get a straight answer. I've already learned that Aoife isn't who I thought she was. She works for Caolán, obviously as a spy, but clearly she works in other ways too. Ways I don't want to think about, but I can't stop myself from asking.

"Have you been with my husband?" The words are just a whisper, but they seem to fill the room. The only thing louder is my heartbeat.

"Yes," Aoife says softly. Then she stands and walks over to me, caressing my cheek. Up close, I can see that her face is bruised too. There are marks around her throat, like she's been choked. And the red bruises on her shoulders ... they're teeth marks.

Choked. Bitten. Hit in the face. Whoever Caolán sent her to isn't human. But ... *why* did he send her to that man?

I can't stop myself from feeling angry. It bites me, sinks its fangs into my heart and I feel the poison of resentment leak into my body. *She deserves this*, is the dark thought that swims through my mind. But there's a brighter part, a *Christian* part of me that cried over the Bible not long ago. That part is filled with empathy. That part can see past Aoife's mistakes. That part forgives her.

I grab her by the shoulders. "Aoife, come with me."

She stares at me. "What?"

"I'm leaving. I have to or else my family will suffer for what I've done."

Her chin dips, almost nodding, but not quite.

"You can't escape," she whispers.

There's the dark truth I've been hiding from. No one leaves this life. If they could leave, Tony wouldn't be spying on us in exchange for help from Caolán. If they could leave, Aoife would have walked away from Caolán when he told her to go with the man who hurt her. If anyone could leave, I would have run away when I was overseas in England. But I didn't. Because I knew there was no escape. My family would have hunted me down. Caolán would have hunted me down. The result would have been the same, just more painful along the way.

So ... then, why am I trying to leave now?

Because, for the first time, the problem in front of me looks worse than what may be waiting in my future. Caolán could fix things. He could somehow work things out with both families. But if he doesn't.

If he *doesn't...*

I shake my head, even shake Aoife too. "You have to come with me. I'm leaving tonight. This is our chance to get away together. We can start over."

Aoife's eyes are so pretty, even filled with tears. They look like liquid crystals, and every time she blinks, they spill down her cheeks like a bitter spray of glitter. "Ria ... Ria, I can't leave."

"Why not? You don't *like* working for Caolán, do you? Don't you want to get away from all of this?"

She doesn't answer. Which is an answer all on its own. Her words from earlier drift to the surface of my mind and I hear them so clearly, it's as if she's spoken them again.

He doesn't even love you.

No. But she thought he loved her because she loves him. That love will keep her trapped here. That love will kill her. It's the same love that killed my sister, but I won't let it kill me.

A gate closes over my heart. I hear it slam shut, bolts creaking, gages screaming in a howl of glee. It blocks out everything I once felt for these sad people around me. Caolán, Aoife, Mother, Father—everyone in the mafia. Love cannot exist in this world; it will only be used against you.

"If you won't leave with me then at least help me get out," I say.

Aoife doesn't respond.

"If you were ever my friend, then help me." I reach out and grab her hands, squeezing them. "I don't care that you lied to me. I don't care what you've done with Caolán. I care about what you choose to do right now. Help me, Aoife. As the friend you once were."

It takes her a second to decide but, eventually, Aoife nods and wipes the tears from her eyes. "What do you need me to do?"

19

Caolán

I don't have a great plan to fix things. I know I preached a big, brave game to Gloria, but the truth is that all I can do is ask for privacy during the ceremony and allow the witnesses to check the bed afterward instead of watching it live. That way, I can just prick Gloria's finger and put her blood on the sheets. Problem solved.

My grandparents were granted privacy for their consummation, so the request won't be out of the ordinary, but it will raise some eyebrows. For now, I have to survive the awkward brunch my mother has planned for both families and all the witnesses. It's supposed to introduce everyone, and possibly help us relax? I don't know, but I've taken the liberty of getting to Gloria's house early to pick her up so we can arrive together.

I haven't seen her since last night, didn't even send a text to say good morning. That seemed a bit too casual after everything we did. I'm sure she'd rather hear details about my plans to fix this instead of reading a good morning text anyway. That's why I've come in person. I want her to know that I'm trying. That I'm taking this seriously.

Billy follows me up the front steps, he's acting as my driver for now. Says I've inspired him to move up in the organization, so he's driving me around on his days off. It's nice to know he'll be spending his time running my errands when he isn't killing people but I'm not excited to have him following me everywhere. Billy is my favorite cousin, but he isn't exactly wonderful company, especially if you aren't used to him.

The woman who answers the front door certainly isn't used to him. She doesn't even look at me as I introduce myself, she's busy staring at Billy with his unkempt hair and his split tongue and his facial tattoos. He winks once he notices her gaze.

"Mornin' love, can we come in or what?"

The woman bristles but doesn't say anything. She should honestly be thankful Billy's in a good mood. Apparently, he had a great time with Aoife, I heard all the lurid details on the drive up.

The woman is still guarding the door, angered by Billy's nonchalance, but instead of responding, she steps aside and lets us in.

"Wait in the foyer?" I ask, walking into the mansion.

To my surprise, she says, "Mrs. Jackson has requested that you report to her study when you arrive."

Her study...? A million questions shoot through my head, and I can't think of a single answer as I follow the small woman through this large, echoey house. My shoes tap against the tile floor, sounding more like stones dropping rather than feet walking. When we arrive, my heart is hammering.

The woman opens the door to a small study, and I see Mrs. Jackson standing behind her desk, staring down at a pile of torn clothes. To my complete shock, Aoife is sitting in a chair across from her. Neither of them looks at me nor Billy when we enter. Somewhere in the back of my head, I hear the door close behind us, then we're engulfed in silence. Not even Billy speaks, which is somewhat of a miracle.

"Good morning," I say.

Mrs. Jackson looks up, for a moment her eyes drift to Billy, but her focus snaps right back to me the next instant. "We have a problem."

It would seem so. She isn't even dressed yet, and neither is Aoife. Both women are in pajamas; Mrs. Jackson's hair is still tied up in a bonnet. Aoife looks like she just showered and threw on a big t-shirt. I'm positive she isn't even wearing underwear, if the wet outline of her breasts is any indication. The sight doesn't turn me on in the least; it makes me nervous.

Why aren't they dressed? What is going on?

My eyes widen. "Where is Gloria?" I hadn't noticed she wasn't in the room. *Has she gotten cold feet? Or worse... did she confess what happened to her mother? Was I called in here to rearrange the contract?*

"Where is Gloria?" I ask again.

Mrs. Jackson wipes her red, puffy eyes. "I don't know."

I step back. "What?"

"Tell him." She snaps her fingers at Aoife who jumps in her

seat, then she hugs herself and I hear her sniffle. She isn't facing me so I can't see her expression, but her shoulders bounce and her breaths come out in choppy pants; it's obvious she's crying.

Mrs. Jackson has no sympathy for her tears. She slams her fist on the desk, shouting, "Tell him!"

"I ... I tried to stop her."

My body feels cold. "Stop her from what?"

"From leaving."

Mrs. Jackson shoves the pile of clothes off her desk, and they tumble toward Aoife's feet. "You did this," she hisses, and I'm shocked to see that her attention is focused on me. She's glaring at me, eyes spilling tears down her swollen cheeks. "You did this," she repeats.

I have no idea what she means until I look down at the clothes and realize they aren't clothes at all. It's a pile of sheets. Sheets with a red stain. They've been ripped and torn up like someone had been trying to get rid of them ... but had gotten caught.

My eyes drop onto Aoife's shoulders, and like she's drawn to my rage, she finally turns in her seat to look at me. There are tears running down her face, racing to the point of her delicate chin, but I know Aoife well enough not to be fooled.

"I tried," she whispers. "I caught her changing her sheets and she confessed everything. She told me she was leaving. I ran to take the sheets to her mother, but when I returned, she was already gone. Her balcony doors were left open."

"I have men combing the property. She couldn't have

gotten far," Gloria's mother says.

"I'll help search." Billy leaves in a rush.

"Check the security cameras. They should have picked up something," I say.

"I had Anthony check already."

I squeeze my eyes shut. Why *him* of all people? If Anthony checked, then they didn't find anything because he would never turn on Gloria. He might have been spying for me all this time, but I am not so foolish to believe that if he had to choose between us, he'd pick me. I'm only surprised *Aoife* didn't pick me.

My vision blurs with anger as I stare at her. She has betrayed me. *Again.* And she helped Gloria betray me, too. I was too reliant on her feelings for me. Too reliant on her blind obedience. But even if I never loved Aoife back, why did she do this to me? She has to know I will never forgive her for—

I suck in a little gasp as Mrs. Jackson goes on about their security system. Apparently, it was down for maintenance the whole night. Anthony verified it.

Aoife didn't do this because of unrequited love. She did it because of *me*. Because I sent her away with Billy.

Only now do I notice the scratches on her shoulders, the fading bruises around her neck, the red kisses on her cheeks that I know are marks left from Billy biting her face. He's kinky like that. And I *knew* he was kinky like that. It's why I sent her with him. I wanted to punish her for slipping information to Tadhg, and now she's punishing me in return.

Gloria is gone. And Aoife helped her. She's the only one

who could. Aoife worked for me as a spy—I *trained* her. I taught her to hide in the shadows. I taught her to pry information out of people without giving herself away. I taught her to remain hidden. Undetected.

Even if the security system hadn't gone down for a conveniently scheduled maintenance run, there would be no evidence. Aoife is skilled enough to have escorted Gloria away without ever being seen on camera. And I'm the one who taught her how.

"I'm sorry," Aoife says through tears.

What a lying whore.

"This isn't your fault." Mrs. Jackson steps around her desk and plants her hot gaze on me. "You need to explain yourself, Caolán O'Rourke."

"Mrs. Jackson—"

"Did you touch her?"

"Yes."

"Why?"

"Because she wanted me to."

Mrs. Jackson stares like that was the last thing she expected to hear. I don't know why the truth is so shocking. Is it difficult to believe that good little Gloria could ever *want* me to touch her?

I blink. "Did you honestly think I'd *raped* her?"

Her vision falls to the floor, giving me her answer.

Aoife makes a noise and then sniffles. It sounds like she's crying again but I'm not fooled. She'd *laughed* and covered it with a sob. She's sitting there laughing at me.

I shouldn't be surprised. I look at my hands, covered in skeleton tattoos. The middle fingers completely black. I look like a rapist. I look like a murderer. I look exactly like the man I am. But Mrs. Jackson knew who I was when she sold her daughter to me. She doesn't get to judge me now. How so very Christian of her. Sin now, repent later, judge others once you're a step higher on the moral ladder. But who is she to look down on me?

"I took Gloria's virginity last night," I say. My tone is no longer apologetic; I don't care what trouble I've caused. I'm focused only on the headache this is giving me.

How could Aoife do this to me? How could Gloria? *Why* would Gloria?

She left me. She slept with me and then crawled out of bed and left like it meant nothing to her. I feel cheap and used.

"So, you admit it," Mrs. Jackson says. She looks like she's ready to claw my eyes out. I hope she tries.

"Yes. I admit it."

"That's why she left." Aoife covers her mouth with the back of her hand. "She was afraid of what would happen once everyone found out."

"Are you sure that's it?" Mrs. Jackson asks. She turns back to Aoife and kneels in front of her, even reaches up to take her hand. "Did she run because of the consequences? Or because of something else."

Something else... She still thinks I raped her daughter. She thinks I forced myself onto her because I couldn't wait until the ceremony, and that Gloria ran away in fear once it was over.

It must be so easy for her to swallow that version of events. She believes my brother killed her oldest daughter. And now she's convinced I've hurt Gloria. It doesn't matter what Aoife tells her; Mrs. Jackson has already formed her own opinion. She will never see me as an innocent man in this. Still … Aoife glances up at me before she answers. She might hate me for what happened with Billy, but she's still here. She knows her punishment for this is coming, the truth is her only chance at getting any mercy from me. I have to wonder why she stayed, knowing I would not react kindly to her *second* betrayal. I could convince myself she did it for Gloria. To ensure her escape and keep the Jacksons running in circles for as long as possible, but I'm not stupid. I know Aoife, and I know the hatred I see in her eyes is real.

This moment is why she stayed. A moment where she holds all the power in her own hands. A moment where I am entirely at her mercy. A single moment where I could lose everything.

Aoife looks back down at Mrs. Jackson. "She ran because she feared the consequences. She told me she'd made a mistake."

"It was her choice," I echo. "A mistake she made of her own free will."

Mrs. Jackson doesn't move. She remains on her knee, staring up at Aoife, squeezing her hand so tightly I can see it trembling. I don't know if she's angry or hurt.

Finally, she nods and pulls away. "I see."

"I can fix this—"

"I think you've done enough."

"She is my wife with or without the ceremony. You are not the only one who has been slighted by this, Mrs. Jackson. We are all at risk now."

"Who do you think they will blame once word gets out?" She shakes her head. "They will say our family is cursed. That my daughters are unfit for the organization. Darren Jr. will never find a suitable wife." She covers her face and begins to sob, the sound of it breaks my heart, but not because she is sad. I'm heartbroken for Gloria. Her mother was concerned when she thought her daughter had been raped, I'll give her credit for that, but once she realized the fault was all Gloria's, she stopped caring. She's upset because her reputation is ruined, and her son won't have good options for marriage. She doesn't care that Gloria is gone. She isn't worried about her survival. She's worried for herself.

Gloria was right to leave these people. They didn't care about her. But I did. I cared and she left me anyway.

"I'll get her back," I say, turning away.

"So, you're going to hunt down my daughter?" Mrs. Jackson says this like it's wrong, shouting at my backside as I move toward the door.

I turn back. "Yes. I am going to hunt down my wife and bring her back home where she belongs."

"Do you honestly think you'll find her?"

"Before I was the underboss of the Middle Finger, I was a hitman. Hunting people was my job, and I was quite good at it, Mrs. Jackson. If there is any chance for us to fix this, it starts with me getting Gloria back. Do you understand?"

It pains her, but she nods agreement.

"Have you told anyone else she is missing?"

"No. Only you and…" she pauses to think, "the other young man."

"Billy. He's my cousin, we can trust him." I look down at Aoife, enjoying the way she squirms in her seat at just the sound of his name.

Mrs. Jackson nods. "I didn't want to risk word getting out and starting fires that don't need to happen. We are the only ones who know. I told the men searching that Gloria left the property without permission. They don't know she's completely missing. Neither does her father. He is still resting; I haven't woken him yet."

"That was wise. Call off the men searching your property, they've made enough of a scene."

Mrs. Jackson nods again, nervously sanding her hands together.

"Once I leave, you will get dressed and attend the brunch where you will tell your family and my own that Gloria and I performed the ceremony this morning. You and Aoife will testify as the witnesses." I nod to the shredded sheets on the floor. "You can show them the bloody sheets as proof."

"But they're torn apart—"

"Then put blood on new ones." I step toward her. "You have to make this work, do you understand, Mrs. Jackson?"

"I do, but what do we tell them about your absence?"

"You can say we left on an early honeymoon."

"What if they don't believe that?"

"Then make them believe it."

Her jaw tightens like she has more to say, but I don't have more time. I need to get on this as quickly as possible. "You have your instructions," I say. "Do not try to contact me, I'll reach out to you when it's safe." I shift my gaze to Aoife. "I'll walk you back to your room."

She's smart enough not to argue, rising in silence and walking toward the door behind me. We don't exchange any words until we've made it to the staff quarters where Gloria banished her before.

Aoife stops outside her small bedroom. "I did it because I care about her."

"Get inside," I tell her.

She hesitates like she doesn't want to, but she knows better. Stiffly, Aoife turns and unlocks the door—I shove her inside and kick it shut behind me. She squeals and falls onto the floor, crawling backwards and gasping apologies.

"I'm sorry!" Her voice is high and cracks on each word. "She wanted to leave; I couldn't make her stay!"

"You could have notified me. You could have called, text, anything. But you didn't."

"Caolán—"

I step forward and she literally screams, as if sounding some sort of alarm. I have half a mind to silence her, but I keep my hands firmly at my sides, knotted into fists.

"Be quiet, Aoife, I'm not going to hurt you."

She stares in disbelief.

"Answer my questions and I won't hurt you."

She nods.

"What time did Gloria actually leave?"

"Last night."

I thought so. I told Billy to return Aoife by midnight, if he honored my promise then she wouldn't have strolled into the estate at the crack of dawn and caught Gloria changing her sheets. She would've found her last night, probably just after I left.

"Where did she go?"

Aoife shrugs one shoulder and I take another step, the action makes her scoot backwards again. "She didn't say!" Aoife shouts. "She wouldn't tell me where she's going because she didn't want me to get into trouble." She gives me a nasty look, nose wrinkled, eyes squinted to hateful slits. "Or to have it tortured out of me."

I lunge forward—Aoife is quick, darting to the side, crawling away, swift as a cat—but I'm quicker. I grab her by the hair, and she flails as I lift her from the floor, kicking her long legs out, bucking against me. She doesn't settle down until I wrap my free hand around her throat and squeeze.

"Do you really think I can't tell when you're lying?" I hiss into her ear. "I'm the one who taught you how to lie."

I shove her to the floor and watch her crawl away, sobbing.

"Where is she?"

Aoife hugs her knees, rocking slowly.

"Tell me, Aoife."

"N-New York City. I have family there who may be able to hide her if she can make it there in time."

Why didn't I figure that out? Aoife was born in upstate New York, she was part of the old sector of the White Hand. NYC should have been my first assumption, but I've been blinded by my anger and shock.

I grunt, pinching the bridge of my nose. "How is she traveling?"

"By foot."

I blink and she flinches. "I'm telling the truth! She left here on foot with ten thousand dollars in cash. New York City is the goal, how she gets there is on her. That's all I know."

I stare at her, taking in her watery eyes, her disheveled clothes, her bruised skin. I believe her. She's telling the truth.

"I understand," I say calmly.

"I'm sorry, Caolán. I had no choice, I had to—"

"Thank you for your honesty, Aoife. Billy will escort you to brunch with Mrs. Jackson. He'll also make sure you get home afterward. And look after you while I'm gone."

Her eyes eclipse her face. "Y-You said you wouldn't hurt me."

"I won't. But I can't make any promises for Billy."

I turn and leave, closing the door to the sounds of Aoife's wails. I could have more sympathy, show some mercy, but the truth is that I don't care. I have never been the kind gentleman Gloria wanted me to be. This is who I am. This is who I'll always be—it's who I need to be to bring my wife back.

20

Caolán

Gloria is going to New York City. She has very limited options on how to get there, so I don't bother checking airlines, I head straight to the bus station and then realize I'm screwed. The bus schedule is enormous. New York is across the country; there are no Greyhounds running from California to NYC, that means she could have taken any bus out of town and chosen her own route from there. Hopping from city to city, constantly changing buses and traveling at her own pace. She had thousands in cash and nothing but time to kill.

I'm screwed.

"There may be a way out of this," Anthony says when I climb back into my car. I confronted him about his betrayal, and he immediately confessed. Considering he was nearly killed just last night, I let him off by blackening his other eye. He deserves more than that, but with Billy back home, I need someone at my side. Anthony is as good as it gets.

I could pull connections and have every bus station on this

side of the state shut down, but I can't do that without drawing attention to what's really happened. My family, and now Gloria's family, believe that we've left on an early honeymoon. Bringing Anthony along was already a risky move because, why would I invite him to join me on my *honeymoon*? But there's no way I could justify shutting down a bus station.

If I want to keep things quiet, then I've got to move quietly. But that only gives Gloria more time to get away. Unless Anthony has a grand plan.

I lean my head back against the cushion of my leather seat. "What way do we have out of this?"

"Let her go to New York."

"What?"

"We don't have the resources to stop her right now, so just let her go and find her later."

I pause. He's got a point. We already know exactly where she's going, we could fly there now and simply wait. Maybe even set up connections with people who will help us. Aoife said her family might help Gloria. If I get there first, I can convince them to betray her. But that might backfire. They could alert the Hand to what I'm doing and the whole thing could go up in flames.

No. I shake my head. *I'll need better connections than that.*

"Take me to the airport," I tell Anthony.

He starts the car with a confused look on his face. "Are we flying into the City?"

"Not New York City. We're going somewhere else. Somewhere nearby."

Benton, New York is exactly 45 minutes outside of New York City, and home to a beautiful woman named Serena Vittore, princess of the Italian mafia of Benton. The White Hand and Black Hand have a history of bad blood, so the Irish and Italians don't normally get along. At least not within the mafia. But what I have with Serena has nothing to do with the mafia. She isn't just a connection; she's a woman I care about.

It only takes a single phone call, and she agrees to meet me at a bar on the outskirts of the city. I sit in a booth with Anthony who fidgets and squirms until I snap at him.

"Relax, you're drawing attention."

It doesn't help that I'm a flaming, redheaded Irishman, and he's a muscular Black guy. We're both painfully out of place in this Italian bar, but this seems like the sort of pub that won't mind so long as we don't cause any trouble.

I wave a waitress over and order two drinks. When she brings them, I slide them both to Anthony. "Drink."

He stares at them.

"You need it."

He gulps down both shots of whiskey and then takes a long, deep breath, nostrils flaring.

"Relax," I say again. "We're meeting a friend. Everything will be fine."

Just as the words leave my mouth, I look up to see Serena pushing through the backdoors of the bar. She looks beautiful. Smooth tan skin veiled by tattoos, a trail of chocolatey brown hair dancing around her hips which sway as she walks confidently in pointy heels no mafia princess should ever wear.

Serena Vittore is not your average mafia woman. She runs a percentage of her father's organization, has a college education, and is still single despite being in her mid-twenties. Most mafia girls are married off at eighteen, if not engaged before then, like Gloria. But Serena has eluded the altar all these years. I'm partly responsible for that.

The reason Serena is unmarried is because she isn't a virgin and no high-ranking man in his right mind would ever pay for damaged goods. Yes, I'm the one who damaged her. It happened years ago, when I was passing through Benton, hunting a name for the Hand. I stopped at this very bar for a drink and ended up in the alleyway with Serena.

In my defense, I didn't know who she was at the time. She was just a pretty woman in a dimly lit bar who was drunk enough to follow me out back when I asked if she was up for some fun. It *was* fun, and then it was over. I zipped up my pants, she yanked down her skirt, and we went our separate ways. It would be another year before I even learned Serena's name.

I bumped into her at a neutral-ground hotel while doing business with my father. She strolled into the lobby with a bodyguard at either side, didn't even glance my way. Just walked by like she didn't see me. My father had smacked my head and scolded me for staring, but I couldn't help myself. There was the slutty girl I'd hooked up with, suddenly wholesome and businesslike and ... in the Italian mafia?

My father said, "I don't blame you for staring. Serena

Vittore is the worst kept secret of the Italian mafia. Everyone stares at her now."

"Worst kept secret?"

"Didn't you hear? Her engagement fell through after she failed her examination."

Meaning, her doctor reported that her virginity had been taken.

My father had harrumphed. "Vincent Vittore has been reaching out to everyone, searching for new matches. But no one will bite. I wouldn't be surprised if she was sold to a low-rank guard, at this point."

That had been the end of the discussion, but it wasn't the end of my fling with Serena. She'd walked right by me in the hotel, but that night, I got a knock on my door and a sweet little visit from a beautiful Italian woman.

We've kept in touch since then, our meetings far and few. My father had called Serena the worst kept secret of the Italian mafia, well, I had become her best kept secret. As furious as her family was that she'd damaged herself, they were never able to find the guy responsible. I don't know why she didn't snitch on me, but I'm thankful for her silence. It's been the fuel that has kept a tiny smile on both our faces, our own middle finger to the mafia.

She slides into the booth across from me now and waves for a drink. "Caolán O'Rourke." Her voice is the sound of chocolate. Dark and smooth and sexy.

"Serena. It's been a while."

"What brings you through Benton?"

"I'm heading to New York City."

She glances at Anthony who is staring at her abundant cleavage. "I'm guessing this is a business trip."

"Isn't it always?"

That makes her laugh, but she cuts it short, and sets her elbows on the table, pierces me with her dark gaze. "I cleared my schedule for this. I don't normally do that last minute."

"I promise it'll be worth it." I have no idea what I can offer her now, but if she helps me, I'll make it up to her later. No matter what. It isn't easy for Serena to get away from her family. She might hold more power than any other mafia woman I've met, but she's still a woman, and her older brother, Luca Vittore, is notorious for being overprotective of her. I hear things have gotten worse since the Vittores lost their youngest prince. A teenager who was shot dead in an alley. I wonder how Serena feels about it. She doesn't show much emotion as I stare at her now, then again, this isn't the time nor the place for grief.

"What's going on?" she asks.

"I need connections in New York City. People who will give me eyes and ears."

"Manpower."

I nod.

"You haven't told me what's going on."

"I'm looking for someone."

"A kill?"

I hesitate for half a heartbeat and Serena pounces on it. A smile pulls up the corners of her mouth. "You're tracking someone you want to see."

When I don't answer, her eyes drop to my hands resting on the table, focusing on the silver band around my ring finger, but she doesn't comment. Serena's been running her father's organization long enough to pick up on certain things.

"So, you want to keep this quiet."

"I do."

"Is that why you haven't bothered contacting what's left of the White Hand in New York?"

"Yes." And the fact that what's left of the White Hand is too tiny to make a difference in this situation. I need someone with real connections and influence.

Serena sighs as the waitress arrives with her drink. She tosses the whole thing back and then waves for another. "You know the Vittores aren't allied with the De Lucas, right?"

New York City is run by five different mafia organizations, one for each borough. Queens is ruled by the Spanish mafia, the Russians own Staten Island, the Italian family—De Luca—rules Manhattan, the Willis Stronghold runs the Bronx, and the Germans hold Brooklyn.

Before the Italians took over Manhattan, the Irish White Hand reigned over that territory. But that was more than a generation ago, before Lucky Luciano or the Gambinos came along, certainly before the De Lucas who hold the reins of power now. But I don't need Italian connections.

I lean forward, halfway across the table. "Actually, I'm not interested in speaking with the De Lucas."

"Good," Serena says. "Their empire is on fire anyway."

I raise an eyebrow to which she shrugs in response.

"Their princess ran away."

"Seems to be a trend lately."

She laughs. "Her older brother got her back, but who knows how this will play out? I think my father may introduce her to Luca."

"This may be a good opportunity to establish a relationship with New York City."

"We're doing just fine here in Benton."

"Sounds like you're not interested in expansion."

"Not if it means latching ourselves to a sinking ship." She sighs. "And anyway, there are rumors she's being sold to the German mafia."

"The Jägers?"

"Uwe Jäger has two unmarried sons."

"You know an awful lot about Germans."

She smiles. "I have a friend in the City."

"So do I. I think you might be able to convince him to help me."

Serena stares at me for a long moment, tapping her black acrylic nail against the rim of her glass. "Conrad Jäger," she says.

"He owns a bar in Brooklyn."

"I've visited."

Of course she has.

"I bought a whore from that bar a few years ago. Conrad overcharged me on her."

"So what? You want me to ask for your money back years

later?"

I make a face. "I want you to remind him that he's a scumbag who owes me a favor."

"On a deal you stupidly agreed to?"

"Serena."

She lifts a hand. "I'm just laying all the cards out. I need to know what I'm walking into, okay?"

"So, you'll give him a call?"

"Why should *I* call him if he owes *you* a favor on a whore *you* bought?"

"Because we both know that's not a good enough reason for him to take a meeting with me. But if he's your friend—"

"You want me to stick my nose into whatever drama you've stirred up across the country?" She leans back. "Caolán, this is crazy. Even for you."

"I need one favor, Rena. One meeting with Conrad. That's it." I reach for her hand, shocked that she lets me take it. "Can you do that?"

Serena's eyes flutter shut, but after a moment she pulls her hand away and then glances back at the bar. There's a man wiping down the counters who pays us no mind. He looks older than me. Tough. Experienced. Italian. I wonder if he's her newest fling. Or maybe he's more than that.

"I'll give him a call," she says, then she gathers her purse. "I can't guarantee he'll see you. It might take me a few days to convince him."

"I've got a little time."

"What will you do until then?" She bites her lip, and I can't tell if she wants to see me or not, but that doesn't matter. I'm a married man now—I've *been* married. Yes, I've broken my vows over the years, but now the marriage has been consummated. I have to take it seriously. Even if Gloria won't.

"I'm going to lay low," I tell Serena. "Give me a call when you've got an answer for me."

She nods, her expression unreadable. "I'll let you know what happens next."

21

Ria

The music is so loud, I feel it in my bones. My entire body vibrates with each thump, each boom of the heavy bass that fills the club. I am sweaty, hot, and sticky with foul joy. My body feels like it's on fire, each breath a burning gasp of air. But I don't stop dancing. I'm celebrating my freedom. Celebrating my glorious escape from the mafia.

It's been a week since I left home. The escape itself wasn't all that dramatic; it was everything that came after that served as a test of my determination. I didn't run to an airport or a bus station like everyone thought I would. Instead, I stayed in California, just three blocks from my house, for 48 hours, *then* I booked a plane with the fake papers Tony gave me.

Aoife helped me off the property, but she was smart enough to let Tony handle the rest. Caolán had trained her; he'd be able to tell if she was lying to him. But he'd never paid much attention to Tony. He would never even think to question him. I can't blame him for making that mistake. Aoife is the one with all the secret spy training, anyway. Tony was just my bodyguard. And he'd made it clear to Caolán that he wanted to escape the mafia which would indicate he didn't have the connections to get away on his own.

He didn't. Aoife is the one who told him how to get his hands on fake papers for me. Now, he *does* have the connections he's been looking for. He doesn't need Caolán's money or information to start over. I just hope he takes advantage of that and gets out while he can.

I got away. Flew straight to New York City where they don't ask for your ID, they ask for your affiliation. NYC is ruled by the mafia. Criminals like my husband roam freely through the streets; they have no fear or respect for the law because they have become the law themselves.

When I land in the City, I have only one question to answer. *What gang do you belong to?* I tell the airport security that I'm not affiliated with any gang. I'm just a girl visiting the City for fun. They don't believe me, and I'm hounded with questions until I confess that I'm from California. I thought I'd given myself away. That these burly men with scars and tattoos would hold me until my family or Caolán arrived to get me, but they didn't. They offered me hospitality. A place to stay, food to eat, and clothes to wear. I'm a mafia princess, and I've been given the royal treatment.

The music bleeds into my very soul, filling me with an energy I can't explain. I dance until I feel dizzy. Sway my hips until a man's arms wrap around them and we move together in this sea of sweaty bodies. The flickering lights reveal flashes of his face. It's a handsome face with red eyebrows and a shaved head. I've seen him every night this week, the man who's shown me kindness I never expected.

"Let's get out of here," he says. His breath is hot, and his words are wet against my ear.

I nod and I feel his hand grab mine as he pulls me through the club toward a back room. The music hushes behind us and I feel blind and deaf for a dizzying moment as he clears the room. There are people smoking and kissing and moaning on the couches, even on the floors. They're gone by the time my eyes adjust to the light. I'm glad. With a deep sigh, I throw myself onto the sofa, kick off my heels, and watch my new companion with a drunken smile. He moves to the drink display to make us something, his shoulders broad and strong. He's rich and handsome and owns part of the city. Says he's a prince from a mafia I've never heard of, but I believe every word he tells me. The proof is on the back of his head. A bullseye tattooed onto his skull.

The mark is the sigil of the Jäger family, leaders of the German mafia. In their language, *Jäger* means hunter, so I guess the bullseye is a fitting symbol.

"Wolfgang Jäger." His name dances off my lips and I smile at the sound of it filling the room.

He turns, smirking. "Yes, Darling?" That's the name on my fake ID. He knows it's not my real name, but he calls me that anyway. Says it suits me.

"I had fun tonight."

Wolf walks over and passes me a glass. "The night isn't

over."

"So, neither is the fun."

"Drink," he says.

I do. Deeply. I drain the glass and then wipe my mouth and pass it back to him. I know it's spiked. Everything he gives me has something in it that makes my mind too fuzzy to focus. But Wolfgang hasn't touched me. He hasn't done anything to me since I met him. The men at the airport worked for him, so when I was first apprehended, they gave him a call, and he personally arrived at the airport to see who he was dealing with.

I told him everything, fully expecting him to ship me home but he said he would do no such thing. He said he was happy to have me. And it isn't until now that I think I understand what he meant.

I'm his now. His own little mafia princess to play with. If anyone from California wants me back, they'll have to pay him handsomely. And if they don't. Then I'm stuck here. With Wolfgang Jäger.

Perhaps it was stupid to trust him. I'm completely at his mercy now. But what choice did I have? Aoife told me how to contact her family here, but it'd be dumb to think no one from California would ever look for me. Once they sniff out my trail to New York, it'd only be a matter of time before Aoife's family becomes the top suspects. They don't deserve to be targeted for helping me. So, I looked for help wherever else I could find it.

Wolfgang was the best I could get.

It's not all bad. He's put me up in an apartment, given me

food, clothes, and a new phone. All he's asked for in return is a partner to dance with when he goes out. So that's what I've been doing for the past week. Partying like a normal eighteen-year-old. Forgetting that I'm a mafia princess. Forgetting that I used to think of myself as a Christian woman. I've shed every part of my old life. The despair and the hope too.

I had my first drink a few nights ago. A German beer that tasted like licorice and urine. I nearly gagged at the taste, but Wolf grabbed the can and held it to my mouth, tilting it so I could chug the rest. He didn't pull away until I drank the whole thing right there. I was instantly drunk, tripping around the dance floor, everything around me blurring and mixing together until all I heard was noise and all I saw was flashing lights. I woke the next day back in my apartment. Tucked into bed. None of my clothes were disheveled. No part of my body felt sore. I had a pounding headache, and I couldn't keep my breakfast down, but I was fine otherwise.

When Wolf texted me his location that night, I put on the dress he had delivered and followed the same routine. It's been that way for days now. Endless parties at night, and severe headaches during the day. But I can get through this. I can do whatever I need to do if I want to survive here.

Wolfgang takes the glass from me and licks the rim. I watch his tongue slide over my lipstick stain and feel myself shiver.

"How do you feel?" he asks.

I hum and then giggle. "Like I'm floating."

"Good."

He leans over and I let him kiss me, his tongue sticky in my mouth, his hands large and groping. He pulls back for air, his forehead pressed against mine. "How old are you?"

"Eighteen." I giggle again.

He smiles, and this time, his voice is a growl. "*Good.*"

His mouth covers mine, but he's too aggressive. I can't breathe with how hard he's kissing me. I pull back, and he takes the moment to slide his hands up my tiny, sequined dress.

"Wolf," I whisper, but he kisses me again, shifting us so he's lying on top of me. His hands go up my dress again, rolling my panties down my legs.

No matter how drunk I am, I'll never be able to escape the natural clarity that fear provides. I can feel my heart pounding, feel my palms getting slick with sweat. I press them against Wolf's chest and push hard.

"Wolf, wait!"

He leans back, his eyes flicking down to the glass he'd dropped onto the floor, as if to check that it's empty. I get it now. I shouldn't be fighting him like this. I shouldn't be resisting him. But I am. Because I don't want this. I want to get away from my home. I even want to party. But I don't want to sleep with Wolf.

"I-I'm not ready," I whisper.

"You a virgin?" He cocks an eyebrow.

"No, but I am married."

He laughs. "That doesn't matter much, princess."

He dips his head and kisses me again, but this time, his phone rings and interrupts.

When he answers, his voice is a snarl. "*What?*"

I am frozen beneath him, my eyes large and my mouth pressed into a thin line. I don't know what I should do in this situation. Should I kick him and run? Should I lay here and wait for him to finish?

Wolfgang ends the call and sighs, sitting up straight and staring at the wall across the room. "I have to go," he mutters. "One of my men will drive you to your apartment."

With a nod, I scramble from the sofa and walk barefoot to the back exit across the room.

Wolf's voice stops me at the door. "Darling?"

I look back. "Yes?"

"I'll see you tomorrow."

It's a statement that carries so much weight. So much meaning. Not just a promise that I'll see him soon, but a reminder that this isn't over. Tomorrow, we'll pick up where we left off. Tomorrow, I won't be able to get away so easily.

I reach down and tug on my tiny dress, hoping no one can tell I'm no longer wearing underwear. My panties are across the room, still in Wolf's hand. He holds them in his fist, rubbing the strap of the thong between his fingers.

I inhale very slowly, peeling my eyes away. "Goodnight, Wolf."

"Goodnight, Darling."

O.O.O

Winter birds wake me the next morning. My head is pounding. My vision is blurry. When I step out of bed, I can't seem to get my balance. I don't even know how I got into bed. All I remember is swiping my card to get into the building and then punching the elevator button. Everything after that is a complete blank. But I'm wearing the blue pajama set Wolf bought me and my body feels fine. I've even got on a leopard print bonnet that keeps my natural curls nice and silky. I snatch it off as I stare into the bathroom mirror. I hardly recognize the girl who stares back. My makeup has smeared around my eyes and mouth, so I look like a raccoon and a clown mixed into one very ugly person. I'm missing one of my fake lashes. And I have a hickey on my neck, courtesy of Wolfgang Jäger.

I sigh and run the faucet. The water is cold and wakes me right up so I'm fully alert when I enter the small kitchen and find my roommate, Krista, sitting at the table. Her head is down, tucked into a thick book, so she doesn't see me until I stumble into the garbage can and swear.

Her head pops up. "Morning, Darling."

I grimace and hope it looks like a smile. "Morning, Krista."

"Did I wake you?"

"No." How could she? She was in here reading, it's more like *I* disturbed *her*. I don't say this, of course. I don't really say much of anything to Krista, honestly. I met her a week ago and I've made it very clear that I have no intentions of being her friend. It's bad enough that I'm connected to Wolf, I don't need to hang around some other mysterious girl. I've very quickly learned that I can't trust anyone in this city. Especially the nice ones, and Krista is plenty nice.

She agreed to take me in as her roommate without notice,

and has never made a fuss about it, even though she lives in a one-bedroom apartment, so we have to split the room down the middle. Wolf had one of his men squeeze a twin bed into the corner of the room, so we live like dorm buddies with a tiny bedside table between us. My clothes are crammed into a box at the end of my bed.

Still, Krista has never been rude to me. Never had anything to offer except smiles and coffee, which she crosses the room to pour for me now. Regardless of her pretty smile, I don't trust her. She knows Wolfgang, which probably means she's associated with the German mafia somehow. Wolf never mentioned that he knew her. He said the landlord of the building owed him a favor, so he agreed to put me up rent free. But why stick me with Krista? She must be mafia.

I stare at her as she adds cream and sugar to my mug, chatting about her morning the whole time. She's a small girl, just an inch or two taller than me, with pretty blonde hair and bright blue eyes. She never wears makeup so I can see her natural freckles and the way her cheeks blush babydoll pink when she stands in the sun. She's a perfectly innocent girl, but I can't get myself to see past her German features, and I'm certainly not fooled by the cross hanging around her neck. I used to wear one too.

"I hope you slept well." Krista passes me the coffee she made. "You certainly needed the rest."

I wrinkle my nose. "What's that supposed to mean?"

She flushes. "I—well, y-you stumbled in so late last night. I had to help you into bed—"

"That was you?"

"Who else could have undressed you?"

I take a moment to sip my coffee. It tastes as good as it smells. "Thanks," I mutter.

Krista shrugs as she returns to her seat and starts packing up. I notice the cover of the book she'd been reading when she closes it.

"You were reading the Bible." The words leave me before I can stop them, but the smile on Krista's face lets me know I haven't said anything wrong.

"Yes." She nods. "I was."

"Why?"

She laughs. "Because I love the Lord. This is how I spend time with Him."

That makes me fidget. I thought I loved God once. Now I have no idea how I feel about Him. I spent my teenage years praying to God for a way out of my marriage and He never answered. I spent two days, after running away from home, praying to God for a way out of that mess and He never answered. I had to get myself out. I had to get myself to New York City. Now, I'm stuck with Wolfgang Jäger, and I want to pray for help again, but what's the point? God doesn't listen to my prayers.

I stare at Krista as she packs the rest of her things. Pink spiral notebooks with flowery covers, gel pens of every color, pastel tabs which she's stuck into her Bible, fat from notes taped to the pages and streaked with neon highlights. She is exactly the sort of innocent, modest girl that comes to mind when you think of a Christian woman. She *looks* like a Believer. Unlike me, with my hangover and headache and ugly scar. A scar that has plagued me for years now. I suppose my spirit and my face finally look the same. Marred. Broken. Grotesque.

But Caolán never cared about my scar. And Wolfgang doesn't now.

Neither does Krista, I remind myself as she prattles on about the Bible. Krista has never commented on my scar or asked about it either. When she looks at me, she looks into my eyes, not at the side of my face. Even now as she brushes her hair behind her small ear and smiles, she looks like she's talking to an old friend. Not a stranger who was forced into her home and stumbled in drunk last night. She doesn't judge me for what I've done or who I am. Not a single time. Maybe she is different from Wolf. Maybe she isn't involved with the mafia.

"What were you reading?" I mutter, and I hope I said it softly enough that she didn't hear and can go on about her business, but she pauses and blinks at me.

"I was reading the twenty-third Psalms."

"Oh."

"Do you know it? It's pretty popular."

"I've heard it," I say truthfully. I did go to a Christian boarding school, after all.

She smiles. "That's wonderful. My favorite part is verse four; Yea, though I walk through the valley of the shadow of death, I will fear no evil—"

"For thou art with me; Thy rod and thy staff they comfort me," I finish the scripture and then take a sip from my mug just to avoid her gaze.

"You know it," Krista says, like she doesn't believe it. It's not like I've given her any reason to believe I know anything about the Bible.

"I used to read the Bible a lot."

She nods slowly. "Well, if you ever want to read it again or if you have any questions, I'd be happy to answer them."

"Cool."

Krista takes the hint and turns to leave, but she stops at the door and looks back. "Darling, I don't mean to cross any boundaries, but I go to a small Bible study on my university's campus, you're welcome to join us anytime."

"You go to university?"

The question throws her, and she laughs to cover her confusion. "Yes, I'm a student. That's why I'm living here in New York City."

"What's school like?"

"Um…" she adjusts the strap of her Bible bag on her shoulder.

"Sorry. I don't mean to pry."

"No, no. You aren't prying. I was just thinking; you can shadow me if you want? I mean, you're not in school, right?"

"I'm looking for schools," I lie. It's already weird that I'm eighteen and asking dumb questions about college like I've never heard of the place. But Krista doesn't know that I dropped out of high school to get married and will likely never see the inside of a lecture hall in my entire life. Mafia girls don't go to college. We don't need to. We never work a day in our lives, that's the point in marrying someone rich and powerful like Caolán. He provides everything I need, so there's no use for an education and a job would make him look weak. Like his wife has to help put food on the table.

"Well, this is great timing!" Krista sounds excited. "If you're looking for schools, you must shadow me! I think you'd love it!"

"I hope so."

Krista looks me up and down. "I think you should probably rest for today, but you can shadow me tomorrow. And then maybe we could go to Bible study together?"

"Yeah," I say. "Maybe."

I watch Krista leave, listening to her footsteps click down the hall. I guess she's on her way to class now. On her way to live a life I could only dream of. This was supposed to be my fresh new start, but it seems like I've jumped from the frying pan into the fire.

Maybe this is *my fresh start*, I think, washing out my coffee mug. God never answered my prayers before, but going to Bible study could change things. It could be good for me. Until then, I'm going to rest up for the day and try to find a way out of seeing Wolfgang tonight.

22

Caolán

Conrad Jäger is not happy to see me. When I enter his bar, aptly named, *The Club*, he is sitting at a booth with a drink in one hand and a stack of money in another. There is a dancer on a pole in front of him, body glitter her only clothing, and a troop of women standing off to the side watching quietly. His security might have had the instinct to stop and search me if they hadn't also been watching the show. As it stands, I stroll into The Club without a problem, marching right up to Conrad as he shouts at the woman on the pole.

When he finally notices me, his face withers and he releases a string of angry German words. "Cut the music!" he shouts.

The music pauses and the woman on the pole stares between us, unsure what to do.

"Take five, ladies," Conrad announces. "We'll pick this up later."

The women clear the room in a hurry while Conrad's bodyguards follow them out. I nod at the retreating men. "Is it wise to leave you here alone with me?"

Conrad doesn't like my joke. "We both know you came here to beg for help, Caolán. You ain't gonna shoot me. Not in my own bar."

"You've added new dancers since I was here."

"Yeah, well, they can't dance worth a dime. Waste of money."

"Aoife was a fine dancer," I say. She was. That's why I first took an interest in her, turns out she had other talents too. Talents she ended up using against me.

"Aoife was a gem," Conrad admits. He leans back in his booth and offers me a drink.

I shake my head. "Aoife is why I'm here."

"That's a lie. Aoife is what got you through the door, but we both know you've got something else on your mind so just spit it out."

"I need eyes and ears here in New York."

"You need men."

"Just a few dozen."

"A few dozen is an awful lot."

"New York is a big city."

Conrad stares at me over the rim of his glass. He's got a bullseye tattooed onto the knuckle of his middle finger. The rest of him is covered in thick, dark hair. His beard is neatly trimmed, only disturbed by a scar that slices through his chin. I wonder what he did to get it. Rumor has it, Conrad is more of a businessman than a mafia grunt. He likes dancers and money, not drugs and guns. I don't care what he enjoys, I just need him to give me manpower while I'm here.

"You owe me, Conrad." I lean toward him. "I came all this way just to speak to you."

"I don't owe you for a whore you made the mistake of overpaying on."

I pause, unsure how to lay this out, but what else do I have to lose? With a sigh, I dig into my pocket and retrieve a tiny bag of silver powder. I lay it on the table in front of Conrad and watch as he picks it up, almost amazed.

"Fog," he whispers.

Cocaine is the drug of choice here in New York, but sometimes I leave fog with Serena, and she makes deals with Conrad who gives it to his dancers so they can perform to his liking. Or the liking of the men he sells them to by the hour.

"I've got a small supply with me," I tell him. I could have led with that information, and he would've agreed to help me in a heartbeat, but I'm going over Serena's head right now. She never would've set up the meeting if she knew I planned to cut her out of a deal. I was hoping Conrad would help me without me having to bribe him with drugs, but it is what it is.

Conrad stares at the fog, probably thinking of what excuse he'll use when he doesn't buy Serena's next shipment. That's really not my problem. Only a fool would pass this up.

I pull out a large bag, kept in my waistband, and place that on the table. An entire kilo, worth at least fifty grand. He could double it if he's the businessman everyone says he is. That's why I know he'll take this deal. I'm handing him easy money and good drugs; all I want in exchange is a few dozen men to help me find my wife.

Conrad snatches the package from the table and snaps his fingers. A security guard runs into the room and quickly takes it back outside. I guess we have a deal.

"Come with me," Conrad says, and then he stands and leaves before I can reply.

I scramble from the booth and follow him to the backroom. It's dark inside, save for a small orange glow coming from the lamp across the room. Once my eyes adjust, I can tell it's an office. There's a desk, a comfy chair in front of it, and a sofa against the wall. There's even a drink display with a tall figure pouring himself a whiskey. He doesn't react to our presence right away, not until Conrad says something in German. Then he pauses, his head turning slightly so I can see the side of his face. I recognize him immediately.

It's Amory Jäger, underboss of the German mafia.

"Caolán O'Rourke," he says softly. His accent is slight, much easier to understand than Conrad's. "You came to this bar as soon as you arrived in New York. Your business must be urgent."

"You knew I was in the city."

He turns to face me fully. I'm older than him, but there is something mature about Amory, something that makes him seem more like a *boss* than an underboss. Maybe it's because he is the first in line for his father's throne, while I am a cheap replacement for mine. I wonder if he can see that in my face, in the slight droop of my shoulders. His are straight and broad, pushed back slightly as he lifts his chin. His grey eyes sharpen on me like a hawk's, and when he speaks, he doesn't sound conversational. Each word is chosen carefully, leaving no room for question or interpretation.

"It is my job to know who enters my city. Now, what do you want, White Hand?"

He knows my name, my gang, and that I came here on business. For the first time, I feel nervous, and I wonder if leaving Anthony in the car was a good idea.

"I need eyes and ears—"

"Yes, Conrad told me. What for?"

"I'm looking for someone."

Amory blinks.

"For my wife."

"Why don't you know where your own wife is?"

"She ran away from me."

Amory's jaw tightens. "How interesting."

"If you know who enters this city then you would know where my wife is at," I say.

"It is not my job to keep up with Irish foolishness."

"She isn't Irish."

Amory's expression shifts slightly, his eyes open just a bit more. Probably the closest he'll ever come to looking interested in anything.

"Your wife is not Irish," he repeats.

"She's a Panther of LA."

"A Black woman."

He knows the mafia better than I give him credit for, even across the country.

"Yes," I say. "My wife is Black American."

For some reason, Amory's entire demeanor shifts. He doesn't look like he hates me anymore. When his grey eyes land on me again, he looks empathetic.

"I'm getting married soon," he tells me, and that's when I notice the band on his finger as he takes a sip of his drink. "My wife will not be German."

"I'm guessing she wasn't your choice."

He exhales sharply, which I suppose is his way of laughing. "Not my choice in the least."

"Do we ever get to choose in this world?"

"No." His voice is soft. "We do not."

"Amory, I only need—"

"Speak with my little brother," he says over me. "Wolfgang Jäger."

Conrad says something in German, but Amory completely ignores him.

"My brother found himself a new toy not long ago. A girl I've never seen in the city before."

My heartrate quickens.

"She has a scar," Amory says. "Ring a bell?"

I can't get myself to speak because I'm not sure if I'm relieved or outraged. Amory called my wife another man's *toy*. What does that mean? Is she giving herself away or being abused?

"Please understand I am sharing this information with you because I have business to deal with and this drama will only cause more headaches," Amory says. "It will be easier for all of us if you simply collect your wife and go. Find Wolf and you will find the scarred woman."

"If your brother—"

"My brother is not to be touched." Amory's voice sharpens, his accent grows thick and his face wrinkles in anger. "He is a prince of the German Hunting Grounds. The second son of the Jägermeister. If you touch a hair on his head, I will treat it as an act of war, Caolán of the White Hand."

He used my gang's name on purpose. To remind me that causing trouble with him would cause trouble for my entire organization ... which is across the country. I am alone in enemy territory. If I want to walk out of here with Gloria alive, I'll have to do it Amory's way.

"What if he ruined my wife?" I challenge. "She is mafia royalty—"

"Then she was ruined the moment she left you." Amory turns away, done with the conversation. "I told you where to find her. Everything else is your problem to solve." He waves his hand and Conrad moves toward me, guiding me to the door. I let him escort me out, glancing back at Amory one last time. As the door shuts between us, I see him staring down at the drink display, probably thinking of his own wife and what his marriage will be like. Hopefully, it's nothing like mine.

Back in the main section of the bar, Conrad stops and offers me a drink one last time, but I turn him down. "You really think I want a drink after that?"

"Honestly, yeah. Seems like you need one." He looks coy. "Unless you prefer something a little stronger."

"No thanks."

Conrad's brows come together. "I thought—"

"I'm clean now, Conrad. I don't use anymore."

He nods and looks away, embarrassed.

"Amory didn't tell me how to find his brother," I say, changing the subject.

"Wolfgang likes women. Start by checking the local clubs or the topless bars."

"I need more than that. There are hundreds of clubs in New York City."

He takes a slow breath, glancing back at the office door like Amory might tear it down and shoot us at any moment.

"I can get you more fog," I offer. "We can turn this situation into a lucrative deal."

Conrad surprises me by shaking his head. "We have a deal with the Morenos."

The Spanish mafia.

"They run cocaine," I say. "This is fog."

"Doesn't matter. New York is a snow city. Not much fog in our area. Not unless the Morenos are dealing it, and even then, they'd have to get the Volkovs to agree to ship it."

The Volkovs are the head of the Russian mafia here in New York. They rule Staten Island, which gives them control over the shipping docks. So, it doesn't matter what the Morenos want to deal, they can't refill their supplies without the Volkovs involved.

I nod slowly. It was a bold idea, but not a good one. Deals like this are complicated. They take years, lawyers, meetings, and sometimes marital contracts to seal them. It was foolish to think I could walk into this bar and make a deal so large with one bag of product and a handshake.

Conrad sighs. "Look, all I know is that Wolf's been hanging out in Manhattan lately. He thinks Amory doesn't have eyes there because it's beyond the Brooklyn perimeter." He sniffs. "But Amory's fiancé is a De Luca princess; she lives in Manhattan, so we're allowed to have men stationed there for her protection, you know?"

His wife is Italian. I wonder how that was arranged.

He passes me a slip of paper. "That's the club Wolf's been going to lately. I can't promise he'll be there tonight, but it's a good place to start."

I snatch the paper and turn away. "Thanks."

"Don't touch him, Caolán!" Conrad calls behind me. "No matter what you find, just don't do anything stupid."

No matter what I find? Just who is this guy, and what has he done with my wife?

23

Ria

College is amazing. Krista attends a university in Manhattan, and it is HUGE! The campus covers multiple blocks with a dozen different buildings and thousands of students—there are even parking garages! I've never been so excited to go to school in my life. We get to ride the subway, which Krista complains about, but I don't see the problem at all. Yes, it's sticky and smelly and some of the people seem a bit disturbed down there, but it's like peering into an entirely new world.

I follow Krista around with my mouth open, gaping at everything, realizing just how large the world is. That sounds strange coming from someone who has lived in two different countries and crossed the United States alone, right? But I did all that under strict surveillance and discretion. In England, I couldn't explore, and Aoife never left my side. But here in NYC, no one knows who I am, and no one cares.

Except Wolfgang Jäger.

It's been three days since I last saw him. I've waited with

bated breath, clutching my phone, jumping every time it buzzes in my hands. But I never got the call or text I was expecting. He never asked me to meet him anywhere. Even now, I stare at my phone as I wait beside Krista for her History 202 class to begin. My messages are blank. No missed calls. Nothing. It's like Wolf has disappeared.

Krista bumps me with her elbow. "Whoever he is, I'm sure he'll text soon."

I blush, mostly because it's weird that Krista would think I want a guy to text me. Then again, isn't that the problem with, like, all college girls? I've been shadowing Krista for a few days, and I've seen the skimpy clothes and the wandering eyes. Every interaction between guys and girls is like watching something I'm not supposed to see in public. Plus, *everyone* in college is a model—the guys too. Their shirts bulge with muscles and their pants tent with far too much testosterone. I don't know if I'm the only one who's noticed or if we've simply normalized male immodesty, but I have to keep my eyes glued to my phone to avoid them getting poked, and now that's attracted Krista's attention.

She smiles warmly. "What's his name?"

"Uh…"

"Sorry. I know it's none of my business, it's just that you're always checking your phone. So, I assumed." She laughs. "Boy problems. You know?"

"We've all got them," I joke.

"Maybe he's busy with school."

I can't tell her he isn't in school, so I just nod. "He doesn't live in Manhattan. When he's busy, its tough for us to see each other."

"What borough is he from?"

"Brooklyn."

"Oh!" Krista gasps. "He's probably caught up with the wedding. I hear all of Brooklyn has been shut down for it. Or at least major parts."

"Wh-What wedding?"

She shrinks and lowers her voice, though I can't tell if it's because of what she's about to tell me or because students have begun to file into class. She scoots her chair closer to mine. "You know? The *mafia* wedding. Between Rosa De Luca and Amory Jäger."

The name Jäger rings a bell because of Wolf, but I have no idea who Rosa De Luca is—and I don't know why Krista would expect me to know this. Has she found me out? Does she know my real identity? Maybe Wolf told her. Maybe she's mafia and has known all along, fooled me the way Aoife did.

Krista leans back, frowning. "Gosh, you really have no clue. You aren't from New York, are you?"

"Guilty." I laugh nervously.

Krista glances around and then tugs a magazine out of her backpack. She discreetly slides it over to me and I stare at the cover.

Teen45Oh! All the juicy mafia gossip you want in one cool spot!

"What… What is this?" I glance back at her to see her eyes shining with joy.

"Okay, don't tell anyone, but it's a gossip column." She laughs. "Teen-Four-Five-Oh is a magazine that talks about all the hottest mafia drama. It's written for teens so there aren't any raunchy details, but it's still so juicy." She exhales and looks off at the ceiling, undoubtedly fantasizing about the *juicy* things she reads in this magazine.

I stare at her. Who knew Krista the Christian girl loved mafia gossip? Then again, it's not like there's any celebrity gossip anymore. In a lawless place like New York City, mobsters *are* celebrities now. Magazines like this glorify them and make good girls like Krista drool over bad boys like Wolfgang. I see his name on the cover, talking about his brother's upcoming wedding.

A wedding to remember! THREE organizations united by two pounding hearts. How long will the power couple last? Check page 32 for photos of the couple we caught last week! PLUS, a photobomb of Wolfgang Jäger, the best man of the event!

"That's where I get all my info," Krista says, tapping the magazine.

"I see. It looks ... thorough."

She exhales. "Oh gosh, I've said something wrong."

"No! I just didn't know you were into this kind of stuff."

"I try not to get into it. My pastor says gossip is a sin, you know?"

"Right."

I glance back down at the magazine, scanning the bold headlines. There's a picture of a couple on the front. A woman with light brown skin and dark curly hair standing beside a man in a dark suit. He's got the same German features I've seen on Wolf. I wonder if that's his brother. The man getting married to some mafia princess Krista is obsessed with.

The caption below the photo says,
See page 46 for an interview with Giovanni De Luca on what it feels like to give his little sister to a rival boss. Is this Rosa's redemption for betraying her organization? Are the rumors about her Christian faith true? We've got all the gossip you need!

"She's a Christian," I mutter.

Krista nods beside me. "Rosa De Luca? I heard she converted after she ran away."

"She escaped the mafia?"

"Her brother eventually tracked her down, but yeah. While she was gone, she became a Christian." Krista smiles. "That's why I like her. I've been following her story for a while now, trying to see what difference her faith makes in this situation."

How much difference could it make? She escaped and gave her life to God, but then God let her brother drag her back and sell her to some German boss. If her husband is anything like Wolfgang, then I feel sorry for her.

"How could her faith do her any good?" I whisper, running my fingers over the magazine cover. She isn't even smiling in the picture. Just staring at the camera. I wonder when it was taken, if she enjoys being the center of all this attention.

"Maybe it will give her strength to survive in this world. It isn't easy," Krista says.

"Why couldn't it give her what she needed to stay away? To stay *safe*. She made it out, and now she's back. After everything, God let her get taken again. How can anyone believe after all that?" I turn to Krista when she doesn't reply. She's staring at me with her eyes wide open, confusion knitting her brows together. The rest of the room is staring too. Heads turned in my direction. Eyes blinking like they're all trying to figure out what's wrong with me.

I hadn't realized I'd begun to yell. I hadn't realized how much I cared.

Without thinking, I snatch the magazine from the table and run out of the room. I dash down the hall, turn two corners, and then rush down the stairwell. When I finally stop, I'm in a quiet lounge where students sit with headphones covering their ears and their noses tucked into books or tablets. No one pays me any attention. No one seems to notice me.

I walk to the back of the lounge and sit on a cushion, then I guiltily open the magazine again. Rosa's story is there. Princess of the Italian mafia, nicknamed the Rose of Manhattan. She ran away from home, just like Krista said, and her brother Giovanni tracked her down and brought her back. Now she claims to be a Christian, even though she's marrying the underboss of the German mafia. *This marriage will restore her honor*, the article says, *solidifying her place in our society as a mafia princess. Her sins will be forgotten the moment she says, 'I do,' then Rosa De Luca will no longer be called the Withered Rose.*

I lean back on the cushion. They're happy for her. Whoever wrote this article, whoever published this magazine, the people who read it... They're all happy that Rosa is back. They want her to embrace her role here in the mafia. They don't want her to be a Christian. To them, her faith will get in the way. Marrying this mafia boss will wipe away her sins. The sin of leaving. The sin of wanting a better life. The sin of trusting God.

Where does that leave me? Will I end up just like Rosa? Tracked down and dragged back to the mafia. Where I belong. If there's no hope for her, then what hope do I have?

"Darling?"

My head snaps up to find Krista standing over me, a guilty look on her face.

I shoot to my feet. "Sorry. I didn't mean to run away like that."

"It's okay."

"Did you leave class early for me?"

She shakes her head. "The professor gave us a take-home test, so we got out early. I've been searching for you for a while, though. The campus is huge, I'm glad I found you."

"Yeah." I hand her the magazine. "Here. It's yours."

She doesn't move. "Keep it. Seems like you've enjoyed it."

"I don't know how I feel about Rosa De Luca. About her being a Christian but also in the mafia."

"I see." Krista brushes by me and takes a seat on a cushion beside the one I'd been sitting on. "I think sometimes people forget that Christians are human too. We make mistakes and poor decisions that sometimes lead to bad circumstances."

"Being in the mafia is more than just a bad circumstance."

"But it isn't a circumstance that Rosa chose. Not any more than Queen Esther chose for herself."

I tilt my head to the side. "Queen Esther?"

"She was a Jewish girl who ended up in an arranged marriage with the king of her enemies. His royal officials wanted to slaughter the Jewish people. That's the man she was married to. But she didn't have a choice. Just like Rosa has no choice."

And I have no choice.

"Oh," I say. "I guess I understand a little."

Krista stands. "Come on, let's grab something to eat and forget all this happened."

I stand to follow her, still clutching the magazine. "What happened to Queen Esther in the end?"

Krista looks back. "God used her to convince her husband to spare the Jewish people. She became a hero, and her marriage was an example of what God can do with bad circumstances."

I hope she can't see the blush on my scarred cheek. "That sounds cool."

"It's in the Bible, The Book of Esther, if you ever want to read it."

I do want to read it. More than anything.

24

Ria

I read the Book of Esther. Every single chapter. It was amazing. Esther was just a girl who didn't ask for anything she'd faced. She was thrown into chaos and married to a man who ruled over her *and* her nation. She couldn't even speak to him without risking her own life, but she did it anyway. My favorite verse in the entire Book was in chapter four when she said, *If I die, I die.* Esther was determined to carry out God's will, even if it meant standing against her own husband. Even if it meant getting herself killed by his own hand.

I am nothing like Queen Esther. I didn't stand against my husband and square off with the mafia, I cowered and ran away. I don't even know if my marriage serves any sort of purpose like Esther's. At least she was married to a king who could make a difference, but what can Caolán do except kill people?

I sigh, rolling over in bed. Do I want Caolán to make a difference? That would mean staying in this marriage. Staying with him…

I don't know if I want that. But I don't think I truly want to live without him either. I never wanted to leave him anyway. I only wanted to leave the mafia. But I can't have one without the other. Caolán would never leave, even if he had the chance.

"What's the point?" I whisper.

My eyes slowly close and I feel myself drifting off to sleep again. It's the middle of the day, I should be up by now, but I slept in instead of going to class with Krista. Almost a week of shadowing her and her professors are starting to give me dirty looks now. I don't think I'm welcome anymore, especially not after I caused a scene yesterday. Besides, I didn't know how taxing school could be. Waking up early every day, sitting in long classes, concentrating for hours. Now, I'm alone in our apartment and sleep is my only friend.

I drift away with thoughts of queens and war on my mind—and then my phone buzzes against my cheek and my eyes pop open with a gasp.

The screen is blurry when I hold it up, but I manage to make out one word. Wolf.

I answer on the fourth ring. "Hello…?"

"Darling. It's been a while."

"I thought you lost my number."

"Not quite. I got a little busy with family drama."

"I hope everything is okay." I honestly don't care at all, but it seems like the right thing to say.

Wolf chuckles into the phone. "How sweet of you. Everything is alright but seeing you would make it better."

I pause. Here it is; the moment I've been waiting for and dreading at the same time.

"Let's hang out tonight," Wolf says. "I'll send a dress for you to wear and pin my location. My driver will call when he arrives."

"What time?"

"He'll call."

Wolf hangs up and I stare at the phone. I may be nothing like Esther, but I know for a fact that Caolán is nothing like Wolfgang. He's the real monster I need to escape from.

God, I pray inside, *if You help me out of this, I promise I'll get my life together. I promise I'll start over and do things right. But I can't do that if I'm stuck under Wolf's thumb.*

I wait for a reply, but nothing happens. It's not like I expected the sky to split open and the ground to rumble anyway, so I toss my covers back and head to the shower. Krista is in our bedroom when I emerge in a cloud of steam. She's sitting on her bed brushing her blonde hair.

"How was school?" I ask.

"Odd without you. I think I got used to you being there already."

"Miss me?"

She snorts. "Just a little."

I flop onto my bed. "Well, I'm back now."

"Wanna go out for dinner?"

I pause. "I, uh, I have plans tonight."

"Is it the mystery guy from Brooklyn?" She laughs as she says this and I try to force out my own laugh too, but nothing about seeing Wolf is funny. He drugged me the last time we were together. He'll probably do it again tonight to make me compliant enough for him to finish what he started before.

"Yeah." I swallow. "It's the guy from Brooklyn."

"You don't seem so excited."

I shouldn't tell Krista any of this, she doesn't deserve to be dragged into my drama, but now that I've opened that door, I don't think she's going to step back through it. She scoots to the edge of her tiny bed and says, "You can talk to me, Darling."

"Why are you so nice to me?" I blurt. "You don't even know me."

It's true. I was forced into her apartment without notice and she's never complained. She's been nothing but nice to me since the day she met me. Never even asked questions about where I came from or if I have plans to leave.

Krista adjusts on the bed. "The building superintendent told me he would reduce my rent by half if I agreed to take in a roommate. It was a deal good enough to keep me from asking questions." She stares at her hands. "I knew something weird was going on, but I've learned that asking questions can get you in a lot of trouble in this city. So I let it go and enjoyed the discount on my rent." She shrugs. "You turned out to be nice, anyway. So I figured your past didn't matter. Everyone has a story, but that story isn't everyone's business."

"Wise words," I whisper with a laugh.

"If something is going on, you can tell me, Darling. I won't judge you."

She's already seen me act like a lunatic at her school, so I believe she wouldn't judge me. But still… I just can't get myself to open up to her. I don't trust anyone anymore and I wouldn't want Darling involved in this even if I did trust her. So instead of asking for help, I say, "Are you any good with makeup?"

Krista is such a girl. She has a delicate hand that expertly applies eyeliner and mascara. We are nowhere near the same skin tone with her pale pink color and my dark brown skin, but she does give me a serum that makes my skin feel vibrant and fresh, then she helps me take down the braids I'd put in before my shower. They leave my hair springy and wild in a way that makes Krista clutch her invisible pearls once my dress is delivered.

"You're going to look amazing in this!"

She helps me into the free clothes, a ruby colored minidress that comes down *just* enough to cover my butt. Wolf also sends a set of lingerie for me to wear; it's nothing more than a pair of nipple covers and a ruby thong. Krista passes them to me without a word, keeping her promise not to judge me. Then she grins at the six-inch stilettos he dropped off.

"Any woman who can walk in heels this high has all my respect," Krista says.

I step into the shoes and then teeter across the room. "How do I look?"

"Like a movie star."

When the driver rings, I give Krista a long hug. She rubs circles on my back and then waits by the door in a pair of pajamas and matching slippers. Her hair is pulled into a sloppy bun, and her face is bare. In that moment, she looks just like Aoife. One of the prettiest girls I've ever seen. I wonder what it's like to be so good looking. To never have to worry about the side of your face. No one here has said anything about my scar, not even Wolfgang. I haven't decided if that's made me more self-conscious or not. It's like I'm waiting for them to bring it up, holding my breath while they smile and stare. But Wolf doesn't care about my face because he has plenty of other reasons to smile and stare. That's why he's dressed me up like this; his own personal princess. A runaway bride with nowhere else to go, leaving me entirely at his mercy. Tonight, he'll ask me to pay him back for all his hospitality. My only prayer to God is that He doesn't let that happen.

Wolf is waiting in the back of a shiny black car when I walk outside, holding the diamond studded clutch he left for me. His eyes drag up and down my frame when the driver opens the door for my big reveal.

"You look marvelous," he says, flashing a wicked grin.

"Thanks."

"Get in."

I slide onto the leather seats, and he quickly tucks me against his side, beneath his arm. He isn't a large man, but all the evidence of his masculinity fills the car. I can smell his strong cologne mixed with the distinctly sour smell of whiskey. He's already been drinking. Does he need alcohol to get this done? Does his drunkenness cover the guilt? Will it quiet my screams?

Wolfgang leans close enough for me to smell his whiskey

breath as he speaks against the shell of my ear. "I couldn't wait to see you tonight."

I feel his hand slide over my knee. He keeps it there like he owns it, rubbing his thumb back and forth.

"Wolf, you hardly know me," I say, trying not to fidget.

"Then tell me more about you."

"You already know I'm a mafia princess."

"That's what I like about you."

That's the only reason I'm here. He wants to have something that's supposed to be off limits. But I've stupidly offered myself to him on a silver platter. I'm not a virgin anymore, so even if Wolf is caught, he won't be the one responsible for damaging me. And I've run away from home… that means I'm already damaged. Whatever happens here will be viewed as my own fault. The mafia might even blame Caolán for not being able to control his wife. Plus, the fact that no one knows I'm here. If I scream, who will help me?

I'm in this alone.

Wolf pulls me closer, smooshed against his body as the car rides along. He's got his heavy arm draped over both my shoulders, making me feel so small compared to him. His fingers graze my bare shoulder, tickling the skin. The action should make me flush with heat. I should feel the hairs on my arms stand up one by one—and I do, but not because this feels good. Every part of me feels disgusted.

Wolf leans closer, inching his hand past my knee to my thigh. "Tell me about your scar," he murmurs.

The last person I talked about this with was Caolán. My

husband. That story belongs to him now. Just as the story of his brother and mother belong to me. We had sex that night, but it was our confessions afterward that tied us together. Our words were intimate, the sex was just fun. But I won't share either one with Wolfgang. I refuse.

"Are we almost there?" I ask, changing the subject and scooting slightly away from him.

"Why the rush? Aren't you enjoying yourself?"

"Well, sure, but—"

"Relax," he cuts me off with a quick kiss and then scoops me into his lap, but his driver hits a turn and throws us. Wolf bangs his head against the window and shouts in German, long leg whipping up to kick the partition between us. I see the driver jump behind the glass and then the car pulls off to the side of the road.

We're parked now. I have no idea where we are, but I don't get to look around because Wolfgang shifts us so that I'm lying on the leather seats beneath him. I can't see anything except his face leering down at me now.

"Wolf—"

"Relax," he says again.

I feel his hands roaming my body. I feel his wet lips on my skin. I feel his need pressing into my thigh as he rolls his hips against me.

"A-Aren't we going somewhere?" I try to remind him.

"We'll get there soon."

My eyes burn and I blink away tears. "Please don't do this." My voice is a pathetic whisper that Wolf either doesn't hear or chooses to ignore. He slides his hand up my dress and I gasp, lifting my knee to his groin.

He grunts and I feel his weight shift as he leans back to glare at me. "What's your problem?"

"I'm *married*, Wolf."

"If that mattered, you wouldn't have run away." He runs his hand over his shaved head. The fuzz on his scalp matches his red brows and the sight makes my heart ache. It's nothing like Caolán's hair but it's red all the same. Like sparks of fire on his face.

I miss him... I roll onto my side, hoping my tears will blot out the image of his face that appears in my mind. We didn't love each other, we barely *liked* each other, but what we had was better than this. Caolán might not have loved me, but he did care about me. For nine long years, he cared. And I tossed that away to gain a cheap taste of freedom that's done nothing but put me in danger.

Wolf touches my arm, and I flinch.

"Calm down," he says, then he gets a good look at my face and a curse slips between his lips. "Are you crying?" He curses again and then reaches into his pocket, pops a mint into his mouth. "Let me make it better."

Wolf pulls me closer and kisses me before I can stop him. I feel his tongue wiggle into my mouth, and with it comes the mint he was eating. But I know it isn't a mint. It's something that will make this all *better*. Something that'll stop me from fighting back.

I try to force the pill back into his mouth, but Wolf jerks

back and quickly clamps a hand over my face. "*Swallow*," he hisses, holding the back of my head in place.

I can't breathe with his hand over my nose and mouth. I struggle against him, clawing at his hands, slapping his arms, but he responds by slamming me against the car door. My head whips back and smacks the window so hard I see stars, but the fact that I still can't breathe keeps me focused.

I clutch Wolf's strong arms as he holds me, suffocating me.

"Swallow," he says again and this time I understand. He'll let me breathe if I take the pill.

A single tear trickles down my cheek, over his hand. *God please...* I don't even have the strength to finish my prayer. Black dots speck my vision, and my body starts to go numb. There's no point in being stubborn. It would be so much easier to simply swallow the pill and get this over with. It would've been easier to give Wolf what he wanted when I first got into the car. Maybe we'd be happily having dinner by now if I hadn't resisted.

But I'm not being *stubborn*, I'm standing up for myself. I'm standing up for what I want. I'm fighting for what I believe in. If resisting Wolf costs me my life, then so be it.

If I die, I die.

Something *pops!* outside and then the window shatters behind us. It scares Wolf so badly that he jumps away, eyes blinking in fear. I suck in a deep gulp of sweet air, it hits my lungs with a satisfying burn, and I cough on my next breath, spitting out the pill. Meanwhile, Wolf fumbles to get his gun from his waistband, but another *pop!* goes off and he ducks for cover, screaming at his driver. The chauffeur throws the car into drive, giving me exactly two seconds to react.

My hand finds the handle of the door and I yank hard. Wolf's eyes grow large when he sees my door flying open. He reaches for me, but I get my leg up and kick him hard in the chest. The force sends me tumbling backwards. I hit the sidewalk with a thud that knocks the air out of me, but there's no time to dwell on it. More *pops!* go off around me, punching holes into the black car. *Someone is shooting at us! Someone wants to kill us!* I have no idea which one of us is the target, but I don't plan to stick around and find out. Sadly, neither does Wolfgang. He doesn't even hesitate to order his driver to pull off.

The car screams away from the curb, forcing me to roll to avoid the open car door. I don't spare another second on that scumbag. With bullets popping around me, I push to my feet and break for the nearest alleyway, praying the entire time.

Please get me out of here, God!

I run as fast as I can, squeezing between two buildings where there's barely any room for the bags of trash I hop over. I land poorly and my ankle rolls. A scream fills the air as I tumble to the sticky ground. My hands slap the pavement, clawing at the cement for perch. I drag myself down the alley, tears streaking my face, hair unraveling and sticking to my wet forehead. I'm sweaty, covered in dirt, and aching all over. By the time I make it to the end of the alley, I have no dignity left. I claw myself to my feet, kick off my stupid shoes, and begin a slow limp back to my apartment. I'm barefoot and dressed like a hooker, but a taxi stops for me halfway down the street. I offer my diamond-studded clutch as payment and the driver agrees to take me home. It's honestly a miracle, and I thank God with every step I take up to my apartment door.

When I limp inside, the place is dark, but the bedroom light flickers on when I trip into the tiny table crammed into the corner of our small kitchen. Great, Krista is awake.

She walks into the kitchen the next moment, groggy with sleep, even though it isn't even very late yet. "Darling? You're home already?"

When she switches on the kitchen light, I hear her gasp and then her feet rush toward me. I have my face buried in my hands, sobbing already.

Krista doesn't ask what happened. Doesn't ask what's wrong. She simply guides me to the bathroom and starts the hot water. As the steam clouds around us, she kneels in front of me and begins peeling my sticky clothes away. She brushes back my matted hair, wipes my smudged makeup away, and then kisses my forehead.

"It'll be okay," she whispers.

I nod because I believe her.

"I had one prayer," I say, grabbing her hands when she turns away.

Krista faces me again. "What do you mean?"

"Before I left, I prayed and asked God to get me out of that date." I laugh; it makes my sore throat burn. "I wasn't rescued like a princess, but I did get out of there."

Krista squeezes my hands. "God saved you."

"He did."

She pauses, biting her lip. "Darling … Do you know the Sinner's Prayer?"

"I've heard of it."

It's the prayer a sinner says when they want to convert and give their life to Christ, making them a Believer.

"Do you want to say it with me?" Krista asks.

"Are you asking if I want to become a Christian?"

"Aren't you tired of being a sinner?"

I am.

"Being a Christian doesn't mean you won't sin anymore," Krista tells me. "But it does mean you'll be covered under God's grace and Christ's blood. It means you won't have to go through this alone, Darling. Even if you don't tell me everything, you'll be able to tell God. And as His Child, you can expect Him to fight for you."

She squeezes my hands again. And I squeeze back.

"Okay," I say softly. "Help me say the prayer."

25

Caolán

I stand in the middle of Gloria's apartment. It's small, like her. Smells nice, like her. It's an apartment with pale walls and wooden floors hidden beneath cheap plush carpets. The fridge has rainbow magnets and there are slippers left by the door. The shampoo in the bathroom smells of coconut and vanilla. The coffee mug left on the counter has a cat's smiling face printed on the front. This is exactly the sort of place I would expect two young women to settle down and call home.

Gloria, I turn in a circle, taking in everything around me, *did you feel safe here?*

She certainly didn't feel safe with Wolfgang Jäger. If his grabby hands weren't enough of a threat, then my bullets certainly were. Yes, that was me shooting at her car last night. It took me a few days to track Wolf down. He does frequent clubs, and he definitely loves women, like Conrad said, but Amory's wedding has kept him busy. He hadn't gone out much until last night.

I waited in the shadows for days, stalking him across the city. Moving between boroughs to keep up with him. He was predictable, but I still found myself staring with flared nostrils and wide-open eyes when I saw Gloria walk out of this apartment.

She didn't look like herself. She looked like she belonged on one of the poles in Conrad's club. But there she was. My innocent wife, dressed like a whore. I could only imagine what she's been doing here in New York, and that outfit pretty much solidified my worries.

My brother found himself a new toy…

The words pierce my skull, giving me a headache. *Why, Gloria? Why did you leave me for this?*

I walk through the kitchen, past a slice of half-eaten toast, past the coffee maker, which was left on, past the dirty wash rag tossed onto the side of the sink. In the bathroom, I see a hamper that spills dirty clothes onto the floor. A pile of dark purples, navy blues, and coral pinks. There are sweatpants, pajamas, and a tangle of panties. I can't tell which clothes belong to Gloria and which ones belong to the girl she's staying with. So I don't touch them. I walk to the bedroom and find two twin beds, wondering how on earth they fit in those things.

Gloria is small, not just because she's 18, she's small in general. Tiny, to my 6'1 height. It hits me then that she's so young. Still a girl. Yet, she is my wife, and I want her back the way a dog wants his bone. She belongs to me. For the rest of her life.

One bed is neatly made, the pillows fluffed, a stuffed animal resting against them. The other looks like a child made it and I immediately know it's Gloria's. Mafia princesses don't make their own beds; this is probably the first time Gloria has ever folded a sheet in her life. She even had maids in England, perks of attending a rich boarding school.

I sit on the edge of her bed. There's a cardboard box of clothes at the end, mostly sweatshirts and leggings. Curiosity digs into my mind, grabbing hold of every thought until all I can think and wonder is what's in that box.

I pull out each article and hold them in my hand, lift a shirt to my nose and inhale the fragrance of cheap detergent. She has socks and pajamas and a sequin dress that looks uncomfortable. At the bottom is a bundle of underwear, I take that out too.

Did Wolf buy these? Most of them are tiny thongs, nothing more than three strings looped together with a triangle of material in the middle. I have never seen Gloria in panties like these. The fact that she might have worn them for another man infuriates me.

Without thinking, I take every single pair of her underwear and cram them into my pockets. They're small enough to fit. Then I toss the rest of her clothes back into the box and rise from the bed, rolling my shoulders back. It's time for me to leave. I know she's on campus with her girlfriend, finding her exact location won't be too hard. Now that I've gotten into the rhythm of hunting again, this part should be easy. Fun, even.

I haven't been on a hunt in so long. Twelve years…

To come back into the game for my own silly wife is an

embarrassment, but the faster I get this over with, the faster I can go home. I've already done the hard part, chasing off Wolfgang Jäger, now I just need to take Amory's advice. Collect my wife and go.

I place a gift on Gloria's bed before I walk out, leaving the rest of the apartment exactly as I found it. Her university isn't too far from here. A thirty-minute train ride, and then another fifteen minutes on foot. I could use the time to think, to map out the campus, to plan how I'll get this done. I can't afford a scene, but I will retrieve my wife no matter what it takes.

26

Ria

The lounge is quiet. I'm sitting in the same spot before, when I ran away and read that silly gossip magazine. Krista is in class right now; she invited me to come along but I only agreed to go if I could rest here. I don't think her professors want to see me again.

So far, the day has been peaceful. I've spent my time shamefully reading that magazine again. Rosa's story was interesting, but I read everything else too. The interview with her brother, the photos of Wolfgang.

I stare down at the magazine, thinking about this hopeless, crime-filled city. Maybe not all hope is lost. Maybe Rosa can do something about this. Maybe God will listen to her prayers. He listened to mine. My heart still flutters when I think of how narrowly I escaped rape and death. *You answered*, I pray inside, *even when I didn't entirely believe it. You came through.*

I tuck the magazine away and stand, feeling my back pop as I stretch. Enough with the gossip column, since I officially became a Christian, I think I should probably read the Bible. I don't have one. Krista said I could borrow hers, but it's all marked up with highlights and notes. There's nothing wrong with that, but I feel like reading through her notes would be an invasion of privacy. Some people write their prayers into their Bibles, sometimes their notes are personal. I don't want to snoop around, especially not on a spiritual level.

I could download a Bible app on my phone, but I ditched it after last night. Wolf gave me that phone. Holding on to it felt like I was keeping something I shouldn't. Plus, I didn't want to make it easy for him to contact me again. Of course, he could just drop by the apartment anytime he wanted, but something tells me I won't be seeing him soon. He seemed more afraid than I was.

Since I don't have a Bible of my own, I decide to try the library, but on my way out of the lounge, I see something from the corner of my eye that stops me in my tracks. A flower.

It sits on the table right beside the exit, like someone left it there the same way you'd leave a pencil or a slip of paper. Something forgotten. None of the other students seem to notice the flower, they don't even pay me any attention as I walk over and pluck it from the table. That's when I feel a sudden wave of dizziness.

It's a morning glory.

See you soon, love.

I sway on my feet, reaching out to grip the edge of the table. I almost drop the flower, but I manage to hold on to it, nearly crushing it in my grasp. *Who left this?* My mind wanders in a dozen different directions, but each path leads to one person. Caolán O'Rourke.

I feel a ghost whisper his name into my ear and I turn a circle, scanning the lounge. *Where is he?* He must be here. I *know* he's here. I can feel his eyes on me as easily as I feel the thorns of this flower puncture the flesh of my palm.

Caolán is here. Somewhere.

How did he find me? I carry the mystery with me as I rush to the library, like the stacks of books can save me. Caolán could be my hero or the monster I've been running from all along. My knight or my nightmare. I can't tell, and I won't know until I see him but I'm too afraid to take that chance. I could leave and escape again, but I don't want to abandon Krista. She would have no idea what happened to me. At the very least, I could stay until her classes end and then tell her goodbye. Until then, I just need to lay low.

I make my way into the back of the library, past the study section and into the stacks of books no one reads. This is the nonfiction section, filled with dusty books that probably haven't been touched by anyone since I was born. Sadly, I find a Bible buried in the back. It's covered in dust and someone ripped out the first few chapters of Genesis, but I'm glad I've got it anyway.

I already read the Book of Esther, but I have no idea where to start after that. There are 66 books in the Bible and half as many authors. Each book, each chapter, each individual verse serves a purpose. With that in mind, how could I ever pick a place to begin?

I flip through the pages until I see a name I recognize—it's Moses in the Book of Exodus. I don't remember much about Moses except that he was in that kids' movie, *The Prince of Egypt*. I have no idea how biblically accurate the film was, but I remember being obsessed with it as a child. Now is as good a time as any to look at the original story.

Right away, my worries and frustrations begin to trickle down my back. I'm immersed in a world of sand and gold and plagues and mourning. For some reason, I'm just now realizing that many of the heroes of the Bible didn't have perfect lives. Many of them weren't much better off than me. Moses's family was broken—his own mother had to send him away to save his life; in a way, mine did too. I have so much more in common with the Bible than I thought. Pain, grief, temptation, misery, confusion, anger; everyone in the Bible felt those things too. Even God got angry sometimes, that's why He sent plagues against the Egyptians, because they were abusing His children. So ... What will He do for me?

I become obsessed with Moses and Pharaoh and the rest of Egypt. I don't know how long I sit there, but I ignore my growling stomach and my cramping legs. I'm so engulfed in the story of Moses that I don't notice when someone sinks into the chair across from me, exhaling a lazy sigh.

"Hello, darling."

I freeze.

His voice makes my heart flip for so many reasons. I lift my gaze to take him in, his crisp suit, so out of place on this college campus, his loosened tie, his flaming hair, tousled and wild like he just ran his large hand through it. His eyes are on me, as they always are, sharp and focused, filled with emotion.

I see anger, it's the loudest and sparks in his eye like a flame. But that flame heats him up and leaves a sense of warmth that calms my racing heart. I know there is joy beneath his anger. He's as relieved to see me as I am to see him, but there's a wall between us we must tear down first, each brick a mass of pain, hate, and bitterness.

We stare at each other, saying more through our eyes than our words ever could. As he holds my gaze, I hear his raspy voice in my heart. *You left me.*

I glance away. *I had no choice.*

I hear him sigh and I know what he's thinking. *You didn't give me a chance.*

I dare to glance up. *I'm sorry.*

He doesn't blink. *So am I.*

"We're leaving," Caolán finally speaks.

"I can't."

He stands and buttons his suit jacket like he didn't even hear me.

I don't move. "I can't leave, Caolán."

His eyes heat with rage but his voice remains calm. "I chased you across the country. I groveled at the feet of other mafia bosses to get help in finding you." He leans across the table, splaying his hands on the smooth wood. "You are done making me look like a fool. Now, you can walk out of here or I can drag you out. But we are leaving, Gloria."

I remain seated, and before I know it, Caolán is across the

room. He grabs me by the wrist, and I yelp as he yanks me to my feet.

"I'll scream!" I say quickly, trying to wriggle free. "I'll scream if you try to make me leave."

The threat makes him pause, but only for a moment—long enough to understand what I just said. Once the threat sinks in, Caolán's grip on my wrist tightens and he yanks me around, so my back is flush against his chest.

When he speaks, I feel the rumble in his ribcage before the words reach my ear. "Go ahead and scream," he says hotly. "See if anyone here can stop me."

This is New York City. Any security guards here are gang affiliated. Caolán may be from the White Hand, across the country, but he's still an underboss. I'm positive people here know his name, which means they won't challenge him. They won't intervene if he starts a scene. And they won't help me if I scream.

"My friend," I whisper, tears burning my eyes, "she's expecting me after class. I don't want to leave her."

"You can text her goodbye."

"I don't have a phone."

Caolán chuckles. "That's too bad." He tugs me away from the table and I follow him without a fight. I can't see past the tears that blur my eyes, so I clutch his hand and walk out of the library like a child being led away from the playground. Caolán ignores all the strange stares we get, brushing by pockets of confused students and nervous professors who pretend they don't see us. I'm an eighteen-year-old girl being dragged away in tears by a man in his thirties, but no one seems to care. That's the reality of living in New York. For some reason, I thought this would be the perfect place to hide. But it's caused me nothing but trouble.

Caolán says nothing as we trudge three blocks up the road and head into the subway station. He keeps me close, squeezing my hand, refusing to let me go in the crowd. We stand in the subway together, two faces in a sea of New Yorkers. No one pays us much attention except a woman who sidles up to Caolán and tries to make small talk. She makes a comment about the weather and then complains about there being no seats, then she cracks a joke about stealing one of the accessible chairs which makes me scowl as I glance at her. That's when I see what she's doing. She's flirting with my husband.

For the most part, Caolán ignores her, grunting out a noncommittal response to each of her statements, but when he sees me shoot a glare at her, he blinks and then a lightbulb flickers on in his head. Now, he gives her his full attention and I see an easy smile crawl across his face, I see his shoulders relax and his free hand slides into his pocket.

Oh my gosh… He's flirting back.

Caolán smiles as he chats, tosses his head back so a bubble of laughter can pop from his mouth. His voice is heavenly as it fills the train, a deep rasp with a sharp accent which makes him sound exotic. He looks so normal it makes my heart ache with a different sort of pain. Is this what our lives could be like without the mafia? Could we ride the subway, hand in hand,

and casually chat about the weather or the café or the discount deals at the grocery store?

There's no point in wondering because there is no Caolán without the White Hand.

When we exit the train, the chatty woman passes Caolán her number, scribbled down on the back of a Starbucks receipt. He smiles and thanks her and then tosses the paper away as soon as she turns around.

"Did you enjoy that?" I ask.

"Did you enjoy all of your hot little dates here in New York?" he shoots back.

I shake my head. If only he knew what my dates were really like.

We finish the walk to my apartment in silence, riding the elevator with my hand still stuck in his. Caolán doesn't release me until we're standing in the tiny kitchen.

"Go pack," he instructs, shutting my door firmly.

I do as he says, trudging to my bedroom, only to stop at the entrance when I see the morning glory left on my bed. "You were here before," I whisper.

Caolán appears behind me, and although I don't turn around, I can tell he's smiling as he says, "The place is cute."

"Why didn't you get me earlier?"

"I enjoyed watching you from a distance."

I pivot and shove my palms into his chest. He stumbles a few steps back, and I yell, "Did you enjoy watching that jerk force himself onto me last night!? Was that *fun* to you? Or did you think it was just another *hot little date*?"

His brows pinch together. "That wasn't any easier for me to watch as it was for you to live through."

"Oh, you're so compassionate," I sneer.

"Who do you think shot at him?"

I pause. "That … That was you?"

"I couldn't kill him because I made a deal with his older brother. I would have picked you up afterward, but I stuck around to make sure his car didn't circle back to get you." Caolán steps closer, his hand going to my face, his thumb brushing my cheek. "I would never let anyone touch you, Gloria. I'm sorry I didn't come sooner."

I … I don't know what to say. I'd prayed and cried that God would rescue me last night, and He did. But He did it in a way that leaves me speechless as I blink at my husband now.

God sent *Caolán* to save me.

Will he be my knight or nightmare? I think I know the answer now. But I don't know how to tell him this. I don't know how to respond to what he's just revealed. In the silence, I hear the bricks begin to crumble and the wall between us cracks as we work together to tear it down.

What do I say? I don't realize the words are a prayer until God answers. His Voice is sweet and calming, something I recognize without question.

Tell him the truth.

"I didn't run away from you," I whisper. "I ran away from the mafia."

Caolán tilts his head to the side, thrown by the confession.

"You were one of the reasons I wanted to stay. But I

couldn't, Caolán. I couldn't be trapped in that life, and I can't go back to it now."

"The mafia is not an easy life," he says. "But it doesn't have to be so hard. We can go through it together."

He offers me his hand and I stare at it, almost in fear. I told him the truth, just like God said to do. But I'd expected the truth to open his eyes. I expected him to understand where I was coming from, to tell me everything would be okay, that he would help me pack and we would run away from the White Hand and the Panthers together. Instead, he's telling me to return with him. To go back to the very thing I ran from.

I don't understand. What was the point in telling him the truth?

"Gloria?" Caolán says, hand still extended.

I hear the question he didn't ask. *Will you come back? Will you give me a second chance?*

There it is. The reason for the truth. This is my second chance. Not to return to the mafia, but to return to my marriage. To get along with Caolán, and then, when the time is right, to leave again. But next time, I'll leave with him by my side.

When I reach forward, I don't just take Caolán's hand, I slide my fingers between his and I step close enough to wrap my free arm around his neck. He blinks in surprise, but the shock melts into desire when I kiss him right on the lips.

Caolán kisses me back, moaning into my mouth, gasping like this moment is all he came for. The very reason he's even alive. I feel the intensity of his passion as he backs me into the bedroom, his hands running down to my waist. He kicks the door shut behind him and lifts me from the floor, never breaking our kiss.

This feels nothing like the night I had with Wolfgang. Caolán's mouth is sweet, his breath is warm, his body radiates with heat and desire. Tangled up like this, we don't even make it to the bed. Caolán trips over my dirty pajamas and we end up on the floor but that doesn't stop us. He finds my lips again and I kiss him like he's the last man alive. The exchange is desperate, needy, each panting breath a plea for more.

Caolán's calloused hands slide up my sweater dress and I feel the material of my underwear rip. When I gasp, he laughs into my mouth and says, "Hold on to me."

I obey without question, listening to the jingle of his belt. The last time we made love, it was spontaneous and lusty and forbidden. This time is only marginally different. Caolán's raspy voice is in my ear, each grunt setting me on fire. I want to scream, want to rake my nails down his back until I draw blood. But I don't do any of that. I can barely breathe, let alone think or scream or scratch.

Something unfurls inside of me, something alive and hungry. It storms through my body, feeding on the passion that burns between us, searching for a release. I can't hold it in, though I desperately try.

"Caolán—"

"Hold on."

"I *can't*."

Lightning strikes. My heart stops. I see stars. Caolán's entire body jerks and he buries his face into the crook of my neck, fist pounding the carpeted floor. The lightning fizzles into fire and the fire cools into embers. I feel like I can breathe again, but what happens next catches my breath for an entirely different reason.

I hear footsteps in the apartment.

"Caolán," I whisper, "someone's here."

"Darling? Are you home?"

It's Krista! And it sounds like she's coming this way. But Caolán hasn't moved. He's still collapsed on top of me, his heavy body completely covering my own. We're in the middle of the floor, Caolán's between my legs, his pants yanked down to his knees. Krista cannot see us like this. She would never understand. She would never forgive me.

"Get up!" I whisper, shoving Caolán. "She's coming! You have to get up."

Caolán pushes onto his elbows just as I hear Krista's voice again. "Darling? You in there?" Her hand grasps the doorknob, I hear it wiggle as she begins to turn it.

"Hold on!" I shout. "I'm getting dressed!"

She stops. "Oh, thank God you're okay. Why'd you leave? A friend from another class said she saw you run out with a man?"

"I ..." I stare at Caolán as he tucks himself away and zips his pants. "I got sick. A man helped me get home."

"Are you okay?"

"I'll be out in a minute."

There's a long pause and then, finally, the doorknob slides

back into the default position. I hear Krista sigh. "I'll get started on dinner, then. Come out when you're ready."

"Okay. Thanks!" I try to sound perky and friendly, but my voice cracks and I have to cough to cover it.

Once I'm sure Krista is gone, I finally look at Caolán again. He's standing by my bed, his hair a mess, his lips puffy and swollen from everything we just did. But he looks relaxed, perfectly calm and satisfied.

He smiles. "That was nice."

"How can you say that?"

"Should I say you're bad at sex and I had to do all the work?"

I blink, trying to figure out if he means that.

"Come on," Caolán says, pushing from the bed. He wipes his hand through his hair, which does nothing to tame the red flames, and then approaches the door while I frantically shove down my dress.

"Wait! You can't go out there!"

"Why not?"

"Because my roommate is home. Didn't you hear her?"

"That's why I'm going out there. To meet her."

"But ... You can't."

He frowns. "Why not?"

I can't really think of a reason except that I don't want him to. Krista is my friend. My secret here in New York. Introducing her to Caolán is like bringing a lamb to slaughter. She doesn't deserve to be tangled up in our dangerous lives. But I can't explain any of this to Caolán who is already reaching for the door.

"Wait! I'm not dressed!"

Caolán leans against the wall as I toss clothes out of the cardboard box at the end of my bed. I'm looking for a new pair of underwear since he so gracefully ripped mine off earlier.

After a few moments of rummaging, I take a step back, blushing, hating to admit this. "I—I don't have any panties."

Caolán grins. "You don't need any." Then he turns and opens the door before I can stop him, leaving me no choice but to scurry out and hope that Krista doesn't mind a mafia boss joining us for dinner.

27

Ria

When Caolán steps out of our shared bedroom, Krista's eyes widen, and her body goes ramrod straight. She stands perfectly still in the middle of our kitchen, wearing a Hello Kitty apron with strawberry-colored slippers. She's got her hair pulled back with a thick scrunchy, but a few strands of silvery blonde hair have fallen loose. They wave as she shakes her head like she can't believe what she's seeing.

"What's going on?" she whispers.

"I'm sorry," Caolán says.

Krista blinks rapidly, thrown off by his thick accent.

"I'm Gloria's husband."

"Gloria?" She looks at me, then shakes her head again like his last word just sank in. "*Husband?*"

How do I explain that everything she knows about me is a lie? I don't have the heart to do it, so I just stand there and stare at the whiskers sewn onto her Hello Kitty apron as Caolán takes the lead.

He steps forward, full of charm and smiles and deep, throaty chuckles. Even I have a hard time keeping my heartbeat steady as I listen to him. The teenager in me wants to squeal as I watch him lean over the counter, introducing himself to my roommate. Krista is wary, but she is not immune to Caolán's blue eyes. I see the way her body begins to relax. I watch the color return to her face. And then I watch as she brushes a stray hair behind her ear, surrenders a self-conscious smile, and then it happens.

Caolán says, "I hope you don't mind the intrusion."

And Krista says, "No. Not at all. It's sudden, but totally welcome."

She laughs. Krista lets go of a feminine giggle and her body sways toward Caolán like she would fall into his arms if the counter didn't stand between them. My husband does not have a handsome face. I find him attractive because his face is something I've seen since childhood, but in the clarity of my adult years, I see Caolán for who he truly is. Scars like rivers of pain drawn down the sides of his face, hollow cheeks, tired eyes forever half-lidded. But … his hair is like tongues of fire, his jaw is square and strong, and he has an accent that sounds like a gentle purr. Caolán knows how to use the good parts of himself. However unattractive he is, no one can resist his charm for long.

In just a few moments, Krista is flushed pink, cheeks stained with a gentle blush that I cannot ignore. She is under his spell, completely swooned by his charm.

It's amazing, watching my husband go from a dangerous

mafia boss to this smiling, chuckling man asking a young girl to dinner. He's like two different people, picking and choosing the persona that benefits him most.

"So, have the plans changed?" I interrupt Caolán's stupid joke about grocery prices and unexpected guests.

Krista cuts her laugh short and blinks at me like she's just remembered my presence. With that reminder comes the realization that Caolán is a married man and that his wife is right in front of her. The pink in her cheeks turns angry red and she huffs.

"I don't have enough for three. I guess we can all go out together."

I glance at Caolán. *Is that a good idea?* Caolán avoids my gaze and leans against the counter, lazily resting on his elbows. "I can have my driver pick us up, so we won't have to take the subway."

"There's no need for that," I say, but Krista interrupts in a cheery tone that none of us can argue with.

"I'm not in the mood for the subway, and I'd like to get to know your *husband*."

I don't miss the way *husband* rolls off her tongue.

She reaches up to untie her apron. "Just let me change my clothes and spruce up a bit."

I follow Krista into the bedroom as Caolán opens his phone to call his driver. As soon as I close the door, Krista turns and folds her arms.

"What is going on?"

I'm momentarily stunned by how fast she can change her

mood. What happened to the giggling and flirting she was doing moments ago?

"Krista, you said everyone has a story, remember? My name isn't Darling, it's Gloria O'Rourke. I'm not the person you thought I was."

"That much is obvious." She throws her hands up. "You're *married?* And you had your husband in our apartment. In our bedroom." She looks around, hugging herself like she's disgusted with the room. I don't blame her. On the floor between us is my ripped pair of panties, torn off by Caolán and discarded like trash. There hadn't been time to snatch them up and hide them earlier, so now they're on display for Krista to see.

She knows what happened in this room. Even without the panties, I know she can see it in my face. In the way I can't hold her gaze anymore. I know she can hear it in my voice, how much it trembles when I speak. And she can smell it in the air. The room still holds the heady scent of sex and desire. It's so thick I want to cover my nose, but I don't. I've already embarrassed myself enough, I won't add salt to the wound by admitting that we stink.

Sex isn't as sexy as those romantic novels make it out to be. The truth is that it's sweaty, tiring, and causes an awful lot of complications. Even though I'm married.

"Krista," I say calmly, "I can't tell you everything. But I promise that everything I've kept from you was for a good reason."

"How many lies have you told?"

"Enough to keep myself alive."

She looks angry, but I see a wave of empathy roll over her and she replies with a sigh. "Is he really your husband?"

"Yes."

"Is he the reason you came to New York?"

"Part of it."

"Is he the reason you're returning?"

I hesitate. "I don't know."

"So, you're going back?"

"Yes, but only because I think that's what God wants me to do."

Her anger returns with an exasperated sigh. "Are you pulling my leg?"

"Krista, I lied about a lot of things, but not my faith. That was real."

It was. Faith isn't something I would ever lie about. I didn't learn much at my school, but I learned enough to know that God doesn't like fake people. People who pretend to be Christian. Christians who curse you out and then end their rant with a very pleasant, *God bless you!* Christians who open a bottle of wine on Saturday night and their leather Bible on Sunday morning. The ones who wear crosses around their necks but forget the cross that was carried for them. We call them lukewarm Christians, but I'd take it a step farther and say they aren't Christian at all. Not because they make mistakes, but because they don't see their behavior as a mistake to begin with. They justify their actions and feel comfortable repeatedly sinning. They are the Christians who will cry bitter tears and gnash their teeth when they stand before God and He says, *Depart from Me ... I never knew you.*

Not long ago, I was one of those people. I knew who God was, but I didn't live the way He wanted me to. In a way, that made me no different from Satan himself. But I'm not that girl anymore. I've accepted Christ into my life and I'm trying to live for Him. God is the one who told me to tell Caolán the truth. Though, He *didn't* tell me to sleep with him on my bedroom floor.

Is that a sin? I've heard the bedroom is undefiled, but at a Christian high school, the only time they even dared to talk about sex was to tell us that it was for married people. Our classes didn't cover anything else, as if married couples don't have questions about their bedroom. Like ... What do I do when I accept Christ and my husband doesn't? Should we divorce? Should I drag him to church with me? Is it sinful for me to share my body with him before he gets saved?

I don't know, but I don't think Krista has the answers. She doesn't want to discuss my love life anyway. She can barely wrap her head around the fact that I'm married to begin with.

"My faith in God is real," I tell her. "I'm sorry I've lied to you, but I never lied about that. I'm trying to do what's right by God, but I don't know how."

She doesn't speak, choosing to gnaw on her lower lip instead.

"You said everyone has a story."

"I guess I never thought your story could be so complicated."

"I'm sorry, Krista. I know I'm asking a lot of you right now."

"What exactly are you asking?"

"For you to stay calm and just go along with what's happening. Don't make a scene. Don't ask questions. Just enjoy dinner and then move on."

"So, you're really leaving, then?"

I nod. "I am."

She nods too. "I think that's for the best."

Her comment stings, but I don't let the pain fester. She's right, after all. Not just because I've lied to her, it's best for me to leave because she doesn't know who I truly am. Who Caolán truly is. He told her he was here on business. While she smiled and giggled, he explained that we got into an argument, and I took off to have some time to myself. Now he's come to get me. That isn't a total lie, but it completely downplays who we really are and what business Caolán has in the city. Krista doesn't need the details anyway. She's agreed to have dinner and then turn a blind eye once I leave. That's the best I can ask for, so I'll take it without complaining.

Krista turns to find a change of clothes, leaving me in an awkward silence. I take the hint and grab a dress from my cardboard box before dashing to the bathroom. I fill the sink with water and clean myself up with a soapy cloth, but I still can't find any underwear. Every single pair I own is missing, and I am positive Caolán has something to do with that but there's no time to make a fuss. With my cheeks burning in shame, I slip on a new dress and walk out the bathroom to greet my husband and roommate.

"Ready?" Caolán asks.

I lift my eyes to answer, but I can't find any words when I see the person who's joined us.

It's Tony. Caolán's driver.

I stare at him as Caolán introduces him to Krista. He doesn't meet my eyes, just keeps his gaze on his shoes or steadfastly focused on Krista who shakes his hand and laughs at something Caolán says that isn't even funny.

How could you? The question burns the backs of my eyes as I feel bitter tears rise, but I refuse to shed them. Instead, I turn to my husband and Krista. Caolán is saying something about the restaurant now, but I cut him off by abruptly marching to the door. "Let's go," I grunt, "I'm hungry."

We ride the elevator down in silence but once the doors ding open, Caolán cracks a joke about his appetite and Krista starts talking about a complicated fast she was on last month. Something about Daniel and raw vegetables.

Krista and Caolán are so engrossed in this conversation that neither of them notices me walking three steps behind them. But Tony notices. He sidles up to me with an apology falling from his mouth before I can even turn to face him.

"Ria, I'm sorry."

"You're not."

"I am."

"You hunted me down," I hiss the words, but I really want to scream them. Except screaming would draw attention, so I swallow my rage and hope Tony can hear the loathing in my voice as I say quietly, "Have you ever cared about me?"

He looks wounded. "That's why I did this."

"You sound insane."

"It's my job to keep you safe, Ria. But I believe the safest place for you is with Caolán."

"A mafia boss."

"Isn't that Wolf guy in the mafia, too? Was he any safer than Caolán?"

I snap my vision toward him, ready to bite his head off, but he keeps talking.

"I didn't have much of a choice."

"Why did you even bother giving me hope when you knew I'd come right back?"

"Because you wouldn't have listened if I had tried to convince you to stay."

"So, you lied to my face. Again."

"Helping you escape meant leaving you at the mercy of a world you've never been in. Look where you ended up, Ria. You're safer here with Caolán. He isn't so bad. He won't hurt you. Not like Wolf would have." Tony closes his eyes for a moment, and I see his shoulders drop. He cares. He really does, but he doesn't see this the way I do.

This isn't about Caolán hurting me. It's about living in the darkness of the mafia. Living a life that I've never wanted for myself, and that God doesn't want for me now. But Tony doesn't understand that. He never will. So I don't even try to explain it, I just shake my head and pick up my pace.

"Gloria," he calls.

"You're a traitor." Those are my last words to him before I climb into the car. Once I'm inside, I block out his voice and wall off my heart.

The ride to the restaurant is frustratingly awkward, but only for me. Krista finds Caolán absolutely charming, and he bathes in the attention she gives him. He is once again full of smiles and chuckles and witty little jokes, none of which he has ever told me. The two seem more like best friends than strangers who just met, leaving me to sulk in silence as I try to digest everything happening around me. Believe it or not, I'm more upset about Tony's presence than anything else.

I was fooled again. This is more proof that no one in the mafia can be trusted. Not my best friend. Not my childhood bodyguard. Not my husband.

But what about me?

In a way, I'm a traitor too. I've betrayed the mafia by converting to Christianity. I've betrayed my family. I've betrayed everything that we stand for and believe in. And no one has a clue. But what do I do now that I have faith? Should I start preaching to people? Should I speak in Tongues and prophesy the downfall of the Panthers and the White Hand?

"Darling?" Caolán's voice stabs into my thoughts. He's reaching for me, stretching his long arm across the seats.

I hadn't even realized we'd arrived. Krista is already standing on the sidewalk beside Tony. Both of them are staring at me.

"Are you coming?" Caolán asks.

Yes—is what I mean to say. I even reach for Caolán's hand, but I never speak the word. I never even get to touch his hand. The next moment, something loud cracks behind us and I see a spray of red mist burst into the air.

The world is silent for a moment. Everything slows down, and I feel like I'm moving underwater. Caolán's face freezes in shock, then darkens in anger. Some of that red mist got on him. The side of his face is speckled crimson, darker than his hair. It's on his tie. It's on his shoulder. I see it staining the tips of his bangs.

Something crashes into him. It's heavy and dark—it takes me a moment to realize it's a body. Tony's body. He's fallen into Caolán like he's just fainted. Caolán trips sideways, trying to hold him up. More cracks split the air. Somewhere in the distance, I can hear screaming, but I don't know if it's coming from me or from Krista outside.

"Gloria!" It's Caolán's voice, a loud bark that startles me enough to bring me into focus.

Everything snaps into place. Time speeds up. My heart beats again. Now I can understand what's happening.

The cracking noise ...

"Gunshots," I whisper.

The red mist...

"Blood."

And Tony...

"Is dead."

I inhale a breath and exhale a scream. Tony was shot and he fell into Caolán who is crawling into the car now, dragging his limp body with him. He's shouting something, but I can't hear it because I'm shouting too. There aren't any words coming out of my mouth, just incoherent shrieks. Panic, raw fear, every dark emotion I ran away from has caught up to me now.

I did not leave the pain in California. I did not leave the misery at home. It's right here in my lap. Tony's shattered skull is on my legs, his wide eyes rolled to the back of his head. The car is moving now, I think Caolán got into the driver's seat. I don't know where Krista is. All I see is red.

So much blood...

Tony is sprawled across the backseat of the car. Dying. I press my stained palms onto his chest and try to perform some sort of CPR, but the car is moving, and his body is swaying. I can't even see past my tears to find his mouth, and even if I could, it's too late now. His body seizes right there in my lap, legs jerking and twitching.

I scream again, sobbing like I'm the one who's been shot. That's what it feels like. There's a black hole in my heart now. It was formed by the same bullet that punched through Tony's skull. The same bullets that ping off the car as it speeds down the highway.

Caolán shouts for me to keep my head down as he makes a sharp turn, yanking hard on the steering wheel. I can hear Krista crying in the passenger seat, but her sobs are different from mine. She is crying out of fear; I am crying out of heartbreak.

Tony is gone. He's dead and it's my fault.

28

Caolán

I drive for an hour, in no particular direction, with no destination in sight. The goal is simply to get away. I have a sobbing woman beside me and my hysterical wife behind me. That's what bothers me most, that Gloria was dragged into this.

I know who did this. Dead eyes drift into my mind as I grip the steering wheel.

Amory Jäger.

I shot at his brother. I chased him away from my wife. And now he's retaliated. But why? We had a deal. Sure, I pulled the trigger, but Wolfgang walked away unscathed. I made sure of that. Amory has no reason to hunt me down like this.

Unless it wasn't him.

Wolf's vulpine grin slithers into my head. He is all I can see until I blink away the image and pull the car to the side of the road. I switch it into park and sit there breathing.

Wolfgang did this. I had a deal with his older brother, but

there was never an agreement with him. He probably doesn't even know who I am. He just hunted down the car that followed him the night he was shot at. Or maybe he was aiming for Gloria, and I was simply in the way.

Through the rearview mirror, I can see Gloria leaning over Anthony's body. His blood is smeared all over her clothes and hands. Tears chase down her cheeks. She's rocking back and forth, making little whimpering noises.

This is bad.

Gloria is one thing, but Krista is here too, and she isn't in much better shape. She's still crying, her eyes squeezed shut, mouth open. There's a draw of snot trailing from her chin, dangling like a string of rubber.

I pass her the handkerchief from my breast pocket. "It'll be okay."

She stares at me. "W-What?"

"It'll be okay."

"How can you say that?"

I blink. I have no idea how I can say that. I don't even believe it, it just seems like the right thing to say. What else *should* I say here? That I'm sorry? That won't cut it. That I didn't mean for this to happen? That's true, but it won't make a difference. Clearly, my little bit of encouragement won't change things either, so I settle for the truth.

"Fine. Things won't be okay. We're being tracked by a mafia prince who wants to kill me because I wouldn't let him sleep with my wife. He's a bad shot, so he ended up killing my driver instead. Now I'm going to find him, kill him, and take my unruly wife home. But before I can do any of that, I'm going to drug you, wipe your memory, and then drop you off at a hotel where you will stay until it's safe to return to your crappy apartment." I tilt my head to the side. "Is that what you want to hear?"

"Y-You're going t-to … to drug me?" Krista wipes the snot from her nose as she stares at me. "I don't understand."

I open the armrest and retrieve a tiny bag of fog. Billy said I might need this for Gloria, and I almost shot him for even thinking that I would ever drug my wife. But now I'm glad he made the suggestion. This is the only way I can keep Krista safe. She won't be able to give the Jägers any information about me or Gloria or where we went. And if she forgets all this, she won't just lose the memories, she'll lose the pain too. I think that's the part that matters most. She doesn't deserve to live with the darkness I've brought her. Gloria wouldn't want that.

"It won't hurt," I say.

Krista shakes her head, sobbing. She tries to speak again, but she's crying too hard. So instead of begging me not to do this, she yanks the door handle and bolts from the car.

I sigh. Glance into the rearview mirror. Gloria is staring wide-eyed. "I'm going to get your friend back," I say calmly. "Please don't leave the car."

She nods.

I'm in good enough shape to chase Krista down quite easily. She makes it half a block before I snatch her into a nearby alley, hand clamped over her mouth. She kicks, screams against my palm, and then tries to bite me. I let her go and grab her by the hair, just to hold her still while I pull out the fog again. When she sees the bag, she loses it, screaming like I'm trying to kill her. My gut reaction is to slam her face into the wall, but she's a friend of Gloria's, so I won't treat her that way. Instead, I shove her to the ground and straddle her legs. While she slaps at my chest, I stick two of my fingers into my mouth and then cram them into the bag. They're coated with spit and silver powder when I pull them back out.

Krista stares at my fingers. "What is that?"

"It won't hurt."

"Please don't."

Tears leak from the corners of her eyes. I watch them dip into her hair. If I were any other man, I might've been moved by her pleading, but I have a wife who needs me, so I take a breath and say, "I'm sorry," then I grab her chin.

Instead of screaming, Krista clamps her jaw shut, curling her lips into her mouth. That doesn't stop me. I simply pinch the sides of her jaw, ready to crack it if I have to. She holds out longer than I expect but when I add more pressure, her jaw drops with a painful shriek, and I shove my fingers into her mouth.

She bites me. I slap her so hard my hand hurts, but she lets me go and I stagger to my feet, holding my injured fingers. One of them is bleeding.

Krista tries to sit up, but her body isn't working right. The drug hits her hard, probably because she's an innocent Christian woman who's never even held a vape before. When she tries to stand, her legs buckle, and she falls into the concrete wall. Her eyes loll in her skull, rolling from one direction to the other. Her mouth moves, but nothing coherent comes out. After a moment, she starts laughing hysterically, and then she doubles over and vomits.

I watch the show with a blade of pity slicing through my heart. I didn't want this. But it had to happen. Please don't judge me. It's almost over.

"I'm sorry," I tell her, though I know she doesn't hear me. Krista is lost in whatever hallucination has gripped her mind. She's still laughing, so I guess it's a good one. Better than screaming or crying or getting shot at.

High as a kite, it's much easier to get Krista into the car. She lets me scoop her up, bridal style, and shouts, "Giddy up!" as I walk out of the alley

Mercifully, Gloria is still in the car when I get back. She doesn't ask any questions or add any comments. She just sits there and sniffles as I buckle Krista in. When I drop into the driver's seat, I check the rearview mirror once more. Our eyes meet but neither of us speaks. I'm too tired, she's too sad. I almost don't care.

I drive an hour to a hotel in Staten Island. It's an expensive place run by the Russian mafia. The Bratva and the White Hand aren't allies but we aren't enemies either, so when I walk into the hotel, the concierge doesn't ask questions. Once he hears my name, he gives me a room and promises to look after Krista for three days. By then, the drugs should be out of her system, and it should be safe enough for her to return to her apartment.

"Now," I mutter, wiping my bloody hand through my hair, "I've got to deal with my wife."

She's still in the car when I leave the hotel, cradling Anthony's stiff body. I hate seeing her like this, but I don't know how else we're supposed to travel. I won't dump Anthony's body. I want to take him back home with us so his family can bury him.

"Sit up front," I tell Gloria, watching her through the rearview mirror.

She shakes her head. "I'm not leaving him."

"He's already gone."

She sniffles and I look away. Now, everything hits me. I feel the grief, the pain, the misery of what I've done to my wife. I got her friend killed and her roommate drugged. I am the monster she tried to escape.

"Gloria—"

"It's my fault," she whispers.

My breath hitches.

"If I hadn't run, he'd be alive."

She's blaming herself.

I want to tell her that she's wrong. That this is the mafia, anyone could die at any moment. But I don't think she would believe me. She's sitting in the back of my car with her bodyguard's blood on her hands. Gloria wouldn't listen to a word I said. So I don't say anything at all, I put the car into drive and pull off.

We don't stop by the apartment again, there is nothing there for either of us. I can buy new clothes for Gloria, and I'm sure

Krista will appreciate the 10K in cash Gloria left under her mattress. She took it from home when she ran away but with Wolfgang providing for her, she never had to use it. The money doesn't make up for everything we put Krista through, but I'm positive she's going to keep it.

In the car, I kill the engine and yank the key from the ignition. I squeeze the jaggedly carved metal in my hand, feeling it dig into my bloody finger. The pain isn't so bad, its an external reminder of all the bad things Gloria feels inside. The things I block out and bat away every day.

I stare at her through the mirror, watching her tears fall, wishing I could catch them or kiss them away. I wonder if her tears taste the same as her blood. What an odd thing to wonder.

"We're here," I say.

Gloria looks up and then her eyes go in a circle as she looks around. We're at a private airport outside the city, in Benton. Anthony and I used my private jet to get here. We were supposed to fly back together, the three of us. Technically, that's still happening, but not the way I planned.

"We need to leave," I tell Gloria. "We'll fly to a hotel and get ourselves cleaned up. We'll take Anthony home with us, but I need to make some calls so we can get his body prepared. Okay?"

Gloria nods, staring out the window at the plane.

"Let me take you inside."

She nods again and I get out and open her door. She is surprisingly compliant, letting me lift her from the car. I carry her to the plane like a bride, but she clings to me like a child.

Her arms wrapped around my neck; her face pressed into my shoulder. I feel the weight of her emotions and I swallow to choke them of their pain. I can't let it in now. We're almost back home.

The plane can seat six, so I let a stewardess sit beside Gloria while I go back down to handle the bloody mess in the car. Amory was my only connection here in New York; I had to beg Serena for help and bribe Conrad with drugs just to get a meeting with the guy. Then Wolfgang tried to kill me. I have no one I can call to help me with this. So I have to handle this myself.

I take off my jacket and roll up my sleeves, this isn't a big deal. It's not like I haven't dressed a body before. I delivered the body of my own brother to the White Hand years ago. I stood over him as he knelt on the ground. I pressed a gun to his forehead. I looked him in the eye as he whispered his last words. And then I pulled the trigger.

I remember the feel of the gun in my hand. I remember the sound of the bullet smashing through his skull. I remember the warm spray of his blood on my chest and face. And I remember the sound of his body hitting the ground. **Thud.** He was so heavy. Even heavier when I had to lift him into my car. But I did it, with my teeth grinding and my eyes watering, I dragged his body to my car and forced him into the trunk. He almost didn't fit, so I had to break his legs to fold him up and make room. It was the most gruesome thing I've ever done. That's why Anthony's body doesn't faze me.

I drag him out of the car and onto the cement ground. A

stewardess from the plane brings me gloves and plastic bags, they're nowhere near the size I need, but they'll work well enough. She's brave enough to help me wipe most of his blood away, then she rolls Anthony over so I can wrap him up in the bags I've cut open and unfolded like sheets of plastic.

"You're good at this," I grunt, hoisting Anthony's body over my shoulder.

She smiles. "It's part of the job." Her accent is Russian, and every question I have about her suddenly has an answer.

The Russian stewardess stays back while I load Anthony into the baggage hold beneath the plane. She didn't fly here with me, I only have three staff members; two stewards and the pilot, but she waves goodbye as I enter the plane, and I make a mental note to reach out to Mikhail Volkov once I'm home again. He's the leader of the Russian mafia here in New York. His hotel let me in without question and now his staff has helped me without asking for anything in return. But nothing in the mafia is free.

I know the Russians are at war with the Germans right now. Amory's wedding might have momentarily paused the friction between them, but I'm certain things will pick up again. When they do, Mikhail will remind me of the kindness his organization showed me. And of the bullet Wolfgang gave me.

My pilot greets me when I step back onto the plane. His face is solemn. He only gives me a nod. I know he saw me loading a body into the hold, but he doesn't offer any condolences. I appreciate that more than anything. I don't want to hear apologies; I just want to go home.

"Straight to LA?" the pilot asks, his Irish accent thicker than mine.

I shake my head and glance into the passenger area. Gloria is in her chair, wrapped in a blanket with her head down, eyes closed. I don't know if she's asleep, but I reply in my mother tongue just to be safe.

"I need you to make a stop."

My pilot raises a brow but obediently nods. "Whatever you say, sir."

After I give him the destination, I settle into my seat. The stewardess offers me a blanket too, but I'm not in the mood for sleep. I want to shower. I want to wash the blood off my hands and clothes. More than anything, I want to figure out how I can make things right. I came to get my wife. She's right beside me now, but I feel like she's back in her apartment in Manhattan. Farther from me than she's ever been.

I drop my head into my hands. *What am I going to do?*

29

Caolán

Anthony's body is cold and stiff. I stare down at his ruined face as the doctor cleans him. He had an awful death; worse than the bullet I would have given him. He died protecting Gloria. But he didn't die free. The only thing he wanted was to get out of the mafia; I could have helped him, but I chose to string him along because it was more beneficial for me.

I'm not so cruel. I'd always planned to cut him loose one day. But that never happened. Anthony is dead. I blame myself; Gloria blames herself. We've both got to pay. The moment we land in California and word reaches our respective organizations, we'll have to answer for what's happened. I just don't know if we'll answer in blood or not. Anthony was the son of a Panther General, but could his death spark another war?

My chest inflates and I slowly exhale the stale air of the examination room. I had my pilot take us to a safehouse on private property I own in Chicago. I don't have many connections or places my family cannot trace, but this house is one of them. We should be safe here for a few days, but I don't plan to stay long. I don't want to take any risks. I've already had to pay everyone here double their rate and in cash just to keep their mouths shut, but it's a price I'm willing to pay for a little more peace.

Gloria is still inconsolable. I had a stewardess from the plane take her to a room when we arrived; she did nothing but sob until she passed out from exhaustion and sorrow. Sorrow I caused. I've got to find a way to make this better, but I can't. Of all the bad things that could have happened ... Why this?

The doctor tells me he'll have Anthony's body dressed and delivered to the plane before we leave. On the way out, I pass a massive deep freezer, and I wonder if that's where he'll store him. I've dumped hundreds of bodies into freezers over the years, but I can't stomach the thought of Anthony in one. It doesn't seem real. It doesn't feel right.

He was there and then he wasn't, and there was nothing I could do about it.

My feet slowly climb the stairs from the basement to the first level of the safehouse as a question bounces around my head. *What was the point?* Anthony survived Tadhg's kidnapping just to be brutally murdered a week later. Right in front of Gloria.

I still have his blood on my clothes. When we landed, I called the mortician and waited in the basement with Anthony's corpse until he arrived. I stayed there as he used scissors to cut away the plastic bags I'd wrapped him in. I watched as he grimaced at Anthony's shattered skull. I held my breath when he drained his body of what was left of his blood. I was there through it all while Gloria sobbed in her bedroom. I carried her sorrows and buried my own, convinced I didn't have any. But now that she's asleep and I'm alone, I feel dead inside. Heavy with emotions I can't name or place and don't want to feel.

I drag myself into the kitchen and search the fridge for a drink. There's a bottle of something in the back, it's half full and doesn't have a label but that doesn't stop me from snatching it by the neck, biting out the cork, and chugging three gulps. It burns and I cough until I vomit, then I drink the rest and stumble into the living room.

I want to lie down on the sofa, feel the tension in my body unwind and melt away in the river of alcohol I've poured into my system, but that's not what happens. I end up tripping over a cord in the dim light and toppling to the floor. When I'm face-flat on the carpet, I begin to laugh.

I laugh until my eyes burn, until I can't breathe, until my jaw hurts and my shoulders shake and my abs cringe. Then I roll onto my side and squeeze my eyes shut, pretending I don't feel tears slipping down my cheeks. That's when the laughing stops and the sobbing begins.

I messed up. I messed up so bad. Worse than I ever have.

But I have to get it together. No matter how bad it gets, I still have to be there for Gloria. With great effort, I sit up and wipe my eyes and nose with my jacket sleeve. It's gross now, covered in tears, mucus, and blood, so I yank it off and toss it to the side. When it lands, something falls from the pocket and slides across the carpet.

My breath hitches. It's a tiny bag of fog. Just one ounce of magic that will wipe away the pain, if only for a moment. It could replace Gloria's sorrow, make her forget the misery I've put her through. It could turn her back into the wife I spent the night with. The one who almost fell for me.

But I don't reach for the bag because of Gloria. I pick it up and cram my sticky fingers inside for me.

I remember the way fog tastes, metallic and slightly sweet. I remember the way it melts beneath my tongue. I remember the way it burns when I inhale it. But I don't remember the way it made me sick or how it took over my mind and turned me into a monster I didn't recognize. Right now, I only remember the good parts. The parts I need. The parts that filled the void in my life, dreams painting streaks of color over my grey reality.

Fog gave me joy, hope, and love. Fog made my mother smile at me. Fog brought my brother back from the dead. Fog made me a man I could live with. I never wanted the drug… I *needed* it. I need it now.

Trembling, I lift my fingers to my mouth. This should be enough for one night, just enough to take the edge off. Then I'll start fresh tomorrow, and I'll fix this whole mess. I'll get—

"What are you doing?"

My head snaps up, and through the spaces between my foggy fingers, I see Gloria standing in the archway between the living room and the hall. Her eyes are wide with confusion and disbelief, staring back and forth between my fingers and my face. She's already heard about my past addiction, but she's never brought it up. Never asked any questions. I'd expected her to when we were lying in bed together, but the moment hadn't come.

It's here now. With me sitting on the floor in a pathetic heap, with silver powder coating my fingers, with salty tears staining my face. Now she can see me for who I truly am. She'd asked me before: *Who is Caolán O'Rourke?* This is her answer.

"What are you doing?" Gloria takes a step closer.

"I thought you were asleep," I mutter.

She stares at my hand. "Is that medicine?"

Gosh. I don't know if she's naïve or hopeful.

"You know it isn't medicine."

She shakes her head. "Why, Caolán?"

"I need it."

"No, you don't."

"You think it's easy to deal with all of this?"

"Do I look like I'm handling it any better?" She reaches up and clutches her necklace. I suddenly can't look at her, not while she's standing there holding my promise in her hands. "I'm hurt too," she says.

"You don't get it." I chuckle. "You're my wife. When you're hurt, I'm supposed to fix it. But what can I do when *I'm* the problem, Gloria? It's my job to protect you, but now you're hurt because of me." I lift my fingers to my face, brush the powder against my lips, but I never get to taste it.

Gloria rushes forward and slaps my hand away, shouting,

"I'm not hurt because of you, I'm hurt *with* you, Caolán!"

That snaps something inside of me. I feel my chest tighten, feel my eyes burn, feel the back of my throat clog with emotion. I want to shrivel away in shame, but I can't move because Gloria is right in front of me now. She drops to her knees, still holding my powdery hand, lacing her fingers between mine.

"Don't touch me," I whisper.

Don't let my sins taint you.

Gloria doesn't care. Doesn't shy away from the powder on my fingers. She holds my hand and pulls me into a hug, my face buried in the crook of her neck. "You're not alone, Caolán."

This ... Can't be real. She isn't disgusted by me—the *real* me. She isn't angry. She isn't running away. Not anymore.

For a second, I wonder if I've taken the fog and this is an illusion. My shoulders shake as I exhale. "Is this real?"

"It's real. I'm right here," Gloria says, tangling her free hand into my hair. "You're not imagining anything."

I don't know if that's good or bad. Gloria accepts me, but now she's seen me. Now she knows how awful I really am. How weak.

"I'm sorry," I say gently. "I messed up."

"I don't care."

"No... You don't get it, Gloria."

"I know you used to have an addiction. I saw what it did to you... In your bedroom."

I stiffen. She saw my secret—my own scar. Hers was

difficult to hide but mine was worse to see. It told more than the story of a broken person, it revealed every foul thing I'd hidden inside. All the reasons Gloria was too good for me. But she'd seen it, and it hadn't scared her away. Just as her scar hadn't scared me away.

"I know this was how you coped," Gloria continues. "I know it probably got worse after you were forced to kill your brother. I know it wasn't easy. I know you're ashamed of it." She squeezes me against her. "But I don't care."

Her words pull a sigh from my lips. She knows. And she doesn't care.

Gloria leans back and looks at me, smiling, almost laughing on her words. "We all mess up. It's okay, Caolán."

"The way I mess up is different."

"No, it isn't."

"Only one of us is a murderer."

She chews on her lower lip, glancing down like she doesn't know what to say. Then she takes a deep breath. Builds her confidence. "You know... Moses killed someone too."

Moses...?

"Gloria, I don't understand."

"He's in the Bible."

Oh, *that* Moses.

"He killed someone and tried to cover it up. But when he ran away, that's where he truly discovered his faith in God. Once he was away from his home and everything he'd ever known, God was able to mold him. Teach him. Nurture him into a man who would lead a nation."

"Why are you telling me this?"

"Because it doesn't matter how badly you mess up. God can still forgive you and use you for great things."

I look away. "You know I'm not a Christian, Gloria."

"Neither was I, until recently." She touches my cheek. "I discovered my faith in God after I ran away from home."

"So, are you like Moses?"

She laughs. "Only in my dreams."

The room folds into silence and we sit there staring back and forth, trying to find words to explain what the heck just happened. What the heck we're feeling right now.

"You were right," I whisper. "About the drugs getting worse after Aidan died."

She nods slowly.

I grew up as a mafia prince, I'd already been experimenting with drugs, alcohol, and women well before I killed my brother, but that changed everything. I didn't want beer after Aidan died. I didn't want a hooker. I didn't want weed or cocaine or heroin. I wanted fog. I *needed* fog after losing Aidan. It wasn't just his death that drove me to it, it was what happened right after.

When I dragged my brother's body before the leaders of the Pointer Finger and saw my mother's face, my world ended. But then she set it on fire when I tried to apologize.

"Mother," I'd said, staring at my bloody hands, watching them tremble. "I-I'm sorry. I killed him, but I didn't know—I didn't have a choice."

She'd made a noise that sounded like a sob, covering her

mouth with the back of her delicate hand. "My boy…"

I moved to hug her, but she shoved me away. At first, I thought it was because I was still covered in blood. *Aidan's* blood. But then she looked at me with hate in her eyes and yelled, "Why couldn't it have been you!?"

I blinked. "W-What?"

"Not Aidan," she whispered, crumbling to the floor. She crawled beside his body, touching his cold face, closing his dead eyes. "Not my Aidan."

I couldn't look at her, with her blonde hair sticking to her wet face, and her makeup smudged around her watery eyes. This woman who had been the image of perfection my entire life had been reduced to a sniveling mess. She wasn't my mother anymore.

I did that to her. I broke her.

"I'm sorry," I said softly. "I messed up."

She cut me off with a hiss. "The only thing you messed up was living."

That had been my great mistake. Living, when everyone else wanted me dead. My mother, my mafia leaders, my enemies.

Fog was the only thing that could get rid of the nightmares and the memories—the truth. Fog replaced Aidan's dead face with a pleasant, smiling one. Fog replaced my mother's tears with bright laughter. Fog washed away her vicious words and gave me whispers of love. A love I have never felt. Until now.

"I needed fog," I tell Gloria. I can't repeat all the details to her. Not now. I'm not ready. But I know from the look on her face that she understands. That she doesn't hold it against me.

"It's okay," she says. And then she adjusts to sit beside me on the floor, still holding my hand. She rests her head on my shoulder, and I lean back against the sofa. We sit there and we don't move.

"We have to go back home," I say.

"I know."

"I'll protect you when we get there."

She squeezes my hand. "I'll protect you too."

30

Ria

It's bright when I wake up. The moment is so unexpectedly peaceful that, for a few seconds, I have no idea where I am. Then I glance around at the fresh bedding and the splash of sunlight spilling in from the windows, and I remember everything. I remember that I'm in a home I have never been to. I remember that my childhood friend is dead, and that I blame myself for it. Then I remember Caolán, who blamed himself so deeply, he wanted to take drugs just to cope with the guilt.

I take a deep breath, bunching my blankets in my hands. *When did I get into bed?* My last memory is sitting beside Caolán on the living room floor. Squeezing his hand. Promising that I would protect him, however I could. Now I'm in a king-size bed, warm and cozy beneath the blankets.

Did Caolán carry me here?

I push the blankets back and pad across the floor to the door. When I open it, I see a man who is tall enough and muscular enough to definitely be a security guard. He frowns down at me, though I can hardly see his mouth behind his blonde beard.

"Mrs. O'Rourke, you're awake."

"Good morning," I say. "Where is Caolán?"

"Mr. O'Rourke has errands. He will be back shortly."

I've never seen this guard, so I don't know his name, but I doubt saying his name will make him surrender more information. He's planted his body in front of the door so that I can't see around him unless I step to the side and tilt my head. It's obvious he doesn't want me to leave.

"Can you take me to Caolán?"

"Is there an emergency?"

"N-No, I just—"

"Why don't you get cleaned up, Mrs. O'Rourke? The underboss will be back shortly."

"I wanted—"

"In the meantime," he says over me, "I'll have breakfast delivered to the room. Do you prefer white or wheat toast with your fruit and yogurt?"

For a moment, I don't know what to say. I've been in the mafia long enough to know when I'm being handled, but that doesn't mean I like it. I thought becoming Caolán's official wife would grant me a bit more freedom but that isn't the case at all. I've been confined to my bedroom and given little information. I can't leave without my husband's permission. Right now, the only choice I have is white or wheat toast with a breakfast I didn't pick. I've gone from being under the thumb of my parents to being controlled by my husband. What a life.

My will peters out with a tired sigh. "Wheat toast, please," I whisper, then I step back as the security guard reaches into the room, grabs the knob, and closes the door in my face. It locks with a soft *click*.

This is my life. This is the second chance I've agreed to walk back into, and I don't understand why. *Is this really what You want?* The prayer fills my head as I march to the bathroom, trying to make sense of things.

Do You want me to love Caolán?

To my shock, God answers me.

I want Caolán to know *My* love.

What does that have to do with me? Why can't he know You by reading the Bible like I've been doing?

Who taught you to read My Word?

Krista taught me. I'd learned about God throughout my years at a Christian private school, but it wasn't until a pretty blonde girl from college told me about Queen Esther that I truly began to understand God's Word, and once I understood, I began to see Him in His Word, and once I finally saw Him, I began to seek Him more. Not just in the Bible but in the world around me. I pray now without even thinking. I ask God for His opinion, for His guidance, for His help.

It happened naturally, without me thinking about it. Like a door suddenly opened, and God stepped through. That door was to my heart, and I hadn't known how long it'd been closed.

But there isn't a door over Caolán's heart, there's a bloody gate with an armed guard standing watch.

I can get past that guard. I can sneak through the gate. I think I already have. Moment by moment, Caolán and I have gotten closer to each other. He let me in, showed me a part of himself that no one else has seen. Last night brought us together. For the first time, I saw him as a man—a *person*—not a mafia boss, not a man I'd been assigned to marry. I cared because he was human. That human side of him planted seeds in my heart that have taken root and are growing into real feelings. What I have for Caolán isn't a childhood crush anymore, it's a real emotion. Something dangerously close to love. I've begun to fall for the former addict, for the troubled son, for the broken brother, and the imperfect husband. That's the Caolán who held my hand, interlaced his fingers with mine, and whispered a promise I know he'll keep. I promised him something too; to protect him. And now I know how I can.

If Krista can lead me to God's Word, then I can lead Caolán to the Lord, too.

That's what You want, isn't it? I ask Jesus. *You want Caolán to see Your love through me.*

God doesn't answer this time, but He doesn't need to. I've got the message loud and clear.

In the bathroom, I finish brushing my teeth and stare at my reflection in the mirror. My hair is wild, my face is speckled with blood and crust from sleep. My clothes are disheveled and stained with more blood. I look awful. I didn't clean myself up yesterday because I was overcome with grief, then I spent the night on the floor with Caolán. Neither of us were in good shape, but a momentary sense of relief budded between us when we admitted that we were in this together. Except, now it feels like we aren't anymore. I don't know where Caolán is, and I don't know when he'll be back. Right now, I'm alone.

I reach for the soap, but stop short, hand extended. It trembles as I stare at it, at the blood crusting each finger. It stains my palms, flakes away from the backs of my hands, it's even caked beneath my nails. Suddenly, I hear the sickening *pop!* of gunfire, and I see Tony's face in my mind. I see the hole in his temple, and his eyes rolled to the back of his head. The scene is a nightmare that I can't get rid of, but I can wash away all the blood.

The bathroom is stocked with supplies. Rich body butters, silky shampoos, and bubble bath that smells like roses and winter. I fill the tub with steaming water and sink beneath the soapy waves with a sigh, but I don't stop there. I go all the way under, submerging until every part of me is covered. I open my eyes and feel them burn. I don't know if it's from the hot water, the soap that floods into my pupils, or the tears I feel stinging the backs of my eyes. I scream beneath the water and bubbles gurgle up my throat, popping on the surface in a wordless cry.

My friend is dead. Tony is gone.

My heart hurts. My chest aches. The pain is almost unbearable, but none of this compares to what Tony felt in his last moments. He died in my arms, and the last thing I'd said to him was that he was a traitor. I never got to make up with him. Never got to tell him that I forgave him. That I understood he was just doing his job. Instead, I watched him choke on his blood and suffer a seizure.

Tony didn't even want to be in the mafia. Everything he did was to get what he needed to leave. I thought he'd gotten that already. Aoife gave him the connections he was missing, but instead of using them on himself, he helped me get away. And then he stayed to look after me. To make sure I didn't get myself killed in New York City.

He was wrong. I'm not the one who came back wrapped in plastic.

But ... why not? Why do I get to live, and Tony doesn't? Is it because God wants to use me to reach Caolán? Did Tony have to *die* for that to happen? How can I lead Caolán anywhere when I can't even find my way through this pain?

Finally, I can't take enough. I jerk forwards and burst from the water, sucking in deep gulps of air. Whatever the reason is for all of this, I won't find it in the bathtub, but I can't get myself to move. My limbs feel leaden, and my head grows cloudy. I'm exhausted, even though I just woke up, but I don't want to do something stupid like falling asleep in the water, so I drag myself from the tub and walk out the bathroom soaking wet.

Breakfast is set up in the middle of the room. There's a small round table with a bowl of pink yogurt and a cup of fruit beside it. Granola has been sprinkled onto the yogurt and a slice of wheat toast left on the side. There's also a glass of water with slices of lemon floating between the ice cubes. A very healthy, very nutritious breakfast that I did not ask for and do not want.

I walk past the display, vaguely wondering when someone

entered my room to leave it. My feet leave soapy footprints in the carpet, but I don't care. I just want to lie down and dream of a better version of this day—of this week. But sleep eludes me.

The blankets stick to my wet, naked body, making me feel hot all over. I toss and turn until I can't take it anymore, that's when I throw the covers back and decide to get dressed. There's a dresser beside the bathroom filled with clothes. They're all masculine. Boxers, slacks, shirts way too big for me, and an entire drawer filled with nothing but black ties.

I pull on a pair of boxers, black sweatpants, and a white t-shirt that drowns me. Then I wrap my afro curls in another t-shirt, use the shea butter bar in the bathroom to smooth down my edges, and fall back into bed, but it's wet from when I rolled around in it earlier, so I get back up and punch my pillows until my arms ache.

I am miserable.

"What am I supposed to do locked in here all day!?" I yell to no one.

The room is spacious with a desk, dresser, and two bedside tables. There's a walk-in closet that I haven't explored, so I stomp over and throw the doors open. There are suits hanging from shelves, a display of shined shoes, and a cart full of drawers which hold cufflinks and earplugs. Caolán wears silver gauges large enough to fit my finger through his lobe. I thought those were strange until he took his shirt off and I realized he also had a naval piercing. My cheeks blush when I think of the silver bar in his belly. That was the first time I'd ever seen one on a man. I don't know if it's okay for me to say I liked it. But I did. I *do*. Except I don't want to think fondly of Caolán right now because I'm angry, so I slam the jewelry drawers shut and stomp out of the closet.

I spend the next hour searching through his drawers, combing through the cabinets in the bathroom. When I'm finally finished in there, I go through the desk, but the drawers are locked, and I nearly drag the desk across the room trying to pry them open.

I don't know why I'm obsessed with finding things in here. Like I'm looking for secrets. But I can't help it. I'm locked inside. I feel like I'm going crazy.

When it becomes clear that I can't get the desk open, I go to the bedside tables and yank open the drawer on the first one. That's when I pause. There's a Bible inside. It's hardcover and in pristine condition which makes me doubt Caolán's ever read it. But just the fact that it's here warms me. I wonder if he has it out of habit or cultural obligation. The Irish mafia is very Catholic just as the Panthers are very Christian. My parents had me Christened and baptized, taught me that sex was for married people, and sent me to private Christian schools all my life. I'm positive Caolán had a similar upbringing, and I'm positive it also had little impact on his personal walk with God.

Reading the Bible doesn't make you a Christian, if that were the case, even Satan would still be saved—he quoted scripture to Jesus Christ in the New Testament.

What matters to God is your heart. God said as much when He sent the Prophet Samuel to anoint David as the next King of Israel. Vaguely, I remember the story from my Bible classes at school, and I flip through the pages to find it. Sure enough, my favorite verse is there in **I Samuel 16:7**, *But the Lord said to Samuel,* **"Don't judge by his appearance or height, for I have rejected him. The Lord doesn't see things the way you see them. People judge by outward appearance, but the Lord looks at the heart."*

Are You looking at my heart? I ask God. *Do You see how broken it is?*

I can't stop the tears that burn my eyes, in fact, I welcome them. Tony's death is all consuming. I don't know how I'm supposed to handle it. I don't know how I can ever get over the sorrow I feel. It's just as heavy as the guilt. I can only imagine how Caolán is dealing with this while I'm locked in this room. At least I can pray to God. At least I can hope.

The thought makes me gasp and I start flipping through the Bible again. It's literally *filled* with hope, but our hope has a purpose, just as much as our pain.

"There…" I whisper, scanning the words of **II Corinthians 7:10**. One of the few scriptures I memorized as a child. It was read at Bethany's funeral. I was just a kid at the time, but I wasn't too young to recognize the feeling I got when I heard our pastor say the Words aloud. I get the same feeling now. It's strong and fervent, like raw passion coursing through my body.

For the kind of sorrow God wants us to experience leads us away from sin and results in salvation, there's no regret for that kind of sorrow. But worldly sorrow, which lacks repentance, results in spiritual death.

I get it now. The sorrow I have inside might be awful, but as a Child of God, my sorrows can lead me right back to God—into His loving arms. That's what that strange feeling was all those years ago. It was *hope*. Hope that the pain of Bethany's death would not overtake me. Hope that God could take that pain and use it for my good.

Now, I hope that He can use it for Caolán's good too. For his repentance and salvation.

Will the sorrow of Tony's death finally open his eyes? I wonder. *Will Caolán finally be able to see the mafia as the monster it truly is?* A monster that will devour us both if we don't get out soon. It's already taken my sister and his brother. Now it's gotten my childhood friend and it's coming for us next. I can feel the whispers of death skirting over my goose pebbled skin. I can feel the hot breath of pain rolling over my neck. It's right behind us, and we can't outrun it. But Caolán doesn't know that. He'll never know it because he doesn't see the mafia the way I do, from a spiritual perspective. To him, this is simply our way of life. It's harder and more complicated but it's just life.

Not the life God wants for us...

"I have to show him that," I whisper. But I don't know how.

31

Caolán

I bring dinner when I get home. My day was crap; making arrangements for Tony's body, placing phone calls to people I hate. My mother, Gloria's mother, Billy (I don't hate him, but I hate the sound of his voice when I tell him the news, *"You really messed up, mate!"*) yeah, I know. I *know* I messed up, so I need to do everything perfectly from this point forward.

A guard I've hired is waiting outside my bedroom door when I get there. "How was she today?"

"Heard some yelling inside, but fine otherwise."

Yelling. Probably some crying too. All the things I would expect from my wife when she's trying to deal with so much. If I could make it better, I would. But the best I got is a nice hug and a bag of fried chicken.

It's not until this moment, as I'm unlocking the bedroom door, that I wonder if bringing her fried chicken for dinner is as offensive as her wearing bright green to the family brunch.

Oh well, it's too late now. The food is here, and fried

chicken is delicious. If she won't eat it, I certainly will.

Gloria is sitting on the bed when I walk inside, her head is down and she's hunched over a book, so intrigued that she doesn't look up when I first enter.

"Evening," I say softly. The room is dimly lit, she hasn't turned on a lamp, so the only light in the room comes from the streetlights outside. I can barely see her, but I leave her alone for now and begin setting out our dinner.

"I brought food," I say, trying to make conversation, but I cut the discussion short as I frown at the little round table in the middle of the room. It's still set for lunch. All the food I had delivered is untouched on a plate. Even the drinks are still full.

I blink at the sandwich, soup, and salad. "You haven't eaten."

Gloria doesn't reply, she keeps staring down at her book.

"Was something wrong?"

Again, no reply. I don't know why it takes so long for me to realize I'm being ignored but once the truth sinks in, a spark of anger flickers to life inside me.

"Gloria!" I bark.

She snaps her head up, eyes ablaze. "What?"

"Why are you acting like a child? Do not ignore me when I speak to you."

"Or what?" She rolls her eyes. "You'll lock me away again? Been there. Done that."

I see...

"You're upset with me."

"Where have you been all day?"

"Handling business."

She looks like she wants to throw that book at me. If I were any closer, I'm sure she'd try. I'm not sure if I would throw it back or not.

"And what am I supposed to do while you're handling business, Caolán?" She shifts so she's sitting on her knees, and I'm momentarily distracted by the fact that she's wearing my clothes. A large t-shirt and a pair of my sweatpants, even has on my socks that are way too big for her. She's got them rolled up twice, so they look puffy around her ankles.

"Umm," I lick my lips, and this somehow makes her angry.

"You're ridiculous," she mutters, slamming her book shut.

I'd be angry about her attitude, but as she climbs from the bed, I notice the cover of the book she'd been reading. It's the Bible. Suddenly, I understand her stress and anger. She needed me. But I'm glad she had God when I couldn't be here.

I wonder what God has to say about me when I *am* here. Is my presence in Gloria's life good or bad? Does He want her to leave me?

"I'm sorry," I say, motioning to the table. "Come have dinner. It's getting cold."

Gloria hesitates but eventually complies, her eyes never leaving my figure like a cat watching prey. She sits across from me with a flop and reaches forward; at first, I think she's grabbing the hot sauce I bought but her hands go past that to touch mine.

"Let's say grace," she mutters, staring at our interlocked

fingers.

I don't really want to. I don't even know why Gloria wants to, but I won't deny her this. She mentioned God yesterday, but that was an intense moment, so I didn't think too deeply on it. Now she's reading the Bible and asking to pray together. I don't know if she's become a convert or—actually, I don't know anything about Gloria's faith. To be honest, I barely know my wife at all.

We've been married for half her life, and I've spent years stalking her from the shadows, yet I can't tell you what she thinks of God.

Is this something she's using to cope with Anthony's death or is her faith real?

I squeeze her hands and take a seat. "Go ahead and pray."

She closes her eyes and bows her head; I follow suit, silently listening as she blesses the food and then asks God to forgive us for our sins and protect us as we go on about our way. I don't know if that's possible for me. The sins I've committed are nothing like the things Gloria has done—if she's done anything bad at all. She's an eighteen-year-old girl and the worst thing I think she's done is marry me.

I'm 33 years old, 15 years older than my wife. I married her when she was a child—without hesitation. While I never touched her until she was of age, I know what I did was wrong. I played a role in snatching Gloria's childhood away. Even if God does forgive me for that, I don't think I can forgive myself.

"Aren't you hungry?" Gloria asks.

I look up, shocked to see that she's already tucked into the food. There's a french fry in her mouth now and a smear of grease along her chin.

I smile. "Yes, I'm hungry."

"The chicken is good."

"Of course, it is. I always stop at this place when I'm in town."

"Where is this place?" Gloria looks around.

"We're in Chicago. At a house I keep for—" I pause, eyes growing large. I stopped myself before the words slipped out, but the way Gloria blanches lets me know I didn't have to say it aloud. She may be eighteen, but she isn't stupid.

"A house you keep for whores," she says plainly.

I nod. "Yes. But I haven't been here in a while."

"How long?"

"A month."

She clenches her jaw.

"The last time I was here, I only—"

"Was Aoife ever here?" she cuts me off.

I do not want to answer that question, but I nod anyway, hating myself even more when Gloria stiffens and then slowly looks around, like she's really seeing the room for the first time. The floor, the bed, the walls, her eyes trace every surface, imagining the women and the things I did with them.

"Thirty days ago, you were here with another woman."

"Gloria—"

"You've had my best friend here. In this house. In the bed I slept in last night."

I set down my food. "You were a child, darling. And I was a different man before you came of age."

She's still a child now. The way she can't even look at me, how her cheeks glow with blush as she thinks of all the things I've done. And quietly wonders if I'll do them with her. She yells when she gets angry. She acts out of impulse. She thinks she's much stronger than she actually is. In so many ways, my wife is still a child, but I've made her a woman in more ways than one.

"Gloria," I say softly, "are you jealous?"

She nearly combusts. "Jealous!? Is that what you think—"

"I don't like the thought of sharing you, either."

That shuts her up. She opens her mouth and then closes it, staring at me through wide eyes.

"I did not honor my vows when you were young." I lean across the table and place my hand over hers. "But you're a woman now."

She lowers her gaze to our hands, her eyes fluttering shut for just a moment.

"Say the word and I'll never touch another woman again."

Honestly, that's a given when you're married, but I want to hear Gloria say it. I'd like to know that she actually wants me to herself. After all the heavy conversation we've had of late, her words will be a delight to hear, but she doesn't give them. She presses her lips into a hard line and stares at the table.

My initial reaction is anger, but I see the hesitation on her face, and I realize she's embarrassed.

"Gloria," I say, "I don't want you to ever look at another

man again. I don't want you to think about men, dream about men, or even stand in the same room as other men. That's how much I want you to myself."

"Is that why you locked me away today?" She pulls her hand back into her lap and I take a big fat breath, filling my lungs until my chest hurts and then slowly releasing it. Honestly, fighting with my wife is like fighting with a teenager.

Oh wait...

"Are you going to answer?" She folds her arms like a child.

For half a second, I debate treating her like a child; yanking her pants down and spanking her bare bottom, but I change my mind and give her what she wants.

"I told you I had business to deal with, darling."

"I don't like being kept in the dark."

"There are some things you don't need to know in this business."

"We said we were going through this together, Key."

I pause, even suck in a little gasp. She just gave me a nickname. I want to smile. I want to spank her for a different reason now, but I keep my hands to myself and raise my eyebrows at her. She doesn't seem to notice what she just did, like the nickname means nothing.

"Yes, we're going through this together," I explain, "but that doesn't mean—"

"I just want to know why you were gone all day."

"You don't need to know everything." *What part of this does she not understand?* "I had to check Anthony's dead body," I say angrily, "I had to make sure the doctor rebuilt his face, so he still looks like himself. I had to call your family and report his death, then I had to call his family to deliver the news and my condolences. Finally, I called *my* family to prepare them for what may come. Would you have liked to help me with all of that?" I stand, running my hand through my hair. "Or would you have liked to call my bank to wire money to Serena Vittore so I could cover the lump sum she lost when I gave free fog to Conrad Jäger? Maybe you think you could have helped me speak to Mikhail Volkov and thank him for taking care of your friend from New York. Would you have liked that, Gloria?"

She stands too; eyebrows flattened across her forehead. "I would have liked to know, Caolán. Is that a crime?"

"I kept you here to be *safe*."

"You locked me up until you were ready to be a husband! There's a difference." She turns to walk away, but I dash around the table and grab her by the elbow, yanking her back to face me.

"Protecting you is part of my job as your husband. You're the one who ran away, now let me clean up your mess the best way I can. If that means locking you away so you don't screw up again, then so be it. You don't have to like it, but you don't get to pick a fight with me over it either."

"So, what should I do?" she sneers. "Enjoy my solitude in your whorehouse?"

"You can start by saying thank you." I shove her away and she trips a few steps back until she bumps into the edge of the bed.

"You're ridiculous."

"And you're a child." I loosen my tie. "I don't have time for your attitude. If you're going to act like this, then you can have the room to yourself until you learn to be more grateful."

Her eyes enlarge, but if she has anything to say back, I don't get to hear it as I turn and enter the bathroom. I close the door behind me just as she starts to speak. Whatever. We can talk once I'm done, hopefully, she'll be easier to deal with by then.

32

Ria

There are no words in my head right now. I watch Caolán walk away from me, and mentally scrape my brain for a response, but nothing comes until he reaches the door.

I bare my teeth and snarl, "Who do you—"

The door closes.

After everything I've done for him. When he held out his hand in my bedroom, I took it. When he said, *let's go*, I didn't fight him. When he put me on a plane, I didn't argue. I peacefully gave him the second chance he asked for, even though it cost the life of my childhood friend. Even though it brought me to my knees with grief. Even though it caused me to question everything I know. I did it for Caolán.

And this is the thanks I get. As soon as I demand to be treated as an adult, as his *equal*, he insults me and locks me away again.

I won't have it.

With a grunt, I storm around the little table and cross the

room. At the bathroom door, I can hear the shower water running, *this* close, I can even feel the heat of the steam trapped inside. I only hesitate for a moment, wondering what will come of this. Wondering if maybe Caolán is right. Am I overreacting? Am I behaving like a child? *Is he behaving like a loving husband?* I counter, and then I shake my head before I change my mind.

The bathroom door is heavy, but I swing it open with one arm and stomp inside. The room is covered in steam, so I don't see Caolán's pile of clothes until they're right in front of me, folded neatly beside the shower door. I can see his frame behind the distorted glass, moving beneath the hot water. It dawns on me then, that he doesn't know I'm inside. I could turn around and walk out, avoid another argument. But I don't.

I snatch open the foggy shower door and savor the momentary shock that crosses my husband's face. For a single second, he looks beautiful. Standing in the steamy little room, his head tilted back, carmine hair pushed from his face, blue eyes blinking away droplets of hot water. He looks like a model, and I wish I could hold that picture of him in my mind forever. Then he feels the slap of cool air when I snatch the door open, and the moment is gone.

Caolán snaps his gaze to me, turning his head so fast, water flicks from the strands of his hair. He is utterly shocked. Eyes wide, brows furrowed, like he never thought I would confront him. Not like this. Not while he was naked and vulnerable in the shower.

Angrily, I lift my hand and wipe the shock off his face. The slap echoes through the room, both of us momentarily stunned. I hadn't expected to hit him, but I acted without thinking. And now it's Caolán's turn to respond.

He moves too fast for me to comprehend what's happening. Before I know it, his large hand clamps down on my arm, and he snatches me *into* the shower. My back hits the wall with a thud, and I yelp, but it's cut off as his hands wrap around my throat.

He only squeezes for a second. Like a scream, his anger is there and gone. We're left staring at each other, both of us rapidly blinking away the running water, trying to see each other's face, trying to look into each other's eyes. Clouds of steam puff around us, fogging my view of Caolán's face, but even through the haze, I can find him. I can *feel* his anger in the gentle grip he uses to hold me. How strange… to recognize rage through peace.

He wants to hurt me. This man I've married. He wants to cause me pain. But he doesn't.

"*Why?*" he grates out, voice like a withheld scream. "Why did you hit me?"

"Why didn't you hit back?" I challenge.

"Do you want me to?" He tightens his grip just a bit, enough to let me know that he could. That he's willing. I can see the hate in his eyes, the bottlenecked anger that he's itching to let out. But instead of squeezing the life out of me, he leans forward and presses his lips against mine.

The kiss is a gasp and then a hiss, like relief and pain wrapped into one. It burns away the anger and leaves only the hate—hate I recognize. Not for each other, but for the world around us. Caolán has never hated me. He has never hated this marriage. He has hated his loss of control.

He was forced into this as much as I was. Then I forced him to chase me down when I ran away. And now I'm forcing him to navigate the complicated planes of marriage, to find love in the chaos between us. We grasp something like it, something close enough to love that we don't see the tendrils of darkness it drags into the room behind it.

The creature is called lust. I hear its whispers in the groan that falls from Caolán's mouth, I hear its wail in my own whimper when he peels my wet shirt from my body. I feel its talons scraping along my flesh when I notice my husband's desire pressed against my inner thigh.

I pull away, breathing heavily, but Caolán holds me close, pressed against the wet wall. "Stop bullying me," he murmurs, kissing me again.

The request leaves me stunned. In what world could a mafia underboss feel bullied by an eighteen-year-old girl? The thought is unfathomable; I've been locked in this room all day; I've been at the mercy of someone else my entire life. But then I think of everything Caolán's done for me, and I finally see what he means. I feel what he feels.

He trusted me and I ran. He tracked me down and I blamed him for the mess I created. He tried to keep me safe, and I slapped him for it. Maybe his methods weren't right, but he's always done the best he could. He's always done things the only way he knew how. I can't fault him for trying. He's the only one in my life who ever has.

"Caolán," I whisper.

He's busy fighting with the pair of his boxers I've got on. He can't just rip them away like he did with my own underwear, so his hands remain busy while his gaze lifts to meet mine.

That's when he stops.

"This—This isn't punishment for anything, Gloria."

"I know."

I think of the hatred I saw in his eyes, blue eyes like his mother's. It almost makes me shiver.

"I would never hurt you," Caolán says. "Even if you wanted me to hit you back. I wouldn't."

I know he wouldn't. I don't know why I challenged him to, but I guess this chaos has brought out the worst in both of us. He didn't ask for a runaway Christian bride, and I didn't ask for a mafia boss with mommy issues, but here we are. A little madness. A little mercy.

"I know you'd never hurt me," I say softly.

Caolán reaches up and strokes my cheek, then trails his hand along my scar, down to my jaw, whispering over my throat. Moments earlier, he'd had his fingers wrapped around my neck but now he looks ashamed of the memory.

"Are you afraid?" he says softly.

Do I fear my own husband? No. But I fear the world around us. I fear the chaos we're living through. I fear what we could become if we don't slow down. If we don't think about the decisions we make. If we allow the darkness around us to consume our hearts and minds and our marriage too.

God wants me to lead Caolán into His presence. I can't do that if I'm slapping him around. I can't do that if every conversation turns into a fight which turns into sex on the floor or in the shower or God knows where else. We can't even communicate properly, let alone live as husband and wife. There is so much we need to fix, and it starts here.

"Yes," I admit, nodding. "I'm afraid, Caolán."

He studies me for a long moment, like he's trying to decide what to do next. I'm in his arms, naked and completely vulnerable. If he wants to have sex, I'll give that to him. If he wants to walk away, I'll accept that too. But he shocks me by doing neither.

Caolán chooses to ignore the lust and the anger around us and pulls me into his chest for a hug. He chooses to give me love.

I crumple against him, choking on my sobs and the shower water and my pain too. I don't know if it's the grief of Tony's death or the fear of returning home or my guilt for mistreating Caolán, but everything collides into one emotional storm I cannot control. All I can do is cling to my husband and pray that he makes it better.

"I'm sorry," he mutters, stroking my puffy hair. "I'm so sorry, Gloria."

I'm sorry too, but I can't get it together enough to tell him that, so I just nod and sniffle.

"This world isn't perfect. I'm not perfect," he says, hugging me so tightly, I feel his heart beating against my own. "But if we try, we can make it bearable."

I nod again. I thought we'd agreed to try last night when we sobbed on the floor and promised to protect each other, but that had been a shallow, spur-of-the-moment thing. This was the real test. The fight that tore the veil of emotions away from our faces and revealed our true selves. It opened our eyes and made us take a hard look at each other. We were experiencing the same pain, but we weren't sharing it. We weren't carrying each other's burdens; we were tossing them back and forth and blaming each other for it.

Now, we're finally on level ground. Now, we can start over and build something together.

A scripture drifts into my mind. *Everyone who hears these words of mine and puts them into practice is like a wise man who built his home on the rock...* Our rock is Christ. I have to lead Caolán there, and I will. It starts here.

"Let's start over," I whisper, pulling back enough to look up into his eyes. "Whatever happens when we return to California, we face it together, Caolán."

He holds my face in both his hands. "Promise me you'll always trust me, Gloria. No matter what happens."

I nod slowly.

He kisses me, long and deep, and when he pulls back, he whispers against my lips, "All I ask is that you don't judge me when it's over."

33

Caolán

We needed this trip. I hate to admit it, but Gloria's great escape saved our marriage. I thought I had to teach her how to be a proper mafia wife. I thought I had to break her will and rebuild her to my liking. But I was wrong. All I needed to do was accept that she was her own person, as imperfect as *me*. All *we* needed to do was get away from all the noise, to find each other in the chaos, and create our own peace.

We did that. In the shower, after viciously fighting, baring our teeth at each other, we set aside the boxing gloves and learned to talk. Learned to trust. Learned to forgive and give second chances.

I didn't touch her after I turned off the shower water. I wanted to, more than anything, but Gloria wasn't in any state to even think about sex that night. I cleaned her off, rubbed oil over her soft skin, and then dressed her in another of my t-shirts. She fell asleep beside me, and I pretended I didn't miss her while she slept. I pretended I wasn't nervous when she woke the next morning. I pretended the conversation between us over breakfast wasn't awkward.

"Nice weather," she'd said.

"Yeah."

"The raspberry jam is good."

"It's my favorite. Because it's red. Like blood."

She had stared at me, fiddling with her toast, not really sure how to respond. So I took the chance to dismiss myself and grab a delivery at the door. I'd arranged for someone to bring clothes for her, so it was good timing. While Gloria dressed, I called the airport and made sure we were set to fly out, by the time I returned to our bedroom, she was dressed and ready to go, the awkward exchange forgotten.

Gloria naps throughout the plane ride, which works well enough for me. I have plenty of business to sort out while she drools on the armrest of her leather chair. My phone is bursting with messages and missed calls from my family and other members of the Hand. Even Tadhg called me.

We're in trouble... the thought drifts through my head as the plane touches down. It's solidified by the sight of my family waiting at the end of the runway. They have never cared when I left or returned. But now they're all here to greet me. To greet *us*. I glance down at Gloria who is stretching and groaning, her arms high above her head. When she sees me watching, she smiles and starts packing her stuff away. She'd been reading her Bible again.

I don't know what's up with that lately, but I don't question it. Whatever helps her cope. Whatever makes her stronger.

Whatever keeps our marriage peaceful. I have a feeling she's going to need her faith as the plane halts and the small crew works to lower the stairs and open the doors.

Mother is the first to greet me with a grand smile and a kiss on both cheeks. "You're back! Welcome, welcome!" She moves to Gloria and holds her at arm's length. "Let me look at you! Oh my, you're glowing! So, the honeymoon was a success." She looks back at me, blonde brows lifted above her sunglasses. It's frigid out but the sun is bright enough that I squint against it to nod back at her.

"Success," I mumble.

"Good! We'll have you checked out before lunch," she says to Gloria which makes me freeze.

"What?" I turn back around, and my mother waves me off.

"We need an heir, Caolán. A pregnancy test should be administered as soon as possible."

"No, it shouldn't." I reach for Gloria's hand to drag her away, but Mother takes her other hand and holds her in place.

"Caolán—"

"Our private lives are not a spectacle, Mother. We're not taking the test."

"Your lives are not your own." The voice belongs to my father, a sound so foreign it halts everything and we all blink at him in silence, even Nolan stares from beside the door. Charles O'Rourke adjusts his tie and then stuffs his oversized hands into his pockets. "You got away with your little honeymoon," he says, "or whatever that was. But this is serious. Take the test, Caolán."

"I'll take it," Gloria says, and when I turn to protest, she squeezes my hand and gives me a stern look, one that says, *trust me*.

I can't deny her request after last night, so I give in with a sigh. "I'll be right there beside you," I say, but my mother interrupts again.

"We have a family meeting."

"It can wait."

"It's urgent," she insists.

"Gloria *is* my family," I growl. "I'm not leaving—"

"I'll be fine." She wraps her arms around my middle and hugs me. "It's just a little test. I'll be done before your meeting."

Everyone watches me, waiting for a response, but Gloria is the only one I care about. I look down at her and cup her face, kissing her until she moans into my mouth. I hear my father clear his throat behind me, even Aifric shifts her weight from one foot to the other. But I ignore them both and pull away to whisper to my wife, "If you need anything—"

"I'll be fine," she insists.

I nod and peck her forehead once more, then I look up at my mother who is studying me sharply. Her eyes narrow when Gloria pulls away. "Well, how sweet."

"Yeah," I grunt.

Quinn meets us in the back entrance to the house, immediately whisking Gloria away. I resist the urge to watch her go. That display of passion was more than enough to tell my family what she means to me, I can't let them catch me wearing puppy dog eyes too. So I keep my face blank when we enter the conference room, though it's not easy to pretend I'm not nervous by the presence of every boss and underboss of each Finger in the room.

Clan O'Connor, Clan Fitzpatrick, Clan Cullen, Clan Hughes, and now Clan O'Rourke are all present. My family is the only one with more than two members in attendance, probably because we are the issue here. But Clan Fitzpatrick is the only one with just *one* representative. As I glance around the room, I don't see Tadhg, the underboss of the Pointer Finger. His father is here, staring at me with a bored, blank face, unimpressed with the up-jumped hitman who has caused him so much trouble.

I flick my eyes to my mother who busies herself with taking a seat beside my father. For the first time, she is quiet, keeping her eyes lowered to the table, keeping her mouth shut like she knows her place for once.

She's afraid. How could she not be? My family is sitting at our own table across from a display of Clansmen who glare at us like we're being presented for a trial. Awaiting judgment. No one speaks. I don't even breathe as I wait for something to happen.

Finally, after an agonizing silence, Balor Fitzpatrick rises from his chair. He unbuttons his suit jacket and then leans across the table, so it falls open to reveal the guns strapped under his armpits. There's also a knife sheathed on his right hip.

"Caolán O'Rourke." His voice is rich and deep, a hollow

beat that clangs against my skull, echoing around the room.

I stand and incline my head, placing a fist to my heart. The Hand's salute; all five fingers united as one, forming a unified weapon and a solid defense.

"Honored Fitzpatrick," I say, embarrassed by how small my voice is.

Balor stares at me for a long time, blinking only once while I fidget and squirm. "How was your honeymoon?"

"Nice."

"Did you produce an heir?"

"We will find out momentarily."

"Yes, my son will deliver the report shortly."

His son? I hold my breath, knowing I can't react. That's what Balor is looking for, any sign of concern. I *am* concerned. I'm outraged because his son is Tadhg who isn't here right now. He's with my wife alone. Administering a pregnancy test.

Who knows what he's really doing?

I resist the urge to look back at my mother. She did this. Whether it was her idea or not is irrelevant to me, I know she wanted it to happen. She lives to please Clan Fitzpatrick, to kiss up to the ones she believes she should have married into. I can imagine the proud look on her face now, gazing up at Balor, the man she should have married. He is larger than my father, a great bear that seems to swallow up more room than any other man around him. The other Clan bosses seem to shrink each time he moves, subconsciously inching to the side, moving out of his way. They do it without thinking, making room for a king. And now I stand before that king, awaiting his judgment.

"I can only hope the result is pleasing to us all," I mutter.

"Clan O'Rourke is long overdue for a son." Balor waves his right hand and the ring on his pointer finger catches the light for a moment. There's a ring on the respective finger of each Clan leader's hand. I imagine my father's black stone ring looking very dull in comparison to Balor's glittering emerald. *Green*, I almost roll my eyes.

"Whatever the results may be," Balor says, "you have plenty of time now to make as many sons as we need. Because we are at war."

"War?"

He looks at me like I'm stupid. "You returned with the body of a Panther. Do you think the Jacksons will let that slide?"

"I did not kill him myself."

"Anthony Jones was the son of a Panther General," Balor says, "do you believe he will take kindly to his son being collateral damage in whatever foolishness you caused in New York?"

I bite my lip and shake my head.

Balor growls, "*Speak*, boy."

"No, Honored Fitzpatrick, I do not believe he will take kindly to that suggestion."

"The death of Anthony Jones is a serious blow. The Jacksons want reparations."

"I will pay—"

"They do not want *money!*" Balor roars, spittle flying from his mouth. He switches to Irish to finish his statement, like the

English words can't find him in his rage. "They want blood, boy. Do you understand? An eye for an eye." He looks over my shoulder and I turn to find Nolan sitting with his hands clasped in front of him, shoulders bunched like he's uncomfortable.

"No..." I whisper. The Jacksons want *Nolan's* head? That can't be right. "He is a prince, not a General's son."

Balor grunts—I think it's a laugh. "They have given us a choice. Nolan's head or the head of William O'Rourke."

Billy... My cousin. My *favorite* cousin. The only one who's been by my side through all of this. The only one I trust as much as I trust Gloria now. Billy has helped me with kills, helped me dismember bodies, gave me fog when I knew I didn't need it, and stayed with me when I couldn't walk home. He's cleaned me up, checked me into rehab, took care of Nolan when I couldn't. Now they want me to kill him.

"I won't," I whisper, and Balor grunts again. This time, I know it's a laugh.

"If we do not produce a head, then we will go to war and lose far more than a prince or a General's son." His nostrils flare. "You have a week to choose. I'll leave it to you."

My choice... But how can I pick between two brothers? Nolan, my brother of flesh, and Billy, my brother in blood.

Balor holds out his hand. "Come here, boy."

I have no choice but to move, walking stiffly to the middle of the conference room to stand before him. He's large enough to extend his arm across the table between us, so his hand hangs in the air. I take it, bow my head, and press my lips to the cold ring on his Pointer Finger.

"Where the Pointer leads, I follow," I mutter against his hand, as expected.

Balor pulls his fingers away and pats my bowed head like a child. "Fix this, Caolán. I know it is a hard decision, but you've done it once before. You can do it again."

He's right. The last time I had a choice, I killed my own brother. Now they want me to choose between my last living brother or my favorite cousin.

But this time is different. This time, I have more to live for than the blank promise of a future. I have a wife who thinks I'm a better man than when I met her. I have a fragile dream of a life of peace. I don't want to murder another member of my family to attain it. But I can't say that while I stand in the room with my Clan leaders. If I do, I'll bring death to my doorstep before the night is up.

"I will get the matter done," I promise, then I straighten and dismiss myself, ignoring the overwhelming silence I hear over my shoulder. I need to find Gloria; there's no time to worry about anything else. While I was in that meeting, she was alone with Tadhg. Only God knows what he's done with her. Only God could keep her safe from him.

Desperately, I find myself praying as I sprint down the halls of my home, *this* close to shouting my wife's name and kicking in doors to find her. *Please*—please—*help her. I don't deserve anything from You, but she's innocent. She's good.*

Only *I* am good.

The Voice is quite but firm, so shocking that it pulls me to a halt for more than one reason. Did God just speak to me? And ... What do His words mean?

I don't get it, I don't understand why that would be His response, of all the things He could tell my hopeful heart in that moment. He says He's the only good thing in this world.

Does that mean Gloria isn't good? That all her innocence means nothing?

The sound of laughter shatters my thoughts. I blink at the door I've stopped in front of. The voice was Gloria's... She laughs again and I barrel *through* the door like I've lost my mind, only to feel embarrassed when I see her staring at me. She's sitting at a table with a lunch display set out before her, wearing a cozy winter dress with her hair pulled back into a massive puff of dark coils. Her scar is there for everyone to see, but that doesn't seem to bother her one bit. I would say she looks beautiful, but the truth is that she looks so frightened she's actually clutching her necklace. The one I gave her.

"Gloria," I whisper.

"I assume the meeting is over?"

My body goes rigid.

Tadhg sits beside my wife at the lunch table. Miniature sandwiches, sliced fruit, a platter of vegetables and an assortment of dips, cured meats, hard cheeses, and a bottle of wine. Only Tadhg has a glass, Gloria has seltzer water in a flute. It looks fancy with cranberries floating in it. But she isn't drinking or eating right now, she's still staring at me, that scared look in her eye. Not because of Tadhg who looks perfectly calm and is smiling at me like an old friend. She looks frightened because I nearly took the door off its hinges coming through the room.

I don't care about the stupid door. I care about my cousin who has no business being left alone with my wife.

"What are you doing here?" I step closer to the table.

Tadhg picks up a sandwich. "Having lunch. You two had quite a day, I thought Ria might need to relax."

I've never liked her nickname, but it sounds even worse coming from Tadhg's lips which stretch and pull into an ugly smirk as he says, "We had a lovely time with the test. Ria deserved a break afterward."

"Did he touch you?" I ask Gloria.

She shakes her head, but it's Tadhg who answers, "I used gloves, Caolán, don't worry. I didn't want to get blood everywhere."

Blood… I close my eyes with a sigh, feeling every muscle in my body unwind and relax. He administered a blood test. In my twisted mind, Gloria lifted her dress and peed on a stick Tadhg held between her legs with his own hands. He's vile enough to do that, just to piss me off. But that isn't what happened.

"You're okay," I say, though the statement is more to myself than Gloria, but she nods anyway.

"I'm fine, Key."

The nickname makes me close my eyes, but only for a second. So long as Tadhg is here, our peace won't last long.

"I'm sure you have other business, Tadhg."

He looks like he wants to laugh. "Putting me out already?"

"I have a busy schedule."

"Don't mind me. I'm fine here with Ria." He flicks his wrist, shooing me away. "I'm sure the Hand's Vampire is very busy these days."

Gloria stares between us which makes Tadhg chuckle.

"Did you know that was what we called him back in the day?" He grins wide enough for me to see his white teeth. "That's how much blood he shed for us. Like he was addicted to it."

"I think you should leave now," I say softly, but Tadhg doesn't move. He just keeps digging the knife in, stabbing the wound, killing me over and over. If I had a coffin, he would open it and spit on my corpse.

"I bet he doesn't remember those days," Tadhg says, and Gloria listens with wide eyes. "Caolán was so cracked out, I'm sure he's missing *years* from his memories." He shakes his head. "Fog will do that to you."

"I remember ending a war when you couldn't," I growl. "Fog didn't take that from me."

Tadhg works his jaw like he wants to speak, but I don't give him the chance to.

"I remember doing what you couldn't. And I've got to do it again."

He stands, but I talk right over him.

"I was just in a meeting with your father. It seems he trusts me with yet another war. While you sit here and enjoy lunch."

Never mind that this war is my fault. Never mind that my own mother wanted me dead instead of Aidan in the last war.

The point is that I'm doing something, and Tadhg is not.

His face goes from ghostly pale to crimson red, but when he speaks, his voice is oddly calm. "Well, here I thought the Vampire's fangs had grown dull over the years. But I see they're as sharp as ever." He straightens his tie. "What happens when your fangs get too sharp?"

I don't have a reply, but something tells me Tadhg isn't looking for one. He holds my gaze as he steps around the table, muttering the answer to his question as he passes by.

"They have to be removed."

I stand there until I hear the door close behind him and hear his footsteps fade down the hall. Then I remain there, staring at Gloria, wondering if I've just put my wife in more danger.

She gets up and practically runs to me, hugging me tightly, but all the passion I had before is gone. I stand there like a statue, my arms at my sides, neither touching Gloria nor pushing her away. I'm numb now, shocked into silence. There is so much going on, so much I can't control and don't understand. We got Anthony killed. They want Billy's head for it. Does Gloria know what her family has proposed? Will they retaliate if I don't give them what they want in a week?

To top it all off, I've just pissed off Tadhg for no reason.

My breath leaves me in a long exhale. I feel Gloria squeeze me even tighter. She stays by my side when we finally leave that room, holding my hand, sitting close to me in the car. She doesn't question where we're going, I think she's just glad we're out of the house. I can't stay there right now, not with my traitorous family and not in my awful bedroom. Gloria would have endless nightmares if I tried to take her there. So, we hunker down in an apartment I keep for myself. Yes, it's another place I've taken women to, but Gloria doesn't make a scene about it this time. She doesn't do anything except hold on to me, like she's afraid I'll fall apart if her hand isn't clasped in my own.

She orders food and we eat together. She makes conversation as we clean up, washing dishes side by side. She runs a bath and leaves the door open so she can hear me moving around in the room. I know she's worried about me, but I'm not like her. I don't run away when I'm upset. Right now, I'm quiet because I'm trying to solve this issue. I'm trying to think of what I can do to make this better. To fix it. But nothing comes to mind.

That night, Gloria reaches for me in bed. Trying to fix me the only way she knows how. I let her kiss me, let her whisper that she's here with me—that she's here *for* me. She wants me to use her, to bury my confusion and anger in her. I want to. Normally, I would without question. But I just can't tonight. I can't give her what she wants or needs, and it makes a small part of me ache inside.

I feel awful as Gloria stares at the limp muscle between my legs, the tips of her ears burning in shame. I know she's blaming herself. Convinced that this is her fault. She couldn't bring out any desire or passion in me. She wasn't enough for her own husband. But that's not it.

I'm sorry, the words are on the edge of my tongue, but I don't say them as she retracts her small hands from my body and settles in the blankets. Now is the time to comfort her, to tell her I don't need sex, I just need her. But I don't say that. I keep quiet as she lays on her side, I remain silent as she leaves me in the dark to drift into her dreams. I don't say a word because if I do, then I'll have to admit that the problem is me. *I messed up*, and I don't think I can fix it.

34

Caolán

The next day, I crawl out of bed like a thief sneaking away, holding my breath as I stare at my sleeping wife. She doesn't stir or move as I replace the blankets, so I slip into the bathroom and get myself cleaned up in peace. She rolls over when I tiptoe through the room, but her eyes remain shut. I'm not avoiding her, despite our awkward night, but I also have no idea what to say right now so I exhale a breath of relief when I step into the hall alone. There are a hundred things I need to take care of; Gloria will have to wait today.

Should I feel guilty about locking her away again? After our last blowout, yeah, I should. But I don't. We are days away from war, this is the safest place my wife could be. My only regret is not talking to her about it. But how do I explain that her family wants me to kill my own kin to make up for Anthony's death? I have no idea how Gloria will feel about any of this, but I know she won't like that I've kept it from her.

She can wait, I tell myself as I climb into my car. I have no driver today—I don't trust anyone and the only guy I'd give the job to is nowhere to be found. Not by outsiders at least. I know where he's at, and I know why he's gone quiet. He's hiding from me because I'm supposed to kill him.

Billy O'Rourke has a handful of places he could hide, but I know about each one. At least, I think I do. As teenagers we made a promise to be there for each other; in the mafia, we call it the Shadow's Vow. If Billy dies, I will find and bury his remains. If there is ever a hit placed on him, I will enforce it. That means I am his personal reaper.

Billy knows I'm coming, I'm sure he's just biding his time.

I spend the morning checking every safe house, apartment, and bar I know Billy frequents, crossing them off my list. By the time my stomach growls, I only have three locations left. With the list narrowed down, I know exactly where to find him, so I head straight there and hope he knows I'm not hostile.

The house looks like a midwestern suburb, complete with a white picket fence and a tulip garden out front, dead from the slow, crawling winter. Billy bought the house in his early 20s, the very first place he ever owned. It was a piece of garbage back then, but he made it a personal project; buying supplies and restoring it by hand whenever he had free time. He never took women here. Never used it to push drugs. Never stopped by unless it was to repaint the windowsills or water his plants. I don't know what he planned to do with it, he never told me, but I had my guesses. It was the home he wished he could have if he didn't have to murder people for a living. As much as Billy likes blood, he's still a human being like me. And you. There's a part of him that hates himself as much as we all do. A part of him that wonders what life would be like in a different color, a brighter shade of red.

I don't bother knocking because I know he won't answer, so I just punch in the security code I have memorized and let myself in. The inside is dim, but I hear soft chatter toward the back. My footsteps feel loud as I pass through the kitchen, but the voices never waver. *Do they know I'm here?* I find my answer when I push open the bedroom door and come face to face with the barrel of a gun.

Billy is at the other end, the television on beside him, volume turned down low. "'Bout time you showed up, mate," he drawls, lowering the gun. "Never knew Death would take so long."

I push the gun aside. "You know I haven't come to kill you."

"Why not? I heard the choice was me or Nolan. Aunt Aifric will never let you near him. I'm as good as dead."

"Is that what you really think?"

His expression slices through me, eyes narrowed, mouth pinched. When he speaks, I catch flashes of his split tongue, and in my head, I see a snake hissing at me. "You're my reaper. It's your job to kill me—that's the vow we made. I didn't even hear about the mark on my head from you. Someone else told me." His nostrils flare. "Because you were too busy."

"That isn't fair."

"Yeah," he laughs mirthlessly, "it really isn't."

"Billy—"

"The Hand's got a grip on you." He steps back and grins, scratching his temple with the tip of his gun. "Of course they do. You're their favorite errand boy. *Prince Caolán*, went from a bloody hitman to an underboss." He chuckles. "Mounted the world and then his wife."

I don't realize I've moved until Billy's head whips back and blood spurts into the air. He stumbles into his desk chair, grabbing the back for support, but it doesn't help him. Momentum takes him backwards to the floor, and he lands with a thud and a groan, the gun spilling across the carpet.

Billy touches his nose. "You broke it."

I shake out my hand. "You deserve it."

"Don't let me die ugly."

I laugh. "Can't help that, mate."

"You really gonna do it?"

"Are you serious?"

He sits up and sighs. "You have to, Key."

"You're my family."

"So was Aidan."

I stare at him, wondering how long he's known, wondering how he found out. I've never told anyone what really happened with Aidan, no one except Gloria. Maybe my mother said something? No—she would never reveal her true nature to anyone, especially not the likes of Billy. She hates him more than she hates me.

Billy reads my mind. "It was after a serious bender. We were high for almost a week, snorted so much fog you got nosebleeds for the next month." He winces as he aligns his broken nose. "At the end of it, you started talking about Aidan. It was near his birthday, so I guess you were missing him. I thought you were hallucinating—I thought *I* was hallucinating. But the look on your face tells me everything you said that night was true. You killed him. Didn't you?"

"I had no choice."

"And you've got no choice now."

"Yes, I do." I squat beside him. "Get out of town, Billy. I can't kill you if you disappear."

"And leave Nolan here for you to take out?"

"You just said my mother would never let me near him."

"My escape will start a war."

"I can handle a war," I say. "I'm not killing another family member."

Billy doesn't speak, he's busy staring at the carpet, weighing his options.

"Listen to him," says a voice from behind me.

I turn to find Aoife standing in the doorway, looking straight through me to Billy. I forgot I left her with him when I took off after Gloria. This isn't how I thought we'd meet again. And this isn't how I thought she'd look when we did meet again.

She ... She looks good. Her skin is clean, free of blemishes and scars, her face is washed so she isn't wearing any makeup, but that doesn't take away from her natural glow. She isn't smiling, but she still looks pleasant. Content. Like a suburban housewife who just walked in on unexpected guests.

"Aoife?" I say, turning to face her.

"Surprised to see me?" She raises her blonde brows.

"Yes."

Billy clears his throat, still sitting on the floor. "She's not half bad. Been here since your wife left you."

I grunt. She left me, but I got her back.

Aoife folds her arms. "Billy isn't so bad either."

After that first night, I thought he might have killed her while I was out of town, but I suppose even depraved men like Billy can be wholesome at times. He's even got Aoife wearing a long skirt with *pleats* in it. Like some kid's hot soccer mom.

"Listen to Caolán," Aoife tells my cousin. "We need to leave town."

We? What exactly happened between the two of them while I was gone? I can't stop myself from staring at Aoife, wondering who this woman is. I see her in the creases of her brow and in the tension of her delicate jaw. She isn't in love with Billy. Nothing even close to that. She's trying to survive, and she knows the best way to do that is to get out of the mafia altogether. Anthony wanted to do that. Gloria wanted to do that. I guess I'm the only one who hasn't gotten the memo. But I can't just leave.

"You've got to go," I tell Billy. "As soon as you can."

"You've still got a few days to think on it."

"My mind is made up. I'm not killing you or Nolan. I'd rather go to war."

"Does Gloria know that?" He looks sincere.

She doesn't know a thing. Not about this hit order or the war. She isn't prepared for either news, but I'll tell her soon. I have no choice.

"I'll take care of her," I say. "You worry about yourself."

Billy nods, but his voice comes out shakily. "I ... I don't know what to do without the Hand, Caolán."

Neither do I.

"Billy," I look him in the eye, "are you afraid?"

The words send a jolt of life through him. I see his eyes light up and then I see a smile slither across his vulpine face. He looks wickedly happy, reliving dark memories in his head.

"Of all the things I've seen and done, who'd ever think *normalcy* would scare me?" Billy pushes to his feet and brushes off his pants. "I'll figure something out, mate." He extends his hand.

"Don't take too long." I take it.

"I won't."

As I turn to leave, Aoife moves to the side so I can get through the door. She doesn't smile at me, but she does incline her head which I suppose is good enough.

"Take care of him," I tell her. I should be saying the opposite, telling Billy to keep her safe and sound, wherever this journey takes them, but after spending time with Gloria, I've realized marriage is the other way around. The husband provides and protects in his own way; a nice house, a decent car, food on the table, good sex in bed. But the things a wife provides are different. Deeper. Impossible to recreate. The things she brings to the marriage are priceless, that's why she's the prize between them. Because I can buy a house, but Gloria can bring me peace. I can get a gun, but she can get a prayer through. Which one do you think matters more?

That's why men like my brother are willing to die for a good woman, because he knows she's more than he'll ever deserve. The Bible says as much, right? *He who finds a wife, finds a good thing.* What does it say about a woman finding a good husband? I don't think it says a thing. But who am I, except a murderer. That's the good husband my wife acquired.

35

Ria

I don't know how to reach him... My handwriting is shaky because my hands tremble every time I think of last night and how Caolán rejected me. It was the single most embarrassing thing I've ever experienced, even worse than revealing my scar to everyone at dinner. Because those people were strangers trying to hurt me. But Caolán is my husband who couldn't comfort me. Who couldn't accept *my* comfort.

I stare down at my new journal; I started a fresh diary using an empty notebook I found in Caolán's room. Even if I had access to my old one locked away in my house, I wouldn't use it. That was the journal of a silly teenager, this is the journal of a married woman of God. I'm not just scribbling the echoes of my soul, hoping no one ever reads them, I'm writing my prayers with the faith that God is listening.

Am I doing something wrong?

Caolán has had a lot of women. He has houses and apartments that he's taken them to. He let go of the womanizing and the drugs, but that doesn't mean he let go of his desire. I thought he didn't need the other women because he had me now. I thought he stayed away from fog because he could cope with his nightmares now. He could talk to me. But he didn't.

Am I not good enough?

I close my diary and reach for my Bible; I took the one from Chicago because I wasn't sure if Caolán would have one here and I still don't have a phone to download a Bible app. I don't know what I'm looking for… Every other time I've read the Bible, I had a scripture in mind. A problem that it could solve. Now, I only have silence and confusion.

I flip to the back and search the concordance, hoping to find inspiration there. What could fix a marriage? First, I have to find the problem. There is so much between us; we're beyond anger and frustration; we're approaching unknown territory that doesn't even have a name.

Fear? Resentment? Confusion?

Honestly, it's easier to focus on what isn't there. For that, I only have one word. Love.

Caolán and I don't love each other, but that's no surprise. We were forced to be together after our siblings lost their lives in a war they started. Our marriage was supposed to bring peace and end the chaos they began, and for a moment, it did. But now we've started another feud between our families, and only we can end it together. But the glue between us is missing, leaving the gaping void that crawled between us last night.

I can't make Caolán love me; I've only just begun to grasp

the strands of love between us myself. But they're only strands. How can I get Caolán to see God's love when we don't even have each other's?

I blow air through my lips, still flipping through the biblical concordance. Suddenly, I get a spark of inspiration and I turn to the list of 'L' words. *Love* appears in the NLT version of the Bible more than 600 times. That fact is enough to drop my jaw, but what really catches my attention is the definition of love. I find it in **I Corinthians 13**.

Love is patient and kind. Love is not jealous or boastful or proud or rude. It does not demand its own way. It is not irritable, and it keeps no record of being wronged. It does not rejoice about injustice but rejoices whenever the truth wins out. Love never gives up, never loses faith, is always hopeful, and endures through every circumstance.

That's what I can show my husband. Even if we don't love each other, he can find God's love in my faithfulness, he can see it in my hope, in the peace I extend to him, instead of starting more fights. He can see my love through my faith in God, and how my faith endures through everything.

That's what I should have offered Caolán last night. Instead of feeding him lust and desperation, I should have fed him hope and faith. It isn't lustful to want my husband, that's called desire. It isn't sinful to offer physical or sexual comfort to him. That's called companionship. But it *is* wrong to think that sex could ever solve the problems between us. Sex isn't a secret key or a solution to anything. That's not what it was created for.

God created sex as an act of intimacy, passion, and *love*.

Couples feel connected when they have sex, some even feel better afterwards—that's why make-up sex is so popular. But the sex isn't what solves the problem, it's the love between them. Sex is merely an expression of it. But if there is no love, then what do you have when you lay together?

You have what I got last night. Emptiness. Distance. Nothing.

I don't have to love Caolán to reach him with God's Word, but he is my husband. I *want* to love him, and I want him to love me back. I've already begun to fall for him, and I think there is room for him to fall for me in turn. But this is about more than just pounding hearts and sweaty palms. It's about his soul salvation. To reach that place, I have to focus on showing him God's love.

As a Christian, I think ... I *think* love begins with faith. It takes faith to believe there is a God at all before you can accept that He loves you. I have faith that God will first open Caolán's heart, and then love can pour in. For now, I'll keep praying.

I reach for my diary to write all of this down, and for the first time, my hand doesn't shake. I'm done sitting around crying in my room all day. I am a child of the Most High God, if I'm going to cry, I'll *cry out* to Him. Those are the only tears that will make a difference.

After I'm done reading and writing, I treat myself to a warm bubble bath and then raid the kitchen. It's late afternoon and I haven't heard anything from Caolán all day but, for the first time, I'm not upset about that. I haven't heard much about what's going on, but you don't have to be a spy to know that war is brewing. Staying here is the safest option for me, especially after Caolán's little spat with Tadhg.

I find potatoes in the cupboard and milk in the fridge. I have very little experience with cooking, but I'm sure I can manage mashed potatoes. I've got a masher in my hands, ready to pound a steaming bowl of peeled taters when Caolán walks inside.

He stops at the door and blinks. "What are you doing?"

"Making dinner."

And there it is. Caolán smiles—a real smile that splits his face and tugs the corners of his mouth up. There's even a little chuckle that slips between his lips, the sound buttery and smooth.

Caolán holds up a greasy paper bag of something that smells divine. "I bought dinner."

"Is it fried chicken again?"

His smile stretches. "That works with mashed potatoes, right?"

"Of course, it does!"

He sets the table while I make the plates, and I can't stop smiling the whole time. This is the closest we've ever gotten to normal. A husband and wife eating dinner together. Talking about our day. Pretending we aren't in the mafia and aren't *this* close to death every day.

Caolán let's me say grace again and even mutters, *Amen*, when I'm done. We crunch our chicken with silly smiles on our faces until he sits back and takes a deep breath.

"I have something to tell you."

I stare at my plate. It was only a matter of time before the peace broke to the chaos.

"The mashed potatoes are bad."

I snort so hard I have to drink some water to stop myself from choking. Caolán laughs too, his shoulders bopping up and down. That breaks the tension, and he reaches across the table, taking my hand.

"I'm sorry about last night. You … You tried to make me feel better—"

"It's all right," I say quickly. I don't really want to talk about this anymore, the sting of embarrassment is still there, stronger than I thought. "I shouldn't have offered myself as comfort. That was silly."

"It was sweet." He squeezes my hand. "You wanted to help the best way you knew how. I can't blame you for that."

How many times have we had this conversation from a different perspective? Now I know how Caolán used to feel when I chastised him for doing his best. His best was often questionable and even made me angry, but I can never say he didn't try.

"Now…" Caolán sits back in his chair, but he tugs on my hand, and I stand, moving around the table to sit on his lap. "There really is something I want to talk about."

"Okay."

"Your family didn't take Anthony's death well."

"Are we not invited to the funeral?"

"It's worse than that, darling."

I blink up at him, waiting for more. What could possibly be

worse than missing my friend's funeral?

"They want blood for his death. Irish blood."

"Why? He wasn't killed by an Irishman."

"But he was killed helping me get you back."

"I don't have Irish blood." I bristle. "I'm Black American, just like the rest of the Panthers."

"But you're married to me." He adjusts me on his lap so he can lean closer, looking me right in the eye. "Your last name is O'Rourke, Gloria. You bleed green now. Not red."

In the mafia, I'm Irish now. As green as my red-headed husband.

"They don't care about me," I whisper. Even worse… "They blame me."

"I have to deliver within a week," Caolán says.

"Deliver what?"

"My cousin's head."

I stare at him. There's no way. There's *no way* my family demanded that of him. How could they? They must know what this will do to me, how it will impact my marriage. How could they ever expect to remain at peace with the Hand if they demand the head of Caolán's own cousin? This will restart the war we've worked so hard to end. If that's the case, what was the point in our marriage?

"Caolán—"

"I know." He wraps his arms around me and buries his face in my puffy afro curls. "I'm not going to do it. I think I already found a way to fix this, but … things might get dangerous, Gloria. I don't know if you'll be safe here."

"I'm not leaving you."

I mean that. We just barely got ourselves together. I'm finally his wife; he can't send me away. I don't care how dangerous it gets.

"Gloria—"

"Why don't we leave together?"

He sits up and frowns.

"We don't have to fight this war. We don't have to put up with *any* of this, Caolán. Look at everything we've been through, all the violence and pain. The mafia is not worth it."

He shakes his head, something I knew he would do. It was a long shot to ever think that he would leave so easily, but I still wanted to try.

"I shouldn't have told you," Caolán mutters, and I reach up to grip his shirt.

"Don't say that. You don't get to shut me out just because I disagree with you."

Some part of him knows I'm right. I see it in his eyes, and then I hear it in his voice. "I'm sorry," he says, and then he hugs me again. "I won't shut you out, but … can I at least admit I don't want to talk about it anymore?"

There's a slight pause.

"I guess so," I mutter. "What do you want to talk about instead?"

"Nothing."

"What do you—*Caolán!*" I squirm as he pulls me closer, turning me in his lap so my back is against his chest.

"I don't want to talk at all." His voice is low, whispered

against the shell of my ear.

"W-Well, there's something I want to do!" I say quickly.

"Me too."

His hands slide beneath my shirt, cupping my breasts, and I squeal.

"I-I want to pray!"

Caolán freezes. He drops his hands. "Did you just say you want to *pray?*"

"Yes—"

"Gloria, look at me." He gestures to his crotch, though I don't need to look at all. I'm sitting on his lap, so I can say, without a shameful doubt, he's more than ready to finish what he couldn't last night.

"I don't want to pray," he murmurs, leaning in to kiss me.

I turn my head, so he kisses my cheek. "Well, I *do* want to pray."

"Right *now?*" He sounds agitated. "Where is all this God stuff even coming from?"

"I've always believed in God," I whisper. "God is the reason I came back with you. He told me to give you a second chance." I reach up and touch the cross pendant hanging around his neck. It's the necklace I gave him years ago. The gesture softens him but doesn't elicit much response beyond that.

Caolán's eyes are filled with a sort of caution I've never seen in him before. He doesn't believe me. But I don't need him to. I know God's Voice when I hear it, and I'm going to follow it whether my husband accepts it or not. I grew up attending churches that told me to blindly listen to my husband. To submit and obey him *even* if he was wrong.

God will correct him along the way! But what if he doesn't listen to God? Is it impossible for a wife to ever be right in an argument or is she always wrong because she isn't a man? Does she never get the final say?

That's not what happened in the Bible. When Abraham and Sarah were frustrated over what to do with Ishmael, God told Abraham to **listen to his wife**. She had been right. She had spoken in wisdom. Yet, I grew up being told that women should throw away their brains and listen to their husbands without question. Because he's a man. Because he's the head of the wife. But what if he is leading me into sin? Or what if I simply disagree with him? Then that makes me a rebellious woman. That makes me a woman who has a problem with submission.

That's not what the Bible says. When Abigail disagreed with her husband, she acted directly against him to carry out God's will. The Bible didn't call her rebellious, it called her a woman of wisdom—and called her husband a fool. When Queen Esther's husband didn't want to see her, she defied him *and* his law to complete her mission. The Bible did not say she had a problem with submission, instead, Queen Esther is hailed as an example to women *and* men of what it means to place God's will above everything else. Even your spouse.

The truth is that submission is not blind at all. Submission requires agreement. The Bible says so when it was written, *How can two walk together unless they agree?* What closer walk is there between two people than that of marriage? An eternal walk sealed by a covenant.

Marriage isn't about authority or power or control. It is about cooperation. When a wife submits to her husband, she doesn't surrender her mind, thoughts, or free will. She doesn't surrender *anything*. She agrees to allow him to support her. She agrees to let him become her provider and protecter and the one who fulfills her needs. Just as the husband submits to her for comfort and wisdom and support.

Of course, I can't explain any of this to Caolán. He's staring at me like I've lost my mind for wanting to pray instead of letting him bend me over our dinner table. But Caolán isn't saved. He can't understand my beliefs because he doesn't see things from a spiritual perspective. Only when he receives the Holy Spirit can we truly connect. Until then, all I can offer is a vague explanation and pray that it's enough.

Please open his heart, I ask my Father.

"I just want to spend some time with you," I say.

"This *is* spending time together." He glowers.

"In a different way. A way that's deeper than sex." I reach up to touch his cheek. "Let's pray first, and then—"

"And *then*?"

I glance away. Well, it's not like I don't want to.

"And then we can have fun."

Caolán smiles again, and it melts my heart.

"Okay." He takes my hands and closes his eyes. "You'll have to lead because I don't know how to pray."

To think there are people who would condemn me for being a woman and daring to lead *my husband in this...*

I take my husband's hands, and I close my eyes, then I begin to pray. I ask God to protect us both and to protect our families. I ask Him to keep the bloodshed at bay and to open the door for us to seek and find Him in this chaos. I ask Jesus to be with us and make His presence known. I ask for peace and understanding. And I ask God to forgive Caolán.

I feel him stiffen as those words leave my lips, and I know what he's thinking. That he can't be forgiven. That he's too far from God for my prayers to reach or make a difference. *That's it,* I realize, *the lock over Caolán's heart is fear.* Fear that he's messed up too many times. Even for God.

Shatter that lock, I pray in my heart, and then I feel a very familiar flicker of hope ignite within, burning on the faith that fuels me.

36

Caolán

Anthony's funeral comes and goes. We are not invited which tears Gloria apart. She hasn't seen or spoken to her family since she arrived back in town. I don't know what to make of that, but she's handling it worse than I thought she would, and being left out of the funeral was like a nail in a coffin. Literally.

I couldn't even take her out to get her mind off all the death and darkness and the looming war. I've still got a few days before I have to produce anyone's head, but I don't trust anyone anymore. I feel like I'm staring over the edge of a cliff, waiting for someone to push me.

Who's gonna do it? I wonder, standing by the bed, watching my wife sleep. She looks peaceful for now, just a girl beneath the blankets, snuggled up in one of my shirts again. She has plenty of clothes here, but she absolutely refuses to sleep in anything else. I don't mind.

Quietly, I lean over and kiss her temple. "Sleep well," I whisper, then I straighten and leave, gingerly closing the door behind me. There's a guard who keeps watch outside, I pay him cash by the hour, but I still don't trust him much. Even so, he's all I've got, so I give him a grunt and a nod as I pass by. He does the same, taking up position outside the apartment door.

Every morning, Gloria prays and reads her Bible when she gets up. This morning will be no different. If I'm still there, she asks me to pray with her. I don't mind—I don't understand anything she says or why she even says it, but I respect it, and I'll admit I even hope her faith is true. I hope God listens to Gloria's prayers. I hope He keeps her safe. Sometimes I find myself hoping that she prays for me too. What could a woman like her have to say about a man like me? She already knows about my past, even told me how she sneaked into my bedroom with Nolan by her side. The fact that she didn't run away right then made me want to hug her. She cares for me—cares enough to want me to pray with her. I don't see her faith as a burden or a restriction, I see it as proof of her heart. She wants to share more than just her life with me, she wants that life to continue in Heaven. Wants our love to transcend time and space and last for eternity.

I stop at a red light and stare straight ahead, squeezing my steering wheel. *Our love.*

I think that's the first time that little word has popped into my head, regarding my marriage, at least. Do I love Gloria? I think that's a strong word for a woman I technically haven't spent more than a month with. But she's the only woman I've been committed to for this long, cared about this deeply, and wanted to have in my life. For all the years I had Aoife by my side, I was never committed to her. Never cared what she thought or did, so long as she followed my orders. But this isn't about Aoife, because even if I did care about her, she isn't my wife.

"My wife is the reason I'm doing this," I mutter, staring at the little house ahead. It's Billy's place, the same house I left him in two days ago. I haven't heard from him since then, but that was expected. I've come to clear out his things, hoping he left something that will tell me where he's gone. It won't be safe to reach out for a long while, but once all the smoke blows over, I'll make contact again.

I get out and march up the front steps, pausing when I reach the door. It's already open. That sets off every alarm in my head—without hesitation, I draw my gun and kick the door in.

There's an odor...

"No," I whisper, moving swiftly through the house. Every step takes me closer to the source, the smell growing more and more pungent. I know what it is before I open the bedroom and see the mess on the floor. It's a smell I've inhaled far too many times. A smell I thought I couldn't escape when I was younger, in the prime of my career as a hitman.

Billy is dead. Aoife is too. She's on the bed with a bullet in her forehead, leaving a tiny hole with blood crusted around the opening. Billy is in worse shape; he's sprawled on the floor, a bullet to his temple, and his mouth is hanging open. I step closer to inspect the bloody hole in his face. He's still got his tongue, but he's missing two teeth. They weren't knocked out in a fight; he would have bruising on his face if that were the case. The gaps in his mouth are clean. Like the teeth were pried out.

This is my fault... I know it as confidently as I know that he's dead. It's clearer than the blood that stains my fingers as I hold Billy's mouth open. The two teeth that are missing are his incisors. *Fangs*. Like a vampire.

That's what Tadhg called me before he left, it's what he said he would do to me. Remove my fangs.

He didn't come for me, he took out Billy instead, forcing my hand in the situation. Now I have no choice but to go after my brother, the only one I've got left. But Tadhg knows Aifric will never let that happen. Now, the only way to prevent this war is to take out the source. Just as I took out Aidan.

That means *I'm* the target now. And not just me, but Gloria too.

With a gasp, I turn and sprint out the room. My mind is racing, my heart is hammering.

"Why didn't you leave!?" I shout into my car, punching the steering wheel. *Why didn't Billy go when I told him to?*

No... There was a *smell*. His body has been sitting there for at least a day, probably longer. Aoife was still wearing that silly pleated skirt she had on when I first visited. That means they were killed that day.

Tadhg might have come for him as soon as I left, he might have followed me there. I wouldn't put it past him—clearly, he's capable of far more than I give him credit for. I never thought this would happen. Never thought that I would be targeted, which was foolish of me. My mother looked me in the eye and said she wanted me dead during the last war. Why would this one be any different? I wouldn't be surprised if killing Billy was *her* idea.

I don't care, I tell myself. I don't care that my mother hates me. In fact, I hope her hatred is real. I hope its strong enough to keep Nolan safe, because now that Billy is dead, I have to go. I have to abandon my baby brother to keep myself and my wife alive. Nolan wasn't built for this world, but he's shown me sparks of strength in the past. He was steadfast about saving Anthony, he was determined to do what was right. Maybe he isn't a murderer like me, but that doesn't mean he isn't a survivor. He'll make it without me. He's got to.

I push all thoughts of Nolan from my head as my tires scream into the parking lot of my apartment complex. My room is on the fourth floor, I have half a mind to scale the building, but I don't want to draw attention, so I force myself to walk calmly through the lobby and then take the emergency stairwell three steps at a time. I'm sweaty and panting when I reach my room, but my heart calms at the sight of my guard still standing outside.

Thank God…

"Is she in there?" I rasp, marching to the door.

He nods. "Hasn't left, sir."

"Good." I shove my key into the knob and hear the latch switch back, then I shoulder the door open and rush inside, shouting, "GLORIA!"

She pops from around the corner, eyes wild, panic gripping

ROBICHAUD, M 7/25

User name: ROBICHAUD, MANDY MARIE
Phone number: 601-757-4872
Email: mandymhall@gmail.com
Pickup library: FRL-SOUTH
Call number: F KLU
Title: Under the whispering door
Item ID: 33222109378175
Current time: 07/18/2025,10:04

M. R. Davis Public Library
8554 Northwest Drive
Southaven, MS 38671
662-342-0102

her features. "Caolán?"

I reach for her. "We have to go."

She nods but turns away. "Let me grab some things—"

"Forget it, we have to go *now*!"

She stops and pivots to face me, but instead of arguing, she points over my shoulder and shouts, "Move!"

I feel his presence at the last second, but as I shift away, I turn and see him. My guard has entered the apartment behind me, he has his gun raised, his finger on the trigger. Almost in slow-motion, I watch him pull it and as the gun fires, my wife screams, my breath leaves my body, and my vision blurs.

I've been shot—but so has he. I've got a gun too, and I managed to lift it in time. Mercifully, my aim was better than his. I'm bleeding from my shoulder, but he's got a hole in his chest. He stumbles back, shock filling his eyes, and then he slumps against the door, sliding down to the hardwood floor.

"Caolán!" Gloria is beside me now, losing her mind as she stands on her tiptoes to see the wound. It burns, but I don't have time to think about it.

"Two minutes," I say, "pack a bag and wait in the kitchen."

"I thought you said we have to leave now!" She calls over her shoulder, running back into our bedroom.

"That guy was supposed to catch me by surprise, it'll be a minute before reinforcements arrive." I stumble into our ensuite bathroom while Gloria throws clothes and money into a duffel bag. There's a first aid kit in the cabinet; I rummage through it for alcohol and almost scream when I press a soaked towel to my shoulder.

"Are you okay!" Gloria bursts through the door, drawn by the noise.

But I ignore her concern and shout, "Finish packing!" and she slips back into the bedroom.

This time, I lock the door. There's a knife in the first aid, but I don't have time to dig the bullet out, so I rip open a closure strip with my teeth and press it over the wound hard enough to make me hiss out a curse. It isn't the right tool for the job, nothing more than a glorified sticker barely holding me together, but it's all I've got for now.

With shaky hands, I wipe away more of the blood with that towel, then I reach for the bottle stored in the kit. It's a little white bottle that holds little white pills. Not fog, just oxycodone, but still… I have a history of addiction. I shouldn't touch this stuff—I don't *want* to touch it, but I need it. I was just shot, and there's no chance of me getting to a hospital any time soon. This pill is my mercy. And my nightmare.

As I pop the lid to the bottle, my shoulder aches and I grunt at the pain. I can still feel the metal inside me. Foreign. Alien. Unwanted. Like I've felt all my life. I need to dig it out, need to cleanse my body—I wonder if that's what the Hand thinks its doing to me. Digging out the last of its problems.

The pills rattle like bones—or teeth—I can't tell. One little dose of heaven falls into my hand, and I stare at it sitting on my bloodstained palm. The last time I took drugs; things went from bad to worse. I want to say this is different. That I took fog for *pleasure*, but the truth isn't so sweet. I took fog because I needed it. The illusions were my escape from the bloody reality I'd been trapped in. And now I need oxycodone to do the same. Escape the pain.

Just one pill, I tell myself, praying to God that I can keep that promise.

I toss it back before I change my mind. It goes down dry, scratching my throat until I slump over the sink and gulp water from the faucet. My throat burns, my eyes sting. I don't know why I'm crying, but I wipe away the stupid tears and slap myself twice before I look in the mirror. Already, I feel the pill working. It doesn't numb the pain; it just moves it. I still hurt everywhere. In all the places fog cannot reach.

Aifric would be so proud to see me now. I am her perfect failure. The knife she could not wield, used to cut down enemy after enemy, name after name. And like a knife grown dull, she has tossed me aside. I'm useless to her now. Useless to the Hand.

I exhale, eyes closed. "Time to go."

When I stumble into the bedroom, Gloria is waiting for me by the door, duffel bag in hand. She looks at the blood on my shirt, at the bottle of pills in my hands, and she says nothing. Maybe she knows what I just did in there, maybe she doesn't.

I wipe my bloody hand onto my pants, stuff the pills into my pocket, and force my legs to move. "Let's go."

Gloria follows me down to the car in silence, sticking close, moving swiftly. She doesn't speak until I grab the handle to the driver door.

"Is it safe?"

I almost laugh. "No, Gloria, it isn't."

"I meant driving."

So, she *did* see the pills.

"I can drive." I've done a lot more with a lot worse in my system, but she doesn't need to know that.

Gloria chooses to trust me, sliding into her seat without another word. I grip the steering wheel like it owes me something. My breath comes out in pants. My mind blurs with the image of my mother. Even in my painful haze, I can still see her perfect lipstick, her sharp smile, black, somber makeup dusting her face. I bet she's already practicing what she will say at my funeral. Mourning the son she tried to kill.

I'm not dead yet.

I throw the car into drive and peel away from the lot, but I jerk to a stop when I near the exit gate. There's someone there, blocking it.

I don't believe my eyes...

"It's Nolan," Gloria whispers.

Has he come to kill me? No—the thought is so unfathomable, I actually squeeze my eyes shut and shake my head. Nolan would never.

"How did he find us?"

"I threw him a party here for his birthday last year," I confess, thankful for the oxy clouding my mind, otherwise, I'd be gifted with an array of vivid memories of my little brother's initiation into manhood. It'd been one crazy night which I enjoyed far more than he did.

"What's he doing?" Gloria asks.

"I don't know," I answer honestly.

Nolan's just standing there, blocking the gate with his own skinny body. There's a car parked crookedly beside the gate; I guess he pulled up in a hurry, decided to wait for me here. I appreciate the fact that he waited outside, it means he expected me to survive that first little sneak attack from the security guard. But now that he knows I'm alive, what is he going to do?

I unlock the driver door, and Gloria says, "Wait—"

"He won't hurt me."

I step out, ignoring the cold slap of winter. I can feel it drying the warm blood still oozing from my arm. Nolan sees the blood and pales as I near him.

"They shot you," he breathes.

"Did you know?"

He shakes his head. "Not until it was too late. I came here as soon as I could but—"

"But you were probably followed."

Nolan steps forward. "Caolán, I tried."

I let him hug me, even though my brain screams at the pain, all that leaves my mouth is a gentle whimper. I hug him back, smearing my blood onto his clothes, dragging my stained hands through his hair. "I don't blame you," I tell him.

"Please don't go."

"You know I have to."

"I can talk to Mother."

He probably could, but he'd never be able to sway Tadhg.

"Nolan, listen to me."

He starts shaking his head, but I give him a slight shake to make him focus.

"Listen. You're on your own now. I've got to get Gloria out of here. I'll contact you again when its safe, but you'll be here alone. You're strong enough to handle it."

He nods. "I know I am."

I had expected tears, even pleading, but Nolan looks fine. Like he expected this. There is confidence in his eyes now, steady and sure, and filled with a truth I hadn't noticed until now. He never asked me if he could come along. He never offered to run away with me.

He doesn't want to leave...

Nolan nods, like he's read my mind. "Someone needs to make sure they don't hunt you down."

I see... He's staying for me.

"You've got to go," Nolan says, stepping back and patting the shoulder that isn't bleeding. "I'll keep them off your trail. Long as I can."

"Thank you, brother."

"Take care of Gloria."

"Take care of Mother."

He smiles. "I'll try."

I slide back into the car with a grunt and a sigh, ignoring Gloria's wild eyes. She's brimming with questions, but gets some of her answers when Nolan steps aside and waves us on. She frantically waves when we drive by, and then she stares over her shoulder until she can't see him anymore.

I drive. And drive. And drive. My shoulder feels like a numb extension of my body, the pain is still there but deeper down, in a place I can only grasp with the edges of my mind. It creeps back to the forefront with every mile that ticks away. Medicine wearing off. When the sun begins to dip toward the horizon, I pop another pill and crunch it between my teeth. Gloria doesn't say a word, not until I swerve the car, then she squeals beside me.

"Pull over!"

"No."

She reaches for the steering wheel, and I snarl, "Not a *chance.*" I'm not trying to be cruel, I just don't want to leave this in her hands. So far out of my control. Like my addiction, like my brother's death, like my entire life. I was never in control. Held firmly in the palm of the Hand. Now I'm doing something on my own, I've got to make it to the end. For both of us.

But I feel my mind clouding from the oxy. I feel my muscles growing heavy. I can't go much longer, or we'll be dead for a completely different reason.

I push myself to my limit, driving until the only light around us comes from the stars. Then I suffer through another twenty minutes before a seedy motel comes into view. The car drags through the lot, bumping the parking block with a jerk. Gloria falls forward, and I slump over the wheel, holding my arm.

"I can't drive anymore."

I hear Gloria fumbling with her seatbelt, then her footsteps running around the car. The chill outside smacks me hard when she yanks open my door, gasping at the sight of me. I bet I look like death, which is funny, I am a reaper, after all.

She pulls my arm over her shoulders and drags me out of the car. If I hadn't taken that second pill, I'd be screaming. The whole thing is sloppy and uncoordinated. First of all, I'm more than a foot taller than my tiny wife, and I'm half high on powerful painkillers. We look awful when we stagger into the lobby of the motel, but Gloria knows what to do. She packed plenty of cash in her duffel bag and she doesn't hesitate to throw it at the old man working the front desk. He helps us to a room and even tells Gloria he can make me a sandwich later—like that'll help. She thanks him and then shuts the door while I lie face down on the dirty bed.

With a grunt, she rolls me over and sits beside me, wiping sweat from my forehead. "I have to look at your arm. I think it's still bleeding."

"Get the bullet out," I whisper.

"I can't—"

"You can. You have to."

"It—It'll hurt."

"I'll be fine."

She pauses, but then I feel her weight lift from the bed, and I hear her fumbling through the duffel bag. When she returns, she whispers softly, "I'm gonna pray first."

I take a deep breath, and hope that God hears whatever she says.

37

Ria

God help me... My hands shake as I fumble through the first aid kit. I took it from the kitchen cabinet before leaving the apartment. I may not have been deeply involved in my parents' mafia empire, but I lived through enough shock to learn that every mafia household has first aid kits in every room. The one I've got is packed with supplies I can't name. In a tired voice, Caolán guides me through the process, telling me what I'll need and how to do it. How to cut him open and get the bullet out of his arm.

"Use the alcohol wipes to clean it first."

Caolán finds the strength to sit up and curses as he peels off his suit jacket and then his torn shirt. There's so much blood; despite the patch he applied to seal it. It's hanging off, soaked by the crimson liquid that spills over his chest.

"You're hurt," I say, as if that isn't obvious.

"Stay with me." He presses his hand to the wound and hacks out a cough. "I need you focused, Gloria."

I nod. Swallow. Hope I don't pee myself.

"Alcohol wipes," he says.

Right...

I tear the wipes open, and he lies on his back, watching the ceiling like it's got all the answers we need written on it. Or maybe he just can't look at me with my shaky hands and trembling nerves. I approach him like I'm walking to my own death, but Caolán stays calm, only offering a curse to the ceiling when the alcohol burns him.

"It's clean," I say.

"The gloves are already sterile. Put them on and then grab the lidocaine." His breathing is shallow, his eyes are half-lidded, but he presses on anyway, shifting to lie on his good side and watch me closely. It probably takes all of his energy to focus, but he's here, showing more concern for my nerves than his.

"Lidocaine," I whisper, snapping my gloves on. *I don't know what the heck that is!*

"It should be in a syringe."

I find it and pop off the cap, then I stand and stare at him. He's covered in his own blood, the stains look so bright against his ghostly pale skin, tinted dark red because of his black tattoos underneath. He moans softly as he leans back into the sheets, and I step forward.

"Let me help."

He waves me off, teeth snapping shut on each word. "Just give me the medicine."

I flick my eyes to the syringe, then back to him. "Is it safe?"

He's taken two of those white pills already. What will this do to him?

He groans. "It's safe, Gloria."

"But—"

"Lidocaine is a local anesthetic, it'll numb the area, not get me high. Just do it."

I lick my lips and then kneel on the bed. I'm wearing a long skirt, so I have to pull it up to make sure I don't trip and fall on top of him. That would be tragic.

"Once you give me the lidocaine, you'll have to feel for the bullet."

"Feel with what?"

"Your fingers."

My stomach roils. "I *can't*, Caolán."

"Yes, you can." He sucks in a breath and then moans on it before releasing. "You have to."

Get it together, girl. I want to slap myself to see if that will help, but there's no time.

I lean closer to Caolán. "How much lidocaine should I give you?"

"The whole thing."

I don't want to do that, but I have no other choice. So I take a deep breath and jab the needle into his bloody arm. He jerks, hands whipping out to grip something. His left hand bundles the blankets into his fist, but his right hand lands on my leg and he squeezes my thigh, leaving a bloody handprint behind.

I don't have time to feel awkward. All I can do is brush his hair from his sweaty forehead and whisper, "It's okay. It'll be okay."

When he releases me, I crawl from the bed and start tossing things around. There are tweezers he told me to use, then I'll need the alcohol wipes, and the saline flush? I think??

I gasp and glance back up at Caolán. He's lying on his back, chest rising and falling. The pace is rapid but as I stare, it slows down until his breaths become shallow. *Is the medicine kicking in?*

I climb onto the bed and hold the tweezers up; my hands are shaking so badly I almost stab the bullet hole when I get closer. Then, to my absolute shock, Caolán snaps his eyes open and sucks in a rugged breath. The action is so frightening that I actually scream.

"Calm down," he says hoarsely.

"I'm sorry!" I'm so scared right now.

He doesn't reply, he's just watching me. Silently, tiredly. When he swallows, his throat moves up and down and I stare at him, then he works his mouth to speak. The sound is sticky, like it's awkward for him to move his tongue now.

"Don't cry," he whispers.

I hadn't realized I was. There are tears running down my face, both cheeks stained with sorrow, even though I'm not the one in pain.

"I'm sorry," I say shakily.

Caolán makes a noise, trying to speak through the haze of injury and too much medicine. "You're so pretty when you cry."

"Thank you…"

I wipe my tears and scoot closer, daring to touch him. When my fingers prod the wound, he grimaces but has no reaction beyond that. His eyes are blue stones set in place, unmoving. I feel his hand grip the blankets again as I prod deeper, inserting my finger into the hole. That's when his eyes finally squeeze shut; he makes a gentle noise in the back of his throat, a soft moan like he wants to cry but doesn't have the energy. He's still gripping the blankets, but the shaky tension isn't there anymore. He's fading now.

"Caolán," I whisper, "please don't go. Please don't leave me here alone."

He exhales slowly, words coming out slurred. "I'm not dying…"

Yeah, but if he passes out, I'll still be alone, and I don't think I can do this by myself.

Crimson liquid spills over my gloved fingers, warm and viscous. I prod even deeper and that seems to bring him back to life. I feel the muscles in his arm grow tense, protectively gathering around the wound.

"Relax," I whisper. "I can't find it if you're stiff like this."

He groans which makes me slightly happy because at least I know he's alive—but when my finger grazes something hard, the groan becomes a grunt.

"I've got it!" I exclaim. In my excitement, my finger pushes too deeply, and Caolán let's out a full-on shout.

He screams. One withered cry peels from his raw throat, a pale gasp, like death inhaling his pain, and then he's gone. Silent.

"I'm sorry!" I shout. "I'm sorry!"

I'm crying so hard; I can barely see past the tears, but the fact that his chest is still rising calms me somewhat. *Get it together, girl,* I tell myself for the second time. I stare at my husband's body, at all the blood and the wrinkled expression on his face. Pained, even when he's passed out. The fact that he's gone is what steels me. *Caolán needs me to focus.* If I don't, he won't be passed out, he'll be dead.

"Lord, help me," I pray, lifting the tweezers. Caolán fainting is a blessing in disguise. Now, I can dig the bullet out without having to hold him down or ignore his cries. The silence gives me peace, though fear and trembling chases at its heels.

God is bigger than my fears, I remind myself. *Fear not,* is one of the most repeated phrases in the entire Bible. God said it so often for a reason. As crazy as this is for me, Jesus knew I would be here in this position one day. He knew me before He created me in my mother's womb. He knew that I would marry Caolán. He knew that Caolán's family would betray us. He knew that I would be crying in a dirty motel, digging a bullet from his shoulder. And He knew that I would call to Him for help. The real test is whether I believe He will answer.

"Please," I sob. "Please help me, God."

My tweezers meet a barricade, and I know I've found the bullet. It takes me a second to get a grip, but once I've got it, I slowly slide the metal out of the hole. It's easier than I thought it would be, but I don't get to bask in my success. I've got to clean and pack the wound now, and time is ticking.

"Okay, okay, okay," I mutter, on my hands and knees

searching through the first aid. I find the saline wash and a pack of sterilized gauze, then I gingerly climb onto the bed again, but freeze when there's a knock at the door.

"Uh—I was just doing a courtesy call," says a voice in the hall. I recognize it as the motel manager, the guy I shoved a wad of hundred-dollar bills at when I first asked for a room. The place is cash-only with just six rooms and no cars in the lot. I'm guessing we're his first customers in a long time, unless he rents the rooms by the hour to cheating spouses and hookers with a hot date. Either way, I know his lips are sealed so I'm not afraid to answer the door. I'm just annoyed.

He won't leave unless I reply, I tell myself, marching to the door. I yank it open and stare at him, hoping he can see the anger in my eyes, but it's the blood on my arms and hands that frightens him. He's a hefty man with a bald spot in the front of his head, leaving smooth, shiny skin on display. He's combed the rest of his hair around the spot, but it doesn't help.

"Oh my," he stumbles backwards. "B-Blood—you're bleeding!"

"It's not mine."

He shifts, eyes climbing over my shoulder to peer into the room. I step to the side to block him. No one needs to see Caolán in this state.

"What do you need?" I ask.

"Just checking. There was a lot of noise."

"My husband was hurt. He's better now."

"Will he need medical attention?"

Like he's seriously going to call the cops.

"No. He's fine now, but he will need lunch." An idea hits me. "Please bring me some bread and grape juice. Knock once and leave it at the door once you've got it."

"Okay, that'll be a ten-dollar charge to the room."

Is he serious?

I shake my head and slam the door in his face, then I run back to the bed and hover over Caolán, staring at his chest. It rises and falls slowly; his breaths are shallow but still there. Still alive.

"Hold on," I whisper, then I puncture the saline wash and flush the bullet hole. I put on another pair of gloves and reach for the gauze; there's another knock at the door, but I ignore it as I stuff the wound with trembling hands. I try my hardest to keep them steady, but it isn't possible with how high-strung my nerves are. Thank God, he's passed out. Otherwise, I'm sure he'd be screaming. I can't take another one of those awful cries. Like a wounded animal, afraid and pained.

"You're gonna be okay," I say, unsure if I'm talking to Caolán or myself.

With a slow sigh, I slide down the bed and sit on the floor of the dirty motel room. Just staring. Just breathing.

It's over.

For now, things are good. For now, things are quiet.

"What have we gotten ourselves into?" There's barely been any time to process the day. Caolán came home and was shot. Then we had to escape and say goodbye to his little brother. Now we're in a motel room paying cash to a sketchy guy and trying not to bleed out.

When I agreed to return to California, I thought I would have to fight to get Caolán to accept my new faith in Christ. But now we're fighting for our *lives*.

"You're still here," I say to God, wiping my bloody hand through my hair. "It's not the fight I asked for but it's still a fight You can win."

With a grunt, I crawl across the room and crack open the door. There's a tray with half a loaf of sliced bread on a plate, butter in a cup, and a bottle of cranberry juice. It isn't grape, but it'll do.

I slide the tray into the room and shut the door, then I lean my back against it and exhale. I packed a Bible in my duffel bag, but I remember the scriptures without it.

Take and eat, this is My body.

I put the bread to my lips and think of Christ's Body, how it was broken so mine could be whole. *And Caolán's,* I pray inside. *God, I take this communion—Your body—in proxy for my husband. He isn't saved. He hasn't committed himself to You yet. But I have. Please, God, heal him for me.*

I take the cranberry juice and almost laugh at myself. Does this still count as the Blood of Jesus?

Technically, the Bible says Jesus took a cup of wine. Last I checked, wine could be pressed from plenty of fermented fruit, cranberries included. Either way, I know God is merciful enough to answer my prayers no matter what juice I drink. I am praying to the same God who parted the Red Sea, raised the dead, and walked on water. If He can do all that, then He can heal my husband.

Drink, Jesus said, *this is My Blood of the Covenant which is shed for the forgiveness of sins.*

"Forgive us both for our sins, Father. Because we are forgiven, we are healed. In the Name of Jesus, I pray. Amen."

I drink the juice and then stare at Caolán, watching his chest like I can see past the bloody skin, behind his ribs, and into his heart. I don't look away, taking each breath as if its my own.

I've never seen him so vulnerable before. So weak. But here he is, the man I married. He is not a myth or a legend. He is not a charming prince. He's just a man, and I think I love him for that.

With my head tilted back against the door, I feel like I can finally breathe. I'm covered in my husband's blood, on the run for my life, and I have no idea what tomorrow holds. But I know we'll make it there, in Jesus's Name, I declare it.

38

Caolán

I feel like I'm floating, and that scares me somewhat because people only feel this way when they're high or dying. I think I might be experiencing both.

I drift down the halls of an empty home, oddly reminiscent of my own. The dream is grayscale, the walls pale cement, void of color and life. But there is a light on at the end of the hall, and I follow it like it's calling me. It leads to a room that I don't recognize at first but as my eyes adjust to the light, I see the dark curtains and the dirty stains on the carpet, and I see the coffin-shaped bed. It's my bedroom.

"You're here."

My eyes laser to the woman standing before the drawn curtains, peering out at the world beyond the windows. That's where all the light comes from, outside this room. Outside this dim, grey world.

"You're here," she says again, and as she turns, her hair sways around her. It's so much longer here, longer than I've ever seen it. And her face is young and pretty, skin smooth as glass, voice rich as syrup.

"Mom?" I don't recognize my own voice, it sounds younger and makes me glance down at myself, as if checking for something. I gasp. My hands and arms are smaller and slimmer than normal. They're younger. Adolescent.

I'm a child again, staring at my beautiful, young mother. She was in her mid-twenties when she had me; I see that youthful glow surrounding her now, like a halo of happiness she never truly had. Neither did I.

"Where are we?" I ask. "Am I dead?"

"No." She laughs and it sounds sad. "Unfortunately, you're alive and healthy."

"Sorry to disappoint you."

"You've done that all your life." She waves. "Don't say sorry now."

"I'm not sorry to you," I tell her. "I'm sorry that I ever cared about your feelings in the first place."

Mother looks up, her eyes going soft and watery. "I was a terrible mother. I know."

"*Why?*" My voice breaks on the word, and I hate myself for it. I don't want to show her this side of me, the side that *does* care for her feelings. The side that needs her to care for mine. "Why did you hate me so much?" I beg her in my tiny child voice. The sound is uncomfortable, a reminder of where her hatred began. I was a child when she looked at me and decided she couldn't stand what she saw.

"I didn't hate you, Caolán. I just…" Her shoulders shake.

"I hated what you were."

"And what was I?"

"A mistake."

The blood obsession, the killing, the fog—and then Aidan died, and I replaced him. I was never meant to be the man I became.

"Well, I'm gone now." I look away. "You don't have to worry about ever seeing me again."

"Where will you go?"

"It's not where I'm going. It's what I'm doing."

"Which is?"

"Moving on."

She laughs. "Do you think Gloria loves you?"

"She cares. That's all that matters." I turn toward the door without waiting for a reply, not that I expect a goodbye from her. She doesn't offer any parting words. She watches me go in silence, the only sound between us is my bedroom door closing. I only wish I could lock it.

When the door closes, I sit up with a gasp. Fire lances up my arm and I'm reminded of the present, and the past. I was shot. But Gloria treated the wound; that's the last thing I remember, her sticking her small fingers into the open wound. It's closed now, stapled shut with gauze pressed over it. I don't even want to know how that happened. I'm thankful I missed it.

The bed is empty, and I search the darkness around me for her, eyes swimming through ink. There's noise from the bathroom, a sliver of yolky light crawling beneath the door. My body settles into the mattress, relaxing now that I know where she's at. I could rouse myself and go to her, but just as the thought enters my head, the door swings open and I see my wife.

She looks tired, wearing a clean shirt and a pair of my boxers. She's barefoot, her wild hair tamed into a sloppy bun atop her head. I watch her stretch and lift her arms above her head, then she looks at me and her body stiffens. It takes a moment for her eyes to adjust to the darkness, but even from my place in bed, I can see them widen when she realizes I'm awake.

"Caolán," she whispers, then she runs to me, crawling into the bed, cupping my face. "You're awake!"

"Of course, I am. Did you really think I would die?"

"You got shot."

"It happens."

She shakes her head. "This isn't funny, Key. I had to... I had to—"

"It's okay." I reach up and stroke her cheek, smiling when she leans into my hand. "I'm sorry I made you worry."

"You were out for three days."

Three? I balk at the revelation. I thought I'd been out for a couple of hours, but the truth is so much scarier, especially for Gloria. She was alone all this time. Watching over me, praying over me, changing my bandages by herself.

"I'm sorry," I say again.

She takes my hand and kisses my palm. "Just tell me we can fix this. What happens next, Caolán?"

I ... I don't know.

I don't realize I've spoken until Gloria adjusts on the bed and says, "I don't know either, but we can figure it out together."

"My family will keep coming for me."

"It's been three days—"

"I know, but..." I stare at the off-white sheets, thinking of Nolan and the goodbye we shared. Sudden and heartbreaking. He promised he would help by keeping the White Hand off my tail for as long as he could. We drove for hours before stopping here, putting good distance between us, but I know it's not enough. There's only so much Nolan can do before they set out to find us. And how long will it take them to track us to this motel?

"We have to go," I say, voice raspy and low.

"Go where?"

"I don't know."

"Caolán—"

"*I'll figure it out*," I snap without meaning to.

Gloria leans away, like she's getting away from me and the mafia too. I reach out and grab her, ignoring the pain shooting up my arm. "Wait—I'm sorry."

"You've already said that."

"I mean it. Cut me a break, Gloria, I was just shot."

"And I was just put through the worst three days of my life."

We glare back and forth, but I give in first, glancing away. "It's not just the bullet. I ... I had a dream while I was out.

About my mother."

She moves back to me, resting on her knees. Her hands twitch in her lap, like she wants to touch me, but she doesn't. "What sort of dream?"

"She told me she's always hated me."

Silence. Pretty much my reaction at the time.

"Yeah." I chuckle bitterly. "Messed up, right?"

"I don't think my parents ever loved me any more than yours."

I scoff. "Gloria, your mother wept to keep you with her as a child."

"But she sold me to begin with."

"Parents make bad decisions."

"Like demanding your cousin's life, knowing that it would cause trouble for me."

"Alright," I mutter, "I get it."

"It's not a competition," she tells me. "Your mother definitely takes the cake for awful parent. But I wanted you to know you're not alone." Finally, she reaches for me. Shyly, like she's afraid I might jerk away. Her fingers trace over my hand, then they fold over mine, interlacing between them until they're united. She squeezes. "You're not alone, Caolán."

My eyes feel heavy, but not from exhaustion, they're weighed down by emotion. Is it fair that I finally get this wonderful gift after everything I've done? I don't deserve Gloria or her kindness, but she's given it anyway. Risking her life for me, patching me up when this whole thing is my fault. Her gentleness is almost surreal. I close my eyes to savor it, then I quickly open them, afraid this is a dream. A foggy lie, like all the other good moments I've lived. But she's still there, sitting beside me, staring at me with her wide, round eyes.

"You're real," I say, squeezing her hand back.

"Of course, I am."

"Can I kiss you?"

Just to make sure.

She doesn't speak, her eyes blinking rapidly. I take her silence as permission, and I lean over, invading her space. I can smell her this close, the fragrance of cheap motel soap. I bet I smell like death, but that doesn't push her away. Gloria remains rooted in place, and I lean closer, lips hovering over hers.

"Can I kiss you?" I repeat.

Her hazel eyes glaze with desire, and she drops her gaze to my mouth, like she can find the kiss herself. "Just one," she says.

I snatch the words away, fast, desperate, almost falling into her. She kisses me back, eyes fluttering like it hurts. *I hurt*—every single part of me. But the sting is good. The pain is pleasure. I've ached for her since all this began, and she's still here now that it's finally over.

The sound she makes sets me on fire; I shift to pull her closer but jerk back with a hiss.

"*Crap*—"

"Your arm."

"I'm fine." I reach for her again, but her hand is pressed against my chest, pushing me away.

"We can't."

"Yes, we can."

She lets me kiss her. Once, twice, another peck against her puffy lips. But the pecks become long, deep exchanges, and she gasps into my mouth, finally giving in to her desire.

Now, she doesn't push me away. Her small hand presses against my chest, gentle, but firmly enough that I get the message and lean back into the pillows.

"I'll be careful," she whispers, having no idea that I don't want her to.

Her concern is heartbreaking, for a second, I wonder how to handle it. What do you do when someone hands you their heart? I have no idea, but I'm not about to hand it back. Gloria is mine, the only thing in this world that's *ever* been mine. In the beginning, her submission had been forced, the duties of a contract. Now, she's here of her own free will. She's here because she wants to be.

There's a fire in her eyes that I know matches my own, but her innocence smothers the flames. She looks down at me with a strike of fear slashing through her passion. She has no idea what to do, and no idea how to speak up.

"It's okay."

She nods, eyes going wide when I place my hands on her hips.

"Like this," I whisper.

A gasp from her and then a noise from me that I cannot describe. It's snatched from my lungs against my will, breath and passion wrapped into one. That's when I realize this is different. A new experience for us both. I've had plenty of sex, but this is the first time I've ever made love. Half-dead, crippled, and grunting through a bullet wound. I wouldn't have it any other way.

I'm breathless when it's over, staring at the ceiling, wishing I could see the stars through them. That's where I've been for the last hour. In Heaven. To think that it could be this way every day is almost unfathomable.

"Gloria," I whisper.

She stirs beside me, exhausted. "Hmm?" she hums, then her voice grows serious, and her words pop from her mouth in frightened concern. "Are you hurt? Is it your arm?"

"No, I'm just making conversation."

"Oh…"

A long pause.

"Do you—" I stop. "Was that… Are you satisfied?"

"Um. Yes."

"I'm sorry. I'm awful at this."

"I think we're both bad at being married." She laughs. "But we're learning."

"Do you want to keep learning?"

I hear the blankets move and she shifts beside me, moving closer. "Yes, I do."

"I'm asking you to stay with me, Gloria. It won't be easy."

"When has it ever been easy?"

She's right, but she doesn't get it.

"We're leaving," I tell her. "We can't stay here. In the mafia, I mean."

"That's good. We don't belong here."

"But I don't know where we do belong."

She sighs. "God will show us."

"Do you really believe in God?"

"Do you really doubt Him after all this?"

She's right again. I can pretend all I want, but I know it was nothing but my wife's desperate prayers that got us through this.

"Okay," I say, slowly moving my arm. Now that the adrenaline of lovemaking has faded, my shoulder feels like it's on fire. "Let's say I do believe in God. Why would He show us where to go? I'm not a good man."

"No one is," she says matter-of-factly. "Only God is good."

The words slap me hard. That's exactly what God told me when I'd desperately prayed for Him to protect Gloria.

"What does that mean?" I ask my wife.

"It means that God isn't like us. We think we deserve good things because we are good people; the world calls this *karma*. An idea that good things happen to good people and bad things happen to bad people. But that isn't how God operates." She adjusts beside me. "Karma isn't real, if it were, then it would negate Christ's sacrifice on the Cross. Because Jesus died for all of us—the good *and* the bad. None of us deserved His Blood. Our salvation is not an exchange of good things to good people; it is freely given to all who grasp it through faith. Even the people we call bad."

I nod slowly, trying to understand.

"Only God is good," Gloria repeats. "That means, without Him, we are nothing but broken sinners. It is Christ's Blood that makes us clean and righteous. Only when we accept Christ can we become good, because with Christ, we have the Holy Spirit dwelling within us. We have *God* with us. God makes us good because He makes us like Him."

"Okay, maybe earthly goodness doesn't matter, but I'm not a Christian, Gloria. Why would God help me out?"

"You can become one."

"Gloria—"

"What's stopping you?" She sits up and looks down at me, eyes glowing in the moonlight. "You already believe in Him, why not accept Him?"

It's not that I can't accept God. It's that I don't understand how He could ever accept *me*. I'm a murderer. A former drug addict. A whore. A reaper. And so much more. I'm not like my wife. I don't have her doe-eyed innocence, her crippling naivety. I've seen the horrors of this world; I've committed part of it. There is no place in God's kingdom for a man like me.

But Gloria is looking at me with so much hope. So much pleading. She wants this for me. She wants me to live for God because she doesn't just care about my heart or my emotions, she cares about my very soul.

"I love you, Caolán," she says, leaning closer to kiss me, the words a whisper on her soft lips. "I want to spend eternity with you."

I want to spend eternity with her, too. But…

I pull back from the kiss, unable to look her in the eye, not when she looks so hurt. Because of me.

"I don't get it," she says softly. "Caolán…"

I dare to glance up, forcing myself to face the pain I've created.

"Do you really want to stay like this?"

"No."

"Then why not accept Christ?"

"I can't explain it."

"Are you afraid?"

The words stab me in the heart. They pierce through every wall built around my soul, every brick cracking, crumbling away. At the center, hidden in the shadows of my brokenness, is a fleshy heart. It's weak and withering but burns to life at the sound of Gloria's words—at *my* words.

Something strikes me inside, the truth hits me, and I look up at Gloria's pretty face to answer, but my reply is a sob.

Yes, I'm afraid.

Afraid that God won't have me. Afraid that I'm not good enough for Him. Afraid that there is no place for me amongst His people. How could there ever be? If my own mother hated me, wanted to *kill* me, how could my Father in Heaven ever love me?

Gloria's love is the only one I've ever experienced, and I've only just grasped it. I can't find God's love now. I don't know how. But like a good wife, Gloria won't let me give up on myself. She scoots closer to me and takes both my hands, looks me right in the eye.

"Don't be afraid. Love has no fear, Caolán. Because God *is* love. He is patient and kind. God is not jealous or boastful or proud or rude. God does not demand His own way. He is not irritable, and He keeps no record of being wronged. He does not rejoice about injustice but rejoices whenever the truth wins out. God never gives up on us. He is ever faithful. God is our hope that endures through everything we face." She smiles, despite the tears that run down her face. "God is love. He won't hurt you, Caolán."

I'm not a Christian man, but I know enough about the Bible to recognize that she just quoted a scripture. For the life of me, I can't tell you which one, but I recognize the words. Like poetry written for my soul, they ease the pain in my heart, chase away the fear.

I nod at my wife. "Okay…"

"Okay?" Her face glows.

I nod again, and I feel her squeeze my hands. I squeeze back.

"This is the Sinner's Prayer," she tells me. "Just repeat after me."

39

Ria

Caolán is doing much better now. We've been in the motel for nearly a week, and he's eating more, walking around, and he took a shower by himself this morning. He's still got a long way to go, but the hardest part is over. There are no signs of infection, he's only getting stronger. Thanks to God. We've been taking communion together every day since he woke up. It's awkward for him, asking for more faith than he has to offer, but he doesn't back away. He holds my hands and listens to me pray. He eats the bread, drinks the juice, and he says amen. He's learning. Taking baby steps.

"I think we should leave tomorrow," he says, walking out of the steamy bathroom. There's a tiny towel wrapped around his waist, but the knot is sloppy because of his arm. As he walks, it slowly unties, and he gasps and then grunts when he reflexively reaches down to catch it. The sudden action puts a strain on his shoulder; I watch him close his eyes and whisper a curse under his breath.

"Language," I say.

He looks angry but doesn't comment. I don't expect him to become a saint overnight, but a reminder of his newfound salvation doesn't hurt.

Caolán takes deep breaths as he holds his towel in place. "Sorry," he finally rasps.

"Are you okay?"

He nods, waving me off when I stand to help. "Let me do it myself, Gloria."

So painfully stubborn, determined to prove that he's okay. Because if he's alright, that means everything else will be too. The rest of this story will magically fall into place, and we'll get our happily ever after. I wish it were that easy, but the truth is that we're still on the run, kept safe by the grace of God. We can't stay here any longer or we may risk our lives. We've got to go before we run out of blessings.

I watch him wrap the towel around his waist again, waiting for him to speak once he catches his breath. "Tomorrow morning," he says.

"I was thinking we could return to New York City."

His eyes fill with anger, but not at me, it's an anger I've felt myself. In my heart and in my bones. Anger toward the mafia, the organization that asked us to sacrifice our lives and our hearts and our minds and then turned on us the moment we caused trouble. It turned our families against us. It turned our lives inside out. It nearly turned *us* against each other. Vicious fights, bitter words spewed back and forth, insults, foul shots, and doors slamming in our faces. We weren't ourselves in the mafia, and even though we're barely seven days free of it, I feel the difference already. It doesn't take years for God's presence to impact you. I felt the shackles of darkness break away the moment I gave my life to Him. As I stare up at Caolán, I wonder if he feels the same. He isn't a great Christian by any means, but he's trying. Perfectly imperfect in every possible way.

"No," Caolán grunts. "Not New York. It's too familiar and I don't have allies there."

He's right. The point is to get away from the mafia, not run into the only mafia ruled city in the country. But where else can we go? We've got around 10K in cash and a few days of supplies left. We've been living on faith and the trembling fear of the motel manager. I appreciate his secrecy, but there are only so many sandwiches I can eat before I go nuts.

"Where else can we go, then?" I ask.

"I think I can make a few phone calls."

"To whom?"

He glances up, his expression almost annoyed, but it softens when his eyes meet mine and he visibly relaxes. This is new for him too. He isn't used to explaining himself, not as an underboss. But he isn't that man anymore, and I'm not that woman. Being a mafia wife means he can answer when he's ready, if he's *ever* ready. He doesn't owe me anything. But we've walked out of that life. When I speak, we're on equal grounds now. When I ask him a question, I expect an answer. Not because I'm demanding anything from him, but because I'm his wife and I deserve the same respect I give him.

"I think I made connections to the Volkov family in New York," Caolán says.

"I thought you said you didn't have allies there?"

"I don't."

"Then who is Volkov?"

"Head of the Bratva in Staten Island."

"Caolán..." I squint. "We're *leaving* the mafia. Remember?"

He walks across the room and starts digging through the duffel bag we've been living out of. I'm sure he's down to his last clean pair of boxers. I watch him slide them on.

"We are leaving, but we still need help. We have no passports. No place to stay. And that cash will run out sooner than you think."

"Maybe my brother can help," I say slowly. Darren was good. Just a kid. He isn't fully tainted by the Panthers yet; he may be willing to help us the same way Nolan has—at least that's what I hope. But the truth is that Darren was there when my family decided to wage war with the O'Rourkes. He never came to my aid. Not when they demanded Billy's head or when they came for Caolán's. I still love my brother, I always will, but I can't pretend that he's my ally anymore.

When I look up at my husband, I know he's thinking the same thing. He holds my gaze, studying me, then he lowers his eyes like he doesn't want to deliver the bad news. Instead of telling me my brother isn't my friend anymore, he says, "We're in hiding, Gloria. We can't trust anyone anymore."

"I know, but—"

"The moment we leave this motel, anyone who spots us

becomes a witness for the White Hand or the Panthers. They are looking for us. Don't forget that."

"I haven't forgotten. But God can protect us," I mutter, "He's kept us safe so far."

We're not even a day away from the city, and no one has found us. It *must* be God's protection. If He's kept us this far, He'll keep us in the future. I know He will.

"We don't need to get tangled up with the Bratva," I say.

Caolán pulls in a long breath, sits on it, and then exhales slowly. "We won't be getting *tangled up*. I just need a flight out of here and a place to stay. Can you agree to that?"

My eyes feel heavy, like stress is knocking at the back of my head. "I don't like this, Key."

"Neither do I."

"We're supposed to live a different life."

"We are," he says, almost angrily. "I'm trying to get to that place, Gloria. The place where we don't have to worry about the Hand or the Panthers. But I need help. I can't get us there without connections."

I know he's right, I just… I don't want help or connections from the mafia. Not even the Bratva. Nothing is ever free in this world. If we ask for help and they give it to us, they will want to be repaid. It might not be today or tomorrow, but they will collect on what they've given us.

Or maybe they won't.

I think of Rahab who helped the Israelite spies, and the centurion who loved the Nation of Israel enough to build their synagogue for them, not to mention the man who helped Jesus carry His own Cross. Throughout the Bible there were Gentiles who helped the Israelites. People who were not part of God's kingdom stepped up to help anyway; some of them asked for nothing in return, others, like the centurion and Rahab, asked for miracles.

Maybe the Bratva is another blessing in disguise. Maybe they can help us without causing harm.

Is this right? I ask God, but Caolán interrupts the prayer, stepping close and taking my hands.

"Let me do this, Gloria."

I have an uneasy feeling about it, but I don't see any other way. What I *do* see is Caolán's shy smile, the pleading look in his eye. He wants this to work. He wants to be the one who fixes this. I don't have the heart to take that from him.

"Okay," I whisper. "We'll contact the Volkovs."

He leans down and kisses my cheek; the smell of bathroom soap invades my nose. "Thank you, Glory."

Glory... The nickname my father used to call me. I was the glory of the family, a cherished prize. I wonder if Caolán cherishes me; he must if he wants to use the Bratva just to keep me safe. I don't know anything about the Russian organization, but I'm choosing to trust my husband. I'm choosing to let him take the lead on this, and I'm praying this isn't a mistake.

"I love you," Caolán says. His voice is shy, he can't even look at me when I glance up from our hands, but he says it again in case I didn't hear it. "I love you, Glory."

"I love you too, Key."

And I know God loves us both. That will have to be

enough.

40

Caolán
6 Months Later

CONGRATULATIONS...

I stare down at the letter we just received in the mail. It arrived in a white envelope, a single card inside. Pink. Swirly cursive writing. Flowers decorating the paper. It's just one word inside, **CONGRATULATIONS**. It's written twice, once in English and once in Russian because neither Gloria nor myself are fluent. We've been here for six months, but it takes longer than that to learn a language. At least for us.

"What's that?" Gloria stops in the kitchen doorway, she's far enough away that I didn't hear her approaching footsteps. Our house is huge, a mansion that rivals my family estate back in California. We didn't need a house this big for the two of us, but the Russians have been generous. They helped us get out of the US, gave us this home, and have allowed me to work in one of their fully legal businesses. I'm not in the mafia anymore, but I am still very much connected to it.

I stare down at the pink card, at the one word in the middle, and I squeeze it until it wrinkles. The edges curl inward, like they're crawling toward me for comfort.

CONGRATULATIONS.

"Caolán?" Gloria steps into the kitchen and I turn away, tucking the card back into its envelope.

"It was nothing," I tell her. "Junk mail from work."

She raises an eyebrow but trusts me anyway, giving a nonchalant shrug. "Okay. I'm going to get started on dinner. Any suggestions?"

I'm not hungry.

"Whatever you make is fine."

For a moment, she doesn't move. I feel the questions rising between us, but she doesn't give them a voice. Gloria smiles, nods, and walks away toward the pantry.

I exhale. We are in a foreign country, working for dangerous people, living off their kindness. And I've just received the first reminder of their power over us.

CONGRATULATIONS. A pink card that makes me want to hurl. I almost take the card out and burn it over the stove, but I don't want to touch it again. I don't want to see that single word, or the picture printed beside it. A baby bottle.

Gloria is pregnant, six months now. We've known for the last three months, but I guess the word is out. Normally, receiving a card like this would make me smile. But now it only makes me worry. This is not the Bratva's way of sending warm wishes and healthy prayers for the baby. It's their way of letting me know that I can't keep anything from them. They are watching us. They are making plans for us. This baby will play a part in it. I don't know how, I don't know when, but the message is clear.

We ran from our families in the US, only to become targets here in Russia.

I can't let Gloria know what's happened. She will never forgive me. *But God will...* I haven't been a Christian long, but I've been praying long enough to know that the Lord is merciful. I *need* His mercy. I need Him to wipe away the mistake I made for this family.

My wife trusted me; she surrendered her own will and gave me leadership to make decisions for us. I led us away from cannon fire into the guillotine. A weapon that is quiet and swift and far more deadly. A cannon could miss, but a guillotine only swings once.

When? I ask myself, staring at the envelope on the counter. *When will they come for my child?*

"You saw it."

I turn to find Gloria once again standing in the kitchen doorway, she's got her hand on her swollen belly, but her eyes are staring over my shoulder—at the kitchen counter.

I glance back at the letter and then look at her again. "What do you mean?"

"I saw the card they sent," she says.

"When?" I frown. The envelope was unopened when I got it.

"They sent two, Caolán. One for you and one for me."

Two separate letters, just to make sure we got them.

"Why didn't you tell me?" I step toward her, looking her up and down like I don't know her anymore. We fought for our lives in California, learned to adjust to life here in Russia, and then discovered we'd be starting a family soon. Gloria and I have become inseparable since we left home. This is the first time she's ever kept anything from me. I don't like the way it makes me feel.

"I didn't know what to say." Gloria takes a deep breath. "I was afraid."

"Don't be afraid." The words are instantaneous, like my heart speaks before my brain realizes it. But I don't take the words back once they're out there. I don't want Gloria to fear a thing. "We'll figure this out," I say. "It's just a card, it could mean anything."

Her face wrinkles like she knows that's a lie.

"We have to be prepared, Caolán. This card is a warning, and you know it."

A warning for what? The Bratva might have helped me when I needed it, but I don't know what I could possibly offer them. Gloria and I cut all ties with our families when we arrived in Russia. I don't have connections to the Hand anymore and she barely held any power in the Panthers. Now, I manage a luxury hotel in Moscow, but that's it. Sure, the Bratva owns the place, but they don't tell me anything. I'm just the guy who makes sure all the rooms are booked and the sheets are changed on time. This is the most normal life I've lived since I was born. Gloria even cooks dinner.

But things are about to change…

"God is with us," Gloria's voice disrupts my thoughts, and I turn back to find her smiling. She's looking down at her belly, like she was talking to our unborn daughter. But now her gaze lifts to find mine and she smiles calmly. "No matter what the cards mean, God is with us, Caolán. We will have this baby, and we will continue to live a peaceful, happy life together. Understand?"

I nod without thinking. Just when I'd almost let fear take over, my wife brought me back.

"We survived everything in California and made it here against all odds," Gloria says. "Do you think God's protection cannot reach us here?"

I shake my head. "I'm sorry. I didn't mean to doubt."

"Don't apologize for being human." She laughs, and it sounds shaky, like maybe she's as anxious as I am. She doesn't have a choice but to be brave, neither of us does. We've got a child who needs us—who needs our *faith*. If there was ever a time to hunker down and believe, it's now.

Are you afraid? The words drift into my mind, and I almost yield to them; in the presence of adversity and ominous warnings, I feel my faith slipping. Until I remember God's answer to that question.

Fear not.

I hold out my hand and Gloria takes it, letting me pull her into a hug, though the embrace is more for me than her. "We're going to be okay."

"We always have been."

"Thank you for trusting me," I say. "Even though I messed

up again."

I feel her laugh as I hold her. "Don't focus on the mistake, Caolán. I don't see this as something you messed up; I see it as a chance for us to learn how to trust God together. As one."

"Ever hopeful."

"One of us has to be."

I laugh and then exhale slowly. "We'll be fine."

She nods against me, offering no words, just a gentle squeeze of her small arms wrapped around my middle. She has nothing to say right now, but I wonder what she'll say in 18 years when our daughter is of age. When the Bratva return, just as I returned for her.

I suppose that's a battle for us to fight at a later time. Until then, I'll keep believing that God is good, and He's already worked everything out. Perhaps it's brash for me to make such claims. I willingly got us into this mess, and now I'm desperately seeking God's help to get out of it. But ... Do you remember what I asked when this story first began?

Don't judge me when it's over.

Epilogue

Sunflower
18 Years Later

We push through the crowd of ballerinas, ignoring their high-pitched squeals. I have a hard time keeping myself from rolling my eyes, but my father seems unbothered. He's used to the attention. I guess that's what happens when you're a retired mafia boss; people stare.

The hotel is at full occupancy because of the Bolshoi Ballet, a famous ballet company stationed right here in Moscow. Their opening season is this weekend, and half the western world just *has* to see it. The last week has been crazy for us; my father is the manager for a hotel just ten blocks from the theater, so we've been working double time for our guests. Now, we've got business to attend but the dancers have all decided this afternoon is the perfect time for them to visit the hotel spa.

There's a line of skinny women that spills out of the spa's entrance and into the lobby. When my father and I enter the foyer, their chatter hushes and their gazes follow us until we disappear around the corner. The attention makes my ears burn in anger and shy embarrassment.

I don't like being watched. I think I get that from my mother. She grew up with an ugly scar dashed across her face, so she's never liked having anyone's eyes on her.

I grew up being raised by two former members of mafia royalty, so I had everyone watching me whether I wanted them to or not.

I never had privacy. Never had the chance to get away from my overbearing Christian parents because they were eternally paranoid of me getting murdered by angry Russians. I don't know exactly where they got that idea from, but the ever-looming threat of death has drifted over my head since I was born. At least that's what my mother tells me.

As I got older, I dismissed my parents' warnings and worries as the rambles of traumatized mafia refugees. For all their fear, I grew up as a normal child. I had birthday parties, I went to private schools, I made friends. When I was old enough, my father started teaching me the business. Now I work as his assistant, helping keep the hotel in order. That's why I'm attending this meeting with him.

We enter the large conference room together, inclining our heads and whispering apologies for our tardiness. There are men in dark suits filling the chairs, but my eyes skip over their grey heads to land on *him*. He's standing in the back corner of the room, casually leaning against the wall, eyes half-lidded, hands crammed into the pockets of his jeans. He looks like he doesn't care to be here.

"Caolán O'Rourke." The voice belongs to Arkadi Volkov, a figure I have seen throughout my childhood. He's a small man with sharp features disarmed by his soft voice. When I look at him, I think of a grandfather who doesn't laugh at many jokes. I've hardly seen him smile.

My father nods. "Volkov, nice to see you."

"I doubt that," he replies.

My father's jaw clenches. He doesn't want to be here, but when your boss summons you, you've got to answer—especially when he's the leader of the Russian mafia.

Apparently, my parents escaped the mafia before I was born, but they couldn't get out without the help of the Bratva. They moved from the United States all the way to Russia just to get away. But now that I'm older, I've realized they never truly got away. I mean, here we are, meeting the Bratva boss in the backroom of our hotel. If that doesn't scream mafia grunts, then I don't know what does. But there's nothing we can do. Arkadi owns the hotel my father manages; if we say the wrong thing, we'll be out of jobs and then out of a home and then who knows what.

"We've called you here today because we've gotten word that your daughter has graduated high school," Volkov says, gaining my attention.

When I glance up, he's looking right at me. "*Поздравления*," he says— *Pozdravleniya,* Russian for *congratulations*.

I was born here, I know the language, so I reply in a perfect accent without hesitation. "*Спасибо*." *Spasibo*, meaning, *thank you*.

My confident response makes Arkadi's eyes crinkle, like he wants to smile. He holds up a black envelope. "A gift for the Irish princess." I'm only half Irish but since I took my father's name, and his red hair, the Bratva only acknowledges that half of me. My mother's Panther lineage doesn't seem to exist in their eyes.

I step forward, holding my breath as my feet move across the carpet. When I reach for the envelope, Arkadi doesn't let go right away, forcing me to look up at his expectant face. "We have thought long and hard about this, Sunflower, I'm sure you will represent us well."

I have no idea what that means, but I nod and take the gift anyway. Behind me, my father clears his throat, but Arkadi doesn't acknowledge him. He's still looking at me.

Nervously, I begin tearing open the envelope while Arkadi explains the gift. "For generations, the mafia has been the subject of dreams and fascination. We are rich, we are influential, we have the police and politicians in our pockets. We exist at the height of society, yet we live in the shadows."

I pull out the thick card inside the envelope. It's heavy and expensive, with loopy handwriting that says in bold letters, *Heights & Shadows.*

"To preserve our way of life and ensure our business can be properly carried out by the next generation, mafia organizations created a place for our youth to learn the ways of this world." Arkadi lights a cigar, the end burns red. "The name of this educational institution is Heights & Shadows University."

I don't get it. "Is this an invitation?"

He shakes his head, sharp eyes narrowing. "It is a summon."

I don't have a choice. Arkadi called me here to tell me that I'm going to this school. A mafia university.

No wonder my father looks so uncomfortable. He knows we can't fight this; it's the repayment my parents have feared for 18 years. And here I thought the Bratva would want *money* as repayment. My parents thought they wanted my *life*. Technically, they were right.

"May I speak?" My father steps forward.

Arkadi waves his hand, granting permission.

"Sunny isn't ready for this. She wasn't raised in the mafia, *Pakhan*."

Normally, my father's disagreement would be met with anger, but the word *Pakhan* softens Arkadi. It means *crime boss* or *Godfather*, a reminder that he's in charge here.

"It is your fault that you did not raise your daughter well," Arkadi says. "She will attend the school."

"Why?"

Arkadi's eyes drill holes into my father. The rest of the room shifts uncomfortably. I feel myself begin to sweat, wondering if he's overstepped his place, but his anger only seems to humor Arkadi whose lips pull back to reveal sharp teeth.

"Because I said so," he replies. "I own your daughter. That is the cost of all you have been given for the last eighteen years, Caolán."

My father opens his mouth, but I interrupt.

"I will attend," I blurt, catching Arkadi's gaze. My father looks shocked, but he must know we have no choice in this. Questioning Arkadi will only make things worse. It's best to just agree and try to work things out later. Also ... I'm sort of interested in Heights & Shadows.

I've spent my life living under the strict rules of my parents, constantly looking over my shoulder, afraid that I would die if I ever stepped out of line. I was never blind to who my parents were, or who they used to be. I grew up knowing everything there was to know about the mafia. Arkadi Volkov is a figure I saw on holidays and even some family events, like a distant grandpa who was too rich and too high class for me to ever approach. But he was there, along with other members of the Bratva.

I look around the conference table now, and I recognize the faces of the powerful men before me. Namely, Ivan Stepanov, an imposing figure who stands as the brother to the Stepanov boss of New York. Everyone here has family in the US, Arkadi is cousins with the legendary Mikhail Volkov who first invited my parents to Russia.

Ivan releases a deep breath, like he's annoyed. "I understand your worries, Caolán. That is why we are sending Sasha with her."

My eyes laser to the boy leaning against the back wall. On cue, he pushes from the wall and stalks forward, his boots hitting the floor in heavy *thuds*. When he stands beside me, I realize how large he is. As tall as my father, and as big as Ivan Stepanov, like he should have been a football player. He wears a hood over his head, his hands are buried in his pockets, his jeans are ripped and stained at the knees. He looks like he couldn't be bothered to even try looking nice. Then again, Sasha's always been that way.

We were raised together, both of us the children of fallen mafia royalty. Sasha is the son of a former Russian mafia princess. His father was imprisoned before he was born. Then his grandfather was murdered by the Italian mafia and his home was burned down with his mother in it. She survived and escaped here to Russia, but she was never the same. Sasha was only a baby when all of this happened, but he *was* there, and the trauma of those events sits on his shoulders today. Weighing him down.

Over the years, he's stayed out of the spotlight within the Bratva. Even changed his name to put some distance between himself and the drama of the US. Sasha is what his father calls him; a name sent in a letter written in the corners of a dark cell. The name he was born with was Italian. Something his mother gave him when she was tangled up with the Vittores, but Sasha denounced it the first chance he got. He won't even speak the name aloud anymore. I'm not sure I blame him.

Since I met him, Sasha has had one goal in mind. To get vengeance on the people who ruined his family. Luca Vittore is the name of the man who caused all this pain, he was boss of the Italian mafia back in Benton, New York at the time. But the drama doesn't end there.

The Bratva has suffered shame at the hands of the German mafia, too. That's where I come in. The Jägers of New York went to war with Mikhail Volkov—it didn't end well for the Russians. But they also gave my father a hard time in New York when he was there searching for my mother. That failed war, plus the Stepanovs getting ripped to shreds by Luca Vittore has left the Russian mafia in a bad place. It's been 18 long years, and now the Bratva finally has a chance to strike back.

They're using us to do it.

I am the daughter of Caolán O'Rourke, a pawn who was shown kindness by the Russian mafia. I will earn the mercy that was given to my father by attending Heights & Shadows and bring honor to the Bratva on his behalf. Meanwhile, Sasha will attend with me and seek his vengeance.

But how?

I glance at Sasha, at the silent anger I see on his face, the rage buried beneath his flattened brows, the hatred bitten back by his clenched jaw, like a withheld scream. Sasha wants to go to Heights & Shadows, like a dog ready to be set loose.

He glances to the side, and I hold my breath, trying not to shrink beneath his judgmental gaze. I'm wearing an outfit that mirrors my father's; a business suit with navy pants and a smart-looking blazer. I thought I looked mature. Serious. But as Sasha stares, I feel like a child who let her dad pick out her clothes.

Sasha looks like he can't stand me. Like he hates my red hair, my stupid business clothes, and even the look on my face. But he doesn't say anything. He stares, he blinks, and then he looks away. Unimpressed.

"I will get the job done," Sasha says in Russian, his voice

thick and his accent rich. "Vengeance will be mine, *Vor.*"

Vor. Another Russian term for crime boss, but this one is old, translating to *Thief.* It isn't an insult but an acknowledgement of who Arkadi truly is. One who doesn't just steal money, he steals lives, joy, and happiness too.

He's stolen my life, holding my future in the palm of his pale hand. All I can do is incline my head and agree while my father sweats in the background. My parents tried to warn me. I thought they were paranoid fools, letting their religious wariness brainwash them into thinking everyone and everything was out to get them. But now I see.

Sasha speaks up again. "I'll keep the girl safe."

He's talking about me.

"I don't need anyone to protect me," I say, trying to preserve my dignity. "I can handle myself at Heights & Shadows."

Sasha makes a noise. "No, you can't." He turns to walk away, glancing at me one last time. The look is withering, like protecting me is the worst thing he's ever had to do. Worse than the grief of losing his grandfather, losing his family home, and falling from royalty to mafia peasantry. He looks at me like he blames me for it all. Or maybe he blames the world, and I just happen to be in it.

Either way, I don't let the look get to me. I keep my chin up as I glance at Arkadi, I ignore my father's anger behind me, I don't even listen to the little voice in the back of my head telling me I should be afraid. I squeeze the envelope in my hand, and I focus on the men at the table before me.

"I will make you proud, Pakhan. I will restore the honor of the Bratva."

He flicks ash from his cigar. "Do not be proud, little girl. You will need Sasha's help."

Stepanov nods. "Heights & Shadows is a school for the mafia. The students are learning to take over their parents' legacies. At this university, graduation isn't the goal. Survival is." He leans across the table, his wide shoulders casting shadows along the wooden surface. "Do you think you can handle such a place, child?"

Child. Girl. They didn't use such terms when they spoke to Sasha. He couldn't even be bothered to pull his hood down or take his hands out his pockets, but I'm the one being treated like an inexperienced child. Then again, I am the one who was raised outside the mafia. My parents both converted to Christianity before I was born. They were open about their past, but they never indulged in it. Everything in my life was filtered, saturated in Christian values and reinforced with scripture.

My parents tried their best to keep their past in the past, but it's hunted them down and sank its teeth into me instead of them.

It doesn't matter, I tell myself, still squeezing the envelope. *I'll show my parents they don't have to worry so much. I'll show them* and *the Bratva that I can handle myself.*

"I can handle this," I finally answer Arkadi.

He chuckles. "Bold words."

"Allow me to prove them."

He sucks on his cigar.

"If I achieve greatness at Heights & Shadows, will you relieve my parents of the debt they owe the Bratva?"

The request stuns Arkadi so much that he coughs up smoke, but the cough becomes a laugh, and he points his cigar at me. "What a foolish girl."

"It would be wise to take this seriously," Stepanov tells me.

They don't think I can do it...

"Is that a, *yes*?" I say snappily.

Both men watch me like predators. My father shifts his weight from one foot to the other. I suppose he did not expect me to respond this way, but the words are out there now. I want this madness and paranoia with the mafia to end. There's only one way I can make that happen.

"Yes," Arkadi shrugs, like he doesn't think I'll get anywhere close to achieving greatness. He probably expects me to die there. "If you excel at Heights & Shadows, your parents will be relieved of their debt and released from the Bratva's command." He inclines his head at my father. "You have my word."

My father looks back and forth between me and the men at the conference table. He can't believe it. After 18 years, he finally has a true way out of the mafia. It will cost everything I can give, but I'm prepared.

Heights & Shadows doesn't scare me. My faith isn't as strong as my parents, but I know enough about God to be confident that the shadows cannot touch me. I don't care what awaits at the school, I will get through it. I will survive. I will thrive and make the Bratva proud, and in doing so, I will win the freedom of my parents. I have no other choice.

"Thank you, Pakhan," I say, turning away.

On my way out, I see Sasha watching me. I dare to meet his eyes, and he holds my gaze. Then he looks away.

See you soon, I think to myself. *Very soon.*

Enjoy these mafia love stories!

Want to know more about Amory's marriage and his Christian bride, Rosa De Luca?
Read his love story in **Withered Rose!**
Don't forget about Luca Vittore! Who is his new bride and what role did he play in Sasha's tragic past? Find out in
Beautiful Lies!

Also check out these other Christian mafia books!
Fractured Diamond
The Woof Pack Trilogy

More books by Valicity Elaine & TRC Publishing!

Christian Fantasy
The Scribe
Cross Academy

Christian Post-Apocalyptic Fiction
The Barren Fields
The End of the World series
MAGOG saga

Christian Science Fiction
I AM MAN series

Christian Romance

My Fellow American

The Living Water

Withered Rose Trilogy

Beautiful Lies

The Gap

Decipis Trilogy

Fractured Diamond

The Woof Pack Trilogy

Singlehood

Christian Children's Fiction

Too Young

ACKNOWLEDGEMENTS

A HUGE thank you to Jesus Christ for bringing me to the finish line! Lord, You know the challenges I faced while writing this one. I can't believe You gave me the strength to make it through!

This book was a journey for me as much as the characters. Thank you so much for giving Gloria and Caolán a chance. As you probably know, low-spice, cracked door, and dark Christian romance in general is a growing genre. Sometimes it feels very lonely as an author in this market. Your support means so much to me. I cannot thank you enough for finishing this novel, and I pray that you enjoyed it.

What do I say now? On to the next, I suppose. I cannot wait to break into *Heights & Shadows*. If you've joined my newsletter, then you've already seen the placement cover and you know I'm working hard already. If you haven't joined my newsletter, now is the chance!

Follow me on **social media!** @valicityelaine to get news on all my books. You can find my newsletter at my website: **WWW . THEREBELCHRISTIAN . COM**

Enjoy sneak peek access to exclusive bonus content and updates on my future releases, like *Heights & Shadows*! I can't wait to see you there.

The Rebel Christian Publishing

We are an independent Christian publishing company focused on fantasy, science fiction, and romantic reads. Visit therebelchristian.com to check out our books or click the titles below!

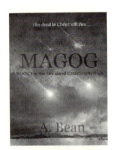
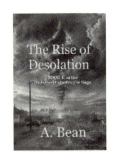

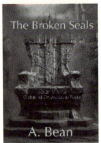
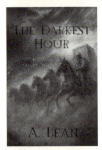
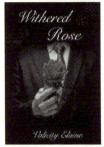
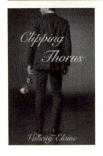

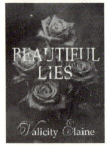

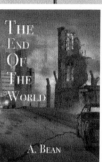

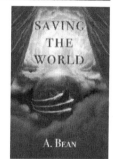

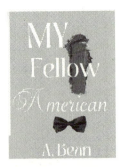
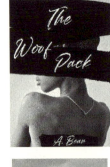
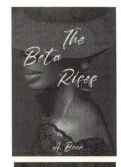
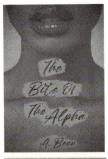
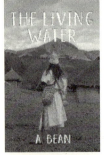
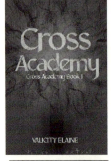
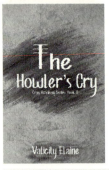
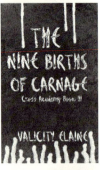

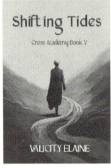
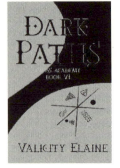

Made in the USA
Columbia, SC
24 June 2025